The Slave

*The author wishes to thank
Miss Elizabeth Pollet for her
assistance in the preparation
of this book.*

Books by Isaac Bashevis Singer

NOVELS
THE MANOR

I. THE MANOR   II. THE ESTATE

THE FAMILY MOSKAT   THE MAGICIAN OF LUBLIN

SATAN IN GORAY   THE SLAVE

ENEMIES, A LOVE STORY

SHOSHA

STORIES
A FRIEND OF KAFKA   GIMPEL THE FOOL   SHORT FRIDAY

THE SÉANCE   THE SPINOZA OF MARKET STREET

A CROWN OF FEATHERS   PASSIONS

MEMOIRS
IN MY FATHER'S COURT

FOR CHILDREN
A DAY OF PLEASURE   THE FOOLS OF CHELM

MAZEL AND SHLIMAZEL OR THE MILK OF A LIONESS

WHEN SHLEMIEL WENT TO WARSAW   A TALE OF THREE WISHES

WHY NOAH CHOSE THE DOVE   ELIJAH THE SLAVE

JOSEPH AND KOZA OR THE SACRIFICE TO THE VISTULA

ALONE IN THE WILD FOREST   THE WICKED CITY

NAFTALI THE STORYTELLER AND HIS HORSE, SUS

COLLECTION
AN ISAAC BASHEVIS SINGER READER

The Slave

a novel by

ISAAC BASHEVIS SINGER

translated from the Yiddish by

THE AUTHOR *and*

CECIL HEMLEY

Farrar, Straus and Giroux, New York

Contents

PART ONE

Wanda

I

1

A single bird call began the day. Each day the same bird, the same call. It was as if the bird signaled the approach of dawn to its brood. Jacob opened his eyes. The four cows lay on their mats of straw and dung. In the middle of the barn were a few blackened stones and charred branches, the fireplace over which Jacob cooked the rye and buckwheat cakes he ate with milk. Jacob's bed was made of straw and hay and at night he covered himself with a coarse linen sheet which he used during the day to gather grass and herbs for the cattle. It was summer, but the nights were cold in the mountains. Jacob would rise more than once in the middle of the night and warm his hands and feet on the animals' bodies.

It was still dark in the barn, but the red of dawn shone through a crack in the door. Jacob sat up and finished his final allotment of sleep. He had dreamed he was in the study house at Josefov, lecturing the young men on the Talmud.

He stretched out his hand blindly, reaching for the pitcher of water. Three times he washed his hands, the left hand first and then the right, alternating, according to the law. He had murmured even before washing, "I thank Thee," a prayer not mentioning God's name and therefore utterable before cleaning oneself. A cow stood up and turned its horned head, looking over its shoulder as if curious to see how a man starts his day. The creature's large eyes, almost all pupil, reflected the purple of the dawn.

"Good morning, Kwiatula," Jacob said. "You had a good sleep, didn't you?"

He had become accustomed to speak to the cows, to himself even, so as not to forget Yiddish. He threw open the barn door and saw the mountains stretching into the distance. Some of the peaks, their slopes overgrown with forests, seemed close at hand, giants with green beards. Mist rising from the woods like tenuous curls made Jacob think of Samson. The ascending sun, a heavenly lamp, cast a fiery sheen over everything. Here and there, smoke drifted upward from a summit as if the mountains were burning within. A hawk, wings outstretched, glided tranquilly with a strange slowness beyond all earthly anxieties. It appeared to Jacob that the bird had been flying without interruption since creation.

The more distant mountains were bluish, and there were others, the most distant of all, that were scarcely visible—unsubstantial. It was always dusk in that most remote region. Caps of clouds sat on the heads of those unearthly titans, inhabitants at the world's end where no man walked and no cow grazed. Wanda, Jan Bzik's daughter, said that that was where Baba Yaga lived, a witch who flew about in a huge mortar, driving her vehicle with a pestle. Baba Yaga's broom was larger than the tallest fir tree, and it was she who swept away the light of the world.

Jacob stood gazing at the hills, a tall, straight man, blue-eyed, with long brown hair and a brown beard. He wore linen trousers which did not reach to his ankles and a torn, patched coat. On his head was a sheepskin cap, but his feet were bare. Though he was out of doors so much, he remained as pale as a city dweller. His skin did not tan and Wanda said that he resembled the men in the holy pictures that hung in the chapel in the valley. The other peasant women agreed with Wanda. The Gazdas, as the mountaineers were called, had wanted to marry him to one of their daughters, build him a hut, and make him a member of the village, but Jacob had refused to forsake the Jewish faith, and Jan Bzik, his owner, kept him all summer and until late fall in the barn high on the mountain where the cattle could not find food and one had to feed them with grass pulled from among the rocks. The village was at a high elevation and lacked sufficient pastures.

Before he milked the cows, Jacob said his introductory

prayer. Reaching the sentence, "Thou hast not made me a slave," he paused. Could these words be spoken by him? He was Jan Bzik's slave. True, according to Polish law, not even the gentry had the right to force a Jew into servitude. But who in this remote village obeyed the law of the land? And of what value was the code of the gentiles even prior to Chmielnicki's massacre? Jacob of Josefov took the privations Providence had sent him without rancor. In other regions the Cossacks had beheaded, hanged, garroted, and impaled many honest Jews. Chaste women had been raped and disemboweled. He, Jacob, had not been destined for martyrdom. He had fled from the murderers and Polish robbers had dragged him off to somewhere in the mountains and had sold him as a slave to Jan Bzik. He had lived here for four years now and did not know whether his wife and children were still alive. He was without prayer shawl and phylacteries, fringed garment or holy book. Circumcision was the only sign on his body that he was a Jew. But heaven be thanked, he knew his prayers by heart, a few chapters of the Mishnah, some pages of the Gemara, a host of Psalms, as well as passages from various parts of the Bible. He would wake in the middle of the night with lines from the Gemara that he himself had not been aware he knew running through his head. His memory played hide and seek with him. If he had had pen and paper, he would have written down what came to him, but where were such things to be found here?

He turned his face to the east, looked straight ahead, and recited the holy words. The crags glowed in the sunlight, and close by a cowherd yodeled, his voice lingering on each note, resonant with yearning as if he too were being held in captivity and longed to thrust himself into freedom. It was hard to believe that such melodies came from men who ate dogs, cats, field mice, and indulged in every sort of abomination. The peasants here had not even risen to the level of the Christians. They still followed the customs of the ancient pagans.

There had been a time when Jacob had planned to run away, but nothing had come of his schemes. He did not know the mountains; the forests were filled with predatory animals. Snow fell even in summer. The peasants kept guard over him and did not permit him to go beyond the bridge in the village. There was an agreement among them that anyone who saw him on the other side of the stream should immediately kill him. Among the peasants there were those who wanted to kill him anyway. Jacob might be a wizard or a braider of elflocks. But Zagayek, the count's bailiff, had ordered that the stranger be permitted to live. Jacob not only gathered more grass than any other cowherd, but his cattle were very sleek, gave abundant milk, and bore healthy calves. As long as the village did not suffer from famine, epidemic, or fire, the Jew was to be left in peace.

It was time for the cows to be milked and so Jacob hurried through his prayers. Returning to the barn he mixed with the grass in the trough the chopped straw and turnips he had prepared the day before. On a shelf in the barn were the milking pail and some large earthen pots; the churn stood in a corner. Every day late in the afternoon Wanda came up, bringing Jacob his food and bearing two large pitchers in which to carry the milk back to the village.

Jacob milked the cows and hummed a tune from Josefov. The sun climbed beyond the mountains and the coils of fog dissolved. He had been here so long now and had become so acquainted with the plants that he could detect the odor of each flower and each variety of grass, and he breathed in deeply as the smells of vegetation were wafted into the barn through the open door. Every sunrise in the mountains was like a miracle; one clearly discerned God's hand among the flaming clouds. God had punished His people and had hidden His face from them, but He continued to superintend the world. As a sign of the covenant which He had made after the Flood, He had hung the rainbow in the sky to show that day and night, summer and winter, sowing and reaping would not cease.

I I

All day Jacob climbed on the mountain. After gathering a sheetful of grass, he carried it to the barn, and then returned once more to the woods. The other cowherds, when he had first come, had attacked and beaten him, but now he had learned how to strike back, and these days carried an oaken stick. He scampered over the rocks with the agility of a monkey, mindful of which herbs and grasses were good for the cattle and which harmful. All those things which are required of a cowherd he could do: light a fire by rubbing wood against wood, milk the cows, deliver a calf. For himself, he picked mushrooms, wild strawberries, blueberries, whatever the earth produced, and each afternoon Wanda brought him a slice of coarse black bread from the village, and sometimes, also, a radish, carrot, or onion, or maybe an apple or pear from the orchard. In the beginning Jan Bzik had jokingly sought to force a piece of sausage into his mouth, but Jacob had refused stubbornly to partake of forbidden food. He did not gather herbs on the Sabbath, but gave the animals feed he had prepared during the week. The mountaineers no longer molested him.

But this was not true of the girls who slept in the barn and tended the sheep. Night and day they bothered him. Attracted by his tall figure, they sought him out and talked and laughed and behaved little better than beasts. In his presence they relieved themselves, and they were perpetually pulling up their skirts to show him insect bites on their hips and thighs. "Lay me," a girl would shamelessly demand, but Jacob acted as if he were deaf and blind. It was not only because fornication was a mortal sin. These women were unclean, and had vermin in their clothes and elflocks in their hair; often their skins were covered with rashes and boils, they ate field rodents and the rotting carcasses of fowls. Some of them could scarcely speak Polish, grunted like animals, made signs with their hands, screamed and laughed madly. The village abounded in cripples, boys and girls with goiters, distended heads and disfiguring birth marks; there were also mutes, epileptics, freaks who had been born with six fingers on their hands or six toes on their feet. In summer, the parents of these deformed children kept them on the mountains with the cattle, and they ran wild. There, men and women copulated in public; the women became pregnant, but, climbing as they did all day on the rocks, bearing heavy packs, they often miscarried. The district had no midwife and mothers in labor were forced to cut the umbilical cord themselves. If the child died, they buried it in a ditch without Christian rites or else threw it into the mountain stream. Often, the women bled to death. If someone descended to the valley to fetch Dziobak, the priest, to confess the dying and administer Extreme Unction, nothing came of it. Dziobak had a game leg and besides he was always drunk.

In comparison with these savages, Wanda, Jan Bzik's widowed daughter, seemed city-bred. She dressed in a skirt, blouse and apron, and wore a kerchief on her head; moreover, her speech could be understood. A bolt of lightning had killed her husband Stach and from then on she had been courted by all the bachelors and widowers of the village; she was constantly saying no. Wanda was twenty-five and taller than most of the other women. She had blond hair, blue eyes, a fair skin, and well-modeled features. She braided her hair and twisted it around her head like a wreath of wheat. When she smiled, her cheeks dimpled and her teeth were so strong she could crush the toughest of pits. Her nose was straight and she had a narrow chin. She was a skillful seamstress and could knit, cook, and tell stories which made one's hair stand on end. In the village she had been nicknamed "The Lady." As Jacob knew very well, according to the law he must avoid her, but if it had not been for Wanda he would have forgotten that he had a tongue in his head. Besides she assisted him in fulfilling his obligations as a Jew. Thus, when in winter, on the Sabbath, her father commanded him to light the oven, she got up before Jacob and lit the kindling herself and added the firewood. Unbeknown to her parents, she brought him barley kasha, honey, fruit from the orchard, cucumbers from the garden. Once when Jacob had sprained his ankle and his foot had swollen, Wanda had snapped the bone back into the socket and applied lotions. Another time, a snake had bitten him in the arm, and she had put the wound to her mouth and sucked out the venom. This had not been the only time Wanda had saved his life.

Yet Jacob knew that all this had been contrived by Satan; throughout the day he missed her and could not overcome his longing. The instant he awoke he would start to count the hours before she would come to him. Often he would walk to the sundial that he had made from a stone to see how much the shadow had moved. If a heavy downpour or cloudburst prevented her coming, he would walk about morosely. This did not stop him from praying to God to preserve him from sinful thoughts, but again and again the thoughts returned. How could he keep his heart pure when he had no phylacteries to put on and no fringed garment to wear? Lacking as he did a calendar, he could not even observe the holy days properly. Like the Ancients he reckoned the beginning of the month by the appearance of the new moon, and at the end of his fourth year, he rectified his computations by adding an extra month. But, despite all these efforts, he was aware that he had probably made some error in his calculations.

As he figured it, this long and warm day was the fourth of the month of Tammuz. He gathered great quantities of grass and leaves; he prayed, studied several chapters of the Mishnah, said those few pages of the Gemara which he repeated daily. Finally he recited one of the Psalms and chanted a prayer in Yiddish that he himself had composed.

He begged the Almighty to redeem him from captivity and allow him to live the life of a Jew once more. This day, he ate a slice of bread left from the day before and cooked a pot of groats over the fireplace in the barn. Having said the benediction, he felt tired, and walked outside and lay down under a tree. He had found it necessary to keep a dog to protect the cattle from wild animals. At first he had disliked the black creature with its pointed muzzle and sharp teeth, repelled by its barking and obsequious licking which had reminded him of what the Talmud said on the subject and how the holy Isaac Luria, along with other cabalists, compared canines to the satanic hosts. But at length Jacob had grown accustomed to his dog, and had even named him, calling him Balaam. No sooner had Jacob lain under the tree, than Balaam sat down near him, stretched out his paws, and kept watch.

Jacob's eyes closed, and the sun, red and summery, shone through his lids. Above him the tree was filled with birds, twittering, singing, trilling. He was neither awake nor asleep, having retreated into the weariness of his body. So be it. This was the way God had willed it.

Ceaselessly he had prayed for death; he had even contemplated self-destruction. But now that mood had passed, and he had become inured to living among strangers, distant from his home, doing hard labor. As he drowsed, he heard pine cones falling and the coo of a cuckoo in the distance. He opened his eyes. The web of branches and pine needles strained the sunlight like a sieve, and the reflected light became a rainbow-colored mesh. A last drop of dew flamed, glistened, exploded into thin molten fibers. There was not

a cloud to sully the perfect blue of the sky. It was difficult
to believe in God's mercy when murderers buried children
alive. But God's wisdom was evident everywhere.

Jacob fell asleep and Wanda walked into his dreams.

I I I

The sun had moved westward; the day was nearing its
end. High overhead an eagle glided, large and slow, like a
celestial sailboat. The sky was still clear but a milk-white
fog was forming in the woods. Twisting itself into small
ovals, the mist thrust out tongues, and sought to evolve into
some coherent shape. Its inchoateness made Jacob think of
that primeval substance which, according to the philoso-
phers, gave birth to all things.

When he stood at the barn, Jacob could see for miles
around. The mountains remained as deserted as in the days
of the Creation. One above the other, the forests rose like
steps, first the leaf-bearing trees, and then the pines and firs.
Beyond the woods were the open ledges, and the pale snow,
like gray linen unfolding, was slowly moving down from
the summits ready to enshroud the world in winter. Jacob
recited the prayer of Minchah and walked to the hill from
which one could see the path to the village. Yes, Wanda
was on her way up. He recognized her by her figure, her
kerchief, her manner of walking. She looked no larger than
a finger, like one of those imps or sprites about whom she
told so many stories, fairies who lived in the crevasses of
rocks, in the hollows of tree trunks, under the eaves of
toadstools and who came out at dusk to play, dressed in

small green coats and wearing blue caps and red boots. He could not remove his eyes from her, charmed by her walk, by the way she paused to rest, by her disappearance among the trees, then by the sight of her, emerging from the woods higher up the slope. Now and again, the metal pitcher in her hand gleamed like a diamond. He saw that she was carrying the basket in which she brought him food.

As she approached nearer and nearer, she grew larger and larger, and Jacob ran toward her, ostensibly to be of assistance, although the pitchers she was carrying were still empty. She caught sight of him and stopped. He was moving toward her like a bridegroom seeking his bride. When he reached her, shyness and affection, both equally intense, mingled within him. Jewish law, he knew, forbade him to look at her, yet he saw everything: her eyes which were sometimes blue, sometimes green, her full lips, her long, slim neck, her womanly bosom. Like any other peasant she worked in the fields, but her hands remained feminine. He felt awkward standing beside her. His hair was unkempt, his pants too short and as ragged as a beggar's. Being descended on his mother's side from Jews who had had constant dealings with the nobility and had rented their fields, he had been taught Polish as a child, and now in his captivity he had learned to speak the language like a gentile. At times, he even forgot the Yiddish name for some object.

"Good evening, Wanda."

"Good evening, Jacob."

"I watched you coming up the mountain."

"Did you?"

The blood rushed to her face.

"You looked no larger than a pea."

"Things look that way from a distance."

"They do," Jacob said. "The stars are as large as the whole world, but they are so far off, they appear to be little dots."

Wanda became silent. He often used strange words which she did not understand. He had told her his story, and she knew that he was descended from Jews who lived in a far-off place, that he had studied books, and that he had had a wife and children whom the Cossacks had slaughtered. But what were Jews? What was written in their books? Who were the Cossacks? All of these things were beyond her comprehension. Nor did she understand his statement that the stars were as large as the earth. If they were really that large, how could so many cluster above the village? But Wanda had long since decided that Jacob was a profound thinker. Who knew, perhaps he was a wizard as was whispered by the women in the valley? But whatever he was, she loved him. Evening for her was the festive part of the day.

He took the pitchers from her and they finished the ascent together. Another man would have taken her by the arm or placed a hand upon her shoulder, but Jacob walked beside her with the timidity of a boy, exuding a sunny warmth and trailing the odors of grass and barn. Yet Wanda had already proposed marriage, or, if he was unwilling to commit himself to that, cohabitation without the priest's blessing. He had pretended not to hear her suggestion and only later had he remarked that fornication was forbidden. God looked down from heaven and rewarded and punished each man according to his deeds.

As if she were unaware of that! But in the village love was a random matter. The priest had fathered a half dozen bastards. Such a proposal as she had made to Jacob would have been refused by no other man. Were not all the villagers pursuing her, including Stephan, the bailiff's son? Not a week passed without some boy's mother or sister approaching her to arrange a match. She was forever receiving and returning gifts. Wanda found Jacob's attitude perplexing and she walked with bowed head thinking about this puzzle which she was unable to solve. She had fallen in love with the slave at first sight, and though over the years they had been much together, he had stayed remote. Many times she had come to the conclusion that from this dough would come no bread, and that she was wasting her youth on him. But the strength of the attraction he exerted upon her did not abate, and she could scarcely endure waiting for evening. She had become the subject of gossip in the village. The women laughed at her and passed sly comments. It was said that the slave had bewitched her; whatever it was, she was unable to free herself.

Thoughtfully she bent down, plucked a flower, and tearing away its petals began, "He loves me; he loves me not." The last petal assured her that the answer was "yes." But if so, how long would he go on tormenting her?

Now the sun sank rapidly, dropped behind the mountains. Accompanied by the croaking and screaming of birds, the day ended. Smoke rose from the bushes and the cowherds yodeled. The women were already preparing the evening meal, perhaps roasting some animal which had fallen into a trap.

I V

In addition to bread and vegetables, Wanda, without the knowledge of her mother and sister, had brought Jacob a rare gift, an egg laid by the white hen, and while she milked the cows, he prepared supper. He placed a few dry branches on the stones, lit a fire, and boiled the egg. He had left the barn door open although it was already dark, and the flames from the pine branches mottled Wanda's face with fiery spots and were reflected in her eyes. He sat on a log remembering the meal eaten before the fast of the ninth day of the month of Ob. An egg was consumed then as a sign of mourning: a rolling egg symbolized the changeability of man's fate. He washed his hands, let them dry, said grace, and dipped his bread into the salt. There was no table in the barn and so he used a pail turned upside down. He gained his sustenance from vegetables and fruit; meat he never tasted. As he ate, he glanced at Wanda out of the corner of his eyes, Wanda who was as devoted to him as a wife, and who every day prepared him something special. "In the mercy of the nations is sin," he said to himself, quoting a commentary on a passage from the Bible and trying to strangle the love he felt for her. Had all this been done by her for the sake of God? No, it was desire for him that had prompted her. Her love depended upon outward show, and should he become a cripple, God forbid, or lose his manhood, her love would cease. And yet such was the power of the flesh that man looked only at the surface and did not probe into such matters too deeply. He heard the sound of the milk falling into the pail and he paused in his eating to listen. Grasshoppers were singing and there was a buzzing and humming of bees, gnats, flies, multitude upon multitude of creatures each with its own voice. The stars in the heavens had kindled their fires. A sickle of a moon was aloft in the sky.

"Is the egg all right?" Wanda asked.

"Good and fresh."

"Could anything be fresher? I saw the hen lay it. The moment it fell to the straw, I thought, this is for Jacob. The shell was still warm."

"You're a good woman, Wanda."

"I can be bad as well. It depends on whom I'm with. I was bad to Stach, peace be with him."

"Why was that?"

"I don't know. He demanded, he never asked. If he wanted me in the night, he woke me from the middle of sleep. In the daytime, he would push me down in an open field."

Her words aroused both passion and disgust in Jacob.

"That was not right."

"What does a peasant know of right or wrong? He just takes what he wants. I was sick once and my forehead was as hot as an oven but he came to me and I had to give myself."

"The Torah says that a man must not force his wife," Jacob said. "She must be wooed by him until she is willing."

"Where is the Torah? In Josefov?"

"The Torah is everywhere."

"How can it be everywhere?"

"The Torah tells how a man should conduct himself."

Wanda was silent.

"That's for the city. Here the men are wild bulls. Swear to me that you'll never reveal what I tell you."

"Whom would I tell?"

"My own brother threw himself on me. I was only eleven years old. He'd come back from the tavern. Mother was asleep but my screams woke her. She picked up the pail of slops and poured it over him."

Jacob paused a moment before speaking again.

"Things like that don't happen among the Jews."

"That's what you say. They killed our God."

"How can a man kill a God?"

"Don't ask me. I'm only telling you what the priest says. Really, are you a Jew?"

"Yes, a Jew."

"It's hard for me to believe. Become one of us and we'll get married. I'll be a good wife and we'll have our hut in the valley. Zagayek will give us our share of land. We'll work our time for the count, and what's left over we'll have for ourselves. There's nothing we won't have—cows, pigs, chickens, geese, ducks. You know how to read and write and when Zagayek dies you'll take his place."

It was some time before Jacob answered.

"No, I cannot. I am a Jew. For all I know, my wife is alive."

"You've said many times that everyone was killed. But even if she still lives, what's the difference? She's there and you're here."

"God is everywhere."

"And it will hurt God if you are a free man instead of a slave? You walk around barefoot, half naked. Summers you spend in the barn, winters you freeze in the granary. Sooner or later they'll kill you."

"Who will kill me?"

"Oh, they'll kill you all right."

"And so then I'll be with the other holy spirits."

"I pity you, Jacob. I pity you."

Both fell into a long silence and in the barn there was quiet except when a cow now and again stamped its hoof. The last embers in the fireplace died, and when Jacob had finished eating he walked out into the open air to say the benediction in a place unpolluted by dung. Evening had fallen but in the west the last shreds of the sunset lingered. Usually, the women who brought food to the cowherds did not loiter on the mountain since at night the way home was considered dangerous. But Wanda would often stay late despite her mother's scolding and the women's persistent gossip. She was as strong as a man and she knew the proper incantations to drive off the evil spirits. She had finished milking the cows and, in the darkness of the barn, she poured milk from the pail into the pitchers. She scrubbed the churn with straw and cleaned globs of mud off the hips of the cows. All this she did swiftly and with great skill. Her tasks accomplished, she went outside, and the dog ran from Jacob to her, wagged its tail and jumped on her with its front paws. She bent down and he licked her face.

"Balaam, enough," she ordered. "He's more affectionate than you," she said to Jacob.

"An animal has no obligations."

"But they too have souls."

She delayed going home, sat down near the barn, and Jacob sat also. They always spent some time together and always on exactly the same rocks. If the moon was not out, she saw him by the light of the stars, but it was as bright this evening as at the full moon. Gazing at her in silence, Jacob was seized by love and desire, and restrained himself with difficulty. The blood in his veins seethed like water about to boil, and hot and cold fire zigzagged down his spine. "Remember this world is only a corridor," he warned himself. "The true palace lies beyond. Don't let yourself be barred from it for the sake of a moment's pleasure."

v

"What's new with your family?" Jacob inquired.

Wanda awoke from her reverie.

"What could be new? Father works, chops down trees in the woods and drags them home. He's so weak the logs almost knock him down. He wants to rebuild our hut, or God knows what. At his age! He's so tired at evening he can't swallow his food, and drops on the bed as though his legs had been cut off. He won't live much longer."

Jacob's brow furrowed.

"That's no way to talk."

"It's the truth."

"No one knows the decrees of Heaven."

"Maybe not, but when your strength gives out, you die. I can tell who's going to go—not only the old and sick, but the young and healthy too. I take one look and it comes to me. Sometimes I'm afraid to say anything because I don't want to be thought a witch. But all the same, I know. There's no change with Mother, she spins a little, cooks a little, plays at being sick. We only see Antek on Sundays, and sometimes not even then. Marisha is pregnant, will be in labor soon. Basha is lazy. Mother calls her the lazy cat. But a dance or a party revives her. Wojciech gets crazier and crazier."

"What about the grain? Is the crop good?"

"When has it ever been good?" Wanda answered. "In the valley you get rich, black earth, but here it's all stony. You could drive a cart of oxen between the stalks. We still have some rye from last year, but most of the peasants eat their knuckles. What little good earth we have belongs to the count and anyway Zagayek steals everything."

"Doesn't the count ever come here?"

"Just about never. He lives in another country and doesn't even know he owns this village. About six years ago, a bunch of them descended upon us in the middle of summer—like now, before harvest. They got the idea they wanted to go hunting and tramped back and forth in the fields with their horses and dogs. Their servants snatched calves, chickens, goats, even a peasant's rabbit. Zagayek crawled after them kissing everyone's behind. Oh, he's high and mighty enough with the people around here, but as soon as he meets someone from the city he becomes a boot licker. When they went away, there was nothing but a wasteland left. The peasants starved that winter; the children turned yellow and died."

"Couldn't someone have spoken to them?"

"The nobles? They were always drunk. The peasants kissed their feet and all the thanks they got were a few strokes with a riding crop. The girls got raped; they arrived home with bloody shifts and an ache in their hearts. Nine months later they gave birth to bastards."

"We do not have such murderers among the Jews."

"No? What do the Jewish aristocrats do?"

"The Jews have no gentry."

"Who owns the land?"

"The Jews have no land. When they had a country of their own, they worked the earth themselves and possessed vineyards and olive groves. But here in Poland, they live by trade and handicraft."

"Why is that? We have it bad, but if you work hard and have a good wife, you at least own something. Stach was strong but lazy. He should have been Basha's husband, not mine. He kept putting off everything; he'd cut the hay and let it lie around until the rain soaked it. All he wanted to do was sit in the inn and talk. The truth was his time was up. On our wedding night I dreamed he was dead and his face black as a pot. I didn't tell anyone but I was sure he wouldn't last long. The day it happened, the weather wasn't bad. All of a sudden lightning struck and came straight through our window. It rolled along like a fiery apple, looking for Stach. He wasn't in the hut, but it went into the granary and found him. When I reached him his face was charred like soot."

"Don't you ever see anything good in your dreams?"

"Yes, I've told you. I foresaw that you would come to us. But I wasn't dreaming, I was wide awake. Mother was frying rye cakes and father had slaughtered a chicken that was starving because it had a growth in its beak. I poured some soup on the cakes and I looked into the bowl which was filled with great circles of fat. A mist rose and I saw you there as plain as I see you now."

"Where did you get such powers?" Jacob asked after a pause.

"I don't know, Jacob. But I've known all along that we were fated for each other. My heart knocked like a hammer when father brought you home from the fair. You weren't wearing a shirt and I gave you one of Stach's. Wacek and I were about to be betrothed, but when I saw you his image was erased from my heart. Marila has been laughing ever since. He fell into her hands like ripe fruit. I saw him at a wedding a short time ago and he was drunk. He started to cry and talk to me the way he used to. Marila was beside herself. But I don't want him, Jacob."

"Wanda, you must get such ideas out of your head."

"Why, Jacob, why?"

"I've already told you why."

"I never understand you, Jacob."

"Your faith is not my faith."

"Haven't I said that I'm willing to change my faith?"

"One can't belong to my faith unless one believes in God and his Torah. Just because one wants a man is not enough."

"I believe in what you believe."

"Where would we live? If a Christian becomes a Jew here, he's burned at the stake."

"There must be some place."

"Perhaps among the Turks."

"All right, let's escape."

"I don't know the mountains."

"I know them."

"The country of the Turks is very distant. We'd be arrested on the road."

The two once more fell into silence. Wanda's face was completely wreathed in shadows. From somewhere in the distance came a cowherd's yodel, muted and languorous as if the singer was expressing Wanda and Jacob's dilemma and bewailing the harshness of fate. A breeze had begun to blow and the rustle of branches mingled with the sound of the mountain stream as it coursed among the rocks.

"Come to me," Wanda said and her words were half command and half entreaty. "I must have you."

"No. I cannot. It is forbidden."

2

1

For Wanda the way down the mountain was more difficult than the way up. She was burdened now by the two pitchers filled with milk, and a heavy heart. But, terrified, she almost ran down the slopes. The path took her through towering grass, underbrush, forests; strange murmurs and rustles came from the thickets. Hostile imps and derisive spirits were abroad, she knew. They might play nasty pranks on her. A rock might be put in the path; the imps might swing from the pitchers and make them heavier; they might weave elflocks in her hair or dirty the milk with devil's dung. Demons abounded in the village and surrounding mountains. Each house had its familiar spirit dwelling behind the stove. Werewolves and trolls swarmed the roads, each monster with its own peculiar type of cunning. An owl hooted. Frogs croaked with human voices. Kobalt, the devil who spoke with his belly, was wandering somewhere in the neighborhood; Wanda heard his heavy breathing which sounded like a death rattle. And yet fear could not dull the pain of love. Her rejection by the Jewish slave intensified her desire. She was ready to leave the village, her parents, her family, and follow Jacob naked and empty-handed. She had told herself many times that she was a fool to be angry. Who was this man? If she wished she could get one of the village boys to kill him, and no tears would be shed. But what was the use of murder when you loved the victim? The ache in her throat choked her. Her face stung as if it had been slapped. Men had always chased after her—her own brother, the urchin who tended the geese. Jacob's spirit was stronger.

"A sorcerer!" Wanda said to herself. "He's bewitched me."

But where was the charm hidden? Slipped into a knot in her dress? Tied to a fringe of her shawl? It might be hidden in a lock of her hair. She searched everywhere, found nothing. Ought she to consult old Maciocha, the village witch? But the woman was insane, babbled out all her secrets. No, Maciocha could not be trusted. Wanda became so occupied with her thoughts she didn't know how she managed the descent. But suddenly she was at the bottom of the mountain approaching her father's hut. It was little more than a hovel with crumbling beams overgrown with moss and birds' nests hanging from the thatch. The building had two windows, one covered with a cow's bladder and the other open to permit the smoke from the fire to escape. In summer Jan Bzik permitted no illumination but on winter evenings a wick burned in a shard or kindling was lit. Wanda entered, and though it was dark inside, she saw as clearly as if it had been day.

Her father lay on the bed. He was barefoot and in torn clothes. He seldom undressed. She couldn't tell whether he was asleep or just resting. Her mother and her sister Basha were busy braiding a rope of straw. The bed that Jan Bzik lay on was the only one in the hut; the whole family slept in it, Wanda included. Years before when her brother Antek had still been unmarried Jan Bzik would have intercourse with his wife before going to sleep and the children would have something to amuse them. But Antek no longer lived at home and the couple had become too old for such games. Everyone expected Jan Bzik to die shortly. Antek who was anxious to take over the house appeared every few days to ask shamelessly, "Well, is the old man still alive?"

"Yes, still alive," his mother would answer. She also wanted to be rid of this nuisance. He wasn't worth the bread he ate. He had become weak, morose, irritable. All day he belched. Like a beaver, he kept gathering wood, but the thin, crooked logs he brought home were only good for the fire.

They scarcely spoke to each other in that hut. The old woman had a grudge against Wanda for not remarrying.

Basha's husband Wojciech had gone home to live with his own parents; he had become despondent after the marriage. Basha had already borne three children, one by her husband, and two bastards; all of them had died. Jan Bzik and his wife had also buried two sons, boys who had been as strong as oaks. The family had become embogged in bitterness and sadness; silent antagonism simmered and bubbled in that household like kasha on a stove.

Wanda didn't say a word to any of them. She poured the milk from the pitchers into some jars. Half of what the cows gave belonged to Zagayek the bailiff; he owned a dairy in the village where cheese was made. The Bziks would use their half the following day for cooking and drinking with bread. The family lived well compared to those around them. In a shed behind the house were two sacks, one of rye and one of barley, and also a handmill in which to grind the grain. Bzik's fields, unlike most, had been partially cleared of stones over the years and the rocks used to build a fence. But food isn't everything. Jan Bzik continued to mourn his dead sons. He couldn't tolerate Antek or his daughter-in-law Marisha. Basha he disliked because of her indiscretions. Wanda was the only one he loved and she had been a widow for years and had brought him no joy. Antek, Basha, and the old woman had become allies. They kept their secrets from Wanda as though she were a stranger. But Wanda managed the household. Her father even consulted her on how to sow and reap. She had a man's brain. If she said something, you could rely on it.

Stach's death had brought her humiliation. She had been forced to return to her parents and again sleep with them and Basha in one bed. Now she would often spend the night in the hayloft or granary, although these places were crawling with rats and mice. She decided to sleep in the granary that night. The hut stank. Her family conducted themselves like animals. It hadn't occurred to any of them that the stream that flowed before their house could be used for bathing. It was the same one that passed near Jacob's barn.

Wanda picked up her pillow; it was stuffed with straw and hay. She walked toward the door.

"Sleeping in the granary?" her mother asked.

"Yes, in the granary."

"You'll be back tomorrow with your nose bitten off."

"Better to have your nose bitten than your soul."

Often Wanda herself was amazed by the words that issued from her lips. At times they had the pithiness and wit of a bishop's talk. Basha and her mother gaped. Jan Bzik stirred and murmured something. He liked to boast that Wanda resembled him and had inherited his brain. But what was intelligence worth if you didn't have luck?

11

The peasants went to bed early. Why sit around in the dark? Anyway they had to get up again at four. But there were always a few who hung around the tavern until it was late. The tavern was presumably the property of the count; it was in fact owned by Zagayek. He supplied its liquor from his still. That evening Antek was among the customers. One of Zagayek's bastard daughters waited on tables. The peasants nibbled pork sausage and drank. All sorts of strange and curious occurrences were discussed.

The previous harvest a malevolent spirit named the Polonidca had appeared in the fields, carrying a sickle and
dressed in white. The Polonidca had wandered around asking difficult riddles and demanding answers of all she met.
For example: What four brothers chase but never catch
each other? Answer: The four wheels of a wagon. What
is dressed in white but black to the sight and wherever it
goes speaks right? Answer: A letter. What eats like a
horse, drinks like a horse, but sees with its tail as well as
with its eyes? Answer: A blind horse. If the peasant didn't
know the right answer the Polonidca tried to cut off his
head with her sickle. She would pursue the man as far as
the chapel. He would become ill and lie sick for many days.

The Dizwosina was another savage spirit. This terrifying
succubus had stringy hair and came from Bohemia on the
other side of the mountains. Recently she had entered the
hut of old Maciek and had tickled his heels until he had
died from laughter. She had taken three of the village boys
as her lovers and had forced them to lie in the fields and do
her will. One boy had become so emaciated he had died of
the phthisis. It was also the custom of the Dizwosina to lie
in wait for girls and win their confidence by braiding their
hair, putting garlands around their necks, and dancing
with them in a circle. But then after amusing herself with
the maidens, she would spatter and cover them with filth.

Skrzots also had been seen this year in the granaries.
This was a bird that dragged its wings and tail on the
ground. As was well known, it came from an egg which
had been hatched in a human armpit. But who in the village
would do such mischief? It clearly couldn't be the men;
only women would have the time and patience for things

like that. In the winter the Skrzot got cold in the granary and would knock at the door of a hut and seek to be let in. Then the Skrzot brought good luck. But in all other respects it was harmful and consumed vast amounts of grain. If its excrement fell on the human eye, blindness followed. The opinion of those in the tavern was that a search party should be organized to find out what women were carrying eggs under their arms. But by far the strangest thing that had happened recently concerned a young virgin. The girl swore she had been attacked by a vampire. The monster had fastened its teeth to her breasts and had drunk until dawn. In the morning the girl had been found in a swoon, the teethmarks on her skin clearly visible.

And yet concerned though they were with vampires and succubuses, they spoke even more about Jacob who lived on the mountain and who tended Jan Bzik's cattle. It was a sin, they said, to maintain an infidel in a Christian village. Who knew where this man came from or what his intentions were? He said that he was a Jew, but if that was so he had murdered Jesus Christ. Why, then, should he be given asylum? Antek said that as soon as his father "croaked," he would take care of Jacob. But the listeners replied that they couldn't wait that long.

"You've seen how your sister crawls to him every day," one peasant remarked to Antek. "It'll end up with her giving birth to a monster."

Antek deliberated before he replied.

"She claims he doesn't touch her."

"Eh, woman's talk!"

"Her belly's flat."

"Flat today, swollen tomorrow," another peasant interjected. "Did you hear about the beggar that came to Lippica? This one was a fine talker and the women followed him around. Three months after he left, five monsters were born. They had nails, teeth, and spurs. Four were strangled but one woman out of pity tried secretly to nurse hers. It bit off her nipple."

"What did she do then?"

"She screamed and her brother picked up a flail and killed it."

"Bah, such things happen," an old peasant said, licking the pork fat off his mustache.

The tavern was half in ruins. Its roof was broken; mushrooms grew on its walls. Two tables and four benches were in the room which was lit by a wick burning in a shard; the single flame smoked and sputtered. The peasants cast heavy shadows on the wall. There was no floor. One of the men got up to relieve himself and stood at a heap of garbage in the corner. Zagayek's daughter laughed with her toothless gums.

"Too lazy to go outside, little father?"

Heavy steps could be heard, and a groaning and snorting. Dziobak, the priest, entered. He was a short, broad-shouldered man; he looked as if he had been sawed in half and glued and nailed together again. His eyes were green as gooseberries, his eyebrows dense as brushes. He had a thick nose with pimples and a receding chin.

Dziobak's robe was covered with stains. He was bent and hunched up, supported himself by two heavy canes. Priests are clean shaven, but coarse, stiff hairs like the bristles of a pig sprouted on his chin. For years the charge had been made that he neglected his duties. Rain leaked into the chapel. Half of the Virgin's head had been smashed. On Sundays when it was time to say Mass Dziobak often lay in a drunken stupor. But his one defender was Zagayek, who ignored all the denunciations. As for the majority of the peasants, they continued to worship the ancient idols that had been the gods of Poland before the truth had been revealed.

"Well, good householders, I see you're all busy with the bottle," Dziobak's hollow voice came from his chest as if from a barrel. "Yes, one needs a drink to burn out the devil."

"Well, it's a drink," Antek said, "but it doesn't burn."

"Does she mix it with water?" Dziobak asked, pointing at the barmaid. "Are you swindling the householders?"

"There's not a drop of water there, little Father. They run from water like the devil from incense."

"Well said."

"Why don't you sit down, Father?"

"Yes, my small feet do ache. It's a hard job for them to carry the weight of me."

Grandiose language was still available to him; he had studied in a seminary in Crakow, but everything else he had learned he had forgotten. He opened his froglike mouth, exposing his one long black tooth which resembled a cleat.

"Won't you have a drink, Father?" the barmaid asked.

"A drink," Dziobak repeated after her.

She brought him a wooden mug filled with vodka. Dziobak eyed it suspiciously and with visible distaste. He grimaced as if he had a pain in his stomach.

"Well, good people, to your health." He quickly gulped

down the liquid. His face became more distorted; disappointment gleamed in his green eyes. It was as if he had been served vinegar.

"We're talking about the Jew Jan Bzik keeps on the mountain, Father."

Dziobak became incensed.

"What's there to talk about? Climb up and dispose of him in God's name. I warned you, did I not, little brothers? I said he would bring only misfortune."

"Zagayek has forbidden it."

"I count Zagayek as my friend and defender. We can be sure that he does not want the village to fall into the hands of Lucifer."

Dziobak peeked at the wooden mug out of the corner of his eyes.

"Just another drop."

III

Jacob awoke in the middle of the night. His body was hot and tense; his heart was pounding. He had been dreaming of Wanda. Passion overwhelmed him and an idea leaped into his brain. He must run down to the valley and find her. He knew she sometimes slept in the granary. "I'm damned already," he told himself. But even as he said it he was aware it was Satan speaking within him.

He must calm himself. He walked to the stream. The brook had its source in glacial snows and its waters were ice cold even in summer. But it was necessary for Jacob to perform his ablutions. What else remained for him but the doing of such acts? He took off his pants and waded into the stream. The moon had already set, but the night was thick with stars. Rumor had it that a water devil made its home in these waters and sang so beautifully in the evening that boys and girls were lured to their destruction. But Jacob knew that a Jew had no right to be afraid of witchcraft or astrology. And if he were dragged down into the current, he would be better off.

"Let it be His will that my death redeem all my sins," he murmured, choosing those words which in ancient times had been spoken by those put to death by the Sanhedrin. The stream was shallow and filled with rocks, but at one spot the water reached to his chest. Jacob walked carefully. He slipped, almost fell. He was afraid that Balaam would begin barking, but the dog continued to sleep in his kennel. He reached the spot that was deepest and immersed himself. How strange. The coldness did not extinguish his lust. A passage from the Song of Songs came to his mind: Many waters cannot quench love, neither can the floods drown it. "What a comparison," he admonished himself. The love referred to in Scriptures was the love of God for his Chosen People. Each word was filled with mystery upon mystery. Jacob continued to immerse himself until he became calmer.

He came out of the water. Before, desire had made him tremble but now he shivered from the cold. He walked to the barn and threw his sheet over him. He murmured a prayer: "Lord, of the universe, remove me from this world, before I stumble and arouse Thy wrath. I am sick of being a wanderer among idolaters and murderers. Return me to that source from whence I came."

He had now become a man at war with himself. One

half of him prayed to God to save him from temptation, and the other sought some way to surrender to the flesh. Wanda was not married, she was a widow, the recalcitrant part of him argued. True, she did not undergo ablution after her periods, but the stream was here, available to her for this ritual. Were there any other interdictions? Only the one that forbade the marrying of a gentile. But this interdiction did not apply here. These were unusual circumstances. Had not Moses married a woman from Ethiopia? Did not King Solomon take as his wife Pharaoh's daughter? Of course, these women had become Jewesses. But so could Wanda. The Talmudic law stating that a man who cohabits with a gentile could be put to death by anyone in the community was only valid if there had first been a warning and the adultery was seen by witnesses.

In Jacob's case the normal order of things had been reversed. It was God who spoke in the simplest language while evil overflowed with learned quotations. How long did one live in this world? How long was one young? Was it worth while to destroy this existence and the one that would follow for a few moments of pleasure? "It's all because I don't study the Torah," Jacob said to himself. He started to mumble verses from the Psalms, and then an idea came to him. Hereafter to occupy his time he would enumerate the two hundred and forty-eight commandments and the three hundred and sixty-five prohibitions to be found in the Torah. Although he didn't know them by heart, his years of exile had taught him what a miser the human memory is. It didn't like to give, but if one remained stubborn and did not cease asking, it would pay out even more than what was demanded. Never left in peace, it would at last return all that had been deposited within it.

To be fruitful and multiply was the first of all the commandments. ("Perhaps have a child by Wanda," the legalist within Jacob interjected.) What was the second commandment? Circumcision. And the third? Jacob could not think of another commandment in the entire book of Genesis. So he began to reflect upon Exodus. What was the first commandment in that book? Very likely the eating of the Passover offering and of the unleavened bread. Yes, but what was the use of remembering these things when tomorrow he might forget them? He must find a way to write everything down. Suddenly he realized that he could do what Moses had done. If Moses had been able to chisel the Ten Commandments into stone, why couldn't he? Chiseling wasn't even necessary; he could scratch with an awl or a nail pried from one of the rafters. He recollected having seen a bent hook somewhere in the barn. Now Jacob found it impossible to return to sleep. A man must be clever in battling the Evil One. He must anticipate all of the Devil's stratagems. Jacob sat waiting for the light of the morning star. The barn was quiet. The cows slept. He heard the sound of the stream. The entire earth seemed to be holding its breath awaiting the new day. Now he had forgotten his lust. Once more he remembered that while he was sitting here in Jan Bzik's barn God continued to direct the world. Rivers flowed; waves billowed on the ocean. Each of the stars continued on its prescribed way. The grain in the fields would ripen soon and the harvest would begin. But who had ripened the grain? How could a stalk of wheat rise from a kernel? How could tree, leaf, branch,

fruit emerge from a pit? How could man appear from a
drop of semen in a woman's womb? These were all
miracles, wonders of wonders. Yes, there were many questions one might ask of God. But who was man to comprehend the acts of divinity?

Jacob was now too impatient to wait for sunrise. "I
thank Thee," he said, rising, and then he washed his hands.
As he did so a purple beam appeared in the crack beneath
the door. He walked outside. The sun had just risen from
behind the mountains. The bird which always announced
the coming of day chirped shrilly. This was one creature
that did not oversleep.

It had become light enough to reach for the hook. Its
place was on the shelf where the milk pots were stored. But
it had disappeared. Well, that was Satan's work, Jacob
thought. He did not wish Jacob to engrave the six hundred
and thirteen laws. Jacob took down the earthen pots, one
by one, and put them back on the shelf. He rummaged on
the ground, searching among the straw. He remained hope-
ful. The important thing was not to give up. Good things
never came easily.

At last he found it. It had slipped into a crack on the
shelf. He didn't understand how he could have missed it.
Yes, everything, it seemed, was ordained. Years before
someone had left the hook there so that Jacob could engrave God's edicts.

He left the barn to find a suitable stone. He did not have
to search far. Behind the barn a large rock protruded from
the earth. There it stood as ready as the ram which Father
Abraham had sacrificed as a burnt offering instead of Isaac.
The stone had been waiting ever since Creation.

What he wrote would be visible to no one; it would be hidden behind the barn. Balaam began to wag his tail and jump as if his canine soul comprehended what his master was preparing to do.

IV

Harvest time was approaching and Jan Bzik brought Jacob down from the mountain. How painful it was for the slave to leave his solitude! He had already scratched forty-three commandments and sixty-nine interdictions into the rock. What wonders issued from his mind. He tortured memory and things he had long forgotten appeared. His was a never ending struggle with Purah, the lord of oblivion. In this battle force and persuasion were both necessary; patience was also required, but concentration was most important of all. Jacob sat midway between the barn and rock, concealing himself with weeds and the branches of a midget pine. He mined within himself as men dig for treasure in the earth. It was slow work; he scratched sentences, fragments of sentences, single words into the stone. The Torah had not disappeared. It lay hidden in the nooks and crannies of his brain.

But now he was forced to interrupt his task.

It had been a dry summer, and though there was never much of a harvest in the village, this year's crop was particularly meager. The stalks of grain grew further apart than usual and their kernels were small and brittle. As always, the peasants prayed to both the image of the Virgin and the old lime trees which commanded the rain spirits.

These were not the only rites. Pine branches, lurers of

rain, were set among the furrows. The village's wooden rooster, a relic of ancient times, was wrapped in green wheat stalks and decked with saplings. Dancing around the lime trees with the decorated image, the villagers doused it with water. In addition to such public ceremonies, each peasant had his own unique rituals which had been handed down from father to son. Relatives of men who had hanged themselves visited the suicides' graves and begged the un-sanctified bones not to cause drought. But rain was not the only problem. As everyone knew, a wicked Baba hid in the stalks and an evil Dziad in the tips. As soon as one furrow was reaped the Baba and Dziad fled and concealed them-selves in another. Even when the whole crop had been bound in sheaves, no one could be sure that the danger was over as tiny Babas and minuscule Dziads sought final refuge in the unhusked kernels, and had to be thrashed out with flails. Until the last small Baba had been crushed, the crop was not safe.

This year all the customs had been scrupulously fol-lowed, but somehow had been of no avail. There was a grumbling among the peasants when they learned that Jan Bzik had brought Jacob down from the mountain. The poorness of the harvest was perhaps his work. A complaint was made to the bailiff Zagayek, but his answer was, "Let him do his job first. It's never too late to kill him."

So from early morning until sunset Jacob stood in the fields, and Wanda did not leave him. It was she who taught him how to reap, showed him how the scythe should be sharpened, brought him the food he was permitted to eat: bread, onions, fruit. The law did not allow him to drink milk now since he had not been present at the milkings.

But fortunately the chickens were laying well and Wanda secretly gave him an egg each day, which he drank raw. He could also take sour milk and butter since the law stated that the milk of unclean animals does not turn. His sin was heinous enough merely eating the bread of the gentile; his soul could not tolerate further sullying.

The work was difficult, and his fellow harvesters never stopped ridiculing him. Here was a man who wouldn't drink soup or milk and never touched pork. This fellow fasted while he worked.

"You'll wither away," he was warned. "The next thing you know you'll be stretched out flat."

"God gives me strength," Jacob answered.

"What God? Yours must live in the city."

"God is everywhere, in both city and country."

"You don't cut straight. You'll ruin the straw."

The women and girls giggled and whispered.

"Do you see, Wanda, how your man sweats?"

"He's the strongest in the village."

Hearing that remark, Jacob cautioned her.

"The man who can control his passions is the most powerful."

"What's that fool saying?"

The women winked at each other and laughed, exchanged lewd gestures. One girl ran over to Jacob and pulled up her skirts. This made the peasants whinny with laughter.

"That's a fine show for you, Jew."

As he reaped, Jacob kept up a constant recitation, repeating to himself Psalms and passages of the Mishnah and Gemara. He had been there when the oxen plowed the fields and the seed was sowed. Now he was harvesting the grain. Weeds grew among the stalks and corn flowers on the sides of the furrows. As the scythes moved, field mice ran from their blades, but other creatures remained in the harvested fields: grasshoppers, lady bugs, beetles, flyers and crawlers, every variety of insect, and each with its own particular structure. Surely some Hand had created all this. Some Eye was watching over it. From the mountains came grasshoppers and birds that spoke with human voices, and the peasants killed them with their shovels. Their efforts were to no avail, since the more they killed, the more gathered. Jacob was reminded of the plague of locusts that God had visited upon the Egyptians. He himself killed nothing. It was one thing to slaughter an animal according to the law and in such a way as to redeem its soul, another to step on and crush tiny creatures that sought no more than man did—merely to eat and multiply. At dusk when the fields were alive with toads, Jacob walked carefully, so as not to tread on their exposed bodies.

Now and again when the ribald songs of the harvesters resounded in the fields, Jacob would take up a chant of his own, the Sabbath service, or the liturgies of Rosh Hashana and Yom Kippur, or sing the Akdamoth, a Pentecost song. Wanda joined in, for she had picked up the tunes from Jacob, singing Jewish chants and recitatives with a voice that had been accustomed to ballads of a different kind. Jacob's soul throbbed with music. He kept up a constant debate with the Almighty. "How long will the unholy multitudes rule the world and the scandal and darkness of Egypt hold dominion? Reveal Thy Light, Father in Heaven. Let there be an end to pain and idolatry and the shedding of blood. Scourge us no longer with plagues and famines. Do not allow the weak to go down to defeat and the wicked to triumph. . . . Yes, Free Will was necessary, and Your face had to be hidden, but there has been enough of concealment. We are already up to our necks in water." So absorbed did he become in his chant that he did not notice that all the others had become silent. His voice sang alone and everyone was listening. The peasants clapped hands, laughed, and mimicked him. Jacob stood with bent head, ashamed.

"Pray, Jew, pray. Not even your God can make this a good harvest."

"Do you think he's cursing us?"

"What language is that you're speaking, Jew?"

"The Holy Language."

"What Holy Language?"

"The language of the Bible."

"The Bible? What's the Bible?"

"God's Law."

"What's God's Law?"

"That one neither kill nor steal nor covet a man's wife."

"Dziobak says things like that in the chapel."

"It all comes from the Bible."

The peasants became silent. One of them handed Jacob a turnip.

"Eat, stranger. You won't get strong from fasting."

v

The crop had been poor, but nevertheless the peasants celebrated. Girls appeared in the fields with wreaths on their heads and the older women assembled also. The time had come for Zagayek to superintend the selection of the maiden who would reap the last Baba. The choice was made by drawing lots and the girl chosen cut the last sheaf of grain, thereby becoming a Baba herself. Once selected, she was wrapped in stalks tied round her body by flax, and paraded from hut to hut in a wooden-wheeled cart drawn by four boys. The whole village accompanied the procession, laughing and singing and clapping hands. It was said that in ancient times when the people had still been idol worshipers the Baba was thrown into the stream and drowned, but now the village was Christian.

The night following this ceremony, the peasants danced and drank. The Baba performed with the boy who was chosen to be rooster. The rooster crowed, chased chickens, did all kinds of antics. He had a pair of wings on his shoulders, a cockscomb on his head and on his heels wooden spurs. Last year's rooster was also there, and the two fought, pushing out their chests, charging each other, tearing each other's feathers. It was so funny the girls couldn't stop laughing. This year's rooster always won, and then danced with the Baba who was now disguised as a witch, her face smeared with soot, and with the broom in her hand on which she rode to the Black Mass. The Baba seated herself in a barrel hoop and lifted her skirts, preparing to make a journey. The peasants forgot their troubles. The children refused to go to bed, sipped vodka, laughed and giggled.

Since it was no longer permissible to drown the real Baba, the boys made an effigy from straw. So skillfully did they model face, breasts, hips and feet, that the scarecrow, with two coals in the head for eyes, seemed alive. Just as the sun rose, the Baba was led to the stream. The women scolded the scapegoat, demanding that she take with her the evil eye and all their misfortunes and illnesses. The men and children spat on her, and then she was thrown into the stream. Everyone watched the straw Baba move downstream, bobbing up and down in the current. As the peasants knew, the river flowed into the Vistula and the Vistula emptied into the sea where bad spirits were awaiting the Baba. Though she wasn't alive, the over-compassionate girls wept for her. Was there such a great difference between flesh and straw? The ceremony over, vodka was passed around, and Jacob was given a drink. Wanda whispered into his ear, "I wish I were the Baba. I would swim with you to the end of the world."

The next day, the threshing began. From sunrise to sunset there was the sound of flails rising and falling. Occasionally a muffled cry or sob rose from the stalks. One of the small Babas was dying. The evenings were still warm enough for the threshers to stay out of doors, and so after supper they gathered branches and lit a fire. Chestnuts were roasted, riddles asked, stories told of werewolves, hobgoblins, demons. The most spine-tingling tale concerned the black field where only black grain sprouted and where a black reaper reaped with a long black scythe. The girls screamed and clutched each other, huddled closer to the boys. The autumn days were brilliant, but the nights were dark. Stars fell; frogs croaked, spoke with human voices from the bogs. Bats appeared and the girls scurried, covering their heads and screaming. If one of these nocturnal creatures entangled itself in a girl's hair, it meant that she would not live out the year.

Someone asked Jacob to sing and he performed a lullaby he had learned from his mother. The song pleased the peasants. He was asked for a story. He told them several tales from the Gemara and Midrash. The one they liked best was about a man who had heard of a harlot living in a distant country whose fee was four hundred gulden. When the man went to the harlot, he found she had prepared six silver beds with silver ladders and one golden bed with a golden ladder. The harlot had sat before him naked, but the fringes of his ritual garment had suddenly risen and struck him angrily in the face. At the end of the story the man converted the harlot to the Jewish faith and the beds she had prepared for him were finally used on their wedding night. The story was not easy to translate into Polish, but Jacob managed to make the peasants understand. They became fascinated by the fringes. What kind of fringes were they? Jacob explained. The glow from the fire lit up Wanda's face. She pulled his arm to her lips, kissed and then bit it. He sought to free himself but she hung to him tenaciously. Her breasts rubbed against his shoulder and the heat she gave off was like an oven's.

The story had been told for her, he knew. In the form of a parable he had promised that if she did not force him to cohabit with her now, later he would take her as a wife. But could he make such a promise? His wife might be alive. How could Wanda become a Jew? In Poland a Christian who became a Jewish convert was put to death; moreover, Jewish law forebade the conversion of gentiles for reasons other than faith.

"Well, every day I sink deeper into the abyss," Jacob thought.

Then on the last day of the threshing, a circus arrived in town. It was the first time Jacob had seen anyone from another district. The troupe included two men beside the owner, and they had a monkey, and a parrot who not only talked but told fortunes by selecting cards with his beak. The village was in an uproar. The performance was given in an open field near Zagayek's house and all of the men showed up with their wives and children. Jacob was permitted to go also. The bear whirled around on his hind legs, the monkey smoked a pipe and did somersaults. One of the men was an acrobat and did stunts like walking on his hands and lying bare-backed on a board of nails. The other was a musician and played a fiddle, a trumpet, and a drum with bells. The peasants screamed with joy and Wanda jumped up and down like a little girl. But Jacob disapproved of such entertainment, which he considered only one step away from witchcraft. More than a desire for amusement had brought him there. Circus men wandered from town to town, and perhaps this troupe had stopped at Josefov. They might have news of Jacob's family. So when the performance was done and the monkey and bear had been chained to a tree, Jacob followed the performers into their tent. The proprietor looked at Jacob in astonishment when he heard his question: had the circus stopped at Josefov.

"What business is it of yours where I've been?"

"I come from Josefov. I am a Jew and a teacher. I am a survivor of the massacre."

"How do you happen to be here?"

Jacob told the proprietor and the man snapped his whip.

"If the Jews knew where you were would they ransom you?"

"Yes, to free a captive is considered a holy act."

"Would they pay me if I told them you were alive?"

"Yes, they would."

"Give me your name. And I must have a way to convince them that I am telling the truth."

Jacob confided to the circus owner the names of his wife and children as well as that of his father-in-law who had been one of the community elders. Although the man could not write, he made a knot in a piece of string and told Jacob that he had not as yet been to Josefov, but he might well stop there. If any Jews were left in the town he would tell them that Jacob was alive and where he could be found.

3

I

After the harvest, Jacob returned to the barn on the mountain. He knew that he would not be there long. Soon the cold weather would set in and the cattle would have no food. Already the days had become shorter and when he gathered grass in the morning, he found the fields covered with frost. Haze hung over the autumn hills and it was increasingly difficult to distinguish between fog rising from the earth and the smoke of camp fires. The birds screamed and croaked more shrilly these days, and the winds blowing down from the summits carried the taste of snow. Though Jacob gathered as much fodder as he could, it was never enough for the cows. The hungry beasts bellowed, stamped on the earth, even pounded with their hoofs while they were being milked. Once more Jacob proceeded with his task of engraving the six hundred and thirteen laws of the Torah onto a stone, but he had little spare time during the day and at night it was too dark to work.

On the seventh day of the month of Elul—according to Jacob's calculations—dusk came quickly. The sun fell behind a massive cloud which covered the entire west. But was it really that date? For all he knew his reckonings might be erroneous and when the ram's horn was blown all over the world and the Rosh Hashana litanies sung, he would be out as usual gathering fodder. He sat in the barn and thought about his life. For as long as he could remember he had been considered lucky. His father had been a wealthy contractor who bought up the gentry's timber, supervised the felling of the trees and floated the logs down the Bug River to the Vistula and from thence to Danzig. Whenever his father had gone off on such trips, he had returned bearing gifts for Jacob and his sisters. Elka Sisel, Jacob's mother, was a rabbi's daughter and came from Prussia where she had been brought up in comfortable circumstances. Susschen, as she was called, spoke German and wrote Hebrew and conducted herself differently from the other women. She had rugs on the floor of her house and brass latches on the door. Coffee, a rarity even among the rich, was served daily in her home. An expert cook, seamstress, knitter, she taught her daughters how to do needlepoint and instructed them in Bible reading. The girls married young. Jacob himself was only twelve when he became engaged to Zelda Leah, who was two years younger, and the daughter of the town's elder. He had always been a good student. At eight he had read a complete page of the Gemara unassisted; at his engagement party he delivered a speech. He wrote in a fine, bold hand, had a good singing voice, and was a gifted draughtsman and wood carver. On a canvas on the east wall of the synagogue he painted the twelve constellations in red, green, blue and purple circling Jehovah's name, and in the corners put four animals: a deer, a lion, a leopard, and an eagle. At Pentecost he decorated the windows of the town's most important citizens and for the feast of Succoth adorned the tabernacle with lanterns and streamers.

Tall and healthy, when he made a fist, six boys could not force it open. His father had taught him to swim side and breast stroke. Zelda Leah, on the other hand, was thin and small—prematurely old, his sisters maintained. But of what possible interest was this ten-year-old child to Jacob? He was more interested in his father-in-law's library of rare books. Jacob received four hundred gulden as dowry, room and board at his in-laws for life.

The wedding was noisy and boisterous. Josefov was only a small town but after his marriage Jacob immersed himself so deeply in study that he forgot the outside world. True, his wife, he discovered, had odd habits. If her mother scolded her, she petulantly kicked off her shoes and stockings and overturned the soup bowl. She was a married woman and had not as yet menstruated. When her period

finally came, she bled like a slaughtered calf. Every time
Jacob approached her, she howled in pain. She was a perpetual sufferer from heartburn, headaches, and back aches.
She screwed up her face, wept, complained. But Jacob was
given to understand that only daughters were always like
that. Her mother was constantly tugging her from him,
but Zelda Leah bore him three children, Jacob scarcely
knew how. Her recriminations and sarcasms sounded like
the babblings of fools or school children; she belonged to
that class of spoiled daughters whose whims can never be
satisfied. Her mother, she said, was envious of her good
looks. Her father had forgotten her; Jacob didn't love her.
It never seemed to occur to her that she should try being
lovable. Her eyes grew prematurely old from too much
crying and her nose turned red. She didn't even take care of
the children. That too became her mother's responsibility.

When the rabbi died, Jacob's father-in-law wanted him
to take over the office, but Zaddock, the late rabbi's son,
had a considerable following. True, Jacob's backer was the
town's elder, a rich and influential man, but the people of
Josefov had decided that this one time they were not going
to let him have his way. Despite himself, Jacob found that
he was involved in a quarrel. He didn't want to become
rabbi, was actually in favor of Zaddock, and because of
this his father-in-law became his enemy. If he refused to
become rabbi, let him at least lecture to the boys in the
study house. Jacob would have liked to stay in the library,
studying the Gemara and its commentaries, meditating on
philosophy and cabala, subjects he preferred even to the
Talmud. From childhood on he had been searching for the

meaning of existence and trying to comprehend the ways of God. He was acquainted with the thought of Plato, Aristotle, and the Epicureans through the quotations he had found in *A Guide for the Perplexed*, the *Chuzary*, *The Beliefs and Ideas*, and similar works. He knew the cabalistic systems of Rabbi Moshe of Cordova and the holy Isaac Luria. He was well aware that Judaism was based upon faith and not knowledge and yet he sought to understand wherever it was possible. Why had God created the world? Why had He found it necessary to have pain, sin, evil? Even though each of the great sages had given his answer, the questions remained unsolved. An all-powerful Creator did not need to be sustained by the agony of small children and the sacrifice of His people to bands of assassins. The atrocities of the Cossacks had been talked about for years before the attack on Josefov. Hearts had long been frozen with fear, then one day death had struck.

Jacob had just turned twenty-five when the Cossacks had advanced on Josefov. He was now past twenty-nine, so he had lived a seventh of his life in this remote mountain village, deprived of family and community, separated from books, like one of those souls who wander naked in Tophet. And here it was the end of summer; the short days, the cold nights had come. He could reach out his hand and actually touch the darkness of Egypt, the void from which God's face was absent. Dejection is only one small step from denial. Satan became arrogant and spoke to Jacob insolently: "There is no God. There is no world beyond this one." He bid Jacob become a pagan among the pagans; he commanded him to marry Wanda or at the very least to lie with her.

11

The cowherds also had their autumn celebration. They had sought by threats and promises to make Jacob join them ever since he had first appeared upon the mountain with Jan Bzik's herd. But, one way or another, he had always put them off. He was forbidden to eat their food or listen to their licentious songs and brutal jokes. For the most part, they were a crippled, half-mad crew with scabs and elflocks on their heads and rashes on their bodies. Shame was unknown to them, as if they had been conceived before the eating of the forbidden fruit. Jacob often reflected that as yet this rabble had not developed the capacity to choose freely. They seemed to him survivors of those worlds, which, according to the Midrash, God had created and destroyed before fashioning this one. Jacob, when he saw them approaching, had acquired the habit of turning his head, or looking through them as if they didn't exist. If they foraged for grass on the lower slopes, he moved up toward the summit. He avoided them like filth. They were crawling all about him on the mountain, yet he went days and weeks without meeting any. Nor was it only disgust that kept him apart from this vermin; they were dangerous and, like wolves, would attack for no reason. Sickness, suffering, the sight of blood amused them.

That year they had made up their minds to seize him by force, and one evening after Wanda had left they surrounded the barn, deploying themselves like soldiers stealthily preparing to storm a fortress. One moment there was a stillness in which only the song of the grasshoppers was heard, and the next, the silence had been broken by howling and shrieking as both men and girls charged from all sides. The attackers were equipped with sticks, stones, and ropes. Jacob thought they had come to kill him, and like his Biblical namesake prepared to fight, or, if possible, to ransom himself through entreaties and a "gift" (the shirt off his back). He picked up a heavy club and swung it, knowing that his adversaries were so debilitated by illness he might be able to drive them off. Soon an emissary stepped forward, a cowherd who was more fluent than the others, and who assured Jacob no harm was intended. They had merely come to invite him to drink and dance with them. The man dribbled, stammered, mispronounced words. His companions were already drunk and laughed and screamed wildly. They held their stomachs and rolled about on the ground. He would not be let off this time, Jacob knew.

"All right," he finally said, "I'll go with you, but I'll eat nothing."

"Jew, Jew. Come. Come. Seize him. Seize him."

A dozen hands grasped Jacob and started to tug him. He descended the hill on which the barn was located, half running, half sliding. An awful stench rose from that mob; the odors of sweat and urine mingled with the stink of something for which there is no name, as if these bodies were putrefying while still alive. Jacob was forced to hold his nose and the girls laughed until they wept. The men hee-hawed and whinnied, supported themselves on each other's shoulders, and barked like dogs. Some collapsed on the path, but their companions did not pause to assist them, but stepped over the recumbent bodies. Jacob was perplexed. How could the sons of Adam created in God's image fall to such depths? These men and women also had fathers and mothers and hearts and brains. They too possessed eyes that could see God's wonders.

Jacob was led to a clearing where the grass was already trampled and soiled with vomit. A keg of vodka three-quarters empty stood near an almost extinguished fire. Drunken musicians were performing on drums, pipes, on a ram's horn very like that blown on Rosh Hashana, on a lute strung with the guts of some animal. But those who were being entertained were too intoxicated to do more than wallow on the ground; grunting like pigs, licking the earth, babbling to rocks. Many lay stretched out like carcasses. There was a full moon in the sky, and one girl flung her arms around a tree trunk and cried bitterly. A cowherd walked over, threw branches on the fire, and nearly fell into the flames. Almost immediately a woolly looking shepherd attempted to put out the blaze by urinating on it. The girls howled, screamed, cat-called. Jacob felt himself choking. He had heard these cries many times before, but each time he was terrified by them.

"Well, now I have seen it," he said to himself. "These are those abominations which prompted God to demand the slaying of entire peoples."

As a boy, this had been one of his quarrels with the Lord. What sin had been committed by the small children of the nations Moses had been told to annihilate? But now that Jacob observed this rabble he understood that some forms of corruption can only be cleansed by fire. Thousands of years of idolatry survived in these savages. Baal, Astoreth, and Moloch stared from their bloodshot and dilated eyes.

He was offered a cup of vodka by one of the merrymakers but the liquid seared his lips and throat; his stomach burned as though he had been forced to drink molten lead like those culprits the Sanhedrin had condemned to death at the stake in ancient times. Jacob shuddered. Had he been poisoned? Was this the end?

His face became contorted and he doubled up.

The cowherd who had given him the drink let out a yell, "Bring him more. Make the Jew drink. Fill up his cup."

"Give him pork," someone else shouted.

A pock-marked fellow with a face like a turnip grater tried to push a piece of sausage into Jacob's mouth. Jacob gave the man a shove. The cowherd fell and lay as still as a log.

"Hey, he's killed him."

Jacob approached the fallen man with trembling knees. Had this also been destined? Thank God, the man was alive. He lay there, foam bubbling from his lips, the sausage still clutched between his fingers, screaming abuse. His comrades laughed, threatened, cursed.

"God murderer. Jew. Scabhead. Leper."

A few feet away a cowherd jumped on a girl but was too drunk to do anything. Yet the two wrestled and squirmed like a dog and a bitch. The surrounding company laughed, spat, dribbled from their noses, and goaded the lovers on. A monstrous square-headed girl with a goiter on her neck and tangled matted hair sat on a tree stump sobbing out a name over and over again. She was wringing her hands, which were as long as a monkey's and as broad as a man's, their nails rotted away. Her feet were covered with boils and as flat as a goose's. Some of the cowherds sought to comfort her and gave her a cup of vodka. Her crooked mouth opened, exposing a single tooth, but she only wailed louder.

"Father! Father! Father!"

So she also cried out, Jacob thought, to a father in heaven. Compassion for this creature who had fallen from the womb deformed and misshapen, a mooncalf, swept over Jacob. Who could tell what frightened her mother at the moment of conception, or what sinful soul had been incarcerated in the girl's body? Hers was not an ordinary cry but the wail of a spirit who has gazed into the abyss and seen a torment from which there is no escape. Through some miracle this animal comprehended its own bestiality and mourned its lot.

Jacob wanted to go and comfort her, but he saw in her half-shut eyes a fury undiminished by suffering. Such a woman might spring at him like a beast of prey. He sat down and chanted the third chapter of Psalms: "Lord, how are they increased that trouble me! Many are they that rise against me. Many there be which say of my soul, there is no help for him in God. Selah."

III

It stormed in the middle of the night. A flash of lightning lit up the interior of the barn, and the cows, dung heaps, earthen pots became visible for an instant. Thunder rumbled. After washing his hands, Jacob recited "The One Who Does the Work of Creation" and "His Power and Strength Fill the World." A gust of wind blew open the barn door. The downpour beat on the roof like hail. The rain lashed Jacob as he closed and latched the door. This was the beginning of bad weather, he feared, and not merely one of those torrential cloudbursts that occur in summer. So it was; for a few hours later, though the rain ceased, the sky remained overcast. An icy wind blew from the mountains. At dawn the storm started all over again. Though the sun had risen, the morning was as gray as twilight. There would be no foraging for grass and other vegetation on the slopes today. Jacob would have to feed his herd with the fodder he had prepared for the Sabbath. He built a small fire to make things more cheerful and sat by it praying; he rose, faced to the east, and recited the eighteen benedictions. A cow turned its head and gazed at him with a blank humility, yet the expression of the black muzzle, wet with saliva and bristling with a few sparse hairs, made Jacob think that the creature nursed some grievance. It often seemed to him that the cattle complained, "You are a man and we are only cows. What justice is there to that?" He placated them by stroking their necks, slapping their sides, and feeding them tidbits. "Father," he often prayed, "Thou knowest why Thou hast created them. They are the work of Thy hand. At the end of days, they too must have salvation."

That morning his breakfast consisted of bread and milk and an apple brought the day before. If the rain continued, Wanda would not come. He would have to sustain himself on sour milk, a dish which he could no longer stomach. He chewed each bite of the apple slowly to savor the full flavor. In his father-in-law's house he had not known that one could have such an appetite and that bread with bran could be so delicious. As he swallowed each mouthful, he seemed to feel the marrow in his bones increase. The wind had died down, the door of the barn was now open, and from time to time he glanced up at the sky. Perhaps the weather would clear: wasn't it too early for the autumn rains? No longer was there a vista of distant places—nothing was visible but the flat crest of the hill surrounding the barn. Sky, mountains, valleys, forests, had dissolved and disappeared. Fog drifted across the ground. Mist rose from the pines as though the wet trees were burning. Here in his exile Jacob at last understood what was meant when the cabala spoke of God's hidden face and the shrinking of His light. Yesterday everything had been bright; now it was gray. Distances had shrunk; the skies had collapsed like the canvas of a tent; the tangible had lost substance. If so much could vanish for the physical eye, how much more could elude the spiritual. Every man comprehended according to his merit. Infinite worlds, angels, seraphim, mansions and sacred chariots surrounded man, but he did not see them because he was small and sinful and immersed in the vanities of the body.

As always when it rained, a variety of creatures sought shelter in the barn: butterflies, grasshoppers, gnats, beetles. One insect had two pairs of wings. A white butterfly with black markings resembling script alighted on a stone near the fire and appeared to be warming or drying itself. Jacob placed a crumb of bread near it, but it remained motionless. He touched it, but it didn't stir, and he realized it was dead. Sorrow overcame him. Here was one that would never flutter again. He would have liked to eulogize this handsome creature which had lived a day, or even less, and had never tasted sin. Its wings were smoother than silk and covered with an ethereal dust. It rested on the stone like a shrouded corpse.

Of necessity, Jacob had to war with flies and vermin which bit both him and the cows. He had no alternative but to kill. As he walked about, he could not avoid treading on worms and toads, and when he gathered grass he often encountered venomous snakes which would hiss and strike at him and which he crushed with a club or stone. But each time something like that happened he judged himself a murderer. He silently blamed the Creator for forcing one creature to annihilate another. Of all the questions he asked about the universe, he found this the most difficult.

There was nothing for him to do that day and so he stretched out on the straw and covered himself with his sheet. No, Wanda would not come. He was ashamed that he longed so much for this gentile woman, but the harder he tried to rid himself of desire, the stronger it became. His yearning stayed with him praying and studying, sleeping and waking. He knew the bitter truth: compared to his passion for Wanda, his mourning for his wife and children and his love for God were weak. If the desires of the flesh came from Satan, then he was in the Devil's net. "Well, I have lost both worlds," he muttered, and through half-shut eyes he maintained his watch. The petals of a flower stirred among the wet bushes. Field mice, weasels, moles, skunks, and hedgehogs were hiding in the thickets. All of these small creatures waited with impatience for the sun to shine. The birds, like clusters of fruit, weighed down the trees and the instant the rain let up, whistling, chirruping, croaking began.

From somewhere far off came a muted yodel. A cowherd was singing in the foul dampness, and his distant voice pleaded and demanded, lamented the injustice visited on all living things: Jews, gentiles, animals, even the flies and gnats crawling on the hips of the cattle.

IV

Though the rain ceased before evening, it was clear that this was only a short respite. Thunderheads lay low in the west, red and sulphurous, charged with lightning, and the air was heavy with mist that might at any moment turn to rain. Crows dived and cawed. There was no hope that Wanda would come in such weather, and yet when Jacob ascended his lookout hill, he saw her climbing toward him, carrying her two pitchers and the food basket. Tears came to his eyes. Someone remembered him and cared. He prayed that the storm would hold off until she reached him, and apparently his plea was answered; a moment after she entered the barn the deluge came, pouring down from the heavens as if from barrels. Neither Jacob nor Wanda spoke much to each other that afternoon. She sat down and immediately began to milk the cows. She was strangely shy and embarrassed and so was Jacob. Now and again a flash of lightning illuminated the twilight of the barn and he saw her bathed in such a heavenly glow that it seemed to him the woman he had known before had only been a sign or a husk. Had she not been created in God's image? Did not her form reflect that emanation through which the Eternal reflected His beauty? Had not Esau come from the seed of Abraham and Isaac? Jacob knew only too well where these meditations were leading, but he could not push them from him. He ate, said the benediction, recited the evening prayer, but still they did not leave him. The weather did not clear; Wanda would be unable to return home. At this late hour, moreover, the road back had already become dangerous.

"I'll sleep here in the barn," Wanda said, "unless you drive me out."

"I drive you out? You are the mistress."

They sat conversing quietly with the ease that intimacy brings. Wanda spoke of Zagayek and his paralytic wife, of their son Stephan who continued to pursue Wanda, of Zagayek's daughter Zosia whom everyone knew consorted with her father. But the bailiff had a dozen mistresses besides his daughter and so many bastards he could not remember their names. He did not conduct himself like a retainer but like a lord or king. He exacted from the peasant brides "the right of the first night," a law that was no longer in force. The peasants he treated as slaves, although they had their own fields and were only required to work for the count two days a week. He whipped them with wet rods, illegally forced them to do his business, levied private taxes upon vodka, performed operations on the sick against their will, tearing out teeth with pliers, amputating fingers with a cleaver, opening up breasts with a kitchen knife. Often he acted as midwife and demanded a handsome payment for his services.

"There's nothing he doesn't want," Wanda said. "He would swallow the village whole if he could."

Wanda's bed was not difficult to prepare. Jacob spread

out some straw and she lay down on it, covering herself with her shawl. He slept in one corner of the barn and she in another. In the silence the cows could be heard chewing their cud. She went outside to relieve herself and returned drenched from the rain. "So modesty exists even among these people," Jacob reflected. They both lay there without saying a word. "I must be sure not to snore," Jacob warned himself. He feared that he would be unable to sleep, but weariness overcame him. His jaw sagged and darkness flooded his mind. Every night he dropped onto his bed like a log. Thank God there was something stronger than his lust.

v

He awoke trembling, opened his eyes, and discovered Wanda lying next to him on the straw. The air in the barn was cool but he felt the burning heat of her body. She caught hold of him, pressed herself against him, and touched his cheek with her lips. Though he was conscious, he submitted in silence, amazed not only at what was happening but at the fierceness of his own desire. When he sought to push her from him, she clung to him with uncanny strength. He attempted to speak to her, but she stopped his lips with her mouth. He remembered the story of Ruth and Boaz and knew that his lust was more powerful than he. "I am forfeiting the world to come," he said to himself. He heard Wanda's hoarse voice imploring him; she was panting like an animal.

He lay numb, unable now to deny either her or himself,

as if he had lost his freedom of will. Suddenly a passage from the Gemara entered his mind: should a man be over-come by the Evil One, let him dress himself in dark cloth-ing, and cover himself in black, and indulge his heart's desire. This precept appeared to have been lurking in his memory for the specific purpose of breaking down his last defense. His legs became heavy and taut, and he was dragged down by a weight he could not withstand. "Wanda," he said, and his voice was trembling, "you must first go and bathe in the stream."

"I have already washed and I have combed my hair."

"No, you must immerse yourself in the water."

"Now?"

"God's law requires it."

She lay there in silence, perplexed by this strange de-mand, and then finally said, "I will do this also."

She rose, and still holding tight to him, opened the barn door. The rain had stopped but the night was mired in darkness and wet. There was not a trace of the sky and the only evidence of the stream was the sound of water churn-ing and bubbling as it rushed downward. Wanda clutched Jacob's hand as they groped blindly and with the abandon of those who no longer fear for their bodies. They stumbled over stones and shrubs, were splashed by the moisture dripping from trees. They were seeking the one spot in that shallow, rock-cluttered torrent where the stream was deep enough for a man to immerse himself. When they reached it, she refused to enter the water with-out him, and he, forgetting to slip out of his linen trousers, followed her in. The shock of the cold water touching him took away his breath; he almost lost his footing, so swollen was the stream because of the rains. They clung to each other as if undergoing martyrdom. Thus, at the time of the massacres Jews had plunged into fire and water. At last, his feet on a firm bottom, Jacob said to Wanda, "Immerse yourself."

She let go his hand and submerged in the water. He reached about, unable to find her. She reappeared, and his eyes, now accustomed to the darkness, made out the dim contours of her face.

"Hurry," he said.

"I have done this for you."

He took her hand and together they ran back to the barn. The cold, he realized, had not extinguished the fire in his veins. Both of them burned with the heat of newly lit kindling. He dried Wanda's naked body with his sheet, breathing heavily, his teeth chattering. Wanda's eyes shone through the darkness. He heard her say to him again, "I have done this for you."

"No, not for me," he answered, "for God," and the blasphemy of his words frightened him.

Nothing could restrain him now. He lifted her in his arms and carried her to the straw.

4

I

The sun rose and red could be seen through the chinks in the door. A purple beam of light fell across Wanda's face. They had been asleep, but awakened by lust they again sought each other. He had never known such passion as hers. She spoke words he had never heard before, called him in her peasant dialect her buck, her lion, her wolf, her bull, and even stranger epithets. He possessed her but it did not quench his desire. She blazed with an ecstasy—was it from heaven or hell? "More, more," she cried in a loud voice, "master, husband." He found himself possessed of powers that did not seem to be his—was it miracle or witchcraft? For the first time in his life he recognized the mysteries of the body. How was such desire possible? "For Love is as strong as Death," the Song of Songs said, and at last he understood. As the sun rose, he sought to tear himself from her. She clung to his neck and again thirstily kissed him. "My husband," she said, "I want to die for you."

"Why die? You are still young."

"Take me away from here to your Jews. I want to be your wife and bear you a son."

"You must believe in God to become a daughter of Israel."

"I believe in Him. I believe."

She was screaming so loudly that he covered her mouth with his hand so the cowherds outside would not hear. He was no longer ashamed before God, but he feared the ridicule of men. Even the cows turned their heads and stared. He pulled himself from her and was baffled to discover morning brought no repentance. The opposite rather! He was astonished now that he had endured his desire. The pitcher had overturned and he could not wash his hands. He didn't even say "I thank Thee," fearing to utter holy words after what had happened. His clothes were damp, but he put them on anyway, and Wanda also tidied herself. He walked out into the cool, clear Elul morning, leaving her with the cows. Dew covered the grass and each droplet gleamed. Birds were singing, and in the distance a cow lowed, the sound echoing like the blast from a ram's horn. "Yes, I have forfeited the world beyond," Jacob muttered, and immediately Satan whispered into his ear, "Shouldn't you also give up being a Jew?" Jacob glanced at the rock on which he had already scratched a third of the commandments and interdictions and it seemed to him like a battered ruin, all that was left to him from a war that had been lost. "Well, but I am still a Jew," he said, quoting the Talmud in an attempt to rally his spirits. He washed his hands in the stream and said, "I thank Thee," and then he began the introductory prayer. When he came to the words, "Lead us not into temptation," he paused. Not even the sainted Joseph had been as tempted as he. The Midrash said that when Joseph had been about to sin, his father's image had been revealed to him. So Heaven had interceded in his behalf.

As he mumbled his prayers, he searched in himself for some extenuation of what he had done. According to the strict letter of the law, this woman was neither unclean nor married. Even the Ancients had had concubines. She could still be a pious Jewish matron. "Something done selfishly may end up as a godly act." But, nevertheless, as he prayed he contrasted, despite himself, Wanda and Zelda, peace be with her. His wife had also been a woman, but frigid and cold, forever distracted. She had been a constant stream of complaints: headaches, toothaches, cramps in the stomach, and always fearful of breaking the law. How could he have known that such passion and love as Wanda's existed? He again heard Wanda's voice, the words she had whispered to him, her groans, the swift intake of her breath, and he again felt the touch of her tongue and the sharpness of her teeth. She had left marks on his body. She was willing to flee with him across the mountains in the middle of the night. She spoke to him exactly as Ruth had spoken: "Where thou goest, I go. Thy people are my people. Thy God is my God." Her body exuded the warmth of the sun, the breezes of summer, the fragrance of wood, field, flower, leaf, just as milk gave off the odor of the grass the cattle fed on. He yawned while he prayed. He recited the Shema and stretched his arms. He had scarcely closed his eyes the night before and lacked the strength to go hunting for grass. Bending his head low, Jacob was aware of his own weariness. During the few brief moments of sleep, he had dreamed, and although he did not remember his dream clearly, its aftertaste lingered. It seemed to him that he had been descending steps into a ritual bath or cave and had wandered across hills, ditches, and graves. He had met someone whose beard was composed of the roots of a plant. Who could it have been? His father? Had the man spoken to him? Wanda thrust her head out of the barn and gave him a wifely smile.

"Why are you standing there?"

He pointed to his lips to signify that she must not interrupt his prayer.

Her eyes shone with affection; she winked and nodded. Jacob closed his eyelids. Did he repent? He did not feel so much contrition as annoyance that he had been placed in a situation which made his sin possible. He stared into himself as though he were looking down the shaft of a deep well. What he saw there frightened him. Like a snake, passion lay curled at the bottom.

11

Rosh Hashana, Yom Kippur, and Succoth, according to Jacob's calendar, were past. The day which he thought to be Simchath Torah, Jan Bzik appeared on the mountain accompanied by Antek, Wanda, and Basha. The smell of snow was in the air; the time had come to drive the cattle down the valley. Both bringing them up and taking them down were difficult tasks. Cows are not mountain goats and do not climb slopes nimbly. The beasts had to be held by short, thick ropes, and restrained at every step. A cow might dig its hoofs into the ground and then one man would be forced to drag the creature while another whipped it. Others might stampede and break backs or legs bolting from the herd. But on this occasion all went well. An hour or so after the cattle had entered Jan Bzik's barn, snow fell. The mountains were no longer accessible, and were enveloped by columns of mist. The village, turned white, looked unfamiliar. Food was not plentiful in the homes of the peasants, but there was no lack of wood; smoke rose from the chimneys. The frames of the windows had been weather-proofed with lime and sealed with straw. The peasant girls had also made out of straw long-nosed monsters with horns on their heads whose task was to tease and annoy Winter.

This year, as every year, Jacob was asked to move into the hut with the family, but he preferred to take up his old abode in the granary. He made himself a straw bed and Wanda sewed him a pillow stuffed with hay; he had a horse blanket for a cover. The granary had no windows but light seeped through the cracks in the wall. Now Jacob longed for the mountains. It was better up there than down here. How strange and remote his peak seemed to him, a giant with a white beard, coiffured in clouds and with curls of mist. Jacob's heart cried out. The Jews were celebrating Simchath Torah, were reciting "Unto Thee it was shown," and circling the lectern. The Bridegroom of the Torah, who would finish the reading of the Pentateuch, was being called up from the congregation, to be followed by the Bridegroom of Genesis who would start once more the Mosaic Books, beginning with the Creation. Even boys were being summoned to the lectern, while those too young to participate were parading with flags decorated with candles and apples. Girls also were coming to the study house to kiss the holy scrolls and to wish for long life and happiness. There was dancing and drinking; people were going from house to house, partaking of wine and mead, strudel, tarts, cabbage with raisins and cream of tartar. This year, if Jacob was correct, Simchath Torah had fallen on a Friday, and the women were preparing the Sabbath pudding, dressed in their velvet capes and satin dresses.

But now all of this seemed dreamlike to him. He had been torn from his home not four but forty years ago! Indeed, were there Jews remaining in Josefov? Had Chmielnicki left a saving remnant? And if so, could the survivors rejoice in the Torah as they once had, now that all of them were mourners? Jacob stood in front of the granary and watched the snow falling. Some of the flakes dropped straight to earth and others swirled and eddied as if seeking to return to the heavenly storehouses. The rotting thatch of the roofs was covered with white, and the clutter of

broken wheels, logs, poles, and piles of shavings was decorated with fleece and the dust of diamonds. The roosters
were crowing with wintery voices.

Jacob reentered the granary and sat down. Some lines
from the Simchath Torah liturgy which he had not thought
of for four years came to his mind:

> Gather you angels
> And converse with each other.
> Who was he? What was his name,
> The man who ascended the heights
> And brought down the strength of confidence?
>
> Moses ascended the heights
> And brought down the strength of confidence.

Jacob started to sing these words to the traditional
Simchath Torah melody. Even the cantor had usually been
a trifle tipsy by the time he reached this song. Every year
it had been the same, the rabbi finding it necessary to
admonish those of priestly descent not to bless the congregation while under the influence of wine. Jacob's father-
in-law had himself brewed beer and vodka using grain
raised in the fields he leased from the town's overlord. At
this time of year, a keg with a straw in it had always stood
near the water barrel of his house, and nearby had hung a
side of smoked mutton. Whoever visited the house sipped
vodka from the straw and took a nibble of the smoked meat.

Jacob sat there in the dark, alone with his thoughts.
Slowly the door was pushed open, and Wanda entered,
carrying two pieces of oak bark, and some rags and string.

"I've made you a pair of shoes," she said.

He was ashamed of how dirty his feet were, but she lifted

them to her lap, and while taking their measure, caressed them with her warm fingers. She took a long time making certain the shoes fit. When she was satisfied, she insisted that Jacob get up and walk about to see if they were comfortable, just as Michael the shoemaker had him do in Josefov.

"They fit, don't they?"

"Yes, they do."

"Why are you so sad, then, Jacob? Now that you are near me, I can take care of you. I don't have to climb the mountain to see you."

"Yes."

"Doesn't that please you? I was looking forward so much to this day."

III

The day began as though it were already ending. The sun flickered like a candle about to go out. Zagayek and his men were in the woods hunting bear, and the bailiff's son Stephan strode about the village in high boots, dressed in a rawhide jacket embroidered with red, a marten cap with ear flaps on his head, and a riding whip in his right hand. Stephan was called Zagayek the Second by the peasants. His career with girls had started early and by now he had his own crop of bastards. He was a short, broad-shouldered man, with a square head, a nose as flat as a bulldog's, and a chin which dimpled in the middle. He had the reputation of being a fine horseman and kept himself busy training his father's dogs and setting traps for birds and animals.

Stephan took over in the village whenever his father went

hunting. On such days he went from hut to hut, throwing open doors and sticking in his head and sniffing. The peasants always had something which by law belonged to the landlord. That morning he entered the tavern and ordered vodka. His half-sister, one of Zagayek's bastards, waited on him, but their relationship did not prevent him from hiking her skirts. Then, after having his drink, Stephan proceeded to Jan Bzik's. Bzik had once been a man of importance in the village, one of those whom Zagayek had taken under his protection, but now the old man was worn out and sick. The day he had brought the cattle down from the mountain he had had a seizure and he now lay on top of the oven as his strength ebbed. He talked, spat, muttered to himself. Bzik was a small, lean man; his hair, long and matted, surrounded a single bald spot. He had deep sunken cheeks, a face as red as raw meat, and bulging, bloodshot eyes underlined by two puffy bags, a few scraggly hairs drooping from his chin. That winter he had been so sick they had measured him for a coffin. But then his condition had improved. He lay, his face turned toward the room, one eye glued shut, the other only half open. Ill though he was, this did not prevent him from running the household and overseeing each detail. "It's no good," he would grumble often. "Butter fingers!"

"If you don't like the way we're doing things, climb down from the oven and do them yourself," his wife would answer. She was a small, dark, half-bald woman, with a wart-covered face, and the slanty eyes of a Tartar. The couple did not live in peace; she kept insisting that her husband was finished and that it was time to cart him off to the graveyard.

Basha resembled her mother. Stocky and dark, she had inherited the high cheekbones and almond eyes of the older woman. She was known for her indolence. At the moment she sat at the edge of the bed studying her toes and every now and again searching for lice between her breasts. Wanda was at the oven, removing a loaf of bread with a shovel. As she bustled about the kitchen, she repeated to herself the lesson Jacob had taught her: The Almighty had created the world. Abraham had been the first to recognize God. Jacob was the father of the Jews. She had never before received any instruction and Jacob's words had fallen on her brain like a shower on a parched field. She had even memorized the names of the Twelve Tribes and knew how Joseph's brothers had sold him into Egypt. When Stephan entered, he stood at the open door listening to her mutterings.

"What's that you're saying?" he asked. "Some sort of an incantation?"

"Close the door, Pan," she directed over her shoulder. "You're letting in the cold."

"You're hot enough to keep from freezing."

Stephan walked into the room.

"Where's the Jew?"

"In the granary."

"Won't he come into the house?"

"He doesn't want to."

"They say he lays you."

Basha opened her wide, gap-toothed mouth in laughter; she licked her lips with delight, hearing her proud sister insulted. The old woman left off spinning, and Bzik wriggled his feet.

"Dirty mouths will say anything."

"I understand you're carrying his bastard."

"Pan, that's a lie," the old woman interrupted. "She just got over her period."

"How do you know? Did you investigate?"

"There was blood on the snow in front of the house," the old woman testified.

Stephan struck his boot tops with his whip.

"The householders want to get rid of him," he said after a slight hesitation.

"Who does he hurt?"

"He's a sorcerer, and that's the least of it. How is it your cows give more milk than anyone else's?"

"Jacob feeds them better."

"All sorts of things are said about him. He'll be done away with. Father will haul him into court."

"For what reason?"

"Don't grasp at straws, Wanda. He'll be taken care of, and you'll give birth to a demon."

Wanda could no longer restrain herself. Not everything the wicked desire comes true, she told Stephan. There was a God in heaven who avenged those who suffered injustice. Stephan pursed his lips as if about to whistle.

"Where did you hear that? From the Jew?"

"Dziobak says so also."

"It was the Jew, the Jew, who told you," Stephan said. "If his God is such a great defender, how come he's a slave? Well, answer that!"

Wanda could think of nothing to say. There was a lump in her throat and her eyes were burning; she could scarcely keep back the tears. She wanted to run quickly to Jacob and ask him this difficult question. With fingers that had become inured to heat, she picked up a fresh loaf of bread and sprinkled it with water. Anger had made her face, flushed already from the warmth of the oven, even redder. Stephan stood surveying her legs and buttocks like a connoisseur. He winked at the old woman and Basha. The latter responded flirtatiously, smiled obsequiously at him with her gap teeth. At length he walked out whistling, slamming the door behind him. Wanda stood at the window and watched him stride off in the direction of the mountain. He was a man filled with iniquity like Esau or Pharaoh. Ever since she could remember he had spoken of little else but killing and torturing. It was Stephan who assisted his father in the slaughtering and scalding of the pigs. It was he who did the actual whipping when Zagayek ordered a peasant punished. Even the trail left by Stephan's boots in the snow seemed evil to Wanda. "Father in Heaven," she began to pray, "how long will You remain silent? Send down plagues as you did against Pharaoh. Drown him in the sea."

"He wants you, Wanda. He wants you," she heard her mother saying.

"Well, he'll just keep on wanting."

"Wanda, he's Zagayek's son. He may set fire to the hut. What would we do then? Sleep in the fields?"

"God will not permit it."

Basha started to guffaw.

"What are you laughing about, Basha?"

Basha didn't answer. Wanda knew that her mother and sister were on Stephan's side. They wanted to see her humiliated. There was a crooked wrinkle on the old woman's forehead and her toothless mouth was fixed in a smile which seemed to say, "Why quarrel over such nonsense? Stephan's powerful. There's no alternative."

The old man lying on the stove mumbled something.

"Did you say something, Father?"

"What did he want?"

The old woman laughed nastily.

"What does a tomcat usually want?"

"Father's forgotten about that kind of thing," Basha said scornfully.

"You did right, Wanda. Don't let him put a bastard into your belly." Bzik spoke haltingly and with the dirge-like tone of the mortally sick uttering a last testament. "The moment you're with child, that skunk will forget you. He has enough bastards already." The old man's singsong voice was mournful, other-worldly. Wanda remembered the Ten Commandments Jacob had taught her; one must honor one's father and mother.

"Do you want something, Father?"

Jan Bzik did not answer.

"Are you hungry or thirsty?"

He had to pass water, he said in a voice which was half cry, half yawn.

"Well, crawl outside," his wife ordered. "This isn't a stable."

"I'm cold."

"Here, Father." Wanda gave him a pan.

The old man sought to raise himself from the oven but the low ceiling interfered. He attempted to pass water and Basha giggled when he couldn't. His wife shook her head contemptuously. His member had shrunk to the size of a child's. A single drop of water fell into the pan.

"He's worthless," the old woman said.

"Mother, he's your husband and our father," Wanda replied sharply. "We must honor him."

Basha began to guffaw again. Wanda felt a cry rising in her throat. Jacob said that God was just, that He rewarded the good and punished the wicked, but Stephan, idler, whoremaster, assassin, flourished like the oak, while her father, whose whole life had been dedicated to work and who had done injustice to no one, crumbled into ruins. What sort of justice was this? She gazed toward the window. The answer could come only from Jacob in the granary.

I V

Jacob in the old days would have considered himself ridiculed if anyone had ever suggested to him that a time would come when he would discuss such matters as the freedom of the will, the meaning of existence, and the problem of evil with a peasant woman. But one never knows where events are leading. Wanda asked questions and Jacob answered them to the best of his ability. He lay close to her in the granary, the same blanket covering them both, a sinner who ignored the restrictions of the Talmud, seeking to explain in a strange tongue those things he had studied in the holy books. He told her that God is eternal, that His Powers and Nature have existed without beginning, but that, nevertheless, all that was possible for Him had not as yet been accomplished before Creation. For example, how could He have been Father until His children were born? How could He have shown pity until there was someone to pity? How could He have been redeemer and helper until there were creatures to redeem? God had the power to create not only this world but a host of others. However, Creation would have been impossible if He, Himself, had completely filled the void. So that the world might appear, it had been necessary for Him to dim his effulgence. Had He not done this, whatever He created would have been consumed and blinded by His brilliance. Darkness and the void had been required, and these were synonymous with pain and evil.

What was the purpose of Creation? Free Will! Man must choose for himself between good and evil. This was the reason God had sent forth man's soul from the Throne of Glory. A father may carry his child, but he wishes the infant to learn to walk by itself. God was our Father, we His children, and He loved us. He blessed us with His mercy, and if now and again He let us slip and fall, it was to accustom us to walking alone. He continued to watch over us, and when we were in peril of falling into ditches and pits, He raised us aloft in His holy arms.

Outside, frost glowed everywhere, but it wasn't too cold in the granary. Wanda snuggled close to Jacob, her body tight against his, her mouth leaning toward his. He spoke and she continued to question. At first it seemed to him that he was both a fool and a betrayer of Israel. How could a peasant's brain comprehend such profundities? But the more Wanda questioned, the more obvious it became to him that she grasped his meaning. She even posed problems he could not solve. If the animals did not possess Free Will, why was it necessary for them to suffer? And if the Jews alone were God's children, why were gentiles created? She clasped him so tightly he could hear her heart beating; her hands dug into his ribs. She lusted for knowledge almost as fiercely as she did for the flesh.

"Where is the soul?" she inquired. "In the eye?"

"Yes, in the eyes, but in the brain also. The soul gives life to the entire body."

"Where does the soul go when a man dies?"

"Back to heaven."

"Does a calf have a soul?"

"No, it has a spirit."

"What happens to the spirit when the calf is slaughtered?"

"It sometimes enters the body of the eater."

"Does a pig have a spirit too?"

"Yes. No. I guess so. It has to have something."

"Why can't a Jew eat pork?"

"God's Law forbids it. It is His Will."

"When I become a Jew, will I also be God's daughter?"

"Yes, if you let Him enter your heart."

"I will, Jacob."

"You must become one of us not because of love for me but because you believe in God."

"I believe, Jacob. Honestly I do. But you must teach me. Without you I am blind."

A plan was forming in Wanda's mind; they would run away together; she knew the mountains. True, a Christian could not become a Jew, but she would disguise herself as a Jewess. She would shave her head and not mix meat with milk; Jacob would teach her to speak Yiddish. She insisted that he begin immediately. She said a word in Polish and he repeated it in Yiddish. *Chleb* meant bread; *wol* was an ox; *stol*, a table, and *lawka*, a bench. Some words were the same in both languages. Wanda asked him if the two tongues were really identical.

"The Jews spoke the sacred tongue when they lived in the Land of Israel," Jacob replied. "The tongue they speak today is a mixture of many languages."

"Why aren't the Jews still in their own country?"

"Because they transgressed."

"What did they do?"

"They bowed down to idols and stole from the poor."

"Don't they do that any more?"

"They don't worship idols."

"What about the poor?"

Jacob considered this question carefully before answering it.

"The poor are not treated justly."

"Who is ever just to the poor? The peasants work hard all year round and yet go naked. Zagayek wouldn't think of soiling his hands, but he takes everything, the best grain, the finest cattle."

"Every man will have to make an accounting."

"When, Jacob? Where?"

"Not in this world."

"Jacob, I must go. It's almost sunrise."

She clung to his neck, pressed deeply into his mouth, kissing him one final time. Her face became hot once again, but finally she tore herself from him. As she threw open the granary door, she murmured something and smiled shyly. There was no moon but the reflection of the snow fell across her face. Jacob recalled the story of Lilith, she who seeks out men at night and corrupts them. He and Wanda had now lived together for weeks, and yet each time he thought of his transgression he shivered anew. How had it happened? He had resisted temptation for years, then suddenly had fallen. He had changed since he had cohabited with Wanda. At times he didn't recognize himself; it seemed to him his soul had deserted him and he was sustained like an animal by something else. He prayed but without concentration. He still recited Psalms and portions of the Mishnah but his heart did not hear what his lips uttered. Whatever was within him had frozen. He no longer hummed and sang the old melodies, and was ashamed to think about his wife and children and all the other martyrs whom the Cossacks had slaughtered. What connection did he have with such saints? They were holy and he, unclean. They had sacrificed themselves for the Sacred Name while he had made a covenant with Satan. Jacob could no longer control his thoughts. Every kind of absurdity and non sequitur crammed his brain. He imagined himself eating cake, roast chicken, marzipan; drinking wine, mead, beer; hunting among the rocks and finding diamonds, gold coins, becoming a rich man, and riding around in coaches. His lust for Wanda reached such intensity that the moment she left the granary he began to miss her.

As with the soul, so with the body! He grew lazy and wanted only to lie on the straw. He suffered more from the cold that year than any other. When he chopped wood, the ax stuck and he couldn't pull it free. When he shoveled the snow from the yard, he tired quickly and had to rest.

How strange it was! Even the cows he had reared sensed his predicament and turned nasty. Several times they tried to kick and gore him when he was milking them. The dog barked at him as if he were a stranger.

His dreams changed also. His father and mother no longer appeared in them. The moment he fell asleep he was with Wanda. Together they roamed through forests, crawled through caves, fell into pits, ravines, abysses, sank into swamps filled with putrefaction and filth. Rats and beasts with shaggy tails, large udders, and pouches chased him; they shrieked with strange voices, dribbled, spat, and vomited upon him. He awoke from these nightmares in a cold sweat but still burning with passion. A voice within him called out constantly for Wanda. He even found it difficult to stay away from her on those days when the Mosaic law declared her unclean.

v

The moon shone in a cloudless sky. That night, it was nearly as bright as day. Jacob, standing at the door of the granary, looked up at mile upon mile of mountains. Crags rising from the forests resembled shrouded corpses, beasts standing erect on their hind legs, monsters from another world. The silence in the village was so intense Jacob's ears rang as though a multitude of grasshoppers were singing under the snow. Although it had stopped snowing, occasional flakes drifted slowly to earth. A crow started from sleep and cawed once. In the granary and surrounding sheds, field mice and weasels scratched in their winter burrows as if expecting the sudden advent of spring. Even

Jacob awaited a miracle. Perhaps summer would come more quickly than usual this year. There was nothing beyond God's power. The Almighty, if he wished, could remove the sun's cover as he had in the time of Abraham. But for whom would the Lord perform such a miracle? For Jacob the profligate, Jacob the sinner? He looked about him at the trees in the yard, snow hanging from their branches like white pears, petals of ice dropping from the twigs. He listened intently. Why didn't she come? The hut was dark, it seemed like a mushroom protruding from the drifts. Yet Jacob thought that he heard footsteps and voices. The door of the hut opened and Wanda appeared, but not as usual barefooted and enveloped in a shawl. She had on shoes and a sheepskin coat and she carried a cane. "Father is dead," she said, walking over to Jacob.

His mind froze.

"When? How?"

"He went to sleep like always, groaned, and that was the end of it. He died as silently as a chicken."

"Where are you going?"

"To fetch Antek."

They stood there in silence, and then Wanda said, "Hard times have begun for us. Antek's no friend of yours. He wants to kill you."

"What can I do?"

"Be careful."

She turned away from him; Jacob stood and watched her move into the distance, diminishing in size until she appeared no larger than an icicle. There had been no tears, but he knew she was grieving. She had loved her father—at times she had even used that word "father" addressing

Jacob—now she had lost him. Whatever soul a peasant possessed had deserted the old man's body. But where was it now? Still in the hut? Or had it already begun its ascent? Had its departure been like smoke through the chimney? The custom of the village required Jacob to visit the family and say a few words of comfort. But he was doubtful whether he ought to go. Without Wanda the hut was a nest of snakes. He was not even certain Jewish law permitted him to make this condolence call, but at length he decided to. He opened the door of the hut. The old woman and Basha stood in the middle of the room; a wick was burning in a shard. On the bed lay the body, its appearance altered by death, the face yellow as clay, the ears chalk white, only a hole where once the mouth had been. How difficult to imagine that only a few minutes before, this corpse had been alive. Yet in the wrinkled eyelids and sockets a hint of the live Jan Bzik remained, a smile, the look of a man who has encountered something both comic and propitious. The old woman sobbed hoarsely.

"He's gone, finished."

"May God comfort you."

"There wasn't a thing wrong with him at dinner. He ate a whole bowl of barley dumplings." Her remarks were only half directed at Jacob.

He stood there while the neighbors gathered. The women arrived in shawls and battered shoes, the men in sheepskins and boots made of rags. One woman wrung her hands, forced tears from her eyes, crossed herself. The widow kept repeating the identical sentence. "He had barley dumplings for supper and ate every morsel." With these words she was accusing death and giving evidence of what an exemplary wife she had been. All the faces were immersed in shadow, filled with the mystery of the night. Soon the air became fetid. Someone went to fetch Dziobak; the coffin maker arrived to take Jan Bzik's measure. Jacob slipped out of the hut. He was an alien among these people, but not as much a stranger now since Jan Bzik could almost be regarded as his father-in-law. The thought of this frightened him. "Well, aren't we all descended from Terah and Laban?" he said to himself. He was cold and his teeth were chattering. Jan Bzik had been good and just, had never ridiculed him, nor called him by a nickname. Jacob had become accustomed to him. There had been a secret understanding between the two men as if Bzik had somehow sensed that some day his cherished Wanda would belong to Jacob. "Well, it's a mystery," Jacob said to himself, "the profoundest mystery. All men are made in God's image. Perhaps Jan Bzik will sit with the other God-fearing gentiles in paradise."

Again he yearned for Wanda. What was keeping her? Well, from now on there would be an end of peace. The dog barked; more and more peasants were entering the hut. Zagayek arrived, a small rotund man dressed in a coat of fox pelts, felt boots, and a fur cap similar to those Jews wore on the Sabbath. Zagayek's mustaches flared underneath his thick nose like the whiskers of a tomcat. Dawn broke and the stars faded. The sky paled and turned rose. The sun blossomed behind the mountains and reddish specks of light glistened on the snow. The shrill voices of winter birds were heard, chattering. Jacob entered the barn and found that Kwiatula, the youngest of the cows who only a short time before had been a heifer, was about to give birth. She stood with bloated stomach, saliva dripping from her black muzzle. Her moist eyes looked straight at Jacob as though imploring his help.

He started to prepare the feed. It was also necessary to milk the animals. He mixed chopped straw, bran, and turnips together. "Well, we are all slaves," Jacob murmured to the cattle, "God's slaves." Suddenly the door opened and Wanda came in. Her cheeks were moist and red. Wanda, taking hold of Jacob, cried out as had his mother, peace be with her, before she rolled the large candle preparing for Yom Kippur Eve. "Now I have no one but you," she said.

5

I

The scarcity of food in the village was rarely discussed, and Christmas was celebrated with great pomp despite the dearth. Though many of the peasants had already slaughtered their hogs and suckling pigs, there was sufficient meat for the holiday meal, nor was there a lack of vodka. Children went from hut to hut singing carols. The older boys collected gifts, leading around one of their company dressed as a wolf. Since the roof of the chapel leaked, the creche showing the birth in the manger had been set up in Zagayek's granary; there, too, was put on the pageant showing the arrival of the kings and wise men come to adore God's newborn son. Staffs, flaxen beards, the gilded star, everything required for the play was on hand, having been used year after year. But the sheep were real and the sound of their bleating cheered up the dejected spirits of the peasants.

The winter had been a hard one. Sickness and pestilence! The number of small and large graves had increased in the cemetery, and gales had toppled most of the new wooden crosses. But now the time to be merry was here, Zagayek distributed toys to the children and he gave white flour to the women so that the wafers could be baked. Wanda now knew from Jacob that the Jews believed in a God who had neither son nor division into persons. Yet she had to participate in the holiday and go with the others Christmas Eve to Midnight Mass. She even took part in the pageant, stood near Stephan with a halo around her head looking like one of the saints. Stephan wore a mask, a white beard, and a miter. His breath stank of liquor, and he surreptitiously pinched Wanda and whispered obscene words into her ears.

Time after time Wanda had begged Jacob to enter the hut and take part with the others in the feasting. Even Jacob's enemy Antek sought to make peace during the holidays. Inside the hut stood a Christmas tree hung with ribbons and wreaths. The old woman had made pretzels, baked pork, stuffed cabbage, and a variety of other dishes. An extra man was needed to even out the number of guests, but Jacob remained stubborn. None of the food was kosher; all of this was idolatry, and it was well known that it was better to die than participate in such ceremonies. He stayed in the granary and ate dry bread as usual. It hurt Wanda to see him separate himself from the others and hide. The girls ridiculed him and her as well since he was her lover. Her mother openly spoke of the need to rid themselves of that accursed Jew who had brought bad luck and disgrace to the family. Now Wanda was more careful about seeking him out at night, knowing that the boys were planning to play all sorts of tricks on him. They considered dragging him out of the barn and forcing him to eat pork. Someone suggested that he be thrown into the stream as a sacrifice to the river spirit or be castrated. Wanda had brought him a knife so he might defend himself. She began to drink vodka to dispel the bitterness in her heart.

On the third day after Christmas, the village celebrated the sacred day of Turon that honored the ancient god of horses and courage, wind and power. Dziobak demanded the abolition of this pagan holiday, pointing out that with Jesus' birth all the idols had been deprived of their power, and in addition that no one in the large cities ever remembered such days. But the village paid no attention to him and there was dancing at Zagayek's house and in the huts. The musicians fiddled, banged cymbals, beat drums, played "The Little Shoemaker," "The Shepherd," "The Dove," "Good Night," and the "Dirge of a Dying Man," the last of which brought tears to the eyes of the women. The boys and girls danced a mazurka, a polka, a cracowiak, a goralsky. Everyone forgot his troubles. Sleighs crowded with young people raced across the snow, the bells on the reins and harnesses of the horses jingling. Here and there a sled yoked to a dog passed. Wanda had promised Jacob not to participate in these pagan revels, but with each passing hour she grew more restive. She had to dance and drink with the peasants. As long as she stayed in the village, it was impossible not to be one of them. The very fact that she planned to run away with him and accept his faith made the avoidance of suspicion more necessary. She hurried into the granary, her face flushed, and her eyes shining. Hurriedly she threw Jacob a few kisses, put her face on his chest, and started to sob. "Don't be angry with me," she said. "I've already become a stranger in my own home."

I I

This was the first of the month of Nissan according to Jacob's calendar, two weeks before Passover. Not once in his captivity had he eaten bread during that holiday, subsisting those eight days on milk, cheese, and vegetables. The cold had set in again and a heavy snow had fallen. Antek had gone to buy another cow in a nearby village, and had taken Wanda along to get her opinion. She had been forced to agree to the trip, fearing to quarrel with her brother as long as Jacob was there. Jacob spent the morning milking the cows and chopping wood for the fire, which was the work he liked best. His ax rose and fell and the chips flew. The heavier pieces he split by hammering wedges into them. Little by little the pile grew until there was a sizable quantity. He went into the granary to rest, lay down, closed his eyes and dreamed of

Wanda, but this dream did not have the village as its setting. Suddenly he felt himself being poked and he opened his eyes. The granary door was ajar and Basha stood near him. "Get up," she said. "You're wanted at Zagayek's."

"How do you know?"

"He's sent one of his men."

Jacob rose, realizing only too well what had happened. Zagayek had learned of his plan to escape and this was the end. Only recently Stephan had prophesied to Wanda that the Jew would be disposed of. "Well, my time has come," Jacob thought. All through the years he had been expecting this outcome. His knees trembled, and crossing the threshold, he bent over, picked up a handful of snow, and rubbed the palms of his hands with it so that he might pray. "Let it be Thy Will that my death redeem all my sins," he mumbled. For one instant he thought of making a break for it, but then saw how useless it would be. He was barefoot and without a sheepskin. "No, I won't run," he decided. "I have sinned and earned my punishment." Zagayek's man was waiting outside; he was unarmed. "Let's go," he said to Jacob. "The gentlemen are waiting."

"What gentlemen?"

"How the devil do I know?"

"So they are going to try me," Jacob said to himself. The barking of the dog brought the old woman out of the hut; she stood there, broad and squat, yellow-faced, neither joy not pity in her slanty eyes. Basha stood next to her mother, another one of those who, cow-like, accept docilely. The dog became silent and his tail drooped.

Jacob was relieved that Wanda was not there; by the time she returned it might be all over. He thought of reciting, "Hear, O Israel," but decided he should do that when the noose was fixed about his neck. His stomach felt heavy; he was cold. He hiccupped, belched, started to recite the third chapter of Psalms, but paused when he came to the verse, "For Thou, O Lord, art a shield to me, my glory, and the lifter of my head." It was too late for such hopes. When he nodded at the old woman and Basha, they remained as unresponsive as stuffed images. The one thing that astonished Jacob was that not only was his attendant unarmed but he made no attempt to manacle him. "Well, there is an end to everything," Jacob thought, walking with bowed head and measured steps. For years he had been curious about what lay on the other side of flesh and blood. He was only anxious to get the death agony over with, and was prepared to sanctify God's name if he were asked to deny or blaspheme Him.

Women came from their hovels to stare blankly. Barking dogs ran after him; others peacefully wagged their tails. A duck waddled across his path. "Well, you'll outlive me," Jacob comforted the creature. He bid the world and the village goodbye. "Do not let anxiety make her ill," he prayed, thinking of Wanda. She had not been destined to reach the truth and he sorrowed for her. He raised his eyes and saw that the sky was once more blue and vernal. The only cloud resembled a single horned beast with a long neck. The mountains looked down on him from the distance, those hills to which he had planned to flee from slavery. "It has been ordained that I be with them," he said, thinking of his father and mother and his wife and children.

The man led him to Zagayek's house and there in front of the building stood a covered wagon hitched to a team of horses. Jacob didn't think that either the wagon or the team were from the neighborhood. The horses were covered with blankets and their harnesses were decorated with brass; a lantern hung from the rear axle of the vehicle. Jacob walked up a meticulously scrubbed staircase to the second floor. He had almost forgotten staircases existed, but here, it seemed, was a piece of the city in the center of this hamlet. As he walked down the hall, he smelled cabbage cooking; the midday meal was being prepared. He passed doors which had the kind of brass latches his parents' house had had. Straw mats lay before them. A door was thrown open and what he saw was strange and dream-like. Three men sat at a table, Jews with beards, sidelocks, and skull caps. The coat of one was unbuttoned and a fringed garment peeped through. Jacob recognized another but in his confusion forgot where he had met him. Jacob stood with his mouth open, and the Jews gaped back. At last one of them addressed him in Yiddish, "Are you Jacob from Zamosc?"

Everything went dark before Jacob's eyes.

"Yes, I am," he answered, speaking with a Polish accent.

"Reb Abraham of Josefov's son-in-law?"

"Yes."

"Don't you recognize me?"

Jacob stared. The face was familiar but he couldn't place it. "So this is not the day of my death," he thought.

He still was unable to grasp what was happening, but he was ashamed that he was barefoot and dressed in peasant clothes. Inside of him all was still and frozen and he became as tongue-tied and shy as a boy. "Perhaps I am already on the other side," he thought. He wanted to say something, but couldn't utter a word. For the moment Yiddish eluded him. Another door opened and in walked Zagayek, short and stocky, red-nosed, his pointed mustaches resembling two mouse tails. He had on a braided green coat and low boots. The riding crop he carried had a rabbit's foot for a handle. Though it was early in the day, he had already drunk enough to make him walk unsteadily. His eyes were bloodshot and watery. "Well, is this your Jew?" he shouted.

The man who had just addressed Jacob spoke hesitantly. "Yes, this is he."

"All right, then, take him and go. Where's your money?"

One of the Jews, a small, pampered-looking man with a broad fanlike beard and dark eyes set widely apart, silently pulled a purse from his coat and commenced to count out gold pieces. Zagayek tested each of the coins by placing them between his thumb and index finger and trying to bend them. Only now did Jacob realize what had happened. These Jews had come for him; he was being ransomed. The man with the familiar face was from Josefov, one of the town elders. Suddenly Jacob felt terribly awkward as though the nearly five years he had lived in the mountains had taken effect this very instant and changed him into an uncouth peasant. He didn't know where to hide his calloused hands and dirty feet. He was ashamed of his torn jacket, and his unruly hair, resting upon his shoulders. A desire to bow peasant-like to the Jews and grasp their hands and kiss them seized him. The man who had counted out the gold pieces lifted his eyes.

"Blessed be Thou who revivest the dead."

III

The speed with which things now happened to Jacob was eerie. Zagayek extended his hand and wished him a pleasant trip. A moment later, the Jews escorted him outside and told him to get into the covered wagon. A number of peasants had gathered at Zagayek's house, but none of Jan Bzik's family was in the group. Before Jacob could say anything, the gentile driver—Jacob had not noticed him before—snapped his whip and the wagon careened downhill. Jacob thought of Wanda, but he didn't mention her. What was there to say? Could he ask that his peasant mistress be taken along? She was not in the village and so he couldn't even say goodbye to her. With the same suddenness that he had been enslaved he had now been ransomed. In the wagon the men spoke to him all at once and confused him so he scarcely knew what they were saying. Their speech sounded almost like a foreign tongue. A quilt was thrown over his shoulders and a skull cap placed on his head. He sat among them feeling naked. Slowly he grew accustomed to their words, gesticulations, odor, and asked how they had known his whereabouts. "A circus proprietor informed us," they said.

He became silent again.

"What happened to my family?" he asked.

"Your sister Miriam is alive."

"No one else?"

They didn't reply.

"Should I rend my clothes?" he inquired, intending the question not merely for them but for himself also. "I have forgotten the law."

"Yes, for your father and mother. But not for your children. More than thirty days have passed."

"Yes, that is now a distant event," Jacob said, employing the technical term.

Although he had known all along that his loved ones were dead, he sat there grieving. Miriam was the only one of the family who had survived. He feared to ask for details, kept looking straight ahead; the men spoke, for the most part, to each other. They discussed the clothes he must have: a shirt, a fringed garment, trousers, shoes. One of them remarked that his hair must be cut, and another untied a leather sack and rummaged in it. The third offered him cake, vodka, jam. Jacob refused to eat: he must remain in mourning for at least one day. Now he recollected the name of the man from Josefov: Reb Moishe Zakolkower, one of the town's seven most prominent citizens. The last time Jacob had seen him, he had been a young man sprouting his first growth of beard.

"It's exactly like Joseph and his brethren," one of the men remarked.

"Now we have lived to see this, we must say a benediction," another interjected, and he started to intone, "Oh, Thou who hast sustained me and made me live to reach this time."

"And I must say 'Thou hast done mercy,' " Jacob mumbled as if to prove that he too was a Jew and that no error had been made in ransoming him. But even as he said this, he was conscious of having erred. The correct thing was to praise God without further ado, but his voice sounded so coarse to him, he was embarrassed to speak before such fine people. His companions were small in stature but his head touched the roof of the wagon. He felt penned in, and so unfamiliar was the smell of the vehicle, it was difficult for him to keep from sneezing. These men should be thanked, but he didn't know the correct words for the occasion. Each time he tried to say something, Yiddish and Polish mingled in his head. Like an ignoramus about to talk to learned men he knew in advance that he would make a fool of himself. But he did ask finally, "Who is left in Josefov?"

The men appeared to have been waiting for this question and all started talking at once. The Cossacks had nearly leveled the town, had killed, slaughtered, burned, hanged, but there had been some survivors, widows and old men mostly, and a few children who had hidden in attics and cellars or taken refuge in peasant hamlets. The men mentioned some names Jacob knew, but others, since Josefov had acquired new inhabitants, that he had never heard before. The wagon continued to roll downhill, sunlight seeping through the covering, and the conversation remained elegiac. Every sentence ended with the word "killed." Now and then Jacob heard "died in the plague." Yes, the Angel of Death had been busy. The massacres and burnings had been followed by sickness, and people had died like flies. Jacob found it difficult to comprehend so much calamity. But as always, there was a saving remnant. The speakers appeared weighed down by an enormous burden and Jacob bowed his head. It was as if he had slept seventy years, like the legendary Choney, and awakened in another age. Josefov was no longer Josefov. Everything was gone: the synagogue, the study house, the ritual bath, the poor house. The murderers had even torn up the tombstones. Not a single chapter of the Holy Scroll, not a page from the books in the study house remained intact. The town was inhabited by fools, cripples, and madmen. "Why did this happen to us?" one of the men asked. "Josefov was a home of Torah."

"It was God's will," a second answered.

"But why? What sins did the small children commit? They were buried alive."

"The hill behind the synagogue shook for three days. They tore out Hanan Berish's tongue, cut off Beila Itche's breasts."

"What harm did we do them?"

No one answered these questions and they raised their eyes and stared at Jacob as if expecting him to reply. But he sat in silence. The explanation he had given Wanda that free will could not exist without evil nor mercy without sorrow now sounded too pat, indeed almost blasphemous. Did the Creator require the assistance of Cossacks to reveal His nature? Was this a sufficient cause to bury infants alive? He remembered his own children, little Isaac, Breina, the baby; he imagined them thrown into a ditch of lime and buried alive. He heard their stifled screams. Even if these souls rose to the most splendid mansion and were given the finest rewards, would that cancel out the agony and horror? Jacob wondered how it had been possible for him to forget them for an instant. Through forgetfulness, he had also been guilty of murder.

"Yes, I am a murderer," he said to himself. "I am no better than they."

6

Passover was at an end. Pentecost came and went. At first each day was so crammed with incident it seemed like a year to Jacob. Not an hour passed, scarcely a minute, without his coming upon something new or something he had half forgotten. Was it so trivial a matter to return to Jewish books, clothes, holidays, after years of slavery among the pagans? Alone in the mountain barn or in the Bziks' granary, he had felt that no trace of this world remained. Chmielnicki and his Cossacks had wiped out everything. At other times he had been half convinced that there never had been a Josefov and that all his memories were illusions. Suddenly he found himself dressed again as a Jew, praying in synagogues, putting on phylacteries, wearing a fringed garment, and eating strictly kosher food. His trip down the road from Cracow to Josefov had been one long continual holiday. Rabbis and elders had greeted and feasted him in every town. Women had brought their children to be blessed and had asked him to touch coins and speak incantations over pieces of amber. The martyrs were beyond help, and so everyone's goodness was lavished on this man who had been ransomed from captivity.

His sister Miriam and her daughter Binele awaited him in Josefov. Besides these two only a few distant relations were left to him. Josefov was so changed it was unrecognizable: grass was growing where houses had once been, buildings now stood where goats had pastured. There were graves in the middle of the synagogue yard. The rabbi, his assistant, and most of the elders came from other towns. Jacob was given a room and the authorities scratched together a yeshiva class so that he could support himself teaching. His sister Miriam had once been well-to-do, but now she was toothless and in rags. Meeting Jacob, she ran to him with a wail and never stopped sobbing and crying until she returned to Zamosc. He feared she was out of her mind. She screamed, pressed against him, bobbed up and down, all the time wringing her hands, pinching her cheeks, and enumerating all the tortures the family had undergone. She made Jacob think of those mourners and hand clappers who in the old days, according to the Talmud, had been hired for funerals. Her voice became so shrill at times that Jacob covered his ears.

"Alas, poor Dinah, they ripped open her stomach and put a dog in. You could hear it barking."

"They impaled Moishe Bunim, and he didn't stop groaning all night."

"Twenty Cossacks raped your sister Leah and then they cut her to pieces."

Jacob was not under the misapprehension that one had a right to forget how the dead had been tortured. What was said in the Bible of Amalek was true of all Israel's enemies. Yet, he did beg Miriam not to heap so many horrors on him at once. There was a limit to what the human mind could accept. It was beyond the power of any man to contemplate all these atrocities and mourn them adequately. A new Tischab'ov and a new seventeenth day of Tammuz had to be proclaimed. The year was not long enough to pray for and lament each of these saints singly. Jacob would have liked to run off and hide in some ruined building where he could remain in silence. But there was no such place in Josefov, which was all hustle and bustle. Houses were being built, buildings roofed; on every side men were mixing lime and carrying bricks. There were new stores in the market place and once again the peasants flocked to town on market day to deal with the Jews. Jacob, returning, was immediately involved in religious activities. It was the time when the matzoth were baked and he helped prepare them for the town's most pious citizens, drawing the water and assisting in the rolling. On the first night of Passover he entertained some widows at his seder, and it seemed strange to him now to speak of the miracles that had transpired in Egypt when in his day a new Pharaoh had brought to pass what the old Pharaoh had been unable to accomplish. There was not a prayer, law, passage in the Talmud that did not seem altered to him. The questions that he asked about Providence became increasingly sharp and searching and he found he had lost the power to stop asking them.

But, as he realized with astonishment, what was so new for him was stale for everyone else. The yeshiva boys laughed and played practical jokes on each other. Alert young men wove chains of casuistry. Merchants were busy making money, and the women gossiped in the same old way. As for the Almighty, He maintained his usual silence. Jacob saw that he must follow God's example, seal his lips, and forget the fool within, with his fruitless questions.

So the days flew by: Passover, Pentecost! Jacob's body had returned home but his spirit remained restless. No, if anything, his condition was worse, for now he had nothing to hope for. To prevent himself from thinking, he kept busy all day: teaching, studying, praying, reciting Psalms. Other towns had contributed a number of worn out, dog-eared books to Josefov and Jacob mended the pages and filled in the missing letters and words. The new study house needed a beadle, and he took that job also. His day began at dawn and did not end until he was ready to collapse from exhaustion. If his thought could dwell only on complaints against Heaven or on memories of lechery in a barn on a mountain, then it was unclean. Let those whose minds were pure indulge in meditation.

Those pious women who took care of Jacob sought to repay him for his years of exile, but an undeclared war developed between them and their charge. They prepared him a bed of down and he stretched out on the hard floor and lay there all night. They cooked him soups and broths, and he wanted dry bread and water from the well. When visitors came to speak to him about his years of absence, he answered curtly. How else could he behave? The windows of the study house overlooked the hill where his wife and children lay buried. He could see cows grazing there in the newly grown pasture. His parents, relations, friends, had been tortured. As a boy he had pitied the watchman in the cemetery at Zamosc whose life had been passed near the cleansing house, but now the whole of Poland had become one vast cemetery. The people around him accommodated themselves to this, but he found it impossible to come to terms with. The best he could do was to stop thinking and desiring. He was determined to question no longer. How could one conceivably justify the torments of another?

One day seated alone in the study house, Jacob said to God, "I have no doubt that you are the Almighty and that whatever you do is for the best, but it is impossible for me to obey the commandment, Thou Shalt Love Thy God. No, I cannot, Father, not in this life."

11

How revolting to lust for some peasant woman and not adore the Creator. Out of contrition, one should bury oneself alive. But what then could be done with the gross body and its desires? How silence the criminal within? Jacob lay on the floor moving neither hand nor foot. The window was open and the night billowed in. He traced the path of the constellation in the ascendant and saw the stars drift from roof to roof, noting how these lights, whiter than the sun, twinkled and shimmered. The same God, who had given the Cossacks strength to chop off heads and rip open stomachs, directed this heavenly multitude. The midnight moon floated in mother-of-pearl and its face, said by the children to be Joshua's, stared straight at Jacob.

Josefov by day was a confusion of sounds: chopping, sawing; carts arriving from the villages with grain, vegetables, fire wood, lumber; horses neighing, cows bellowing; children chanting the alphabet, the Pentateuch, the commentaries of Rashi, the Gemara. The same peasants who had helped Chmielnicki's butchers strip the Jewish homes now turned logs into lumber, split shingles, laid floors, built ovens, painted buildings. A Jew had opened a tavern where the peasants came to swill beer and vodka. The gentry, having blotted out the memory of the massacres, again leased their fields, woods, and mills to Jewish contractors. One had to do business with murderers and shake their hands in order to close a deal. It was rumored that Jews, too, had fattened on the catastrophe, dealing in stolen goods and digging up caches hidden by refugees. Deserted wives were another subject of gossip. These women wandered through town searching for their husbands or for witnesses to testify they were dead. Many Jews had not been strong enough to resist conversion and the Polish government had decreed that those unwillingly baptized might reassume their own faith.

But the greatest sensation of all was caused by the Cossack wives, Jewish women forced into marriage, who now fled the steppes and returned. One of them, Tirza Temma, who had arrived in Josefov shortly before Jacob, had forgotten how to speak Yiddish. Her first husband was still alive, having escaped to the forest where he had lived on roots at the time of the massacre. He had not recognized Tirza Temma and had denied it was she. She had exhibited her evidence in the bath house, a honey-colored speck on one of her breasts and a second birth-mark on her back. But her petition that her husband be forced to divorce his second wife had been denied. Tirza Temma, informed by the court that it was she who would be divorced, had berated the community in Cossack, and still persistently sought to break into her old home and take over the household. Another woman had been possessed by a dybbuk. One girl barked like a dog. A bride whose groom had been murdered on their wedding day suffered from melancholia and spent her nights in the cemetery dressed in her bridal gown and veil. Only now, years after the calamity, did Jacob realize how deep were the wounds. Moreover, new wars and insurrections were feared. The Cossacks on the steppes were again preparing an invasion of Poland, and Muscovites, Prussians, and Swedes stood poised with sharpened swords. The Polish nobility did nothing but drink, fornicate, whip peasants, and quarrel among themselves over the distribution of honors, privileges, and titles.

Only at night was there silence—the song of grasshop-

pers and the croak of frogs. Warm breezes wafted the
smell of flowers, weeds, ripening grain from the fields,
and Jacob recognized each faint aroma. He heard birds
and animals stirring among the thickets. Lately he had
taken a solemn oath, to root Wanda from his heart and
never think of her again. She was a daughter of Esau who
had lured him into adultery, a woman whose desire to accept his faith came from impure motives. In addition she
was there, he here. What good was this brooding? Nothing but sins and imps born of evil thoughts arose from it.
He marshaled the images of the cripples he had seen on
the road and here in Josefov, men without noses, ears,
tongues—each time he lusted for her, he thought of them.
He should be more concerned with the misery of these
unfortunates than with dreams of luxury in the lap of
their torturer's sister. He determined to punish himself:
every time he thought of Wanda he would fast until sunset. He drew up lists of torments: pebbles in his shoes, a
stone beneath his pillow, bolting his food without chewing it, going without sleep. The debt he owed for allowing Satan to ensnare him had to be paid off once and for
all. But Belial was as persistent as a rat. Who was the rat?
Jacob, himself? Some force beyond him? But there was,
as he well knew, a Spirit of Good and a Spirit of Evil. In
his case the latter was more firmly seated in his brain and
had much more to say. The instant Jacob dozed off, Evil
took over, sketched lascivious pictures, brought Wanda's
voice to the sleeper's ears, revealed her naked body to him,
defiled and polluted Jacob. Sometimes he heard her voice
even when he was awake. "Jacob, Jacob," she called. The
sound came from without, not within him: he saw her

working in the fields, grinding the grain, bearing food to the cowherd who this year slept in the barn with the cattle. She had taken up residence within him and he could not drive her forth. She nestled close to him beneath the prayer shawl when he prayed. She studied with him as he sat poring over the Torah. "Why did you show me how to be a Jew if you meant to leave me among the idolaters?" she complained. "Why did you pull me to you only to thrust me away?" He looked into her eyes, heard her sob, walked with her among the cattle in the fields. Once more they bathed together in the mountain stream and he bore her in his arms to the straw. Balaam barked; the mountain birds sang. He heard her panting, "More, more." She whispered, bit his ear, and kissed it.

The matchmakers were busy trying to marry off Jacob, and one of the men who had ransomed him was among those who had found a prospect. Jacob at first said "no" to all these suggestions. He had no intention of remarrying, would remain celibate. But the contention was that he should not travel so dangerous a road. Why endure temptation daily? Moreover, he should obey the precept: "Be fruitful and multiply." A widow from Hrubyeshoyv was among the possibilities and she was to come to Josefov shortly to meet him. She had a drygoods store in the Hrubyeshoyv market and a house that the Cossacks had neglected to burn. The widow was a few years older than he and had a grown daughter, but this was no great handicap. The Jew does not tempt Evil by denying the body but harnesses it in the service of God. Jacob knew that he could never love this woman from Hrubyeshoyv, but possibly he might be able to find forgetfulness with her.

He was exhausted by the struggle within him, sleepless at night, weary during the day. He found he lacked the patience to teach and had lost his taste for Torah and prayer. He sat in the study house longing for the open air, dreaming of gathering grass again, scaling crags, chopping wood. The Jews had ransomed him but he remained a slave. Passion held him like a dog on a leash. The hounds of Egypt bayed but he could not drive them off.

One day when he was seated in the study house explaining the procedures involving the horns of rams sacrificed as burnt offerings, a small boy entered and said, "My father would like to see you, Reb Jacob." Jacob shivered as he always did now when he saw a child.

"Who is your father?"

"Moishe Zakolkower."

"Do you know what he wants with me?"

"The widow from Hrubyeshoyv is here."

The class burst out laughing and Jacob, becoming confused, blushed. "Recite the Gemara while I am gone," he directed. But even before he left the building, he heard his pupils pounding on the table and arguing querulously. Active boys, accustomed to playing wolf and goat, hide and go seek, tag, they were forever joking among themselves and laughing boisterously. One of the principal objects of their humor was gloomy Jacob seated before them lost in somber thoughts, and, now that he was being led away to meet a woman, they had something more to ridicule. Jacob walked beside the boy, having decided not to go home to change to his Saturday gabardines. The child, who had not even been alive at the time of the massacres,

prattled about a bird that had flown through his bed-
room window. They came to Moishe Zakolkower's newly
erected house, even more comfortable than the one the
Cossacks had burned, and Jacob, entering, found himself
in a hall, smelled food, cutlets, and onions frying. The
door of the kitchen was open and he could see Moishe's
second wife (his first had been killed) standing near the
oven. Another woman was kneeding dough and a girl was
grinding pepper in a mortar. For a moment he caught a
whiff of the past and then Moishe, the man who had
counted out the gold pieces for Zagayek, opened the
living room door and bade Jacob enter. In the room,
Jacob noted the newness of everything, walls, floors,
tables, chairs, newly bound books from Lublin in the
bookcases. The evil ones destroyed, the Jews created.
Once more Jewish books were being printed and authors
were traveling here and there to sign up subscribers. Jacob
felt a stab in his heart every time he saw the past visibly
resurrected. No doubt the living must go on living, but
this very affirmation betrayed the dead. A song he had
heard a wedding jester sing came to his mind: "What is
life but a dance across graves?" Yes, his coming to meet
a prospective bride was a scandal. Only a few feet from
here his wife and children lay buried. Yet better a wife
than this perpetual brooding about a gentile woman.

Moishe and he were deep in a discussion of yeshiva and
community matters when the woman of the household
entered, bringing cookies and a dish of cherries—the hos-
pitality of the wealthy. Blushing, she apologized for not
being properly dressed, and nodded as if to say, "I know
what you think, but you can't do a thing about it. This

isn't a man's world." Finally the widow from Hrubyeshoyv
arrived, a small dumpy woman, decked out in a silk dress
and satin cape, wearing a matron's bonnet decorated with
colored ribbons and pearls. Her round face had so many
wrinkles that it looked as if it had been pieced together,
and her eyes were black and soft, resembling those pulps
found in cherry brandy. From her neck hung a gold chain
with a dangling pendant, her fingers gleamed with rings.
The odor of honey and cinnamon trailed into the room
with her, and she looked Jacob over shrewdly.

"My, what a giant of a man! May the evil eye not fall
on you."

"We are as God created us."

"True, but better big than a midget."

She spoke with a lilt and a sob, and kept wiping her nose
with a batiste handkerchief. The wagon that had brought
her to Josefov had lost a wheel, she said, and they had had
to stop for repairs at a blacksmith's. Then she sighed and
began to fan herself, meanwhile talking about her drygoods
store and how hard it was to get the goods that the customers wanted. She refused the refreshments that Moishe's
wife offered her, and then broke down and drained a glass
of blueberry wine while she swallowed three cookies.
Some crumbs fell on the folds of her cape and she picked
them up and ate them. True, her business was large, thank
God, but the girls she had working for her, on the other
hand, couldn't be trusted. "A stranger's hand is useful only
for poking a fire," she said, quoting the proverb and looking at Jacob slyly from the corners of her eyes. "One needs
a man in the house, otherwise everything goes."

She liked him, Jacob saw, and was ready to sit down and

write the preliminary agreement. But he hesitated. This woman was too old and syrupy, too cunning. He didn't want to spend his life overseeing clerks and bargaining with customers. Such a person needed a husband who was wrapped up, body and soul, in money. She was going to add a new wing to the house, she said, and also enlarge the store. The more she spoke, the more disconsolate Jacob became. I have ceased being a part of this world, he said to himself, the match would be good for neither of us. "I am not a business man by nature," he said aloud.

"Who's born a business man?" she asked, picking up a cluster of cherries with her flabby fingers.

She began to examine Jacob on his years of captivity—a subject usually avoided since the Jews regarded time spent among the pagans as wasted and better not discussed —but such a wealthy woman did not have to conform to convention. Jacob told her of Jan Bzik, of the barn on the mountain in which he had spent his summers, of the granary where he had slept in the winter. "How did you get food when you were on the mountain?" she asked.

"It was brought from the valley."

"Who brought it? The peasant?"

"No, his daughter."

"Unmarried?"

"A widow."

"Did you collect grass on the Sabbath?"

"I never broke the Sabbath. Nor did I eat unkosher food." He was ashamed to hear himself boasting of his piety.

The woman thought over what he had said carefully,

and then remarked as she reached out her hand to take another cookie, "What choice did you have? Oh, what those murderers did to us!"

III

It was noon; the boys went for their midday meals, some to their families and others to the houses where they boarded. Alone in the study house, Jacob prepared a lecture. He was pleased to be once more deep in the study of books, yet he found earning his living by teaching distasteful. Most of his students were bored and the clever ones spent their time in hair-splitting or in complicating the obvious. His years away from Torah had changed his views. Now conscious of much he had not realized, he saw that one law in the Torah generated a dozen in the Mishnah, and five dozen in the Gemara; in the later commentaries laws were as numerous as the sands of the desert. Each generation added its own strictures, and during his years of exile the Shulcran Oruch had been further interpreted and additional forbiddances added. A wry thought occurred to him: if this continued, nothing would be kosher. What would the Jews live on then? Hot coals? And why had these interdictions and commandments not preserved the Jews from Cossack atrocities? What more did God require of his martyred people?

Moreover, as Jacob looked about him, he saw that the community observed the laws and customs involving the Almighty, but broke the code regulating man's treatment of man with impunity. His return before Passover had brought him to town when a quarrel was in progress. Flour for matzoths was scarce and the rabbi, finding no proscription in the Mosaic Law, in the Talmud, or even in Maimonides, had authorized the eating of peas and beans during the holidays. This ruling had incensed certain members of the congregation, some because they wanted to show how pious they were, others because they were angry at the rabbi; and they had broken the windows in the rabbi's house and driven nails into his bench at the east wall. One of the zealots had approached Jacob and sounded him out about becoming rabbi. Yes, men and women who would rather have died than break the smallest of these ritualistic laws, slandered and gossiped openly, and treated the poor with contempt. Scholars lorded it over the ignorant; the elders divided privileges and preferments among themselves and their relatives and exploited the people generally. Money lenders gouged their clients—using loopholes in the law against usury; merchandise was kept off the market until it became scarce. Some went so far as to give false weight and measure. But when Jacob entered the study house he met them all: the angry, the haughty, the obsequious, the crooked. They prayed and schemed, erected tall towers of legalisms while they broke God's commandments. The catastrophe had impoverished the community, but the town still had more than its share of hatred and envy. Moishe Zakolkower told Jacob that there were those who were anxious to prevent his match with the widow of Hrubyeshoyv. An anonymous letter had been received denouncing Jacob.

Yet Jacob's thoughts worried him, since he knew his concern with such things was of evil origin. Satan tried to prove that corruption being general, sin could be taken lightly. The Spirit of Good replied: "Why concern yourself with what others do? Look to yourself." But Jacob had no peace. Everywhere he heard people asserting things that their eyes denied. Piety was the cloak for envy and avarice. The Jews had learned nothing from their ordeal; rather suffering had pushed them lower.

Chanting as he studied, he found it difficult now to keep the lilt of the cowherds' songs out of his voice. Moments came when he longed for the barn. His love for the Jews had been wholehearted when he was distant from them. He had forgotten the shifty eyes and barbed tongues of the petty—their tricks, stratagems and quarrels. True, he had suffered from the primitiveness and savagery of the cowherds, but what could be expected from such a rabble?

The marriage contract was almost completed, the date of the wedding set for the Friday after Tischab'ov. The widow, though well along in her thirties, could still bear children and was anxious to have a son. Already flatterers considered Jacob a rich man and showered him with compliments. Yet he lay awake worrying, still uncertain about this marriage. The widow needed a business man, a good mixer; he was withdrawn, a recluse. The years of slavery had estranged him from life; he looked healthy, but was shattered within. He kept rummaging in the cabala and leafing through books of philosophy. Sometimes he was overwhelmed by the desire to flee, but he didn't know where. He doubted everything, with, as the saying goes, the kind of doubt which "the heart does not share with the lips." He had not tasted meat in all the years of slavery and the idea of feeding on God's creatures now repelled him. Meat and fish were both eaten customarily on the Sabbath, but the food stuck in his throat. Jews treated animals as Cossacks treated Jews. The words "head," "neck," "liver," "gizzards," made him shudder. Meat in his mouth gave him the fantasy he was devouring his own children. On several occasions he had gone outside and vomited after the Sabbath dinner.

He was alone in the study house, not studying, but merely leafing through volume after volume. Possibly Maimonides had the answer. Or the *Chuzary*. Might it be contained in *The Duty of the Heart* or *The Vineyard?* He read a few words, turned the page, opened another book in the middle, turned pages again. Putting his hands to his face, he closed his eyes. He longed for both Wanda and the grave. The instant his desire for her left him, he wished to die. "Father in Heaven," his lips said as if possessed of a will of their own, "take me."

Footsteps approached; a charity worker entered, bringing him a bowl of soup. Jacob studied her. Lame though she was, with a wart on her nose and hair on her chin, this woman was a saint. Kindness, gentleness, candor dwelt in her eyes. She had lost her husband and children but exhibited no bitterness, envied no one, nursed no grievances, uttered no slander. She washed Jacob's linen, cooked for him, waited on him like a maid, and would not allow him even to thank her. Her answer to his praise was, "for what other reason were we created?"

She placed the bowl on the table and brought bread, salt, a knife, as well as a pitcher of water for him to wash his hands; and then stood humbly at the door waiting for him to finish. What was the source of her kindness? Jacob wondered. Only the wise behaved as she. Even if she were the sole representative of virtue in Josefov, she would still be a witness to God's mercy, and this was the woman he should marry. Would she consider marriage, he asked, if a proper husband were found for her? Her eyes clouded. "God willing, in the next world with my Baruch David."

IV

Wanda came to Jacob one night as he lay sleeping. He saw her in the flesh, her body surrounded by light, her cheeks tear-stained, and knew she was pregnant. The smell of fields and haystacks entered with her. "Why did you leave me?" she asked wanly. "What will happen to your child? It will be brought up among pagans." Startled, Jacob awoke; the image lingered an instant at the boundary of sleep and waking. When it at last dissolved, the darkness retained an afterglow as if a lamp had just been extinguished. Hearing Wanda's voice re-echo in his ears, Jacob trembled. He could almost feel the warmth of her body. Straining his ears, he waited for her to reveal herself again. He dozed off. She reappeared, wearing a calico apron, carrying a kerchief with a fringed border, and approaching him, threw her arms about him and kissed him. Because of the child she bore, he had to bend to her and he tasted her lips and the salt of her tears. "It's yours," she said, "your flesh and blood."

Once more he awoke, and did not close his eyes again that night. He had seen her, she was carrying his child. Jacob began to recite Psalms. The eastern sky became scarlet; he rose and washed his hands. All was clear to him now. The law obliged him to rescue Wanda and his child from the idolaters. He had money, for as sole heir of his father-in-law he had received fifty gulden for the property in the market place where the old house had stood. He threw his belongings into a burlap sack and walked to the study house. Reb Moishe, always one of the first ten to enter God's house, had his Gemara already open, and was busily studying. His dark eyes grew large seeing Jacob approach with a sack slung over his shoulder.

"What are you up to?"

"I'm off to Lublin."

"But the date of the wedding's been set."

"I can't go through with it."

"What'll happen to your class?"

"You'll find another teacher."

"Why? And so suddenly?"

Wanting neither to lie nor tell the truth, Jacob said nothing. He counted out twenty gulden from a small bag. "Here's part of the money the town spent ransoming me." Astonished, Reb Moishe tugged at his beard. "Repaying the community," he mumbled. "We can expect the Messiah any day."

"It should be of some assistance."

"What do I tell the widow of Hrubyeshoyv?"

"Say we weren't meant for each other."

"Are you coming back?"

"I don't know."

"What's your plan—to become a recluse?"

Without waiting for the arrival of a quorum, Jacob turned his head and began the morning prayer. He had learned the day before that a wagon would leave for Lublin in the morning, and quickly finishing his devotions, he set out to find Leibush the carter. If he passed someone carrying a filled container, he had decided that would be an omen that there would be room on the wagon, and that Heaven approved of the trip. Lo and behold, there was Calman the water carrier lugging two pails of water. "Well, we can always squeeze in one more," Leibush said.

The morning was warm; the village quiet. It was late in the month of Sivan. Shutters opened. Sleepy-eyed women poked out their bonneted heads. Men converged on the study house carrying bags containing their prayer shawls and phylacteries. Cows were being led to pasture. A great golden sun was aloft in the east, but dew continued to fall on the grass and the young trees planted after the destruction. Birds sang and pecked at the oats fallen from the horses' feedbags. On such a morning it was difficult to believe this a world in which children were slain and buried alive, and that the earth still drank of blood as in the days of Cain. "You sit with me on the box," Leibush said to Jacob. The other passengers were mostly women off to buy goods in the Lublin stores.

One woman had forgotten something. Another had to run home to nurse her baby. A man arrived with a package to be delivered to the Lublin inn. So the wagon did not start immediately as scheduled. Two men, storekeepers, who were seated among the women whiled away the time swapping spicy stories and innuendoes with the giggling matrons. Jacob heard his name mentioned and then the name of the widow of Hrubyeshoyv. Unintentionally, he had humiliated her. No matter what one does one stumbles into sin, he thought. He had been reading books of ethics, filled with the best advice on how to avoid the pitfalls of evil, but Satan always outwitted one. He participated in all business transactions and marriages; no human enterprise proceeded without him: touch something and you hurt someone. Have a little success, and, no matter how decent you were, you provoked envy. But why was he on his way to Lublin? He told himself he didn't know. He wanted advice from the city's wisest rabbis and would do as they recommended. Yet all the time he was aware he was traveling to Wanda, like one of the Israelite rabble that had wanted to turn and march back to Egypt and slavery for a kettle of meat. But did he dare let his child grow up among the pagans? He had not thought that the gentile woman would become pregnant. Generally he had withdrawn and spilled his seed like Onan.

Well, it makes no difference whether I go or stay, Jacob remarked to himself. I'm lost either way. The wagon had begun to move without his noticing it, and was now passing fields where the peasants were weeding and transplanting. How beautiful the countryside was and how contrary to his despair. Doubt, dissension, discord dwelt within him, but the fields exuded harmony, tranquillity, fruitfulness. The sky was blue, the weather warm with the mercy of summer, the air fragrant as honey, each flower exhaling its own perfume. A hidden hand had shaped and modeled each stalk, blade of grass, leaf, worm, fly. Each hovering butterfly's wings exhibited a unique design; every bird sang with its own call. Breathing deeply, Jacob realized how much he had missed the country. Grainfields, trees, every single growing thing refreshed his eyes. If only I could live in perpetual summer and do harm to no one, he murmured, as the wagon entered a pine wood which seemed less a

forest than some heavenly mansion. The trees were as tall
and straight as pillars and the sky leaned on their green
tops. Brooches, rings, gold coins were embossed on the
bark of their trunks. The earth, carpeted with moss and
other vegetation, gave off an intoxicating odor. A shallow
stream coursed through the woodland, and perched on
rocks in the water were birds Jacob had never seen in the
mountains. All of these creatures knew what was expected
of them. None sought to rebel against its Creator. Man
alone acted viciously. Jacob heard the women behind him
slandering the whole of Josefov. Raising his eyes, he gazed
through the screen of branches and needles where jewels
glittered. The light which filtered through shone with all
the colors of the rainbow. Cuckoos sang, woodpeckers
drummed. Gnats circled quickly, dark, eddying specks.
Jacob closed his eyes as though begrudging himself the
sight of so much splendor. A roseate light seeped through
his lids. Gold mingled with blue, green with purple, and,
out of this whirlpool of color, Wanda's image formed.

v

Great crowds filled the community house in Lublin. The
Council of the Four Countries was not in session, but the
Council of Poland was. Deserted wives petitioning for
the right to remarry, "Cossack brides" returned from the
steppes and Russian Orthodoxy, widows whose brothers-
in-law had refused to perform the Levirate ceremony or
had insisted on being payed exorbitantly to do so, moved
through the rooms. Mingled with them were husbands
whose wives had run off or gone mad and who needed the

consent of a hundred rabbis to remarry, fathers looking for prospective sons-in-law, authors asking religious authorities for endorsements, contractors seeking partners to invest in the lumber business, and individuals who merely wanted witnesses for wills. Both social and commercial activity went on in the Lublin community house. Merchants passed around samples; jewelers and goldsmiths displayed their wares; authors hawked their books and met with printers and paper jobbers; usurers discussed loans with builders and contractors; managers of estates brought objects their gentile patrons wanted to pawn or sell—a carved ivory hand ornamented with rubies, a lady's gold comb and hairpins, a silver pistol with a mother-of-pearl handle studded with diamonds.

Despite the upheaval, Poland's commerce remained in the hands of the Jews. They even dealt in church decorations, although this trade was forbidden them by law. Jewish traders traveled to Prussia, Bohemia, Austria, and Italy, importing into the country silk, velvet, wine, coffee, spices, jewelry, weapons, and exporting salt, oil, flax, butter, eggs, rye, wheat, barley, honey, hides. Neither the aristocracy nor the peasantry had any real knowledge of business. The Polish guilds continued to protect themselves through every form of privilege, but nevertheless their products were more expensive than those of the Jews and often inferior in workmanship. Nearly every manor harbored Jewish craftsmen, and, although the king had forbidden Jews to be apothecaries, the people had confidence in no others. Jewish doctors were sent for, sometimes from abroad. The priests, particularly the Jesuits, harangued against infidel medicine from their pulpits, published pamphlets on the subject, petitioned the Sejm and the governors to disqualify Jews from medical practice, but no sooner did one of the clergy fall ill, than he called in a Jew to attend him.

Jacob had come to Lublin to get advice from the local rabbi or from the members of the Council, but he loitered in the city doing nothing. The Sabbath came and went. The more he reflected on the question perplexing him, the clearer it became that no one could advise him. He was familiar with the law. Would he find a man anywhere who could determine the authenticity of a vision or who could weigh in the scales which was the greater transgression, the abandonment of one's issue to the idolaters or the conversion of a woman lacking a true vocation? Once more Jacob remembered the saying, "Something done selfishly may end up as a godly act," and argued accordingly. Cakes, candies, and almonds were given a child starting cheder to encourage him to love the Torah. Didn't one speak of a convert as new-born? Who could know all the motives of those who had become Jews in the past? No saint was entirely selfless. Jacob decided to take the sin upon himself and instruct Wanda in the tenets of his faith. Now that the Polish government permitted converted Jews to return to their religion, Wanda could pass as one of them. No one would bother to investigate. She would shave her head, put on a matron's bonnet, and he would teach her every single law.

In Lublin, Jacob was known as that man from Josefov who spent so many years a slave. Speaking thus, they set him apart. The scholars addressed him as if he were a simpleton who had forgotten all he learned. When they mentioned a Hebrew word or quoted the Talmud, they translated it into Yiddish for his benefit. In his presence they whispered among themselves and smiled patronizingly as city people do when they converse with bumpkins. The elders were interested in how he had conducted himself in slavery: had he kept the Sabbath and the dietary laws? How odd that he had not attempted to escape but had waited to be ransomed. Jacob became convinced they knew something dreadful they dared not say to his face. Could they have been told about Wanda? Zagayek might have passed a comment to the group who had come to ransom him. If so, his secret was traveling from mouth to mouth.

From the first he had noted the difference between himself and the others, and the longer he stayed in Lublin, the sharper the contrast seemed. He was tall, blond, blue-eyed; they, for the most part, were short, dark-eyed, black-bearded. They liked esoteric scholarly jokes, used snuff, smoked tobacco, knew the names of all the rich contractors, were acquainted with who had married whom, and what Jew was the favorite of which nobleman. All this was foreign to Jacob. I have turned into a peasant, he said, rebuking himself. But he recalled that it had not been so different before the calamity. The rabbis, elders, and rich men in the old days had also been of one party and he of another. They had eyed him suspiciously as if they suspected he had gentile blood. But how could this have been? Descended from an eminent family, his grandfathers, and their fathers also, had all been Polish rabbis.

Stranger than this, however, was the attitude of the
Jews who, having just survived their greatest calamity,
behaved as if they no longer remembered. They groaned
and sighed, but without feeling. The rabbis and elders were
again quarreling over money and power. The problem of
the deserted wives and "the Cossack brides" was for them
an opportunity to display their casuistic brilliance in long,
time-consuming discussions little connected with the spirit
of the law. The unhappy petitioners waited weeks and
months for verdicts that could have been handed down in
a few days. The Council of the Four Countries had taken
upon itself the task of collecting the Crown taxes in addition to those which went for its own support, and everywhere complaints were heard that the burden of the tax
was inequitably distributed and the rate excessive. Occasionally an accuser pointed a finger at these eminent
men, threatening to complain to the administration, to
stand up in the synagogue and denounce them before the
reading of the Torah, or to wait for them outside and give
them a good beating. The man was immediately made a
member of the elite, offered a few crumbs, and sent out to
sing the praises of the very individuals he had been defam-
ing. Jacob even heard of emissaries who misappropriated
money they collected or took too high a percentage for
themselves. The catastrophes over, the stomachs of many
of the rabbis and elders had increased in size; their necks
wrinkled with fat. All this flesh was dressed in velvet, silk,
and sables. They were so heavy they wheezed; their eyes
shone greedily. They spoke an only half comprehensible
language of innuendoes, winks, and whispered asides. Out-

side the community house, angry men proclaimed these rulers robbers and thieves and warned prophetically of the plagues and afflictions their sins would produce.

Yes, it was clear to Jacob that these, the grabbers, were worthless, but there were also the givers, and more of these than the others. Thank God, not all Jews were community elders. Men still prayed, studied, and recited Psalms in God's house. Many of them still bore the wounds they had received from the Cossacks. Jacob saw cripple after cripple, men deprived of ears, fingers, noses, teeth, eyes, and all sang: "We will sanctify"; "Bless ye." They listened to the sermons, sat down to pore over the Mishnah. Anniversary candles were lit and men continued to mourn.

Wandering through the narrow alleys, Jacob saw how great the poverty was. Many lived in what were only dark burrows; tradesmen worked in shops that looked like kennels. A stench rose from the gutters; ragged women, often on the point of giving birth, foraged for wood shavings and dung to be used for heat. Half naked children with scabby heads and rashes walked around barefoot. Many of the urchins had rickety legs, sores on their eyes, puffed bellies, distended heads. There was some kind of epidemic in progress and hearses with corpses in them passed constantly, each followed by lamenting women. A beadle rattled his alms box and cried out, "Charity will preserve you from death." The insane were everywhere, wild in the streets, another remembrance of the Cossacks.

It shamed Jacob that he thought so much of Wanda. People were starving before his eyes. A groschen here could save a life. He was continually changing silver to smaller coins and distributing his money. But what he gave was little when confronted with this vast need. Bands of beggars pursued him, clutched at his coat, blessing and cursing him. They hissed, spat at him, threw lice in his direction, and he was barely able to escape. Where was God? How could he look down on such want and keep silent? Unless, Heaven forbid, there was no God.

7

Jacob traveled from Lublin to Cracow by wagon. Changing to peasant dress, he proceeded on foot from Cracow to
the mountains. The sack slung over his shoulder contained
bread, cheese, a prayer book and shawl, phylacteries, a
volume of the Mishnah, and presents for Wanda: a matron's bonnet, a dress, a pair of shoes. He had made his plans
in advance; he would avoid the high road and take meadow
and forest trails. The sun had gone down before he left

Cracow, and all night he walked, aware of the dangers around him. Wild beasts and robbers lived in the hills; he remembered Wanda's stories of vampire owls disguised as cats and of witches' mares galloping through darkness on their evil errands.

The roads were dangerous at night, as Jacob knew. The King's Daughter, filthiest of witches, confused travelers and shoved them into bogs. The demonic Lillies made their homes in caves and the hollows of tree trunks. Ygereth, Machlath, and Shibta enticed men off the highways until they defiled themselves with nocturnal emissions. Shabriry and Briry polluted the waters of springs and rivers. Zachulphi, Jejknufi, Michiaru, survivors of the generation that had built the Tower of Babel, confounded men's speech and drove them mad or into the mountains of darkness. But Jacob's longing for Wanda made him willing to take any risk. Even though the journey must result in sin, he sang Psalms and begged God to keep him safe. His investigations of the cabala since his return had uncovered the doctrine that all lust was of divine origin, even Zimri's lust for Kozbi, the daughter of Zur. Coupling was the universal act underlying everything; Torah, prayer, the Commandments, God's holy names themselves were mysterious unions of the male and female principles. Jacob thrashed this way and that, constantly seeking exoneration: a soul would be saved from idolatry; his seed would not be mingled with that of Esau. Such virtuous acts must tip the scales in his favor.

The summer night passed, but Jacob could not have told how. The sun rose and he discovered himself in a forest with a stream close by. Washing his hands, he recited the

Shema, and said the morning prayer in his shawl and phylacteries. He breakfasted on bread, dried cheese, and water, and then, having said grace, rested his head on the sack and fell asleep. The analogy between him and his Biblical namesake had already occurred to him. Jacob had left Beersheba and journeyed to Haran for love of Rachel and had toiled seven years to win her. Had she not been the daughter of a pagan? Awaking with such thoughts in his mind, he resumed his own journey, heading upstream past mushrooms and blackberry brambles in bud, noting which plants were edible. Uncertain of the road, he kept his eye out for the blazes the Gazdas notched into trees. Cows bellowed close at hand; he could see camp fires. As long as the path climbed, it was taking him to Wanda.

Late in the afternoon, when the sun was moving westward, a strange figure appeared as if risen from the earth. White-haired, bearded, the man wore a brown robe and felt boots. A rosary and crucifix hung from his neck. He stopped before Jacob, leaning on a crooked staff. "Where are you bound for, my son?" he asked.

Jacob told him the name of the village.

"There is the way," the old man said, and he showed him the path.

Before leaving, he blessed Jacob. If it had not been for the cross he wore, the old man might have been mistaken for the prophet Elijah. But, perhaps, Jacob thought, he was an emissary of Esau, sent by those powers who wished Jews and gentiles to mate. Jacob was now nearing the village, and he lengthened his stride. He felt anxious: Wanda might have remarried or fallen ill. God forbid, she might be dead. She might be in love with someone else.

The sun went down; though it was midsummer, it became cold. Columns of mist rose from the mountains. In the distance, a huge bird, an eagle perhaps, hung suspended in mid air, wings motionless as though kept aloft by cabala. The moon rose and one by one, like candles being lit, stars appeared. Suddenly there was a noise, a kind of roaring. An animal or the wind? Jacob wondered. Though he was prepared to fight, he recognized that Providence would be justified in allowing some predatory creature to destroy him. How had he deserved better?

Stopping, he looked about him. He was as solitary here as the original Adam, with no sign anywhere of man and his works. The birds silent, only the song of the grass-hoppers and the bubbling of a stream were heard. Glacial breezes blew from the mountains. Jacob breathed in deeply, savoring the familiar odors. Strange how he had missed not only Wanda but this. The stale air of Josefov had been unbearable, windows tightly shut, nothing but books all day. Tired though he was from his exertion, the journey had invigorated him. The body required use as well as the soul. It was good for men to haul, drag, chop, run, per-spire, to hunger and thirst and become weary. Raising his eyes, he saw more stars appearing, large and brilliant here in the mountains. The workings of the heavens were visible to him, each orbiting light going its prescribed way and fulfilling its function. Notions he had had as a boy returned to him. Suppose he had wings and flew in one direction forever, would he come to the end of space? But how could space end? What extended beyond? Or was the material world infinite? But if it was, infinity stretched both to the east and west, and how could there be twice infinity? And what of time? How could even God have had no beginning? How could anything be eternal? Where had everything come from? These questions were impertinent, he knew, impermissible, pushing the inquirer toward heresy and madness.

He continued to walk. How strange and feeble was man. Surrounded on every side by eternity, in the midst of powers, angels, seraphim, cherubim, arcane worlds, and divine mysteries, all he could lust for was flesh and blood. Yet man's smallness was no less a wonder than God's greatness.

Pausing, he took some dry cheese from his sack and refreshed himself. Would he find Wanda today or have to wait until tomorrow? He feared the peasants and their dogs. He began to mumble prayers—a slave returning to bondage, a Jew again putting on Egypt's yoke.

11

Jacob entered the village at midnight, stealing through fields and pastures at the back of the huts. The moon had set, but it was light enough for him to recognize each house and granary. The mountain where he had spent five summers was visible also and he constantly lifted his eyes to it. Those years seemed dreamlike now, a vanished miracle, an interlude achieved by sorcery. Thank God, the dogs slept. His feet no longer felt heavy and his steps were faunlike; his body was buoyant from lack of food. He broke into a run, down the hill leading to Jan Bzik's hut, his single desire to find Wanda. Was she in the house? In the granary? Could she have gone to Antek's? He thought of his life and was amazed at what had happened to him. He had been taken captive; his family had been wiped out. Now, disguised as a peasant, he was hurrying to find his beloved. This was the sort of ballad his sisters had told or sung when his father was absent, not daring to when the pious man was at home, knowing that he regarded the female voice as lascivious.

Jacob stopped and held his breath. There it was, Jan Bzik's hut. He was trembling. He could make out every detail: the thatched roof, the windows, the granary, even the stump on which he had chopped wood. The kennel in the center of the yard appeared to be empty. Tiptoeing toward the granary, he smelled an odor he only now remembered. Was Wanda there? Could he be sure she would not cry out and wake everyone? He recollected the code she had used during those months when he had feared an attack by Antek or Stephan—three knocks, two loud and one soft. He rapped out the signal. There was no answer. Now for the first time he realized how dangerous this undertaking was. If he were discovered, he might be killed as a thief. And what if he did find Wanda, where could they go? This adventure was putting him in constant jeopardy. The Christians burned gentiles who became Jews. Nor would the Jews accept the convert. It was still not too late to turn back, he knew. He tingled with anxiety. Where had passion led him? Quietly he pushed open the granary door, meanwhile defending himself—I am no longer responsible for my acts. He heard breathing. Wanda was there. Hands ready to stifle her scream, he approached. Now he saw her in the darkness: she lay on the straw, her breasts exposed, half-naked. The story of Ruth and Boaz floated through his brain. He was awake, yet dreaming. He put down his sack.

"Wanda."

Her breathing stopped.

"Wanda, don't scream. It's me, Jacob." He broke off, unable to say more.

She sighed. "Who is it?"

"Jacob. Don't scream."

Thank God she did not, but sat up like someone delirious from fever.

"Who are you?" she said uncomprehendingly.

"Jacob. I've come for you. Don't scream."

At that very instant she did. Her scream made Jacob shudder and he was certain those in the hut must have heard. He fell to the straw, and, struggling with her in the darkness, he clamped his hand over her mouth. She freed herself, got to her feet, and he clutched her again, glancing at the open door, expecting to see peasants running toward the granary.

"Be still," he said, his breath coming in gasps. "They'll kill me. I've come for you, Wanda. I couldn't get you out of my mind."

Scarcely knowing what he was doing, he pulled her closer. They dared not stay there, the granary was a trap. He was breathing hard and sweating; his heart was pounding. "We must leave here while it's still dark," he whispered.

No longer struggling, trembling now, she pressed herself to him, her teeth chattering as though it were winter. "Is it really you?" he heard her say:

"Yes, I. Hurry, we must go."

"Jacob. Jacob."

The scream must have gone unnoticed as no one was coming. But perhaps the peasants lay in wait outside. Now, for the first time, it occurred to him that this was not the Wanda of his vision. There was no indication that she bore his child. A dream had deceived him. Her arms about his neck, she whimpered like a sick animal, "Jacob, Jacob." He could not doubt that she had been longing for him. But every minute counted now. Over and over again he cautioned her that she must dress quickly and come with him. He grasped her by the wrists, shook her, begged her not to delay—they were in great peril. She pulled him to her again, pressing her face against his. In his anxiety he couldn't make out what she was saying. "We must leave," he warned her.

"One minute."

Turning, she ran from the granary. He saw her enter the hut and wondered if she would tell the old woman. He lifted his sack and walked out into the open air, prepared to run for the fields if there was trouble. It was difficult for him to believe that the woman he had awakened was Wanda. She looked smaller and thinner than she had been, more like a girl than a woman. Outside it was dark and still—that moment before dawn when night borders on day. Sky, earth, and mountains waited in an expectant hush. Though he remained terrified and shocked at what he had done, there was also a silence in Jacob. His mind seemed frozen. He no longer cared what the outcome of this adventure would be. His fate was decided. He had passed beyond freedom, was both himself and another. The still point within him watched as though his actions were those of a stranger.

He waited, but Wanda did not come. Had she decided not to leave with him? The sun must have risen already on the other side of the mountains. He stood enveloped in the chill darkness of dawn. Suddenly Wanda ran from the hut, now wearing shoes and with a kerchief on her head. A sack was slung over her shoulder. "Did you wake them?" he asked.

"No, they sleep like the dead."

III

Wanda chose another route to leave the village than the one he had had in mind. Like an elusive shadow she ran before him scarcely visible in the darkness. His legs shook from too much walking and too little sleep. He stumbled over rocks, slid into ditches. He wanted to call to her not to get too far ahead, but dared not raise his voice. How could she run so quickly bearing a sack? He felt drowsy; he kept dreaming. Something rose from the darkness. He drew back startled and instantly the image dissolved. An alien voice spoke inside him. Things were happening, but he didn't know what. Wanda had dressed and packed without waking her mother and sister—how? An absurd idea, patently false, came to him: could she have strangled them?

That instant a fragment of day fell on the mountains and made them shine. The east reddened and the sun lifted itself behind the peaks. Jacob caught up with Wanda and saw that they were in a meadow at the edge of the forest. He noticed that she had on the fringed kerchief and the calico apron she had worn in his dream. Yes, she had altered, was shrunken and emaciated. Though her face was tinted purple by the sun, nevertheless her complexion was as pale as that of a consumptive. Her eyes had grown large and protruded from their sockets. It was even more difficult now to understand how she could have run so swiftly.

"Let's stop for a moment," he said.

"Not here—in the forest," she answered in a whisper.

But they did not stop immediately upon entering the woods. Among the trees Wanda's figure became more elusive than ever, and Jacob feared he would lose sight of her. The grade became steeper. He slipped on the pine needles. Wanda climbed like a bear, or a doe. He had returned to a changed woman. How could she have altered so quickly?

The forest grew lighter as if a lamp had been lit. Golden light fell over everything. Birds whistled and sang. Dew fell. Wanda stopped at the narrow opening of a cave. She threw her sack into the aperture and crept in head first, her feet kicking outside for a second. Jacob pushed his sack in and followed her through the opening. He recalled the commentary in the Talmud on the passage in the Bible, "And the pit was empty, there was no water in it." The Talmud added, "There was no water in it, but there were snakes and lizards." Well, whatever happens, happens, Jacob said to himself. It was as if he had entered the mouth of an abyss. He slipped and Wanda gripped him by the shoulders. The dampness choked him. He stumbled into her, and they fell over the sacks. Finally the cave became larger and he was able to sit up. When he spoke, his muffled voice sounded far off and unfamiliar to him.

"How did you know about this cave?" he asked.

"I knew. I knew."

"What's wrong with you? Are you sick?"

Wanda did not speak immediately.

"If you'd waited a little longer, you would have found me dead."

"What's wrong?"

Wanda paused again.

"Why did you go away? Where did they take you? I was told you'd never come back."

"You knew that the Jews had ransomed me?"

"All they said was that some devils had seized you."

"What do you mean? They paid Zagayek fifty gulden. They arrived in a wagon."

"When I was out of the village. But I knew I wouldn't find you when I got back. I didn't need the women to tell me."

"How did you know?"

"I know everything, everything. I was walking with Antek and the sun became black as night. The horse Wojciech was riding began to laugh at me."

"The horse?"

"Yes, and then I knew that my enemies would revenge themselves on me."

Jacob considered what she had told him.

"I was lying in the granary, when your sister came to call me."

"That! I know. As soon as I came into the village, they

all laughed at my bad luck. How did the Jews know where you were?"

"I spoke to that circus proprietor and he carried the message."

"Where to? Palestine?"

"No, to Josefov."

"You didn't even say goodbye to me. It was as if the earth had swallowed you up, as if there had never been a Jacob. Stephan came to me but I spat in his face. He got back at me by killing the dog. Mother and Basha said I was either possessed or crazy. The peasants wanted to tie me to a tree trunk but I ran away to the mountains and I stayed there until they brought up the herd. For four weeks I didn't taste a thing but snow and cold water from the stream."

"It wasn't my fault, Wanda. The Jews came and took me. What could I have told them? The wagon was waiting. When Zagayek sent for me I thought I was going to be hanged."

"You should have waited. You shouldn't have left me like that. If I'd had a child by you I would have had some comfort. But all I was left with was the stone behind the barn and what you had scratched on it. I beat my head against it."

"But I did come."

"I knew you would. You called to me but I didn't have the strength to wait. I went to the coffin maker and had myself measured. I had the priest confess me and I chose a grave next to father's."

"But you told me you no longer believed in Dziobak."

"What? He sent for me and I came. I fell on my knees and kissed his feet. All I wanted was to lie near Father."

"You'll live, but as a daughter of Israel."

"Where will you take me? I'm sick. I can't be a wife to you now. The witch told me what to do—it was she who brought you here and no one else."

"Wanda, what are you telling me? One cannot use witchcraft."

"You didn't come of your own free will, Jacob. I made a clay image of you and I wrapped it in my hair. I bought an egg laid by a black hen and buried it at the crossroads with a piece of glass from a broken mirror. I looked into it and I saw your eyes. . . ."

"When?"

"After midnight."

"One mustn't do such things. That's sorcery. It's not allowed."

"You wouldn't have come by yourself."

Suddenly clutching him, she let out a wail that made Jacob shudder. Crying, she kissed his face, licked his hand. A howl tore itself from her throat.

"Jacob, don't leave me again, Jacob."

PART TWO

Sarah

8

I

Once more the Cossacks attacked Poland, once more they slaughtered Jews in Lublin and the surrounding areas. Polish soldiers dispatched many of the survivors. Then the Muscovites invaded from the east and the Swedes from the north. It was a time of upheaval and yet the Jews had to conduct business, supervise the tilling of leased fields, borrow money, pay taxes, even marry off daughters. A house built today would be burned tomorrow. Today a girl was engaged, a few days later raped. One day a man was rich, the next poor. Banquets were held one day, the next funerals for martyrs. The Jews were constantly on the march, from Lemberg and back to Lemberg, from Lublin and back to Lublin. A city that was secure one day was under siege the next. A wealthy man would wake to find he must carry a beggar's sack. Entire communities of Jews turned Christian and though some later reassumed their own faith, others remained in darkness. Poland teemed with deserted wives, raped women, brides run away from their gentile husbands, men who had been ransomed or who had escaped from prison. God's wrath poured down on his people. But the moment the Jews caught their breath, they returned to Judaism. What else could they do? Accept the religion of the murderer?

A handful of Jews, survivors of burned-out and pillaged towns, gathered in Pilitz, a village on the other side of the Vistula, having gained the consent of the overlord to settle there. The Swedish war had ruined Adam Pilitzky, but not even the Swedes could steal earth, sky, and water. Again the peasants plowed and sowed. Again the earth, soaked with the blood of the innocent and the guilty, brought forth wheat and rye, buckwheat and barley, fruit and vegetables. The retreating Swedish army had set fire to Pilitzky's castle, but a rain storm had extinguished the blaze. A revolt of the peasantry had followed the withdrawal of the Swedes and one of Pilitzky's marshals had been stabbed. Arming his retainers, Pilitzky attacked the rebels, hanging some, and flogging others to death. He ordered the heads of the executed to be placed on poles and publicly exhibited as a warning to the serfs. Birds pecked at the flesh until only naked skulls remained.

Pilitzky had no time for his manor and was a poor manager; his Polish bailiffs were drunkards, drones, and thieves. True, the Jews also swindled if they got the chance, but the owner could brandish a whip over them. A Jew could be flogged like a peasant, imprisoned in a sty, even beheaded. Moreover the Jew was thrifty, saved money, and put it out for usury. One could always go bankrupt and make a settlement with him.

Though Adam Pilitzky was already fifty-four, he looked much younger. He was tall, dark, had brown hair untouched by gray, black eyes and a small goatee. He had spent his youth in France and Italy and had returned with what he termed new ideas. For a time he flirted with Protestantism, but that mood passed and he soon became a zealous Catholic and an enemy of the Reformation. The neighboring landowners found him strange, spoke of him as an "odd bird." He continually predicted the collapse of Poland. All of the prominent leaders were rascals, thieves, scum. He himself had taken no part in the Cossack and Swedish wars but accused his countrymen of cowardice. He swore by all that was holy that everyone in Poland could be bought, from the smallest clerk in a town hall to the king. Phrases from the diatribes of the priest Skarga were perpetually on his lips, though he drank heavily and was considered a libertine. The *jus primae noctis* (obsolete elsewhere) was in force in his estates. It was said that his daughter had drowned herself after having been possessed by him. His son had gone mad and had died of jaundice. The rumor was that his wife Theresa was his procuress and had taken the coachman as her lover. Another report was that she copulated with a stallion. Both wife and husband had recently become religious enthusiasts. When the monastery at Czestochow was besieged and Kordecki put up his heroic resistance, they had worked themselves into a religious frenzy.

Pilitzky's castle was crowded with his and his wife's relatives, who, though they belonged to the aristocracy, did the work of maids and lackeys. Once when Lady Pilitzky found a hole in the tablecloth she emptied a glass of wine over a female cousin. She required that the tablecloths, towels, shirts, underwear, silver, and porcelain be counted weekly. When Adam Pilitzky became angry, he took a rod and beat the old maids. The great fortune he and his wife had inherited between them had been dissipated. The neighborhood joke was that all that remained of Theresa Pilitzky's jewelry was a single gold hairpin. At every opportunity Adam Pilitzky warned that Poland would have no peace until all Protestants, Cossacks, and Jews were killed—particularly the Jews who had secretly bribed the traitor Radziszewski and conspired with the Swedes. Pilitzky had given his word to the priests that when Poland was rid of its enemies, no Jew would lay foot on his property. But, as usual, he did the opposite of what he said. First he permitted a Jewish contractor to settle. This Jew began to complain that he needed a quorum. Soon the Jews were granted the right to build a synagogue. Someone died and a cemetery was necessary. Finally the Jews of Pilitz imported a rabbi and a ritual slaughterer. So now Pilitz had become a community. Adam Pilitzky cursed and spat, but the Jews had done much to get him back on his feet. It was they who saw to it that the peasants plowed, harvested, mowed hay. They paid cash to Pilitzky for grain and cattle, repaired the pond in which he stocked fish, built a dairy. They even brought beehives for honey into the estate. Pilitzky no longer had to go looking for a tailor, a shoemaker, a furrier, a bell maker. Jewish craftsmen repaired his castle, patched the roof, rebuilt the ovens. Jews could do anything; rebind books, mend parquet floors, put glass in windows, frame pictures. When someone was ill, a Jewish doctor bled him or applied leeches and had a stock of medicines ready. A Jewish goldsmith made a bracelet for Lady Pilitzky and took a note instead of cash. Even the Jesuits, despite their slander and pamphlets, dealt with the Jews and used their handicraft.

At first Pilitzky had kept count of the number of Jews who settled on his property. But before long, he lost track. He didn't know their language and could scarcely tell one Jew from another. He warned constantly, "Unless the Poles change radically, there'll be another Chmielnicki. Anyway, everything's collapsing."

11

One day a man and woman trudged into Pilitz, sacks on their shoulders, bundles in their hands. The Jews emerged from stores and workshops to welcome the newcomers. The man, tall, broad-shouldered, blue-eyed, had a brown beard. Wearing a kerchief, seemingly younger than her husband, the woman looked almost gentile. The man was called Jacob. Asked where he was from, he mentioned the name of a distant city. The women soon learned that the young wife was a mute, and at first were amazed that so handsome a man should have made such a marriage. But, then, was it so astonishing? Marriages were made in heaven. Jacob gave his wife's name as Sarah, and she was immediately nicknamed, "Dumb Sarah."

The Jews inquired if Jacob was a scholar because they were looking for a teacher. "I know a chapter or two of the Pentateuch," Jacob said hesitantly.

"That's all that's needed."

It was springtime, the period between Passover and Pentecost. So now Pilitz had a school. Jacob and his mute wife were given a room and promised a house of their own if Jacob proved a good teacher. Pilitzsky owned many forests and lumber was cheap in the town. The new teacher was supplied with a table, a dunce's stool, and a cat-o'-nine-tails; he whittled a pointer and printed the letters of the alphabet on paper. Most of the children were in the early grades and the class assembled under a tree. Jacob sat with his charges in the shade, teaching them the alphabet, how to read syllables and words, instructing each child according to his age and knowledge. Because of the great amount of construction in progress, logs and lumber were piled all around, and the children built swings out of the boards and made little houses from chips and shavings. The town had no woman teacher and some of the parents sent daughters as well as sons to the cheder to learn their prayers and master a little writing. The girls made mud pies and sang and danced in a circle. The smaller boys and girls played house. The husband went to the synagogue to pray, his wife fixed supper for him and served it on a broken plate. The bread was a sliver of bark, the soup sand, the meat a pine cone. Jacob misplaced his cat-o'-nine-tails. He never whipped the children or scolded them, but lovingly pinched their cheeks and kissed their foreheads. These children had been born after the catastrophe.

The community liked Jacob immediately and pitied him for having a mute wife. True, Dumb Sarah behaved as a Jewess should, went to the ritual bath, soaked the meat and salted it, on Friday prepared the Sabbath pudding, burned a piece of chalah dough, blessed the candles; on the Sabbath, she stood in the woman's section of the synagogue and moved her lips as though praying. But sometimes she behaved in a way unbecoming a teacher's wife, took off her shoes and walked barefooted, laughed unrestrainedly, exhibiting a mouthful of unblemished peasant-like teeth. Dumb Sarah labored with the skill of a country woman, chopped wood, tended a vegetable garden she had planted behind the house, washed clothes in the river. When her own washing was done, she helped other women who had small children. She was remarkably strong and worked for everyone—and for nothing. Once she undressed in front of the women and swam in the river naked. Certain that she would drown at the spot where the waters swirled dangerously, the matrons, none of whom knew how to swim, broke into screams. But Dumb Sarah fearlessly crossed the whirlpool. Her audience was astounded. Dumb all right! Just like an animal.

This incident was soon followed by another which gave the people of Pilitz more to gossip about. The construction of Jacob's house was begun; and not only did Jacob assist in the work but Sarah also, although she was already pregnant and had stopped going to the ritual bath. Jacob went to the forest and felled trees, trimmed them with his ax and dragged them to the village. Sarah hauled logs and lumber as though she were a man. The house didn't cost the community a groschen. Nor was Jacob as unlearned as everyone had believed. One Saturday the reader lost his voice and Jacob read from the scroll; several times he was observed opening a Gemara in the study house. When he prayed he stood in a corner, swaying piously, and occasionally sighing. He said little about his past and the community concluded that he must have lost his family in the massacres. If they sought to engage him in conversation, he walked away, saying, "What happened happened. One must start over again."

The men respected him and the women liked him. When the matrons sat on their benches in front of their houses Sabbath afternoons, they agreed among themselves that Dumb Sarah had more luck than brains. No one denied that she was young, good-looking, and healthy, but what did a man want with a dumbbell? A husband liked to talk to his wife and hear her opinions. What a calamity, God forbid, if the child should take after its mother. Such things happened. One woman known as a wit remarked: "Well, some men would regard a silent wife as a blessing. No tongue, no torment."

"Oh, that's just talk."

"Well, it's better than having a blind one."

"Have you noticed," a young woman asked, "that as soon as it's dark she closes the shutters?"

"What does that prove?"

"That she loves him."

"Who wouldn't?"

On the Sabbath, Dumb Sarah discarded her kerchief, put on a bonnet, pointed shoes, an embroidered apron, and a dress with flowers that she had brought from far off. Going to synagogue, she held a prayer book in one hand and a handkerchief in the other. [This was allowed since the town of Pilitz had been enclosed in a wire which removed the Sabbath ban against carrying things.] When the women tried to communicate with her by hand signs, she smiled and shook her head, apparently unable to understand. The women poked fun at her, yet agreed she had a kind heart. She visited the sick and massaged their bodies with turpentine and alcohol. She prepared stewed apples and prunes as a treat for her husband's pupils on the Sabbath afternoon. Her stomach swelled, became pointed, and the women calculated she would give birth around Succoth or early in the month of Cheshvan.

Since the mute are also deaf, the women did not watch their words in her presence. Once, while Sarah sat with her prayer book open, a woman remarked, "She reads as well as the sacrificial rooster."

"Perhaps she's been taught."

"How can you teach the dumb?"

"Maybe she became dumb with fright."

"She doesn't look frightened."

"Perhaps the murderers cut out her tongue."

The women asked to see her tongue. At first, Sarah didn't seem to understand, then she began to laugh and her cheeks dimpled. She stuck out a pink tongue, as pointed as a dog's.

III

Wanda, not Jacob, had thought of playing the mute, realizing Yiddish would take her too long to learn; the few words she knew she spoke like a gentile. Her idea of passing herself off as a "Cossack bride" who could now only speak the language of the steppes was discarded because she didn't know that tongue either. She was not an adroit liar and would have been unmasked immediately. Jacob and she underwent many hardships and dangers before she decided on the role of a mute. They went to distant Pilitz because Jacob was too famous in Lublin and the surrounding areas as the slave who had returned. At night when Sarah, as all Jewish converts were called, closed the shutters, Jacob spoke with her and instructed her in their religion. He had already taught her the prayers and how to write Yiddish and now they studied the Pentateuch, the Books of Samuel and Kings, the Code of the Jewish Law; he told her stories from the Gemara and Midrash. Her diligence was amazing, her memory good; many of the questions she asked were the same the commentators had raised. Teaching her, he dared not lift his voice. Not only did he dread the gentiles and their laws, but also the Jews who would expel him from the village if they learned his wife was a convert. Sarah's presence in Pilitz imperiled the town. If the Polish authorities learned that a Christian girl had been seduced into Judaism, there would be reprisals. God knows what accusations would be made. The priests only wanted a pretext. And if the Jews got wind of it, the elders would immediately investigate the circumstances of the conversion and would guess correctly that Sarah had left her own religion because of Jacob—women being little interested in speculative matters; and Jacob would be excommunicated.

There was so much concern with the lineage and matrimonial connections of scholars that Jacob had not divulged that he was learned. The few scholarly books he had brought he kept hidden. He built his house with thick walls and constructed an alcove, windowless and hidden from the world by a clump of trees, where he and his beloved wife could study in secret. True, they had lived together illicitly, but since then they had fulfilled the law of Moses and Israel by standing under the canopy. Sarah now fervently believed in God and the Torah and obeyed all the laws. Now and then she erred, doing things upside down according to her peasant understanding, or speaking in a manner that was inappropriate. But Jacob corrected her kindly and made her understand the reason for each law and custom. Teaching others, Jacob realized, one also instructed oneself; correcting Sarah's behavior, answering her questions, eradicating her errors, many problems about which he would not have otherwise thought were clarified for him. Often her questions demanded answers which were not to be found in this world. She asked: "If murder is a crime, why did God permit the Israelites to wage war and even kill old people and small children?" If the nations distant from the Jews, such as her own people, were ignorant of the Torah, how could they be blamed for being idol worshipers? If Father Abraham was a saint, why did he drive Hagar and her son Ishmael into the desert with a gourd of water? The question that recurred more often than any other was why did the good suffer and the evil prosper. Jacob told her repeatedly he couldn't solve all the world's riddles, but Sarah kept on insisting, "You know everything."

He had warned her many times about the unclean days, reminding her that when she was menstruating she could not sit on the same bench with him, take any object from his hand, nor even eat at the same table unless there was a screen between her plate and his. He was not allowed to sit on her bed, nor she on his; not even the headboards of their beds ought to touch at this time. But these were some of the things that Sarah either forgot or ignored, for she kept on insisting she must be near him. She was capable of running over and kissing him in the middle of her period. Jacob rebuked her and told her such acts were forbidden by the Torah, but she took these restrictions lightly, and this caused Jacob sorrow. She was very scrupulous about less important things. She immersed all the dishes in the ritual bath, and kept on inquiring about milk and meat. At times she forgot she was a mute and broke into song. Jacob trembled. Not only was there the danger of her being heard, but a pious daughter of Israel should not provoke lust with the lascivious sound of her voice. Nor had she let the bath attendant shave her head like the other women's, though Jacob had asked her to. Sarah cut her own hair with shears; occasionally ringlets pushed out from under her kerchief.

Though Jacob had built them a house, Sarah complained nightly that she wished to leave Pilitz. She could not remain silent forever, and she feared what would happen to her child. The young must be taught to speak, and given love. She kept asking whether her Yiddish had improved; Jacob assured her she was doing well but it wasn't so. She mispronounced the words, twisted the constructions, and whatever she uttered came out upside down. Often her mistakes made Jacob laugh. Even a few words dropping from her tongue and there was no mistaking she had been born a gentile. Now that she was pregnant Jacob was more frightened than ever. A woman in labor cannot control her screams. Unless she could endure the birth pangs in silence, Sarah would give herself away.

Yes, the day Jacob had left Josefov for the village where he had been a slave for five years, he had picked up a burden which became heavier with the passage of time. His years of enforced slavery had been succeeded by a slavery that would last as long as he lived. "Well, Gehenna is for people and not for dogs," he had once heard a water carrier say. Yet he had saved a soul from idolatry, even though he had stumbled into transgression. At night when Sarah and he lay in their beds which were arranged so as to form a right angle (the room wasn't long enough to have one at the foot of the other), the couple whispered to each other for hours without tiring. Jacob informed Sarah about the moral life, spicing his text with little parables. She spoke of how much she loved him. They often recalled the summers he had lived in the barn when she had brought food to him. Now those days were far off and as shadowy as a dream. Sarah found it difficult to believe that the village still existed and that Basha and Antek and possibly her mother still lived there. According to the law, Jacob said, she no longer was a member of her family. A convert was like a newborn child and had a fresh soul. Sarah was like

Mother Eve who had been formed from Adam's rib; her husband was her only relative. "But," Sarah argued, "my father is still my father," and she began to cry about Jan Bzik who had had so hard a life and now lay buried among idolaters. "You will have to bring him into Paradise," she told Jacob. "I won't go without him."

I V

The peasants, now busy in the fields preparing for harvest, rarely brought produce to town. Jewish peddlers traveled to the country with packs on their backs to buy chickens, millet and corn. Sarah, needing supplies, picked up a sack and set out, though Jacob had insisted this was no errand for a pregnant woman, much less the wife of a teacher. But Sarah longed for the fields and pastures. The moment Pilitz was behind her, she kicked off her shoes and slung them over her shoulder. The townswomen smirked, seeing her go, asked each other, "Now how will the dumbbell bargain?"

Sarah's presumed deafness left the women free to slander and ridicule her in her presence. She was referred to as a dumb animal, a golem, a simpleton, a cabbage head. Jacob was pitied for having brought home such a goose. The guess was she had a rich father who had given a substantial dowry to marry her off. Still, Jacob was a fool to have led such a nanny goat under the canopy. Sarah had to keep smiling though she could scarcely retain her tears. The peasants were openly scornful. Running their fingers across their throats, they would point toward the road, pretending the Cossacks were coming. Pan Pilitzky, they

said, was infesting Poland with Jewish lice, and they prophesied wars, plagues, and famines, Heaven's revenge for
permitting the God murderers to settle there. Sarah found
it difficult to remain silent.

When she was alone with Jacob at night she cried and
repeated what the Jews said. "You must not repeat such
things," Jacob scolded her. "That's calumny. It's as great
a sin as eating pork."

"So they're allowed to abuse us but I can say nothing?"

"No, they're not behaving properly either."

"Well, they all do it, even Breina, and she's the wife of
an elder."

"Those who do such things will be punished in Heaven.
The sacred books warn that all those who gossip, ridicule,
or speak evil of others, will burn in the fires of Gehenna."

"All of them?"

"There's no lack of room in Gehenna."

"The rabbi's wife laughed too."

"There are no favorites in Heaven. When Moses sinned,
he was punished."

Sarah became thoughtful.

"No, speaking evil can't be one thousandth the sin of
eating pork, or no one would do it."

"Come, I'll show you what it says in the Torah."

Jacob, opening the Pentateuch, translated the text and
told her how each of the sins had been interpreted by the
Gemara. Several times he walked to the door to assure him-
self no one was listening or looking through the keyhole.
"Why do the Jews obey some laws and break others?"
Sarah whispered.

Jacob shook his head.

"That's the way it's always been. The prophets denounced it. The temple was destroyed for that reason. It's easier not to eat pig than to curb your tongue. Come and I will read you a chapter from Isaiah."

Jacob turned to Isaiah and translated the first chapter. Sarah listened in amazement. The prophet said the same things as Jacob: God had had enough of the blood of bullocks and the fat of lambs; people were not to come into his presence with bloody hands. The elders of Israel were compared by the prophet to the lords of Sodom God had destroyed. Late though it was, the wick in the shard continued to burn and moths circled the flame. The shadow of Jacob's head wavered on the ceiling. A cricket chirped from behind the oven. Love and fear mingled in Sarah. She dreaded the angry God who dwelled in Heaven and overheard every word and thought; she feared the peasants desirous of murdering Jews again and burying children alive; she was anxious about the Jews who were provoking the Almighty by obeying only one part of the Torah. Sarah promised not to repeat the evil gossip she heard, though as it was she had not told him everything. It was said in town that one of the storekeepers gave false measure. There was a rumor that a man had stolen from his partner at the time of the massacres. Sarah had been told that the Jews were the chosen people and she wanted to ask how they could be so favored when they committed such crimes. But that Jacob was righteous was evident to her. If God loved him as much as she did, he would live forever.

In her prayers she told God that she had no one but Jacob. She could never love another. She had joined a community but felt like a stranger. Though she had fled the peasants, she had not become one of the Jews of Pilitz. Jacob was husband, father, and brother to her. The moment the candle was extinguished she called him to her bed. "You, gentile," Jacob said jokingly: "Don't you know that a daughter of Israel mustn't be immodest or she'll be divorced without a settlement?"

"What can a daughter of Israel do?"

"Bear children and serve God."

"I intend to bear you a dozen."

He would not lie with her immediately, but first told her stories of upright men and women. She asked what went on in Paradise and what would occur when the Messiah came. Would Jacob still be her husband? Would they speak Hebrew? Would he take her with him to the rebuilt temple? When the Messiah came, Jacob said, each day would be as long as a year, the sun would be seven times as bright, and the Saints would feed on leviathan and the wild ox and drink the wine prepared for the days of redemption.

"How many wives will each man have?" Sarah asked.

"I'll have only you."

"I'll be old by then."

"We'll be young forever."

"What kind of a dress will I wear?"

Lying with Jacob was for her a foretaste of Paradise. She often wished that the night would last forever and she could continue to listen to his words and receive his caresses. That hour in the darkness was her reward for what she had endured during the day. When she fell asleep, her dreams took her to her native village; she entered the hut where she had lived; she stood on the mountain.

Strange events involving Antek, Basha, and her mother occurred. Her father, once more alive, spoke wisely to her, and though she forgot his words as soon as she awoke, their resonance rang in her ears. Sometimes she dreamed Jacob had left her, and cried in her sleep. Jacob always awakened her.

"Oh, Jacob, you're still here. Thank God." His face would become hot and wet from her tears.

v

A coach drawn by a team of four horses, with two coachmen in front and two footmen in the rear, rode into the market place at noon. One of the coachmen blew his horn. The Jews of Pilitz became alarmed. Pilitzky rarely came to town in such pomp, and never in summer before the harvest. He was carrying a sword; he looked drunk. Leaping from the coach, he drew his sword from its scabbard and screamed, "Where is Gershon? I'm going to cut off his head. I'm going to tear him to pieces and pour acid into his wounds—him and his family as well. I'm going to throw the whole batch of them to the dogs."

Some of the Jews scurried off. Others rushed to Pilitzky and threw themselves at his feet. The women began to wail. The children in Jacob's class heard the tumult and came running to have a look at the lord, at the coach, at the horses with their heads held high in their fine harnesses. One of Gershon's sycophants hastened to him and warned him that Pilitzky was drunk and looking for him. Gershon was the most powerful man in Pilitz, since he leased the fields of the manor and managed them as if they were his own. He was known in town as a shady dealer. He'd built himself a large house and had acquired three sons-in-law, all from wealthy families, who had become respectively the town's rabbi, ritual slaughterer and public contractor. The last supplied the flour at Passover and had built the synagogue. Gershon had retained the wardenship of the burial society and charged exorbitant prices for graves, although Pilitzky had donated the land for the cemetery. Gershon also collected the taxes, usurping the function of the town's seven elders as set forth by the Council of the Four Countries. Taxation in Pilitz worked on the principle that the friends and flatterers of Gershon paid little or nothing; all others tottered under the weight of his levies. Gershon was ignorant but had granted himself the title "Our Teacher" and did not allow the cantor to intone the eighteen benedictions until he, Gershon, had said them over to himself. When he got the whim to take a steam bath in the middle of the week, the bath attendant was forced to heat the water at the community's expense.

Those whom Gershon had trampled threatened to denounce him to Pilitzky and to the Council in Lublin, but Gershon feared no man. He had friends who sat on the Council and he held Pilitzky's note for a thousand gulden. He was an intimate of other landowners, Pilitzky's enemies. Gershon, it seemed, had forgotten that the Jews were in exile. Yes, Pilitzky was looking for him and Gershon was advised to take cover in an attic or cellar until the wrath of the lord of Pilitz subsided. But Gershon was not one to have himself thought a coward, and he put on his silk overcoat, his sable hat, wrapped a sash around his waist, and walked out to meet Adam Pilitzky. Though Gershon dressed like a rabbi, he had the florid complexion of a butcher. His nose was flat, his lips thick; his belly stuck out as though he were pregnant. One of his eyes was higher and set in a larger socket than the other. He had heavy, bushy eyebrows. Not only was he aggressive but stubborn. When he rose to make a speech, every third word was a barbarism; he babbled until everyone fell asleep, and the opposition never had a chance to voice its opinion.

Now, walking slowly, Gershon approached his overlord. He did not come alone but accompanied by his entourage: the butchers, the horse dealers, and the men of the burial society whom he banqueted twice a year and who got all the sinecures in town. Before Gershon could open his mouth, Pilitzky screamed: "Where's the red bull?"

Gershon considered the question for a moment and then replied. "I sold him to the butcher, my lord."

"You dirty Jew. You sold my bull."

"Sir, while I lease the manor land, I'm in control."

"So you're in control. Seize him, boys. We'll hang him here." All the Jews shouted in terror—even Gershon's enemies joined in. Gershon tried to speak and retreated a few steps, but the coachmen and footmen caught hold of him. Pilitzky cried out, "Get the rope."

Some of the Jews fell to their knees, prostrated themselves, bowed—as on Yom Kippur when the cantor repeats the ritual service of the ancient temple in Jerusalem. Women screamed. Gershon struggled with his captors. The sash was torn from his waist. Pilitzky shouted, "A pole. Bring me a pole."

"We can hang him from the lamp post, my lord."

Jacob, hearing the clamor which was not unlike that when the Cossacks had attacked Josefov, came running. Gershon's wife was clasping one of Pilitzky's knees, refusing to let go. Pilitzky was trying to shake himself free of her and had his sword raised as if about to sever her head. The women were pushing and milling and wailing insanely. One dug her nails into her cheeks, another clutched her breasts, a third scratched at her husband to do something. Gershon was a crass man. The Jews of Pilitz disliked him but they could not stand by and see him hanged summarily. Gershon's daughters-in-law fell into each other's arms. The rabbi also prostrated himself at Pilitzky's feet; his skull cap having come off, his long side locks dragged in the dirt. It was almost as if the massacres had again begun. Gershon's followers, instead of disarming Pilitzky's servants which they might have done easily, just stood gaping with legs spread wide, amazed it seemed at their own impotence. But when had a Jew ever defied a Polish noble? Then out of the study house walked the beadle bearing the holy scroll as if it would quiet Pilitzky's wrath. There were shouts bidding the old man advance closer; others among the crowd motioned him back, protesting the sacrilege. He stood swaying indecisively on his rickety legs as though about to fall. Seeing him totter, a great cry of lamentation rose from the people. Jacob stood transfixed, knowing he must say nothing, yet equally certain he could not remain silent. Stepping forward, he ran quickly to Pilitzky and took off his hat.

"Mighty lord, a man is not killed for selling a bull."

The market place became quiet. Everyone knew that Gershon had declared war on Jacob because Jacob had taken the place of the reader. Gershon didn't like scholars, would never have tolerated Jacob's appointment if he had known that this was a man who could understand both text and footnotes. Now Jacob came to his assistance. Astonished, Pilitzky stared at the Jew in front of him.

"Who are you?"

"I am the teacher."

"What's your name?"

"Jacob."

"Oh! Are you that Jacob who cheated Esau out of his birthright?" An inhuman laugh burst from Pilitzky's throat.

Hearing the lord of Pilitz laugh, everyone joined in—the Jews, Pilitzky's men; Pilitzky doubled up with mirth. Was it merely a joke, a nobleman's prank such as the Polish landowners often played on their Jewish tenants? These games always terrified the Jews since such fun sometimes turned serious. But the men still held onto Gershon—who was the only one not laughing. His yellow eyes had lost none of their arrogance; his thick, mustached lip was drawn back into a snarl, revealing sparse, yellow teeth. Gershon looked like an animal at bay about to die in a struggle with a stronger adversary. Pilitzky howled with laughter, clapped his hands, clutched at his knees, and gasped. Those who had prostrated themselves rose and, relieved, bellowed with a mad exuberance. Even the rabbi laughed. The women collapsed into each other's arms, their knees buckling, their laughter turning to tears.

"Mommalas, Poppalas, tsitselas," Pilitzky mimicked and started braying again. The whole community joined in, every face with its own particular expression and grimace.

The sight of one old matron, who had lost her bonnet and whose unevenly clipped scalp resembled a newly sheared ewe, started the women off once more, but this time their laughter was genuine.

Then all laughter ceased. Pilitzky gave a final burst and scowled again.

"Who are you? What are you doing here?" he asked Jacob. "Answer me, Jew."

"I am the teacher, my lord."

"What do you teach? How to steal the host? How to poison wells? How to use Christian blood to make matz- oth?"

"God forbid, my lord. Such acts are prohibited by Jewish law."

"Prohibited, are they? We know. We know. Your cursed Talmud teaches you how to fool the Christian mob. You've been driven from every country, but King Casimir opened our gates wide to you. And how do you repay us? You've established a new Palestine here. You ridicule and curse us in Hebrew. You spit on our relics. You blaspheme our God ten times a day. Chmielnicki taught you a lesson, but you need a stronger one. You love all Poland's enemies—Swedes, Muscovites, Prussians. Who gave you permission to come here?" Pilitzky screamed at Jacob, shaking his fist. "This is my earth, not yours. My ancestors shed blood for it. I don't need you to teach Jewish vermin how to defile my country. We have enough parasites al- ready. We're more dead than alive."

Pilitzky ceased his invective and foamed at the mouth. Once more, eyeing each other in dread, the Jews bent, ready to fall to the ground and beg for mercy. The elders signaled among themselves. Picking up his skull cap, the rabbi placed it, still dirty, on his head. The woman whose bonnet had fallen off clapped it back on, askew, its beaded front to the side. Pilitzky's men tugged at Gershon again, as though trying to shake him out of his clothes. The beadle still swayed back and forth with the scroll. Evidently the story was not to end happily. Men and women began to detach themselves from the crowd and to slip away, some going to close their shops, others running into their houses and locking the doors. "Don't run away, Jews," Pilitzky shouted. "There's no escape. I'll strangle you wherever you are. When I finish with you, you'll mourn the day your wretched mothers squeezed you from their leprous wombs."

"Magnanimous lord, we are not running away. Mighty benefactor, we await your pleasure."

"I have asked you something," Pilitzky shouted, turning to Jacob. "Answer me."

Jacob didn't remember the question. Pilitzky reached out as if to grab the teacher by his collar. But Jacob was too tall for him.

"Forgive me, my lord," Jacob bowed his head. "I have forgotten the question."

Pilitzky, having forgotten himself, looked confused. He had noticed that this Jew, unlike the others, spoke good Polish. His anger left him and he felt something akin to shame at having made such a display before these paupers, the survivors of Chmielnicki's blood bath. He had always considered himself a compassionate man. Tears came to his eyes. Prayers to Jesus and the apostles passed through his head. From boyhood on, he had expected to die young; a fortune teller had predicted an early end. Now he looked for some excuse to terminate this saturnalia. His turbulent spirit stood midway between contrition and anger. Should he ask forgiveness of the Jews, that wilful people God had chosen? There was a bitter taste in his mouth and his nose tickled. I wouldn't behave this way if my life weren't chaos. That cursed woman has ruined me. Suddenly he had an impulse to toss coins to the crowd. That would show them that he was no Haman. But when he reached into his pocket he remembered he didn't have a groschen, and he was overwhelmed with self-pity. That's what these Jews have done to me, he thought, bled me dry. Seeing the old beadle, swaying unsteadily with the holy scroll on his shoulder, he yelled, "Why did you bring out the scroll? How can that help you? It would be better if you followed what is written there instead of using it to mask your crimes. Carry it back to the synagogue, you old rascal."

From every side shouts came, "Carry back the scroll. Carry back the scroll." The lord of Pilitz had relented, the Jews sensed. The beadle gave a final sway and bore the scroll into the study house. But the men still held Gershon pinioned. Pilitzky's mood might change again. He surveyed the crowd, a bitter look in his eyes as if searching for another victim. Dumb Sarah walked into the square carrying an apronful of herbs. Having gone into the fields, she had not heard the noise of Pilitzky's arrival and knew nothing of what had happened. She saw the coach and horses, Pilitzky's men, Pilitzky himself, and Jacob, hat in hand, standing humbly before the lord of Pilitz. Sarah raised her arms, wailed, and the herbs fell from her apron. What she had dreaded had come to pass.

Her nightmares had been true omens. Breaking through the crowd, she pushed her way to Jacob, and screaming wildly threw herself at Pilitzky's feet. Pilitzky turned pale and retreated. She followed him, crawling like a worm and clutching at his legs. "Have pity, Pan," she lamented in Polish. "Mercy, gentle lord. He's all I've got. I carry his child in my womb. Kill me instead. My head for his. Let him go free, Pan. Let him go free."

"Who is this woman? Get up."

"Forgive him, my lord. Forgive him. He's committed no crime. He's honest, my lord. A holy man."

Jacob bent to raise her and then paused, terrified. Only then did he realize that Sarah had given herself away: she had spoken. In the confusion, no one appeared to have understood what had happened. Then men spread their hands and raised their eyebrows; women clutched their heads; Pilitzky's servants momentarily let go of Gershon. Even the horses, until then standing silently, lost in equine meditations remote from the struggles of men, turned their heads. Gershon looked baffled and outraged. Like many overbearing men, he resented having things happen he could neither control nor comprehend. A woman slapped both of her cheeks screaming, "Oh, I've seen everything."

"What is this? Who is she?" Pilitzky asked.

"My lord, she's a mute."

"What? A mute?"

"Gracious lord, she's as dumb as a fish. Deaf and dumb."

"Yes, gracious lord, dumb, dumb, a mute." Cries came from all directions.

"Hey, rabbi, is that a fact? Is this woman a mute?" Pilitzky said, turning to the rabbi.

"Yes, my lord, she's the wife of the teacher. She's deaf and dumb. This is a miracle."

"Children, I'm going to faint"—and a woman fell to the ground.

"Help. Water! Water!"

"Oh, my God"—and another woman fainted.

Jacob, bending, pulled Sarah to her feet. Her limp body lay against his shoulder, supported by his arm; she trembled, gasping, sobbing. Pilitzky rested his hand on the hilt of his sword. "What is this, Jew? Some kind of farce?"

"No farce, my lord. She's deaf and dumb. Deaf as the wall and dumb as a fish."

"My lord, we all know she's mute," witnesses from the crowd attested.

"Are you prepared to swear to that?"

"My lord, we've invented nothing."

"Hey, you, Jew, is your wife really dumb?"

"Yes, my lord."

"Always been that way?"

"As long as we've been married."

Jacob did not consider this a lie since Sarah had assumed her role before stepping under the canopy. All around him the townswomen were screaming that it was indeed so, swearing by their husbands and their children that this was Dumb Sarah who everyone knew was unable to talk. Pilitzky's men stood gaping while their master considered this strange occurrence.

"I don't believe you, Jews, not a word of it. This is just another one of your tricks. You want to fool me and make me look ridiculous. Remember Jews, if this is a lie, you'll be flayed alive, I'll herd you into your synagogue and set it on fire. "We'll roast you slowly, as sure as my name is Adam Pilitzky."

"Gracious lord, we are telling the truth."

VI

Pilitzky realized the Jews were telling the truth. Their open mouths and bewildered looks told him this was a miracle. Adam Pilitzky had been waiting for a miracle ever since the start of the wars and invasions. One was needed to save Poland. Prior Chodecki's resistance at Czestochow and Stephan Czanecki's campaign against the Swedes, which had rallied the Polish armies and revived the cause of Catholicism, had seemed to be that miracle. Now from every side came reports of new wonders. An image of the Virgin had wept real tears which the people gathered in a silver chalice. On church steeples stone crosses flamed in the dark of night. Dead armies, dressed in the uniforms of a hundred years ago, marched against the enemies of Poland and drove them from fortified positions. Ghost riders were seen galloping on phantom horses. Legendary heroes, dressed in helmets and breastplates, brandished swords and spears as they led charges. Monks and nuns, long since residents of Paradise, put on bodies again and roamed the countryside comforting the people and urging them to pray.

Here a church bell rang by itself, and there an ancient coach was seen driving down a road into a wall and disappearing as if swallowed up. Birds spoke with human voices and a dog led a battalion out of ambush. In one village it had rained blood, in another fishes and toads. In one instance wine had been lacking for the mass and God's mother had opened her lips and wine had flowed out. An almost blind crone had watched a flaming ship flying the Polish ensign sail across the sky. These signs and portents had invigorated the nation's spirit and renewed its belief in heaven.

Nevertheless, Adam Pilitzky had seen no miracles himself and resented this. The devil subverted and denied the wonders of God in a thousand ways; hidden in every heart was some doubt. Often when Pilitzky lay awake thinking of what was going on in the country, Lucifer came and whispered in his ear: "Don't they all speak of miracles? The Greek Orthodox, the Protestants, even the infidel Turks? How does it come about that God sometimes rides with the Protestants bringing them victories? Why doesn't he visit them with the plagues of Pharaoh or rain down stones as he will on Gog and Magog?" Pilitzky listened to Lucifer; at heart, he may have believed man merely an animal who returns to dust, and hence condoned his wife's licentiousness.

The revolt of his serfs and the cruelties with which he had suppressed the rebellion had further mortified Pilitzky's spirit. He knew that widows and orphans sorrowed because of him. At night he had visions of bodies hanging from the gibbets, their feet blue, their eyes glassy, their tongues extended. He suffered from cramps and headaches; his skin itched. There were days when he prayed for death or planned suicide. Not even wine and vodka could calm him now. Nor were the pleasures of the body as intense as they had been. He was always on the lookout for new sensations to stave off impotency. Because of the perverseness of that witch Theresa, now only her infidelities aroused his lust. He made her describe her affairs in detail. When she had exhausted the catalog of her debauchery, he forced her to invent adventures. Husband and wife had driven each other into an insane labyrinth of vice. He procured for her and she procured for him. She watched him corrupt peasant girls and he eavesdropped on her and her lovers. He had warned her many times that he would stab her, she teased about poisoning his food. But both were pious, lit candles, went to confession, and contributed money for the building of churches and religious monuments. Often Adam Pilitzky opened the door of their private chapel and found Theresa, her cheeks wet with tears, a crucifix pressed to her bosom, kneeling before the altar deep in contemplation. Theresa spoke of entering a nunnery; Pilitzky toyed with the idea of becoming a monk.

Pilitzky could never have described the torments he had endured during the last few years. Only God, aware of all the temptations and pitfalls besetting man, and compassionately viewing His creatures' follies and weaknesses, knew how much Pilitzky had suffered through shame and guilt. What the lord of Pilitz wanted was a sign that some supernal eye looked down and took notice, some proof that more than blind chance governed the world. Now heaven, it seemed, had decided to put an end to his doubts.

Pilitzky looked at Sarah and Jacob, the wife clinging to the husband. No, this was no fraud. He could see the Jews glancing at each other and staring at the couple incredulously. There was a lump in Pilitzky's throat; he found it difficult to keep from crying. Then, remembering that the mute had spoken of Jacob as a holy man, he said in a firm voice, "Forgive me, Jacob. I did not mean to insult you. If you are truly a holy man as the mute has attested, I respect you even though you are a Jew."

"Gracious lord, there is nothing holy about me. I am an ordinary individual, a Jew like all the others; perhaps even less than they."

"What? Saints are all modest. Hey, there, men, let that crook Gershon go. I'll settle with him some other time. You are no longer my tenant, Gershon," Pilitzky said. "Don't step on my land again or let me see your face. If I find you trespassing, I'll unleash the dogs."

"Your excellency owes me money," Gershon said. His voice did not waver; his manner showed he did not fear the bluster of overlords. "I have leased the manor lands. I have a contract and your note."

"Huh? Jew, you have nothing. You can wipe yourself with those papers."

"My lord, this is not just. A man's word is sacred. There is a court in Poland."

"Drag me into court, will you, Jew? You're crazy, Jew. You'd be already swinging and the birds would be eating the flesh of your head, as the Bible says, if what just happened had not. You thief, you swindler. I've heard that you filch from the Jews, even. I intend to investigate and see you're punished. As for the court: I fear no one. I am the court and the law. I rule supreme on my manor. Poland is not France where the king tyrannizes over the nobles. Here we have more power than the king. We make and break our kings. Keep that in mind and you'll also keep your head on your shoulders."

"I have paid for the contract."

"What you paid, you got back a long time ago. I'll have no further dealings with you. Move—before I break every bone in your body."

There was a murmuring among the Jews. Gershon's friends and family whispered to him to leave the market place immediately. His wife and daughter tugged at his sleeves, begging him to come home. But Gershon shook his head; his nose wrinkled and his heavy under lip sagged. Powerless though a Jew was against a nobleman, Gershon did not intend to stand by and see himself ruined. He had friends who were richer and more eminent than Pilitzky. He knew that the lord of Pilitz had broken every law of church and state. Moreover, he was involved in law suits that threatened to ruin him. The nobility still preserved their code and demanded that notes and contracts be honored, even those made with the contemptible Jews. Gershon took a step forward.

"I am still the tenant until the expiration of my lease."

"All you are is a dead dog."

Adam Pilitzky turned violently, drew his sword, and ran at Gershon. The Jews wailed and screamed.

9

I

Jacob saw that he had lost control of himself. Satan fiddled and he danced. "Trangression draws transgression in its train," the Book of Aboth said, and this was surely true in his case. His lust for a forbidden woman had involved him in deception. An entire Jewish community—no, not merely one, a host of them—had been deluded into believing his wife was a mute. Now, grieving women sought out Sarah who was already in her eighth month and begged her to lay her hands on them and bless them. Nor would the elders of Pilitz hear of Jacob not accepting Pilitzky's offer. Gershon had lost the contract; Pilitzky warned that if Jacob refused to become his administrator, he would import one from another town. He even threatened to expel the Jews from Pilitz. A deputation of the elders, led by the rabbi, came to plead with Jacob. Gershon let it be tacitly understood that he was not opposed to this arrangement; Jacob should administer the estate for the time being. Gershon's appraisal was that the teacher, unable to distinguish rye from wheat, would mismanage Pilitzky's interests and this would lead the nobleman to conclude that Gershon was indispensable.

As is usual in the affairs of men, the relationships were complex, and all were based on deception. Woe to the house founded on falsehood. But what could Jacob do? If he told the truth, Sarah and he would be burned at the stake. Sacred though the truth was, the law did not permit one to sacrifice oneself for it.

Lying awake at night, Jacob addressed God: "I know that I have forfeited the world to come, but nevertheless you are still God and I remain your creation. Castigate me, Father, I will submit to your punishment willingly."

The punishment might arrive any day. Sarah would shortly go into labor, and might scream and talk. The truth would sooner or later make itself known. Jacob waited for the rod to strike and worked; there was more than enough for him to do. God had blessed the fields with plenty; the Polish and Swedish armies had not trampled the newly sown crops that year. Jacob woke early and retired late; the lord of Pilitz expected a profit. Gershon also anticipated getting a covert share. However, Jacob, unlike Gershon, received no contract and was only Pilitzky's manager, supervising the peasants and dealing with the grain merchants. He took as wages merely what he needed to subsist.

It was strange to be in the fields surrounded by vegetation again. Sarah and Jacob lived in the house Gershon had built for himself near the castle. Jacob's own house as well as the school he had begun to build remained unfinished. The town was looking for a new teacher—meanwhile someone tutored the children a few hours a day—and the current joke was that since Jacob was managing Pilitz, Gershon should take over the cheder.

Jacob had always been aware that everything in this world is transitory. What was man? Today alive, tomorrow in his grave. The Talmud spoke of the world as a wedding; the poet in the liturgy compared man to a drifting cloud, to a wilting flower, to a fading dream. Yes, everything passed. But never before had Jacob felt the transience of things so keenly. One week a field of grain stood ripening; the next the field was bare. The days were now bright and clear, but rain and snow would soon follow. Jacob had become important in Pilitz; the lord of the manor was now accessible to him. When he passed peasants, they tipped their caps and addressed him as "Pan." The Jews considered him the husband of a holy woman. Jacob knew the end of all this would be disgrace and a walk to the gallows. But meanwhile he saw to it that the grain was harvested, threshed, and stored. He superintended the autumn plowing and the sowing of the winter crop. What he had learned in those years of slavery had become useful. Now when Sarah and he retired at night, they discussed not only the Torah but also the affairs of the manor. Even though Jacob did not keep the account books, little by little he uncovered evidence of Gershon's bad practices. True, Pilitzky in turn stole from the peasantry and he who robs a thief is guilty of no crime; nevertheless Gershon had broken the Eighth Commandment, made enemies for Israel, and committed sacrilege. Well, but everyone has his temptations.

Jacob had risen in the world, but he knew his ascent was of that kind of which it is written, "Pride goeth before a fall." The peasants did not seek to trick him, as they had Gershon, but followed his instructions and even offered him advice. The inhabitants of the castle, Pilitzky's dependents as well as his servants, respected Jacob. The dogs, whose ferocity had made Gershon tremble, for some mysterious reason took to Jacob immediately, wagging their tails when he approached the gate. Everyone in the castle was kind to him, and Lady Pilitzky sent a maid to help the pregnant and mute Sarah. Pilitzky, himself, went out of his way to talk to Jacob and admired the manager's fluent Polish. Gershon had been another sort, an ignoramus unable to answer any of his patron's questions about Jews and their religion. Jacob replied quoting the holy books. Accustomed to discussing difficult questions lucidly, he invented parables the gentile mind could accept. Pilitzky brought up the same problems that had disturbed Wanda.

One day when Pilitzky sat with Jacob in the library showing him a Bible concordance in Latin which had Hebrew marginalia, Lady Pilitzky entered. Jacob rose from his chair and bowed deeply. Theresa Politzky was a small, plump woman with a round face, short neck, and a high bosom. Her blond hair, twisted in a coronet, reminded Jacob of a Rosh Hashana chalah. She had on a pleated, black silk dress, decorated with ribbons, and around her neck lay a gold cross set with jewels. She had a small nose, full lips, bright dark eyes and a smooth forehead. Jacob had been told that she behaved like a whore, but she walked with sprightly steps and seemed almost girlish, despite her stoutness. She smiled upon seeing the men and her cheeks dimpled. Pilitzky winked at her, "This is Jacob."

"Of course, I've seen you many times from my window."

Lady Pilitzky offered her hand to Jacob who hesitated an instant and then, bowing again, carried her fingers to his lips. One more sin, Jacob thought, kissing her hand, and blushing to the roots of his hair. Pilitzky laughed.

"Well, now that that's done let's have a glass of wine together."

"Forgive me, my lord, but my religion forbids it."

Pilitzky's body tensed.

"Oh, so you're forbidden. It's all right to fleece the Christians, but you mustn't drink wine with them. And who forbids it? The Talmud, naturally, which teaches you how to cheat the Christians."

"The Talmud makes no mention of Christians, only idolators."

"The Talmud considers Christians idolators. Your people gave the world the Bible, but then you denied God's only begotten son, thereby turning from the Father. To-day Chmielnicki punishes you; tomorrow another *hetman* will continue your castigation. The Jews will never have peace until they recognize the truth and . . ."

Lady Pilitzky frowned. "Adam, these discussions have no value."

"No, I will not keep back the truth. That Jew Gershon was a crook and a jackass besides. He didn't know a thing, not even his own Bible. Jacob appears to be not only honest but well-educated. That's why I want to ask him a few questions."

"Not now, Adam. He's busy seeing to the fields."

"Where are the fields running? Sit down, Jew. I'm not going to hurt you. Sit here. Very good! Neither Lady Pilitzky nor I believe in forcing our Faith on anyone. We don't have an inquisition here as they do in Spain. Poland is a free country, too free for its own good. That's why it's collapsing. But that's not your fault. Let me ask you this. You've been waiting for the Messiah for a thousand years—what am I talking about?—for more than fifteen hundred, and he doesn't appear. The reason is clear. He has come already and revealed God's truth. But you are a stubborn people. You keep yourself apart. You regard our meat as unclean, our wine as an abomination. You are not permitted to marry our daughters. You believe you are God's chosen people. Well, what has he chosen you for? To live in dark ghettos and wear yellow patches. I've been out of the country and seen how Jews live abroad. They're all rich and all they think about is profit. Everywhere they're treated like spiders. Why don't you take a good look at yourself and throw away the Talmud? Perhaps the Christians are right after all. Have any of you visited heaven?"

"Really these religious arguments are stupid," Theresa Pilitzky protested.

"What's so stupid about them? People have to discuss things. I'm not speaking to him in anger, but as an equal. If he can convince me that the Jews are right, I'll become a Jew." Pilitzky laughed.

"I can convince no one, my lord," Jacob began to stammer. "I inherited my faith from my parents and I follow it to the best of my ability."

"The idolators had fathers and mothers too. And they were taught that a stone is God. But you Jews demanded the destruction of their temples and the annihilation of their children. The Old Testament says so. Doesn't that prove that one doesn't necessarily follow the parents' faith?"

"The Christians also regard the Bible as sacred."

"Naturally. But one must be logical. Everyone but your people and the infidel Turks have accepted Christianity. You Jews consider yourself cleverer than anyone in Europe or the world. All right, God loves you. What kind of love?—your wives are raped and your children buried alive."

Jacob swallowed hard. "Those were the acts of the Christians."

"What? The Cossacks are no more Christians than I am Zoroastrian. Only the Catholics are Christian. The Russian Orthodox are as idolatrous as their allies the Turks. Protestants are even worse. But this is all irrelevant, Jew."

"None of us knows the ways of Providence, my lord. The Catholics also suffer. They wage war against each other . . ." Jacob broke off in the middle of his sentence.

For a moment Adam Pilitzky meditated in silence on Jacob's words.

"Of course we suffer. As the Bible says, man was born to suffer. But we suffer for a reason. Our souls are purified through what we endure and rise to heaven. But the real torment begins for the unbeliever after death."

Theresa Pilitzky shook her head. "Really, Adam, where's this getting you? The truth cannot be proved. It can only be found here." Theresa Pilitzky pointed to her heart.

"Yes, that is true, my lady," Jacob said softly.

"Well, I suppose it is. But of what use is this stiff-necked clinging to your faith? In your misguided way, you are attentive to God, and your synagogues are always filled. Once when I was in Lublin, I walked past your prayer houses. Such ecstatic singing! A song rose as if from a thousand voices. But a few years later ten thousand Jews were slaughtered. I talked to someone who saw the Cossacks enter Lublin. The Jews crushed each other in their panic. More died from being trampled on than were killed by the invaders. While this went on, was the sky any less blue? Did the sun stop shining? Where was the God you praise and beseech, whose dear children you claim to be? How do you deal with these facts, Jew? How can you sleep at night remembering?"

"When you're tired enough, your eyes close by themselves."

"I see you avoid answering me . . ."

"He's right, Adam, he's right. What's there to say? Can we explain our misfortunes any better than he can his? Even searching for an answer is blasphemous. You know that very well."

Pilitzky drew his eyeballs downward and stared cross-eyed at Lady Pilitzky. "I know nothing, Theresa. Sometimes I think that the Epicureans and Cynics were right. Have you ever heard of Democritus, Jew?"

"No, my lord."

"Democritus was a philosopher who said that chance ruled everything. The Church has proscribed his writings, but I read him. He believed in neither idols nor God. The world, he said, was the result of blind powers."

"Don't repeat those heresies," Theresa Pilitzky said, interrupting.

"Perhaps he was right."

"Really, Adam."

"Very well, I'll go and lie down. Your eyes close by themselves," he said, echoing Jacob. "Isn't there something you have to say to Jacob, Theresa?"

"Yes, there is."

"Goodbye, then, and don't be afraid of us. Is your wife really a mute?"

"Yes, my lord."

"That means that miracles also happen among the Jews, doesn't it?"

"Yes, my lord."

"Well, I'll go and take a nap."

11

As he left the room, Pilitzky glanced back over his shoulder. Jacob bowed. Lady Pilitzky slowly moved her fan of peacock feathers.

"Sit down. So! Where do such discussions ever lead?

One has to trust that God knows how to manage the world. When the Swedes took the manor, they flogged me in my own castle. I thought it was the end. But the Almighty wanted me to continue living."

Jacob paled. "They flogged you, my lady?"

Lady Pilitzky smiled.

"My dear Jacob, the rod is not particular about rank. Dukes, ladies, your royal highnesses even, are all the same to it. It strikes. The officers found it more amusing just because I was an aristocrat."

"Why did they do this, my lady?"

"Because I said no to the general. My husband was in hiding and I had no one to protect me. If my suitor had been young and handsome, or at least healthy" (Lady Pilitzky's tone changed) "I might have been tempted. 'All's fair in love and war,' as they say. But not with that ugly ape. One look and I said, 'Sir, death is preferable.'"

"I had thought such behavior was limited to Muscovites and Cossacks."

Lady Pilitzky smiled. "Ah, the Swedes are angels? No, Jacob, all men are alike. Frankly, I don't blame them. Women have only one use for them. A child must nurse and doesn't care if the breast belongs to a peasant or a princess. Men are like children."

Demureness and coquetry met in Lady Pilitzky's smile. She looked Jacob straight in the eye and fluttered her lids slightly. Jacob's neck became hot.

"A man has his wife."

"What? To begin with, in wartime, wives don't count. Secondly, one gets tired of a woman. My tailor makes me an expensive dress; so after I wear it three times I'm bored with it and give it to one of my husband's cousins. Men feel the same way. A woman's no longer attractive to a man when he can have her as much as he pleases—and he's off after another. But why should I tell you this? You're a man—tall and with blue eyes . . ."

The blood rushed to Jacob's face. "The Jews do not behave so."

Lady Pilitzky petulantly shook her fan. "Jew or Tartar, a man is a man. Why, your men were allowed a host of wives. The great kings and prophets had harems."

"Now that's forbidden."

"Who forbade it?"

"Rabbi Gershom, the Light of the Diaspora. He issued the edict."

"The Christians forbid it too. But what does human nature care about edicts? I don't condemn a man for wanting. If he gets a woman to say 'yes' I don't condemn her either. My view is that everything comes from God—including lust. And not everyone's a saint, and not every saint was always saintly. Anyway, how does it hurt God? Some take the position that a secret sin where there is no sacrilege injures no one. My husband spent a few years in Italy. There the ladies have both a husband and lover. The lover is called an 'amico.' When a lady goes to the theater, she is escorted by both her gentlemen. Don't forget this happens in the shadow of the Vatican. The amico is often a cardinal or some other Church dignitary. The Pope knows of it, and, if it were such a crime would he tolerate it?"

There was a pause in the conversation. Finally, Jacob

said, "Nothing like that occurs among the Jews. A man may not even glance at another woman."

"Just the same they do glance. I know a man's a hypocrite if he claims to be only interested in his wife. Let me ask you something."

"Yes, my lady."

"Where are you from? How does it happen you settled here? Don't think it odd that I pry; I have my reasons. It seems strange that you married a mute. Most Jews aren't as good-looking as you, or as well-bred, and you speak good Polish. You could have had the prettiest girl."

Jacob shook his head. "This is my second marriage."

"What happened to your first wife?"

"The Cossacks killed her and our children."

"In what town?"

"I am from Zamosc."

"Well, that is sad. What do they have against the women and children? And where does your present wife come from?"

"From near Zamosc."

"Why did you marry her? There must have been other women."

"Only a few. Most of the women were killed."

"You must have liked her. It can't be denied that she's good-looking."

"Yes, I did."

Lady Pilitzky rested her fan on her bosom.

"I'll be frank with you, Jacob. Your enemies among the Jews—don't think you don't have any—are spreading the story that your wife is not as mute as she pretends. When my husband first heard this, he was out of his mind with rage, and he wanted to put your Sarah to the test. But I dissuaded him. His idea was to shoot off a pistol behind her and see what happened. I told him you don't play such tricks on a pregnant woman. Adam Pilitzky listens to me. He does whatever I tell him to. In this one respect he's an unusually good husband. You understand yourself that the Jews of Pilitz will suffer if there was no miracle. The clergy in this part of the country, particularly the Jesuits, have their own interests to look out for. All that I want you to know is that you have a close friend in me. Don't be shy and secretive. We are all only flesh and blood underneath our clothes. I want to protect you, Jacob, and I am afraid that you may need protection."

Jacob raised his head slowly.

"Who is spreading these rumors?"

"People have mouths. Gershon is sly and even conspires against my husband. He will come to a bad end, but before that happens he will make trouble."

III

Fear such as he had felt when Zagayek sent for him, arose in Jacob. But now Sarah's life was in danger, also. The Jesuits had interests to protect. Pistols were to be fired near Sarah! I am in a trap, thought Jacob. I must flee. But the child must be born first. With winter approaching, where could he run? What course should he follow—tell Lady Pilitzky the truth? Deny the rumor? He sat silent and helpless, ashamed of his cowardice. Lady Pilitzky surveyed him expertly out of the corner of her eyes, a polished smile on her lips.

"Don't be afraid, Jacob. You remember the saying, 'A great wind but a small rain.' Nothing bad will happen."

"I trust not. Thank you, my lady. I can't thank you enough."

"You can thank me later. Have you seen the castle?"

"No, only this room."

"Come, I will show it to you. The invaders did a great deal of damage, but they left something. At times I agree with my husband—everything's collapsing. The peasants report having seen a huge comet in the sky with a tail stretching from one horizon to the other. It's as it was at the end of the first millennium, or during the Black Plague."

"When did they see the comet? I've seen nothing."

"Nor have I. But my husband has. It's a sign that we can expect some cataclysm: war, pestilence or flood. The Turks are sharpening their scimitars. Suddenly the Muscovites are a power. The Prussians, of course, are always ready for pillage. 'Eat, drink, and be merry. For tomorrow we die.'"

"A life lived in constant fear loses its flavor."

"What? Some have the opposite attitude. I've been through one war after another. But I know how to keep calm when others shiver. I laugh when most people cry. 'Draw the curtains,' I order my maid, and say to myself, 'Theresa, you have only one more hour to live.' Do you ever drink in bed?"

"Only when I'm sick . . ."

"No, when you're well. My husband's room is across the hall from mine and so I can isolate myself completely. I prop myself up with a pillow and order the maid to bring me wine. I like mead especially, although it's supposed to be a peasant's drink. They call it 'the nectar of the Slavs' in other countries. But I'm happy when I'm just this side of being drunk. When my mind's a trifle foggy, I don't worry; I lose all sense of obligation. I only do those things that please me."

"Yes, my lady."

"Follow me."

As Lady Pilitzky led Jacob through the halls and chambers, he did not know what to admire first: the furniture, the rugs, the tapestries or the paintings. Everywhere were trophies of the hunt: stags' and boars' heads staring down from the walls; stuffed pheasants, peacocks, partridges, grouse, looking as if they were alive. In the armory were displayed swords, spears, helmets, and breastplates. Lady Pilitzky pointed out the portraits of the lords of Pilitz and their families. Pictures of the kings of Poland were also on the walls: the Casimirs, the Wladislaws, the Jagelos, King Stephan Batory, along with famous statesmen from the ancient families of Czartoryski, and Zamoyski. Whichever way he turned, Jacob's eyes fell on crosses, swords, nude statuary, paintings of battles, tournaments, and the chase. The very air of the castle smelled of violence, idolatry, and concupiscence. Lady Pilitzky threw open the door of a room in the center of which was a large canopied bed. Jacob caught sight of himself in a mirror, but his image, standing as it were in deep water, was barely recognizable. He saw himself hatless, blushing, his hair and beard disheveled, resembling, it seemed, one of the savages portrayed in the other room. "It isn't the best taste to show the bedrooms," Lady Pilitzky said, "but you Jews don't go in tranquilly. "But the lobsters need to be brought in. You need the money. Just because you work to get the bait does not mean the traps can be forgotten. You have a debt to make good."

The old man sat with his elbows on the table, his coffee mug cradled in his cupped hands. He looked over the mug at his grandson and there was no softness in his voice now.

Linn shrugged wearily. He might have known. "Yes, sir," he answered and set the dishes in the sink. He reached for his cap and jacket. "I might as well be on my way then."

With his head bent sulkily, he walked past the well and down the slope toward the fishhouse. It was just plain humiliating to feel like a man one minute, and then be brought down to feeling like a small boy the next, sent off to do his chores. But he shouldn't have allowed himself to think that Grampa was changing his ways. Linn had not forgotten that he owed on the peapod! But did the old man think that if Linn let the traps set over one day he was already sliding into the devil's clutches?

Already the women were streaming around to Wade's wharf to wait for the mailboat. They greeted him pleasantly and he touched his cap. Charles was rolling along behind them, his hands in his pockets, whistling. Nobody was driving *him* out to haul this morning. No, he was his own boss. *I suppose Grampa would call him one of the grasshoppers,* Linn thought wryly.

"Hi, Linn!" It was Polly, yelling happily from her yard. She was taking in a wash from lines strung over ledges that would have twisted less sturdy ankles. Polly covered them like a goat. "When you coming over?"

He scowled under his visor. At the moment he didn't feel like yelling heartily to anyone, even Polly. "I'm on my way to haul!" he called back.

"You mean after you rowed all last night, and going again

tonight?" she demanded. "My land, your arms'll drop off!"

"Ayeh, they're about ready to," he retorted sourly, and then dived past the fishhouse to the wharf before Charles could catch up with him and make talk about Grampa's being a slave driver.

As he rounded the eastern point of the harbor, heading toward his first string, he heard the whistle of the *Jessie M.,* blowing for attention. He wished he could stay and hang around the wharf. He had not seen Cap'n Scott since the day he brought the double-ender home. He certainly deserved a little change of pace, but Grampa didn't think so.

But by the time he had finished hauling the last trap of the string of fifteen that followed the curve of the shore, he felt better. He had twenty-five lobsters, the most he had ever gotten from those traps; the day was fine, the peapod light and swift, and as he rowed on to the next string, turning under the high point of the eastern end of the island, the crying of the gulls was music to him, and he laughed aloud when two fought violently over a scrap of fish that he threw to them.

When he returned to the harbor the *Jessie M.* had unloaded her cargo and passengers and gone, and a siesta-like silence lay over the village. All the powerboats were on their moorings; most of the men were resting after hearty dinners, reading their newspapers.

Walking with his weighty deliberate tread, Wade came down the wharf to buy Linn's lobsters and stow them in the big car. When he saw the good catch, he was enthusiastic. "That's the boy, son! That's what I like to see. No laying around, even if you were up half the night, torching. Those pots paid you off, too."

"I'll be over later to get some salt," Linn said cheerfully.

But his eyes were thoughtful when he pushed away from the lobster car. He hadn't deserved the praise, he knew; but he hadn't wanted to say right out that Grampa had driven him to haul his traps. It sure was a heck of a way things came about. Anyway, he could see Grampa's point; if he paid five dollars on the peapod today, and another five tomorrow, instead of skipping today's haul, it meant he was that much to the good on his debt.

Wiley's wife, Grace, square, breezy, and good-humored, called to him from her dooryard; Grace had always been nice to him, but it seemed to him that there was a new quality in her greeting today, as if he had a special position as a member of Wiley's torching crew. It was a pleasant thought.

CHAPTER EIGHT

Grampa's Philosophy

The work must go on, and there was another night of torching coming up; Linn could not think of his weariness. After his dinner, he trudged off with his grandfather to the shore.

Several of the hogsheads were empty and dry, ready for the new bait. The others would have to be dumped and washed later. While Linn bailed the herring from the floor where they had been lying all day, the old man stood by with a wooden scoop, and tossed rock salt lavishly, yet deftly. He kept murmuring to himself, "Yes, it is good bait."

A shadow fell across the doorway and Linn glanced up to see who was standing there. "Oh, hello, Bert," he said pleasantly. "How's things with you?"

Polly's father lounged against the doorcase, watching the proceedings for a moment without answering. Then he sighed, "Slow, boy, slow."

Grampa sniffed as he tossed a scoopful of salt into the hogshead. "Slow, eh? With some people things would always be slow."

Linn bailed herring with new energy. He hoped Grampa wasn't going to start a lecture. If only the long, scrawny man would go along . . . But he was propped against the doorcase as if he intended to stay there. He coughed discreetly and fished in his pocket for a plug of tobacco, from which he took a sizable bite.

Grampa straightened up. His black eyes were hard and shining, his mouth twitched.

"Well, Mr. Swenson, looks like Linn's going to have his bait in for fall fishing," Bert remarked blandly. "He's lucky he's got your place to keep his gear and stuff. Not many boys his age got anything like this." His eyes roved around the long shadowy bait shed, partially filled with hogsheads. Dip nets of various sizes hung along the wall. Near the door on one wall was fastened the boxlike table, the keeler, where Linn stood to fill the little twine mesh bait bags with herring.

"Linn is *lucky,* you say?" Grampa peered up at Armstrong from his wrinkled russet-like face. "He is no more lucky than you. Linn would not be using this place if he did not work. You can't call that luck, Mr. Armstrong."

"No," Bert agreed pleasantly. "But the place is here for him to use, and that's where the luck comes in."

"Such foolish remarks to make!" Grampa laid down the salt scoop and went to stand directly in front of Armstrong. "There is no luck about this building being here! I worked hard to have this place, I worked hard to get the things to put into it; had I not worked, where would the place be?" He grasped the straps of his overalls and teetered back and forth on his toes. "Without work there can be nothing!"

"Some people can work themselves to death," Bert ventured. "They can be a slave to it."

"There is no danger of you being a slave," said Grampa softly.

"You're darn right!" Bert wagged his head. "It wouldn't make any difference how hard I worked, I wouldn't ever get ahead very far. Too many bills on my neck now."

"You have the children. Is there no thought about them?"

"They'll make out all right," said Armstrong complacently.

"If you don't teach them to work," Grampa warned him, "they'll be no good to themselves or anybody else."

"Lordy, Mr. Swenson!" The lanky man laughed. "Can't you ever think about anything but work? Look at Linn, here. You'll have him wore out and round-shouldered before his time."

Linn wished heartily that Armstrong would take himself elsewhere. But he dared not interrupt. He leaned the dip net against the hogshead and took up the salt scoop.

"You're a fine one to talk, sir!" Grampa shouted. "A man was born to work and take care of himself and not be a burden to others. But *you* wouldn't know anything about *that!* No, you would rather stand around and talk and chew your tobacco."

He pounded his fist into his other hand. "I have worked hard all my life and it didn't hurt me. It made me strong and healthy."

Armstrong kept nodding amiably. Linn wondered if he was baiting the old man intentionally.

"Yes," said Grampa, "I have worked hard ever since I was a little shaver. When I was big enough to do anything, I was put to work doing it. I had no time to loaf, to spin yarns, to play. I learned to knit when I was four years old. I helped to make mittens and stockings, until I was strong enough to do something else."

Linn had heard stories of his grandfather's childhood many times, but they always seemed fresh whenever they were repeated. That childhood, far away in Norway, was like something out of a storybook, and now he stood with the salt scoop hanging from his hand as his grandfather went on.

"My mother and sisters, they took care of the farm when my father went off fishing. When I was too small to go fishing, I helped with the farm. Then I went fishing with my father. We went sometimes a long way from home, to the Lofoten Islands."

"Is that so?" Polly's father murmured good-naturedly.

"And when I was eleven years old I went on board a ship, as cabin boy. Later I got to be a seaman, and it was not easy work. They were square-rigged ships and the food was poor, and the pay was poor. But I saved my money to send home for a long time. Then I came to this country and went fishing in the schooners from Gloucester."

Linn saw the weathered face soften, and the keen old eyes stared out through the fishhouse doorway. He sighed. "Yes, that was a long time ago. I came to this island in 1893, when it was just beginning to grow. A man could make a good dollar with hand line and trawl. Then I built lobster traps. I had a sloop, and a little piece of ground to make a farm." He sighed again, and Linn saw that all anger had left him. Now if Bert Armstrong would just get out and go on about his own affairs. . . .

"You in there, Carl?" A thick squarish figure filled the bait shed doorway. It was Charles' father. He grinned just like Charles. "Thought I heard you sounding off. Say, you happen to have one of them elegant big cabbages lying around that you'd sell me? The wife's got a notion to make coleslaw to go with the beans tonight."

"Ja, I have one." Grampa looked suspiciously at Bert and then at Linn. "You want it right now?"

"Ayeh, but you tell me where it is and I can go pick it up. I don't want to interrupt a man's work, 'specially when he's so set on it." George's laughter boomed through the bait shed. "Scales still in the same place in the barn?"

"I go with you," said Grampa grimly. He wouldn't give anyone permission to go on his property when he wasn't there, even a man like George Kingman, and even if it meant leaving Linn alone with Bert Armstrong, whose shiftlessness he hated as if it were an infectious disease that Linn might catch.

"I'll finish salting here in a minute and be right along home, Grampa," Linn said briskly.

"*Good,*" the old man said with satisfaction. Without a glance at Bert he trotted out to where George Kingman waited, leisurely puffing at his pipe, and the two men walked off together.

Bert grinned under his straggly mustache. "Boy, I never saw anybody who could get mad so quick and look like he was going to bust!" He sobered, threw a furtive glance over his shoulder and muttered, "I was just waiting around to see if I couldn't get a word to you by yourself. I need a baiting of herring awful bad, son. You couldn't let me have it for a few days, could you?"

Linn frowned and scratched the back of his head.

"I wouldn't take it so the old man would notice," Bert argued. "And I'd get it back to you. I'm trying to get somebody to go torching with me. Haven't had much luck yet. If I had a dory and a net, I'd be all right, but I ain't got the tools. And I can't go to haul till I get some bait."

"All right," Linn said. It wasn't the first time he had let

the man have a baiting; everybody gave him bait at one time or another. They laughed at his excuses, but they still gave him bait. Linn didn't laugh at the excuses, and, because of the kindness Bert had always shown him, Linn would never refuse Bert if he could possibly help it. "You'll have to take some of that over there, though," he said reluctantly. "If you took any of this new stuff Grampa would miss it right away and think somebody's been stealing it. If I had some extra—"

"That's all right, son," Bert reassured him. "That's good bait over there in that barrel. I'll come down later, when it's dark, and get out enough to bait eighty bags or so." He turned to go, then came back, his eyebrows lifted. "You happen to have half a dollar on ye? I'm 'bout out of tobacco."

Linn shook his head. "I don't carry any money on me," he said.

"*What!*" Bert was really amazed, his jaw dropped. "A boy like you with empty pockets?"

Linn shrugged. "I hand it all over to Grampa. He takes care of it."

"You mean you have to give him every cent you make? I never heard of such a thing. He's worse on you than I thought."

Linn's face was strained. "It's the bargain we made," he said stiffly. "He thinks money in pockets is a temptation to spend it foolish. He doesn't carry any money himself. When I need money for clothes, rubber boots, paint, salt—anything for my gear—he gets it out of the tin box." He grinned quickly. "I have to bring him back the change if there is any. So if you hear me jingling anything in my pockets, it's not pennies, it's nails."

"I don't think it's funny," said Bert darkly. "You earn the money, you ought to have a right to spend it without him checking it."

"Not to Grampa's way of looking at it," said Linn. "I can't

kick, really. I have what I need, and I help pay the grocery bill. He produces milk, eggs, vegetables—I bring in fish sometimes and lobsters—we don't go hungry."

"Of course not!" snorted Bert. "Everybody knows old Swenson has a full cupboard. He don't have a houseful of kids to feed. But that don't mean he can't let a boy have some change in his pocket. Especially when it's his own money," he added.

Linn felt sorry for Bert. The man was really disappointed to find his friend had no loose pennies to lend. Linn could let him have bait, but that was all.

As Bert turned to go, he said earnestly over his shoulder, "I'll see that you get the bait back, son. Every herring. Don't you worry about it."

"Oh, I won't worry!" Linn couldn't help a faint smile. Armstrong always added on that little speech when he came begging or borrowing. Linn watched him stalk off along the shore, his hands in his pockets, his head set back on his shoulders, as if to show the world he had no cares. But Grampa was right about Bert's kids. Grampa might be a hard taskmaster, but he had known almost from babyhood what responsibility was.

Linn shook his head and started to work again. When he had finished, he stood gazing off across the harbor, serene in the afternoon sunshine. Tonight they would leave at sundown to go torching; he hoped the herring would come rushing the way they had before. It was bad enough to be tired because the herring had come boiling to the surface; but it was worse to spend hours rowing and have no fish to show for the night's work. Then he remembered his promise to Grampa, and started home.

CHAPTER NINE

A Lesson in Ethics

For three days and nights the weather had stayed fine, and the torching went on without pause. Although it was almost a sacrilege to wish for a storm, Linn found himself thinking, as he and Charles trudged with the handbarrow toward the Kingman fishhouse, how wonderful it would be to lie in bed and listen to the wind rising and keening in the treetops, and to know he need not haul in the morning. But such luxury would have to wait. He must go on rowing and bailing and carrying, until there was bait enough stored away for his needs.

He was still grateful for the chance; he would never stop being grateful. It was just that he was so tired that his very bones seemed made of pig iron. He envied the row of gulls perched on the fishhouse roof; nothing to do but sit and watch somebody else work, and then swoop down afterwards to the wharf to fill up on the herring that had been spilled out of the carrier.

It was a fresh sparkling October morning. Around the bright blue-green harbor the water slopped against the rocks, and the skiffs bobbed at the moorings. Almost everyone else had gone out. Only a man whose boat had sprung a leak, and Randy Mears remained behind.

Linn and Charles had just gone inside the bait shed and were upturning the barrow to let the herring slide out when Randy paused by the door. Charles, back to him and whistling between his teeth, didn't know he was there; Linn glanced at Randy through his lashes. He wore new dungarees and a brilliant plaid flannel shirt against the chill of the fall morning. The others wore rubber boots thick with herring scales, but Randy propped one foot nonchalantly on the doorstep as if to show off his darkly polished loafers. He looked like a sport, Linn thought scornfully, like somebody coming out on the boat in summer to take a look at the picturesque natives. He could have got that heavy tan lying around on a beach somewhere.

Of course, to be honest with himself, he thought grudgingly, he couldn't blame Randy or anybody for liking new clothes. And Randy could afford them. Neither he nor Charles nor any of the other boys who were on their own had to hand over their earnings to their families. They just paid board. *After I get my powerboat,* Linn promised himself, *and a big engine to drive her along smart—well, it's more than likely I'll want to dude up some when I'm not working.* He'd never yet had anything new to wear that wasn't an absolute necessity. No, it wasn't Randy's new clothes he resented, but the way Randy stood around watching him and Charles, as if they were some kind of peasants or something, and he'd never in *his* life got messed up with bailing herring.

He felt Randy's cold stare and knew that Randy was no doubt thinking even less complimentary thoughts about him. He gave the handbarrow a violent twist that startled Charles from his whistling. Catching Charles' eye at last, Randy said ostentatiously, "Hi, Charles," and walked on down the wharf and aboard Wiley's boat.

"Hi, Randy," Charles called after him. His round face creased into mirth. "Doesn't look like he's speaking to you, boy."

"I don't care if he never speaks," Linn said. "Come on, we're supposed to be lugging herring, not gassing."

"What are you in such a pucker for?" demanded Charles. "Rome wasn't built in a day, you know." He set his foot on the barrow and took a bottle of strawberry pop off a dusty shelf. "Here, take a swig. Do you good. You're just tired, that's all. And it's making you cranky."

"Who's cranky?" Linn growled. "Who's tired?" He yanked at the barrow and Charles' foot came down. "And I don't want a swig. Come on, let's get these herring lugged. We still got mine and Wiley's to get out."

"Oh, all right." Charles shrugged good-naturedly.

Randy Mears stood on the washboard of Wiley's boat, jingling the change in his pockets. He looked on with a small self-satisfied smirk as Linn swung the hoisting basket toward Wiley. *What's he feeling so good about?* Linn wondered.

Wiley set the basket in place on the herring knee-deep around him. "What you say, boys?" he asked cheerfully. "Randy wants to buy fifteen or twenty bushels. How about it?"

"You mean take enough out of all our shares to make up what he wants, or one of us give up his share entirely?" asked Charles.

"I dunno. We can thrash it out right now."

"What do you think?" Charles turned to Linn. "We've only carried one barrow into my fishhouse, so we could let him have what he wants right now and then divide between us afterwards."

Linn stared across at Randy, who went on jingling change. His black eyes met Linn's with bold assurance.

"I'm not giving up any herring *I* sweated for," Linn stated bluntly. "Let him take the oars and go row for what he wants. It's just as good for his muscles as mine. If you fellers want to let him have your herring, all right with me, but I worked hard for these, and they're going into *my* hogsheads."

Wiley bit hard on his pipe, and Charles, his broad face sobering, started to speak, but Randy waved his hand at him.

"Don't try to soft-pedal it, Charles." He shrugged. "I know what this half-baked mutt is driving at. He's got a chance to pick up some herring without paying cash for 'em, and it's gone to his head. The old man's chewed at him so much, the kid's turning into a second Swenson. Tight as the bark to a tree, and plenty cheap."

"Now listen, Randy," Wiley began, but Randy shook his head. "Forget it. I can afford to lose a few days' haul. I'm not as poor as some critters around here who'd sooner cut off a hand than part with a few herring." He stepped onto the wharf and walked away. As he passed Linn without a look, Linn's rage boiled up uncontrollably, and he took a step after Randy, but Charles pulled him back.

"Now what in time did you go sounding off like that for?"

"You wanted me to speak my mind, didn't you?" Linn's lips felt stiff.

"Ayeh!" Charles snapped. "It's all right to speak your mind sometimes, but it doesn't pay always. Randy's a neighbor, whether you like him or not, and in a place like this you don't keep up a grudge with a neighbor. You know it as well as I do."

"He's the one holding a grudge," argued Linn. "Why didn't he speak to me when he came down the wharf? I'd have answered him. I tried to bury the hatchet a while back —Wiley knows that. But he wasn't willing. I've done *my* part." Charles still looked angry and Linn set his jaw stubbornly.

Wiley's grave judgment broke in on them. "Sure, you were ready to shake hands once, Linn, but that doesn't carry much weight today. Point is, we've got to let him have some bait. He can't go to haul until he gets some."

"Well, let him go rowing in my place!" Linn's eyes smarted with fatigue and anger. "He always did go with you fellers—I can get along with what bait I have already—" He

turned away and started up the wharf. "Let him have my
share that's in the boat!" he flung over his shoulder.

Charles grabbed at him. "For the love of Mike!"

Linn wrenched himself away. At this instant he didn't
want anything more to do with them, or with herring either.

Charles pulled him around. His usually jolly face was
severe. "You listen here! You rowed for those herring, and
you have them coming to you, so don't get your hackles up.
You don't have to let Randy have one single fish if you don't
want to. Wiley and I will let him buy some of ours. What
I was coming at—"

"Oh, I know what you were coming at!"

"I don't think you do. There's certain things you don't do
in a place like this, no matter how mad you get at a feller.
And one of them is that you don't stand in his way of making
a dollar."

Linn stared at his boots.

"Well, let's get back to work," said Wiley quietly. "The
tide's going."

Linn reached for his end of the handbarrow. He tramped
up the wharf behind Charles, his teeth set hard. What a fool
he'd made of himself in front of Charles and Wiley! He'd
been so set up because they'd taken him with them, given
him a man's place and a man's job to do; and he'd shown
himself a regular kid, a swell-headed young one, having a
tantrum. His shame sent the blood racing hotly through
him.

The business of getting out Charles' herring went on in
silence. Linn kept his head down so he wouldn't have to
meet the others' eyes, and with every minute that passed, he
liked himself less. Nobody spoke as Wiley backed the boat
away from the Kingman wharf and steered it across the
harbor to his own dock. Linn took his place in the boat and
filled the basket again and again.

As he worked, he tried desperately to think of something to say. He knew he'd made a serious mistake. Wiley and Charles had had no trouble with Randy, and if they sided with Linn it would be a gesture against Randy which they didn't want to make and didn't intend to. They would see that Randy got bait, even if they went short on their share of the night's work. If they didn't want to let Randy have their herring, they would have to let him go in Linn's place tonight and work for the fish himself. But that would cut Linn's fall supply, and he would have none for spring. He would have to do as he had done before, pick up bait the best way he could; go handlining, if he couldn't do anything better. . . . *So look what you've done, you blasted fool!* he told himself. *Put yourself in a bad spot and Charles and Wiley in a worse one. They want to be fair with me and with Randy too and it looks as if I wasn't helping 'em any.* . . .

Trying to guess what they must be thinking of him, he found himself blushing with disgust and humiliation. As the last herring was dumped into the barrow, he knew he couldn't stand the silence any longer. He swallowed to dampen his throat and blurted, "Look, fellers, I've got to say something. You hauled me over the coals, Charlie, and I've been thinking about it. Doesn't make me feel very good."

Charles grinned at him. "I don't imagine so, chum. But you made things kind of tough for me and Wiley with all that talk you were throwing around."

"Well, look! What we get tonight—you fellers do what you want with it. Sell the whole load to Randy!" he begged earnestly.

Wiley shook his head. "Nope. We'll sell him just what he asked for. That'll tide him over."

Linn felt a little lightheaded with the relief of his apology. He grinned feebly. "I thought you might be planning to fire me tonight, and take him back."

"I guess you'll be going with us till you get your bait butts filled," Wiley drawled.

"A couple more times will take care of what I want," said Linn. "If they keep coming."

With old brooms and buckets of water they cleaned the boat of the myriad of herring scales. Then Wiley said quietly, "Linn," and nodded at the wheel. "Why don't you take her out to the mooring?"

"*Me?*"

Charles laughed, and Wiley said, "Who else? Let's see you make a sweep around the harbor and catch that mooring buoy on the first try."

This was more than he deserved after the way he'd acted earlier, Linn thought excitedly as he started the engine and moved out cautiously from the wharf. The engine, throttled low, made only a faint purring vibration. Charles and Wiley stood on the wharf, watching while he edged out past the ledges that lay submerged just off the shore. Lordy, the boat felt as long as a battleship, but *smooth*—he felt the power flowing from the wheel into his finger tips. He'd handled Charles' *Bouncing Bess* before, but never Wiley's boat. He gave her more gas and she began the wide sweep around the harbor. He felt like a conquerer as he stood tall and straight by the wheel and watched the high bow thrusting toward the horizon, and heard the rush of water along the boat's sides. Then he turned her in a wide graceful arc and she cut a sleek path among the moorings. He knew the exact moment for shutting off the engine and running along the washboards to the bow with the gaff in his hand, to catch the mooring buoy and bring it aboard with one swift continuous motion.

As he rowed ashore in Wiley's skiff, he studied the boat where she lay long and serene in the dancing tide ripples that flowed from her bow to her stern, and he thought with yearning, *How long will it be before I have one like her?*

"Thanks, Wiley," he said back at the wharf, trying to be casual. "That was swell." Charles had gone home.

Wiley, trying to get his pipe to burn, nodded, and for some reason Linn was glad of his silence. "See you tonight," he said quickly and started for home. He wanted to think about the morning—all of it—in the short distance between the shore and Grampa's house.

CHAPTER TEN

A Narrow Escape

The fine autumn weather continued, but the good lobstering was done. At least Linn's traps had said so in the last few days. One morning as he hauled along the east side of the island he got only an occasional too-small lobster, which he tossed overboard in disgust.

He did somewhat better in the coves along the south-east shore, and picked up a couple of traps that had been missing for several weeks. But his catch was hardly worth the trouble of hauling. *Maybe I should have let them set over a day,* he thought. *Or maybe there's a storm coming and they know it, and they've gone into deeper water.* If that was so, it was discouraging. He couldn't follow them too far out. His boat was too small for that.

He ached from a double tiredness as he stood on the car waiting for Wade to come down from the store and weigh his lobsters. Going short of sleep because you were working nights and days both was one thing when you had something to show for it. But now he had plenty of herring, and no lobsters.

Wade came tramping down the wharf. "How they come today?" he asked pleasantly.

"No good." Linn shook his head. "Hardly worth your time coming down to the car."

Wade glanced at the catch and pursed his lips. "Maybe you'll have to do some shifting. Lobsters don't stay in one place all the time. Could be they're moving away from the rocks a little earlier this fall. They have to get out into real deep water before winter sets in."

"I know that." Linn nodded. "But usually they hang around the shore long enough to give me a chance to make at least enough money to buy some winter clothes." He chewed the inside of his cheek. "Maybe I'd better do some shifting, although I got the most lobsters today from the traps that were closest to the rocks." He shrugged. "It's sometimes hard to figure out just what to do. Have to try everything you can think of."

As Wade handed him the money for the catch, he said kindly, "Hope they come better next time, son."

"I hope so too," Linn agreed fervently. "I have to get that double-ender paid for."

He pushed away from the car and rowed around to his own wharf. His movements were automatic as he tossed his oil-pants and bait box to the wharf and then put the double-ender on her haul-off. He was tired and hungry.

As he walked by the fishhouse door he saw that the herring left on the floor that morning were no longer there. He went into the building and looked around. The salt bags were empty. He looked into a hogshead. There were the herring, all salted, all taken care of. He leaned against the doorway, and rubbed his eyes with the back of his hand. Grampa had come down and salted them while he was out hauling. His eyes smarted suddenly. The old man was a driver, and he was stern. But once in a while he came up with something like this.

Grampa had not only salted the herring, he had also dressed some and fried them for Linn's dinner.

"They are very good," he said. "I think we'll salt some down for the winter."

"Good idea." Linn reached for a potato, then remembered, and looked into his grandfather's face. "Much obliged for taking care of those fish, Grampa. I sure appreciate it."

"I paid that Joe Armstrong twenty-five cents to bail them into the hogshead while I salted them," said Mr. Swenson complacently. "I gave him some herring to take home for dinner, too."

"Joe's a good kid."

"He'd be better if he didn't have such a father," the old man chided. "Eat now, and then have some sleep. You got three hours before it's time to go after the herring again. I'll call you when it is time to get up."

As Linn laid his head on his pillow he could not help marveling. That was the way with Grampa; you never knew just what he would do or say, except for one thing—you always knew how he stood on the subject of work.

As the boys climbed aboard Wiley's boat that evening, he told them, "We're not going to Bull Cove tonight. Think we'll try our luck in Tent Cove, over on the east side."

Charles burlesqued a salute. "Aye, aye, Cap'n! You're the boss!" Outside, the boat raced along, cutting close to the shore, avoiding as if by her own will the pot buoys on either side. Wiley stood by the wheel, spare and tall, his duck-billed cap accentuating the forward-jutting cragginess of his profile. He didn't look as if anything ever bothered him, thought Linn. He had his home, his boat, and a devoted wife. And if he was a tightwad, as everyone said, he looked mighty peaceful about it.

Charles sat on the starboard washboard. His round face was creased in an absent-minded smile, as if he never had anything but pleasant thoughts. It could be the memory of a good supper that brought that look to him, Linn thought. As for himself, his meager haul today still haunted him. This was the peak of the fall fishing, and his traps, baited with good rich fat herring, had been as empty as though the season were over. The debt on the peapod made the slim haul a greater worry. Grampa's warnings about debts seemed to rumble like distant thunder in his ears.

The boat passed below a high cliff of granite, and began to rise and fall to the motion of long, easy swells. Dusk settled over the sea in a purpling haze, and off on the southern horizon, five miles distant, the Light began to twinkle. Soon the boat reached a wide semicircular cove with spruces growing thick above the rocky shore. No houses stood here. The paths were only for those who went into the woods to cut spruce boughs for their traps, or to get firewood, or to wander along the shore after the storms in search of traps and buoys that had gone ashore. Grampa's cow ate her fill in the sun-warmed meadow here, and drank at the brook that ran down the slope to the sea.

Tonight it was all one blackness. The herring did not show up well at first; Charles and Linn rowed back and forth across the cove, the light from the torch dancing and flaring in the chilly breath of the night air.

Wiley said from up in the bow of the dory, "Maybe I didn't figure right, coming over here."

"Too late going down to Bull Cove now," said Charles. "We might as well stick it out here and get what we can."

Linn didn't say anything. Sweating under his oil clothes, he pulled steadily on the oars.

Suddenly the herring came, and the dory raced over the water, a foaming, fire-tinted wake spreading behind her as Charles and Linn dug in hard with the oars. It didn't take long to load the dory. In the powerboat the kid boards were all in place, and they transferred the herring quickly, without talk, working in the small circle of light cast by the lantern on the engine box. As Wiley was about to cast off the dory painter, preparing to go for another load, a voice came quietly out of the darkness to them.

"Well, boys, do you think you'll load your boat tonight?"

Wiley's hand jerked in surprise and Charles exclaimed and swung around. It was Linn who answered.

"Tom Lowell! What are you doing around here this time of night?"

The man seemed to rise out of the black sea as he stood up in his small dory and took hold of the washboard of Wiley's boat. His dark eyes gleamed from cavernous sockets, and his sweeping mustache cut across his sunken cheeks like small wings. He wore his usual dark suit and black hat, and as he smiled his teeth shone large and white.

"What am I doing?" he repeated pleasantly. "Just looking around."

"Not much to see, is there?" Charles laughed. "Blacker than the inside of a cow."

"Oh, that depends on what you go looking for," Lowell's voice was cool and slow. He looked into the boat at the shifting silver of herring. "They seem to be running larger than the others you've been catching," he observed. "Much better for all-around fish. You'd do well to dress and salt a lot of those down in barrels. You'd get a good price for them ashore when cold weather settles down."

"Ayeh," said Charles with a grin. "I suppose a feller'd make a real mint of money doing that, now."

"Oh, not exactly a mint," Lowell answered soberly. "But

it would be worth his while. I was thinking I might salt some if I could find some barrels just the right size."

Charles sat on a corner of the engine box in his rustling, scale-spattered oilskins, not bothering to hide his amusement. But Wiley was politely serious. "You'd have to send inshore for barrels like that," he said. "I know the kind you mean. Hold about seventy-five pounds."

"Exactly." Lowell said the word in his precise, leisurely way. "Ex-actly." He pushed away from the boat and sat down to take up his oars. "Good night, boys," he called as he moved off into the shadows. "Good luck with your fishing."

The three stared into the darkness after him. The sound of his oars was swallowed up in the sounds of the night. Charles' grin slid away. He said uneasily, "Now what in time brought him here? Rowing all the way around the island after dark—"

"Maybe he came earlier," said Linn. Lowell's appearance had helped him shed some of his weariness. "Maybe he's been hanging around this side all day."

Wiley slid into the dory. "Anybody setting out with a pretty girl to watch the moon rise wants to look out. Tom Lowell's likely to rise up from behind them and ask how the fishing is."

Charles roared. "I'll have to remind Randy Mears of that, next time he goes walking with a girl." He got into the dory and Linn followed him. They set their oars in place and began to row away from the small island of lantern light towards the dense blackness of the outer cove.

"One thing," Wiley's voice came from where he stood in the bow. "You never want to wonder what Lowell's doing, and why. Nobody ever knows."

"Oh, well," said Charles, "if he was curious about how we're doing, maybe he's satisfied now. Funny how that feller lives. Just goes handlining some, but never set a lobster pot in the water. Must have some money tucked away in an old sock, I guess."

"He doesn't look shabby," Linn pondered aloud, "and he doesn't talk shabby. Sounds like a schoolteacher somehow."

"Maybe he was, once. Maybe he got disappointed in love and retired to Lee's to forget his troubles."

"Talking about Tom isn't getting us any fish," Wiley called back to them. "Keep that torch well oiled, Charles!"

The dory was filled again, and yet again, and the night wore on. Linn tried not to think of the ache between his shoulder blades, or to allow thoughts of his bed to come into his mind. Just a little while longer now, and they would start home. He'd have plenty of bait, plenty of good herring to tempt lobsters into his traps, if only they weren't slacking off already. . . .

"Toss a little more oil onto those rags, Charles!" Wiley shouted, interrupting Linn's thoughts. "The torch is dying out."

Charles shook the oil can. "Oh, heck, it's empty. Have to go back to the boat."

"There's another can," said Linn. "Right there behind you. Isn't that an oil can?"

Charles picked up the can and shook it, then unscrewed the cap from the spout and smelled it. "We got the wrong can aboard here," he said. "It's about empty, and it's gasoline by the smell. I guess I can put some on the torch though." He reached for the wooden bailing scoop. "I'll turn some in the scoop and throw it on the rags." In the dying light he squinted at the liquid that came scantily from the spout. "Gasoline, all right; it'll give us a little more light, maybe."

Linn watched him idly, resting his aching arms from rowing. Beyond Charles, Wiley's oilskins caught what remained of the light, and shone yellow. With the tall dip net beside him, and his head reaching into the shadows, he was a strange figure. *He'd look mighty peculiar to anybody who didn't know what this was all about,* Linn thought vaguely. *We'd all look strange, sitting here in the middle of the darkness, Charles trying to get something out of the can and into the scoop. . . .*

Charles set down the can and swung the scoop, swishing the contents toward the dying torch. Suddenly the torch exploded into flame. Almost instantly the scoop was blazing as well, and the light breeze blew the fire back over Charles' hand.

Charles yelled incoherently and flung the scoop from him. Linn saw it coming toward him, but not in time to dodge it. In the next moment it had struck him over the temple, and almost immediately there was the crisp smell of burning hair. Linn leapt overboard in instant reaction against the fearful heat and brightness. When he remembered it afterward he could recall only the moment when the blazing scoop struck him and set his hair aflame; the next thing he remembered he was overboard, striking the water feet first.

Water billowed up inside his oilcoat, it rushed down into his boots. He held his breath as he clawed frantically toward the surface. Then Charles had him by the collar, and he was dragged into the dory. Wiley was saying in a faster voice than usual, "Easy now. Easy. No need of choking him on top of everything else."

"Well, gosh, I didn't mean to hurt him!" Charles sounded as if he were going to cry. "Are you burned bad, Linn? Are you burned bad?"

"I guess not," Linn said. "But my skin hurts. Around my eyes, and my forehead. I'm wet, too, but that don't matter so much."

"Better get him home as quick as we can," said Wiley.

Linn sat in the middle of the boat, among the herring, with his eyes squeezed shut, while they rowed toward the power-boat. *It didn't get me in the eyes,* he kept telling himself. But just the same he was afraid to force them open. The lids and the side of his face and most of his forehead felt stiff and burning, as if the flame still licked at the flesh. It hurt so that he did not want to move, or even take a deep breath. Inside his oilskins his wet clothes felt like ice.

Charles was mumbling, "How'd I know that cussed flame was going to jump back into the scoop like that?"

"The heat from the torch exploded the gasoline that still stuck to the scoop," said Wiley. "You didn't have that scoop too far from the torch when it went off."

"I should have known you can't fool around with gaso-line," said Charles. "This is a lesson to me, I can tell you that."

"Good thing Linn wasn't any nearer to you," said Wiley. "You'd have conked him plumb in the eyes, and that would have been a mess now, wouldn't it?"

"Probably blinded him," Charles said grimly. "I guess I came near enough as it was."

"Anybody would think I'd passed out, the way you're talking about me." Linn forced his voice out between clenched teeth. "I don't feel anything the matter with my eyes, but the rest of my face and head feels like it was still on fire."

"What a dumb trick!" Charles sputtered. "And it would have to be me to do it!"

"Stop fussing," Linn said. "We all knew what was in that can."

But Charles went on talking as if there were something in him that had to be unwound. Linn felt sorrier for Charles than he did for himself, knowing how he would feel if the situation had been reversed. "If I'd had just sense enough

to drop the scoop overboard, or drop it down in the herring,"
Charles said. "It wouldn't have happened. But it started me
up so when the thing just exploded in my hand. I didn't
know what I was doing. Just goes to show some people
aren't safe to have around—"

The dory bumped the boat, and there was the noise of
shipping oars. Linn took a deep breath and opened his
eyes cautiously; his lids hurt, but lantern light seeped in
where his lashes should have been. For a moment the rest
of the burn seemed to cool down, and he stood up.

Grasping the edge of the scupper-rail on the big boat with
confident hands, he climbed aboard.

"Get that anchor up, Charles!" Wiley was saying. In a few
minutes the boat was on her way to the harbor; the dory, half-
full of herring, tugged astern on her painter. The engine
was wide open and they made good time getting to the mooring.

Charles was all for loading Linn into the dory as if he had
a broken leg, and Linn pushed him off, laughing in spite of
the discomfort it caused his scorched flesh. "I'm still whole!"

"We'll go right to the house with you," Charles assured
him as they went up the beach, "so your grandfather won't
think we just dumped you onto the shore."

"I don't think there's anything at the house for burns like
this," said Linn. "Grampa always uses butter if he burns his
hand on a baker pan."

Astonishingly Polly spoke out of the darkness close to
them. "Who's burned?"

"What you doing, out after dark?" drawled Wiley. "It's
Linn here. We missed blinding him, thank God for that
much."

"Linn!" She came so close that Linn caught the shine of
her eyes in the starlight. "How did it happen?"

"Oh, easy," said Charles sourly. "I threw the bailer at him. It had burning gasoline in it."

"What? Charles Kingman—!"

"Of course I did it on purpose. I always do things like that."

"Stow it, Charles," said Wiley.

And Linn added vehemently, "Oh, shut up, will you! I could've done it to you. And you didn't ruin me, though it hurts like the dickens while we stand here arguing."

"You come right home with me," said Polly, and her hard little hand fastened on Linn's wrist. "I know what to do. Cold tea." She swept the three men along as if she were as big as Grace. "I haven't dumped the teapot yet, but Pa's been in bed for hours, so I know it hasn't been warmed up."

"I'll try anything, if it'll work," Linn said.

"Well, let's get started on it then," Wiley urged. "We've got some kind of salve up to the house, but Polly can start the tea business first, and see if she can get the fire out of it."

Polly ran on ahead of them. She had a lamp already lighted as they came in, still in their oil clothes, their faces blackened with smoke from the torch, their boots thick with herring scales. The warmth of the room revived the pain of the burn to full strength, and Linn leaned against the wall shivering inside his oil clothes. Wiley squinted against the light and ran his hand nervously over his long jaw. Charles watched dubiously as Polly poured tea from the tall agate pot into a saucepan. It was as dark as strong coffee.

"Looks as if it'd kill a man's insides," he muttered. "What do you think it's going to do to a raw burn?"

"Keep still, you," said Polly. "I'm doing this. Sit right down here, Linn, in Pa's old Morris chair." Fumbling at the neck of his oil jacket, he obeyed her. She plunged a piece of soft old sheeting into the pan of tea and then laid it, dripping, against the side of his face, and over his forehead.

It was wonderfully cool, after the first shocking moment. He leaned his head back against the worn cushions and sighed; all the gimp had gone out of him.

But the tea was really helping. He closed his eyes and listened to Charles making weak jokes about Polly's medicine. After a little while Wiley said, "Well, if that's all there is to it, I guess I'll go home. Come on, Charles, I'll get you that salve for him. And I guess he needs some dry duds, too. Good night, Linn. Polly."

"Good night, Wiley. And, Charles, don't worry about me." Linn roused himself. He was warm now, and the first fire of the burn had died out. It was very quiet in the shabby kitchen. On the square table the lamp burned steadily, trying to reach the shadowy corners. Polly sat by Linn, not speaking, dipping the cloth back into the tea as soon as it was warmed by his flesh.

After a few moments of silence Polly said huskily, "What if it *had* hit you in the eyes, Linn?"

"I guess I'd be kind of a sick pigeon by now." Linn grinned, one-sidedly, with caution. "And you don't know how good everything looks to me when I think what might have happened. I'd been feeling kind of sorry for myself today, but now all I can think is how lucky I am."

"I know. That happens to me sometimes. I'm all fussed up and mad with everybody, and the kids are driving me out of my mind—then Joe falls out of Pa's boat in the harbor and when I think how he could've been drowned if Raymond hadn't been there to grab him with the gaff, and if Bart Robinson hadn't just happened to come into his mooring in time to help 'em. Then I get all humble and quiet inside and feel maybe I should say a little prayer and never complain any more."

He let out a gusty breath. "That's it. Seems as if I shouldn't growl about anything, not with Wade helping me get the peapod, and Wiley taking me torching, and you always handing me out good things to eat, and being on hand tonight with this tea business. And Grampa, because if it wasn't for him I wouldn't be here on the island at all."

"I s'pose I shouldn't ever get mad with him then, either," said Polly. "But it's hard to like him when he doesn't like me."

"Oh, he likes *you* all right," Linn began eagerly. "I mean, if—"

"If Pa was different," Polly finished it. "Well, Pa's Pa, and he hasn't much git-up-and-git to him, but *we* like him."

"Well, that's the most important thing, isn't it?" They smiled at each other.

There was a clatter in the dark entry then, as Charles fell over Mr. Armstrong's rubber boots and muttered fiercely to himself. Linn went into the pantry to change into the dry clothes Charles had brought. Then Polly made cocoa for them, and set out a raisin pie. The boys clowned happily over their mug-up; Charles was lightheaded with relief because he hadn't blinded Linn, and Linn was the same because the pain had died down and because of his private conversation with Polly.

When it was time to leave, before Bert and the children should be roused by their good-natured clatter, Polly smeared the salve over Linn's cheek and brow. "You put a soft old dish towel on your pillow tonight," she ordered. "And put more salve on in the morning."

When Linn reached home, a little hand lamp burned on the kitchen table for him. By its dim light he examined his face in the mirror over the sink. His hair was gone on one side of his head and on the edge of his forehead under the visor of his cap; the blisters were puffed and angry, his cheek and eyelids were swollen. But, thanks to Polly and her cold tea, the worst pain was over. He remembered what she said about the dish towel and got a clean one from the drawer, then tiptoed upstairs in his stocking feet. He was so tired all at once that he swayed as he took off his clothes. The clock on the mantel in the dining room below struck two gentle notes.

CHAPTER ELEVEN

Linn's Suspicions Are Justified

The next morning Grampa clicked his tongue and hissed softly when he saw Linn's face and heard the story. "That Charles is a clumsy one," he muttered. When Linn told him about Polly and the tea, he said nothing at all, but his black eyes were thoughtful.

He did not suggest that Linn stay home from hauling for this one day, and Linn did not expect him to suggest it. Grampa had never pampered himself; he certainly wasn't going to pamper a husky boy. The nearest he came to it was to tell Linn to put a thick layer of salve on his face to protect it from the wind.

That night when supper was over, the dishes washed and his Bible chapter read, as he settled down to read his Norwegian newspaper he remarked casually, "There is a dozen eggs in the blue bowl on the dresser. After you take Wiley's clothes back to him, see if maybe Polly can use the eggs. But be sure not to leave the bowl. Her father would be likely to use it to wash his feet in." He cleared his throat and opened his paper.

Linn, too amazed at Grampa's gesture to speak, simply obeyed him. When Polly saw the bowl of eggs, her hazel eyes shone.

"For *me?* From your grandfather?"

"I guess he appreciated your helping me out last night."

"Well, I never! And it wasn't anything, really—just that old left-over tea." Her cheeks were pink. She carried the bowl to the dresser and began transferring the eggs carefully to a cracked old tureen. "I can make a real two-egg cake now, and a big custard pie for Sunday. Imagine your grampa sending me a present!"

"I wanted to give you one," Linn said stiffly. "But I can't do it right now." That morning he had looked longingly at the bright boxes of chocolates in the store.

"I don't want any presents, as long as you keep coming in now and then."

But I'm going to get a Christmas present somehow, he promised her silently.

In a week the blisters of the burn had healed, though Linn's cheek and temple were still red. The accident was a thing of the past, almost forgotten. His bait butts were full, so he stopped going torching. What he had to concentrate on was his lobstering. His traps just weren't fishing, though he had shifted some of them. He suspected that the traps were being molested. But what good were suspicions? They weren't much help in convicting anyone.

By rights he should have had his double-ender all paid for, and be putting extra money into Grampa's tin box to help out in the winter, when he could not haul in a peapod. And any day now Grampa would begin prodding him with discomforting questions about his poor hauls. Oh, sure, Grampa would believe him if he said his traps were being hauled by someone else, but what could Grampa do about it?

One day when he set out to haul, the sky was gray and threatening, and there was a chill in the air that made him shiver, even in his oilskins. It foretold the end of autumn and the beginning of winter. There was no wind, but the deep swells rolled up one by one under the peapod, and from the ledges at Southern Point the muted, sullen roar of the sea's rote was always in Linn's ears as he rowed out from the harbor to his first buoy, by Spar Ledge.

The first two traps were full of lobsters, and his heartbeat quickened. As he measured them and found six counters in the batch, he was ashamed of his suspicions and relieved that there was no need for them. So it was the shifting that did the trick, after all. He had found where the lobsters had gone.

But when he brought the third trap up to the gunwale, he saw the door was open and the bait bag gone. He stood staring at the empty trap, not even a starfish or a sea urchin inside. His scalp tightened. A bait bag didn't loosen itself and float away. It took fingers to untie the firm knot and remove the bag from the trap. Moving automatically, he tied in another freshly filled bait bag, closed the door and buttoned it firmly, slid the trap overboard and rowed onto the next pot buoy.

The condition of the third was the same, and the threat was as plain as if someone had suddenly shouted at him across the leaden-gray swells. His traps had been hauled, their lobsters taken or released, the bait bags removed, in order to tell him one thing.

Take your traps out of the water. You won't make any money fishing them. This is a warning. If you don't heed it, your buoys may be cut off, and you'll lose the traps altogether.

As he completed hauling, each trap was the same. He rowed mechanically, blind and deaf to everything except the pitifully few lobsters in the box. There were enough for the chowder Grampa wanted, but that was all. He put fresh bait in each trap, though it seemed a waste of good bait and bait bags, but he wasn't going to put an empty trap back into the water, nor was he going to take the trap ashore. That would be to admit he was licked.

He had thought the good fishing was over, because his hauls had been so meager. Now he realized that it was only for him that the good fishing was over. The scanty hauls must have been the first warning. Now the real persecution was beginning.

It was Randy Mears, of course. He was sure of it, as sure as if he had seen Randy haul the traps, take out the lobsters and the bait bags, drop the traps overboard again with the doors wide open. And he knew why Randy was doing it. The bait incident on the Kingman wharf had put the finishing touch to Randy's dislike for him. He must have felt publicly insulted when Linn refused to share bait with him, and in front of Wiley and Charles. He would never let that go by, Linn thought. And here was the evidence. But how could he prove it? Linn couldn't tail that high-powered boat in his double-ender, and even if by some miracle he should catch Randy red-handed, it was Randy's word against his. There would have to be an extra witness. So for now at least, Linn would have to say nothing.

A fisherman with money in his strongbox could keep putting out new traps, hoping the enemy would get tired of the campaign. But for a boy like Linn, a pod fisherman, it was the end, unless he could name the aggressor, and prove it with a witness.

He felt older than his grandfather as he rowed back to the harbor. None of the other men was in yet, but Norris Wade stood on the end of his wharf, a huge familiar figure, feet set wide apart and arms akimbo. Linn pretended not to see him and rowed straight to his grandfather's wharf. His misery increased. *What's he thinking about me right now?* he thought. *Figuring I'm no good as a lobsterman? Figuring he never should have backed me up on the peapod deal? Figuring I'm all done before I've even started?*

He did not bother to put the double-ender on the haul-off as he usually did, but set the box of lobsters—a dozen or so—on the wharf, and made the boat's painter fast to a spiling. His movements were slow and clumsy. His throat felt thick.

Wish I could talk to somebody about it, he thought. But in the next breath he knew he wouldn't talk about it if he could; it was his battle, and nobody could fight it for him. If only he could just figure out *how* to fight. . . .

He managed to keep up appearances at dinner with Mr. Swenson. "My pots were a little dry this morning, I thought," he observed casually. "Got to shift them out still farther, I guess."

The old man nodded and went on eating serenely. Linn washed the dishes afterward, and then took his hatchet and set out across the barnyard to the woods. His grandfather, coming out of the chicken house with a basket of eggs, said genially, "You go for funny-eyes?"

"Yep, I thought I'd get an armful and bend them into some heads after supper." *And be alone for a couple of hours,* he added silently, *and try to think.*

"Good, good!" The old man approved of such industry. Linn went on his way, around the corner of the barn, crossed flat granite ledges and jumped a muddy brook.

A stand of spruce rose just beyond the brook, and he would need slender, supple spruce branches to bend into funny-eyes, the hoops that held the openings in his trap heads wide for the lobsters to crawl in; metal hoops could be bought, ready-made, but the wooden hoops cost nothing, and they did not rust away the twine of the heads.

But he did not stop in Mr. Swenson's spruce woods to cut funny-eyes. He had a great need to keep moving, and he passed through the woods until he came to a wide field which bordered the shore. On the southern side of the meadow the land rose steeply; a thick growth of spruce covered it. In Tent Cove, below the meadow and the woods, old squaws and sheldrakes and loons were feeding and swimming, and a few gulls paddled peacefully above their snowy-white reflections. The water was tranquil, a pale shimmering gray except where the reflections of the woods turned it a deep green. A little golden-eyed duck paddling across the green left a long silvery V behind him.

Linn always paused here on the beach when he came this way. He could almost imagine the pointed tepees of the Indians in the shadow of the woods, and the canoes drawn up on the fine white gravel of the curving shore. The Indians had come here often in times long past, crossing the vast expanse of the bay by way of the islands that went like stepping stones into the ocean.

In spite of his unhappiness, Linn smiled faintly, remembering how, when Grampa had sent him to bring the cow home, he had played at being an Indian. He had stalked her without a sound, as if he were tracking a wild deer rather than an old cow whose bell sounded for a long distance, leading Linn straight to her.

Now whenever he went after the cow he strode swiftly along the winding paths, straight for the clang of the bell, with no stopping to listen for strange sounds and nonexistent animals. For these island woods were silent, except for crows and songbirds, or the screaming of a yellowhammer when a hawk was near. There was not one chattering squirrel, or the thumping of a rabbit, or the quick bark of a fox.

He crossed the beach and plunged into the woods, following the twisting trail among tall spruces whose branches were festooned with thin wisps of gray moss. He kept walking till he came at last to another cove, a small deep indentation in the rocky shore. Here he stopped for a breath. He drove his hatchet into a fallen tree and sat down beside it.

The water flowed quietly in among the rocks, splashing as mildly as a lake. In this dun-colored day the towers of the lighthouse shone white on the horizon. There was a boat out by the Seal Ledges, too small against the sea for him to recognize, yet the sound of its engine traveled to him in the clear windless air. Close to him, crows swooped from treetop to treetop, saw him and gave hoarse warning. The gulls flew lazily over him. Wild ducks, which had been feeding close to the shore, moved out a little way, and a seal lifted its sleek round wet head for a moment and then dived from sight under the pewter-gray water.

He had wanted to think, but what was there to think about? He looked around bitterly at all the things he loved. What right had Randy Mears to drive him away from these woods and shores? Or from that long reef out there, where he could see his buoys floating in a staggered line? "No right at all," Linn muttered. "No right at all. But it won't stop him from doing all he can. . . . All because of that cussed dinghy."

"Talking to yourself or to an unseen companion, Linn?"

A deep voice spoke pleasantly from behind him. He recognized Tom Lowell even before he turned and saw him standing there at the edge of the woods. The man's sweeping mustache was as neatly groomed as usual, and he wore his tidy dark suit and shirt, and the black slouch hat. He was a strange figure to behold where Linn had dreamed of Indians.

"Oh, hello, Tom!" Linn forced a grin, and moved over on the log. "Yes, I was talking to myself. Some people would think I had money in the bank, I guess."

"Or else that you prefer to hold conversation with an honest man." Tom sat down beside him, and laid his long pale hands on his knees.

"What are you looking for today, Tom?"

"I'll know when I find it," said Tom, looking contentedly over the sea.

"What about that ship going ashore on Bull Cove Reef?" asked Linn, desperate to think of something else besides his own predicament. "You know; you were telling about it in Bert Armstrong's kitchen one night."

Tom turned his gaze toward the horizon, toward the boat Linn had seen, and stroked his mustache reflectively. "She was a brig," he said at last. "She went ashore on New Year's morning in a driving snowstorm, with all sails set."

"And you say your grandfather saw her? In a snowstorm?"

Tom studied the white boat moving across the pale water toward them. "He had got up early to see if his dog had come home. She'd disappeared the day before. She hadn't come, so he set off around the island in the snow, whistling and calling. He'd got out on Dead Man's Bluff when all at once there was a lull in the storm and he saw the brig. She was like a ghost ship, he said, all white in the gray day." He stopped for a moment. "Randolph Mears is a long time at his traps today, wouldn't you say? Most of the other men are in by now."

The solitary boat was Randy's sure enough. It cut swiftly toward the island, flinging back curling wings of water that shone dazzling white against the cold gray sea. "Ayeh, Randy works hard and long," Linn said dryly. "Let's not waste breath on him. What about the brig?"

Tom shrugged his narrow black-clad shoulders. "There was only the one glimpse of her, flying with all sails set toward Bull Cove Reef, and my grandfather watched, struck dumb, he said . . . and then she hit. He never forgot the sight or the sound of the cries for the rest of his life."

"What happened then?" Linn asked. In spite of the dread that had sent him out here alone, in spite of the way his heartbeat had quickened with rage at the sight of Randy's boat, his imagination had blossomed at the horror of the disaster in the snowstorm.

"He ran around to the harbor, but by the time they could get boats out there, it was too late. The brig was breaking up fast and the men had all been swept away. Never found a one of them." Tom's measured tones gave the simple words a tragic feeling.

He stopped talking. He was gazing intently at Randy's boat, as the drone of the hauling gear began. "Randolph Mears has no traps along that reef," he murmured. "But he's stopping to haul."

"*My traps,*" Linn said. His stomach seemed to tie into knots.

He'd been sure Randy was the one who was bothering them, and to be still and watch him at his mischief was more than he could endure. But there was no way of stopping him; he could only sit there beside Tom, and stare.

Then he realized Randy was not simply *hauling* the traps. He was not just taking out any lobsters Linn's fresh bait had caught since morning, and then taking out the bait bags and dropping the traps overboard with the doors open. Instead, he was going on to the next, most drastic, step. He was coiling each warp and stuffing the rope, toggle and buoy into the trap, and returning the trap to the sea, and there was no sign that it had gone overboard, save for the momentary swirl of ripples on the water, which soon flattened out and disappeared. It was as if there had never been a trap with a red and white buoy watching and marking its location.

"He's sinking 'em!" Linn choked. "He's sinking my pots!"

"He certainly is," Tom said. "And why? Surely there's room enough in the sea for both of you to fish."

Linn didn't answer. He would never see those traps again, and they were good traps; they had cost money to build, money he had worked hard to earn. It was no trouble for Randy Mears to replace any traps *he'd* lost, for he had money he'd saved; but it would be impossible for Linn. Besides, there was the double-ender to finish paying for.

I'm done, I'm finished, he thought. Then his anger chilled and hardened. *But he's going to know about this, even if I can't prove anything.*

"I'll be a witness for you, Linn," Tom was saying, "if you think it'll do any good."

"You know the truth as well as I do," Linn answered bitterly. "Who'd take our word against his? He's got money in the bank, his father's a respectable citizen, and what are we?" He flushed. "I mean, what am I?"

Tom smiled. "That's all right, Linn. What am I but a poor addled derelict?"

"And all he has to say about *me* is that I'm a no-good mainland stump-jumper, a green fisherman who doesn't know where to set his pots so they'll fish, or who loses pots outright and then says somebody's sunk 'em. And who'll stand with *me?*"

"Your grandfather is no fool. Wiley Abbott is fair-minded. Norris Wade—"

The big man's name made Linn flinch with embarrassment. "He thought I was going to be a good fisherman when he lent me money to buy my peapod. He must be thinking now that I'm just a dub. If I hinted to him what was going on, it would sound as if I was trying to make excuses for myself. That's the first thing they always think when somebody starts hollering about being bothered—until he can prove it."

"Perhaps so." Tom fingered his mustache. "I'm not sure, however . . . What about your friend Charles?"

"I'm not going to go moaning to anybody," Linn said. "Not till I can name names."

Randy, having sunk the last of the seven traps in the string along the reef, was heading triumphantly for the harbor, engine wide open.

"Don't you think there are any others who would give you the benefit of the doubt?" Tom asked gravely.

Linn shrugged. "They don't care whether I go or stay. I'm just a kid from the mainland. My grandfather is an old settler, sure, but who likes him?"

"They may not *like* Mr. Swenson in many ways, but most of them respect him. You may have more friends than you realize, Linn."

Linn laughed without amusement. "Maybe so. But one enemy can do a lot of damage. You've just seen a free sample."

"Randy used to break my windows, years ago," Tom remarked thoughtfully. "Not just once. But over and over. I never knew why." He looked hard at Linn. "Why does Randy persecute you?"

"Because I'm an outsider," Linn answered honestly. "And maybe if I hadn't been here, the summer I was ten, Randy could have claimed a dinghy. It came ashore after a storm—must have been lost from a yacht. One plank was smashed in, but it could be fixed. I was out beachcombing, piling up wood on the west side for my grandfather to come and get with the dory, and I didn't know Randy was down there too. I came down into Marsh Cove, and I saw the dinghy lying on her side in the rockweed. I got to her first, so she was mine. Randy didn't come along till I'd got her cleared of the rockweed."

In his mind he saw the trim little round-bellied boat, so beautifully varnished, her dry side and keel shining in the sun, and the name *Sea Sprite* so elegantly lettered in blue and gold across her square stern. He remembered how he had run to her, with tight throat and pounding heart.

"Ayeh," he said aloud, "she was as pretty as a picture. I don't blame Randy for being mad. Maybe I'd have felt the same way. He was thirteen, and he *belonged* here, and I was a little mainland tyke. Anyway, he said she was going to be his and I said I'd found her first. He slapped me around some—made my nose bleed, but I gave him a good hard bunt in the belly, anyway." His mouth quirked. "I stood there trying to stop the blood and trying not to bawl, and he hauled her up out of the tideway and tied her painter to a tree, and said, 'She's *mine*, see?' Then he went off home to get his father to come after her. He didn't know Grampa was on his way down in the dory to collect my wood. I was still bleeding and really howling when he rowed ashore. It wasn't the blood that scared me, I just couldn't stand losing the dinghy. I was fighting mad."

He gave Tom a quick shy smile. "I'd thought of her as mine from the minute I saw her." Tom nodded.

"Anyway, Grampa stopped my nosebleed somehow, and we took the dinghy in tow and went home. We met Randy and his father just leaving the harbor. They stopped, and Grampa backed his oars a little. Mr. Mears leaned over the side of his boat and said, 'Who found that dinghy first, son?' And I said, 'I did.' He asked me if I was sure that was the truth, and Grampa said, real stiff, 'My grandson is no liar.' "

"Did that end it, then?"

"It did for Mr. Mears. Maybe he thought it wasn't worth fighting over. Or maybe he believed Grampa. Anyway, he

turned his boat around and headed for his mooring. Grampa
fixed up the dinghy and I had her to row around in all summer. Once Randy cut her loose, but somebody brought her
back." Before his eyes the gray wintry-looking sea became
the brilliant blue of that magical summer when he was ten,
and had the little dinghy to row in when his chores were
done. "After my aunt took me away, and Grampa thought I
wasn't coming back, he sold the dinghy to somebody. I don't
know who."

They were quiet for a few moments. Then Tom said
softly, "So that is why Randy hates you. He bears long
grudges."

"Ayeh." Linn's shoulders slumped and the breath went
out of him in a dismal sigh. "If I'd have known, I dunno
but what I'd have given him the dinghy then and there."

The good things were over. The few wonderful glistening
mornings when he had hauled with his new double-ender,
and made the first payments to Wade, belonged to the past.
It was like a happy dream which hurt to remember.

"Well—" He picked up his hatchet. "I said I was going
for funny-eyes and I'd better show up with them. Grampa
will find out soon enough what the score is."

Tom stood up. "Don't be discouraged, Linn. Bad spells
of weather have a way of breaking when the moon changes."

"Thanks, Tom," Linn said with an effort. He knew Tom
wished him well; but all the good wishes in the world could
not help him now. Without much enthusiasm he began cutting branches from a nearby tree, and Tom, without a word
or sound, disappeared into the woods as mysteriously as he
had arrived.

Linn was glad Tom had been there to talk to. It had
helped him to straighten out his thoughts, to speak them
aloud. His own words came back to him now, and as they
did his depression melted away before an invigorating rage

that warmed him to his very toes. His hatchet swung faster and faster. Of course he would look like a stupid, soft-headed kid if he complained! That was what Randy counted on. He expected that Linn would run squawking to everyone about his suspicions, and that would give Randy a chance to make a lot of virtuous talk about how Linn was blackening his name with false accusations. And because Randy's father had always had a reputation for honesty, people would listen to Randy and then see Linn as Randy painted him; a bawlbaby, trying to blame everyone else for his own mistakes.

Linn slashed hard at a particularly bouncy branch. *Well, I won't run to anybody!* he promised himself. *Just as I told Tom—I'm not naming names until I have cast-iron proof. But I'll stop Randy if it's the last thing I do. He's got to make a slip sometime!*

CHAPTER TWELVE

Linn Faces a Few Facts

The lamp on the dining table cast a warm glow on his hands as Linn sat working on the funny-eyes and trying to puzzle out what he was going to do about Randy. The scent of spruce was sharp in the warm air as he whittled each branch smooth and made each end flat, and then bent the slender wand into a hoop and fastened the ends together with fine stout twine.

Grampa sat in his rocking chair by the windows. The

curtains were not drawn and through a top pane of glass
Linn could see a big bright star against the dark blue sky.
It was quiet in the room; he heard only the rustle of the
thin dry leaves of the old Bible, as Grampa's fingers gently
turned them. Whenever Linn paused for a moment in his
task, he looked over at the old man and wondered if he
should tell him what had happened. But he was afraid that
his grandfather would go storming to Randy, and Linn knew
Randy couldn't be handled that way.

He wished desolately that he could feel as calm and con-
tented as the old man seemed to. He wondered if his grandfather had ever been faced with the problem that he had
now.

Suddenly he said, "Grampa, did you ever have your traps
bothered?"

The old man looked up over his glasses at his grandson,
his brow wrinkling, but he kept his forefinger on the page
he was reading. "Why do you ask that?"

"Oh, I was just wondering how things were when you
went lobstering?" Linn tried to sound casual.

"M-m." The old eyes sought the ceiling. "Yes, I was bothered sometimes," he said slowly.

"What did you do about it?"

"I watch till I know who bothers me, then we have a little
talk."

"Did talking do any good?" asked Linn, and then he realized that it was a foolish question.

And it angered the old man. He sprang quickly from the
rocker and crossed the room. He thrust his gnarled forefinger almost against Linn's surprised nose.

"Hah! You think I do not know how to talk?" He drew
himself as erect as his bent frame would allow. "People
used to bother me, yes—a long time ago—but they learned
better; they learned I was not fooling when I talked to them;

they learned that I meant every word I said. Yes," his voice mellowed and his eyes changed as he met his grandson's uplifted gaze. "Yes, they learned."

Linn felt a surge of admiration for Grampa as he watched him pass his work-roughened hand over his black hair and then over his weather-beaten face. He was a small man, he scarcely reached to the boy's shoulder; but he had strength and courage. He walked back to the rocking chair and sat down and his dark far-seeing eyes stared off into space. Linn knew that his grandfather was reliving some of the times when he had been faced with trouble and had conquered it.

The boy took up his knife again. The old man wasn't giving away any of his secrets. It would not be right for him to tell his grandfather about Randy. He must fight this thing out by himself, the way his grandfather had done. Grampa had always kept to himself, whether things went well or ill. *It must have been tough on the old man in those times,* Linn thought. *He had a family to think about, not just himself, the way I have.*

The old man did not go back to his Bible-reading, but sat with his hands folded in his lap till Linn was finished with his funny-eyes. Then he said, "It is time for bed, I think."

Linn nodded. He was tired from the strain of thinking, of figuring, what it was best to do and say when he saw Randy again.

The next morning he set to work running out warps by the fishhouse. It was a cloudy, blustery day, with the tide running too fast and free for good hauling. The buoys would be pulled under and hard to find. It would be a waste of time seeking them out. So none of the fishermen had left the harbor, but were all busy with their individual tasks along the shore. Linn measured lengths of rope, stretching each around a short stake driven into the ground fifty feet or so beyond the fishhouse, and when he was satisfied he had the kinks out, he tied one end to a trap, and fastened a buoy to the other end. Halfway between the trap and the buoy he tied a toggle, an empty quart ginger-ale bottle with a rubber stopper. The toggle helped the buoy to keep the rope from lying on bottom and catching around rocks.

After the buoy and toggle were tied on, he coiled the warp and put it with the buoy and toggle inside the trap, where it would be kept until the moment came when that trap was to be set; then, out in his boat, he would take the warp out of the trap, bait the trap and slide it overboard. The warp would run out after it, and the buoy would float on the surface to tell Linn where his trap was. A trap was only as good as its warp, for it was this rope that took most of the stress and strain of lobstering. When a man hauled, it was the warp which must bring up the entire weight of the water-soaked, rock-ballasted trap. That was why rope must be constantly replaced; if it was used too long, it rotted in the water, and if it broke while a man was hauling, it meant the loss of the trap.

Linn was as methodical as his grandfather had taught him to be, though today he couldn't help wondering if he would ever get a chance to set these traps. He had ten done when Randy passed by. He called out to Wiley, in his fishhouse, but he only grinned when he saw Linn. To Linn that mocking smile said just one thing: *Get those traps all ready, kid. All ready for me to sink, the same as I did yesterday.*

Linn stood very quiet till Randy was three steps beyond him, and then he said, "Hey, Randy—wait a minute. I want to ask you something."

Randy looked back over his shoulder. "What?"

Linn dropped the rope he was holding and walked toward Randy. Linn stood with his hands in his pockets, his head a little on one side. "I saw what you did yesterday out by Long Ledge Reef. Don't do any more of it, understand?"

His voice was soft and he had to concentrate to keep it so and to keep his hands in his pockets; even so they made fists as Randy pushed his cap back and pretended to be surprised. "You saw me by Long Ledge Reef? I haven't got pots there."

"I know it," said Linn. "But I have, or did have, till yesterday. Till you sunk 'em."

"Now wait a minute!" Randy's black brows pulled together. "I don't like that!"

"I didn't like what I saw you doing," Linn answered, "and I'm just telling you I don't want any more of it. Understand?"

"Listen, you half-wit," said Randy coldly, "I can see what you're driving at, but because you *are* half-witted I'm willing to let this go. But I'm telling you, kid, you'd better make up your mind to get off this place, and quick. Because you aren't going to last, see?"

"Sure, I see. And I know why you think I won't last. Because you'll do your best to keep me from fishing any traps. You think you'll sink 'em as fast as I put 'em overboard. Well, Randy, I'm putting out some more pots—the next day I haul—and I don't want to find any missing. You get that?"

"You can't prove I touched your pots," Randy's grin came again, and Linn tightened his fists till the nails cut into his calloused palms. "And can I help it if you're so green you don't know any better than to set them in deep-holes where you can't find 'em again? Maybe you've been lucky up to now and kept them out of deep-holes. Maybe you've been sensible enough till now and had enough ballast in them so they won't float off into deep water. But you need more than luck, kid. And besides all that, it's your word against mine, so you haven't really much to go on, have you?" He

turned away toward the store, flinging the last words back
casually over his shoulder.

"What would you say if I told you I had a witness to
yesterday?" asked Linn hoarsely.

Randy came back then, his black eyes narrowed. Linn
watched him approach, knowing this was not the same as
when he stood listening to Grampa in one of his "spells."
This was something entirely apart. He was standing on his
own feet, staring at someone who hated him, someone who
wanted to break and destroy him.

As Linn stood there watching Randy's eyes, he knew that
it wouldn't be Randy who would strike the first blow if it
came to a fight. His tactics were not so open.

"*A witness?*" Randy repeated. "Who's witness to *what?*"
Then he laughed and shrugged his shoulders. "You haven't
got a witness—you're bluffing." Linn didn't answer; he
wouldn't hold Tom up to ridicule.

Randy burst into laughter. "You haven't got a witness to
anything! You're just throwing a big bluff—talking to make
yourself sound wise."

"You know something?" asked Linn, and his tone changed
to leisurely confidence. "I don't need a witness, Randy."
Around his mouth there was the faint twitching of a smile.
"I don't need anything except my two hands. You go on
sinking my pots, clean me out if you think you can. But
I'm just telling you that I'll still be here on the island.
Neither you nor anybody else can drive me off. It's a poor
game that two can't play, you know."

"What have you got to back all this talk? Not a thing!
It takes money to keep setting traps when they don't stay
where you put them."

"I wouldn't even bother to fish any traps," said Linn
easily. "But you wouldn't fish many either."

"Listen, kid," said Randy, no longer bothering to smile.

"You can't prove you saw me doing anything to your traps, so don't go flying off the handle. Might be there's room enough for us both on here. Just don't bother me. Might be there's room, if you keep your distance." He strode off.

Linn stood looking after him, wondering. Was this the end of his troubles with Randy? Had mention of a witness, which Randy called bluffing, caused Randy to pull back, to hesitate about making any more mischief? Linn wanted to think so, but instinct told him not to accept victory too soon.

He went back to work, measuring and coiling warps, and the mailboat whistled outside the harbor before he was done. Soon most of the women were on the way to the wharf. Children too young to be in school, men who were eager enough to leave their workshops for a few minutes, and assorted dogs, they all joined the procession. Charles came along, calling out to Linn, "Break it off a few minutes! Mailboat don't come *every* day!"

Linn shook his head and Charles scowled. "When are you going to stand up on your hind legs and tell your grandfather you're going to breathe by yourself once in a while? Honest, you just got to, Linn, or you'll turn into one of those Roberts."

"One of those *whats?*"

"Roberts," said Charles. "R-o-b-o-t-s. No kidding, Linn, the day's coming when you'll have to speak up."

"It sure is," said Linn enthusiastically, but he didn't mean what Charles did. Charles went along, and Linn kept on running out the warps. Any minute now Grampa might choose to trot down from the house to see if he was busy; and in Grampa's book, anyone who left his job to hang around the wharf when the boat came was in a class with Bert Armstrong.

Also he didn't want to face Wade. Yesterday when he'd come in from hauling his empty traps, he'd seen the lobster-buyer on the wharf, and he had deliberately looked the other way. And now he was bitterly ashamed, but he still didn't want to face Wade and be forced to say, "I can't pay you anything this time."

Methodically he fastened a warp to a trap, tied a newly painted buoy and a glass toggle to the warp. When he had done five more, most of the women had gone home with the mail and groceries, and some of the men were straggling back to their chores. And in Linn's mind the guilt about Norris Wade grew stronger. It was much stronger than his fear of his grandfather; he found himself growing hot and uncomfortable in spite of the chill wind that whipped around him and piled surf on the harbor ledges.

As he finished tying on the tenth toggle, he knew he couldn't bear this uncomfortable sensation any longer. So without giving himself a chance to change his mind, he set off for the store.

Everyone had left but Wiley, who sat in an old chair tilted back against a shelf of canned goods, his long legs sprawled out before him, Cap'n Scott who sat on the scarred old counter, smoking a cigar, and Wade who was in the post office, getting the mailbags ready for the boat.

Linn leaned against the wall, hearing the conversation between Wiley and Cap'n Scott without really listening to it. *I'll just say it right out,* he decided. *Man to man. I guess I won't have the peapod paid for before winter sets in, Mr. Wade. Do you want to take it over, or give me a chance to finish up in the spring?*

Sure, that was the best way. No holler about the pots not fishing too well, or the lobsters crawling out to deeper water where a double-ender couldn't go—or about somebody else hauling them. And sinking them.

Wiley got lazily to his feet and knocked his pipe out

against the stove. "Well, if I set around here much longer, folks'll think I'm as lazy as Bert Armstrong."

"Oh, Bert's not so slow," said Cap'n Scott without a trace of expression on his stolid brown face. "He's just waiting for young Raymond to get big enough to haul pots. Then he can sit on the shore and send the boy out to work."

Wade's deep chuckle sounded from behind the little window. "Might be a good thing, too. Kid might make a better fisherman, and they could live a little more human."

"That's right, now," drawled Wiley. "I should have had me a flock of boys, all about like Linn here, and now I could retire." He smiled at Linn and went out.

"Well, son," Cap'n Scott said. "How does that new peapod go?"

"Like a bird." But Linn's grin felt a little twisted.

Norris Wade came out of the post office, dragging the mailbags. "She flies across the water, all right," he boomed. "Puts me in mind of a medrick, skimming the waves." He dropped the bags and put his big fists on his hips. His pale blue eyes, set in fans of tiny wrinkles, held Linn's. "How come you didn't bring in any lobsters yesterday?"

"I didn't get but a few," said Linn, "and I brought 'em in for Grampa to make a chowder."

"Don't tell me you didn't get more than that!" Wade's amazement was genuine. "What's the trouble with your pots? You've been shifting them around, haven't you? Not just hauling and dumping, the way Bert Armstrong does?"

Linn flushed. "Sure, I've been tending them." This wasn't the way he had planned it. This wasn't right at all. He tried not to sound defensive. "I don't know what's come over them. Maybe they're crawling off—"

He hadn't meant to say that! His flush deepened and he felt sweat trickling down his back.

"Maybe so, maybe so." Wade was wagging his grizzled

head good-naturedly. "But I thought you'd have that peapod paid for by now."

"I did too. I didn't expect trouble." He looked at Wade steadily, and took a deep breath that seemed to reach clear to his toes. "Do you want to take the peapod back?"

Wade's laughter reverberated around his ears like thunder. "By Gorry, son, you're Swenson's flesh and blood all right! I can see the old man right in your eye! No, I don't want the peapod back. I'm not figuring to stand or fall by what you owe me on her! You just tend to your pots the way your grampa taught you, and you'll be all set."

"I'll have a handful of fresh cigars, Norris," Cap'n Scott said. As Wade went to open the tobacco case, Scott slid off the counter and spoke to Linn.

"They've passed a new law saying fellas like me have to hire a deckhand. It's all got to do with the size of the boat, carrying mail and passengers, stuff like that. I'd like to have you, son, if you want the job. You're strong and able, and you ain't afraid of work." His dark-burnt face was as impassive as ever, but his eyes were friendly. "The wife and I can put you up, or you can live aboard the boat. Whatever would suit you."

There was a queer sensation in Linn's chest, as if his heart had actually leaped. For a moment he glimpsed what it would be; a safe paying job on the mailboat where he could still be on the water; the struggle to stay on an island that seemed determined to reject him would be finished. He would be on his own at last, no longer obliged to obey Grampa. Randy couldn't molest him. He would make new friends and be free to associate with them. Maybe being a lobsterman on Lee's Island wasn't the whole world, after all.

He looked out past Cap'n Scott at the cold, gun-metal harbor, the gulls huddled on the ledges, the far spruces black against the threatening sky. It was not a pleasant prospect. There was his double-ender on the haul-off. Working for Cap'n Scott, he could have it paid for in no time. He could spend his money as he pleased, maybe save up enough to buy him a car to drive around in on the mainland. Lee's Island wasn't the only place. . . .

So I'm thinking of running away from it like a scared pup. The words stood out coldly in his mind. *Randy'd always be sure he'd driven me off. And he'd be right.*

The vision of the mailboat job and all it stood for dissolved like fog in the sunshine, and he grinned at Cap'n Scott. "Thanks very much," he said gratefully. "I appreciate the offer a lot. But I've got my feet braced now, and I'm making out all right."

It wasn't a lie, he told himself as he walked back to the fishhouse. *As long as a man's got any fight left,* he thought, *he's making out all right. And I may be fighting in the dark, but they'll have to lay me out with a top maul to get me off this island before I'm ready to go.*

CHAPTER THIRTEEN

Catastrophe

He awoke at dawn the next morning, and when he realized, looking at the sky, that the day would be clear, he felt a new and pleasant excitement. He would take a load of traps out to set, shift some of the others, and find out once and for all if Randy had meant it when he said there might be room in the sea for both of them. Maybe he *had* meant it. Maybe he had respected Linn's stand. Maybe there was something to be said for being old Swenson's grandson, after all! With a good night's sleep behind him, Linn was eager to believe that his luck had turned.

Taking only a couple of cold buttered biscuits for his breakfast, he went down to the shore in the chilly pale light. There was not a sound anywhere, not a thread of smoke from a chimney. He would be out to his first buoy by the time the day was bright enough for him to pick out his colors, while back at the harbor the engines would be only starting to tune up.

He walked out onto the wharf. The tide was half out, the harbor ledges rose from the tranquil, still colorless water in shaggy black humps. The boats at their moorings were like sleeping birds. And he was so sure of seeing the sturdy pea-pod there at her haul-off, with Wiley's big boat lying beyond, that when he didn't see her his brain whirled. For a moment he stood staring, his mouth open; and then he saw that she was there after all, but she was barely in sight. She was full of water.

He ran around to Wiley's wharf, not feeling the weight of his boots, and rowed out to the haul-off in Wiley's skiff. *She's filled, somehow,* he thought. *And how could she?* He could not imagine what had befallen her. When he reached her he held to the gunwale, looked down through the clear flooding water and saw the great jagged hole in the bottom, close to the keel. The oars had drifted away, but his small gaff was caught under the stern thwart.

He sat in the skiff staring at the hole. A little splintered end of one of the ribs kept moving with the motion of the water, like shattered bone held to a wound by flesh. He could almost feel it in his own flesh. He knew what had happened after dark last night; he knew all about the hasty trip out into the harbor with a boulder bigger than a man's head. It must have taken plenty of strength for Randy Mears to smash that boulder down into the peapod.

He reached over and caught hold of the painter, and untied it from the haul-off. It was a slow trip ashore, towing the dead weight of the water-filled double-ender, but he hardly felt it. His rage and grief gave him the strength of a giant. Get Randy by the throat, that was the thing. Shake the truth out of him about the traps and about this for everyone to hear!

But when he had reached the little sand beach below the wharves, and had put Wiley's skiff back, he knew the utter hopelessness of his position. If he caught Randy alone, there would be no one to hear the truth. And if he caught him when there were others around, Randy would laugh in his face and demand his proof. The others would pick it up. *Where's your proof? Can't go making such charges without proof.* Even his grandfather would say it.

He walked across to where the peapod lay awkwardly, no longer a dancing mussel shell, and took hold of her bow. But she was too heavy to be dragged up further on the sand. He would have to wait till the tide left her, and the water drained out through the hole. He sat down on a rock and stared at her, dull-eyed.

The sea and sky took on a tinge of blue, and the stillness was broken by the sound of a punt being dragged down over a pebbly beach somewhere out of sight. A door slammed, a dog let out a sharp bark like a salute to the fine day. Linn stirred himself and climbed the ladder to the wharf. Perhaps the double-ender was ruined; but unless he could find someone to repair her, she was a dead loss to him, and the thought of his debt to Wade only added to his despondency.

The old dory lay bottom up on the beach. He pulled away the canvas that covered her and studied the heavy, lumbering hull. She was meant for two men to row; when his grandfather had used her, it hadn't been for hauling traps, but for carrying bait.

Well, he'd get Grampa to help him launch her, and he'd plod along the best he could. He wouldn't be able to set any more traps; it was more than likely that he would have to shorten the string he already had.

As he trudged back to the house, he heard an engine start up in the harbor, and he wished he could deafen his ears to it. He'd been going to beat them all this morning!

In the kitchen there was a crackling fire and the smell of coffee. His grandfather peered around at him. "You been putting your bait aboard? Now have your breakfast before you go to haul."

"I don't care if I never eat." Linn dropped into a chair.

"What is it now, a boy not hungry?"

"Oh, I just ran into a little hard luck." Linn tried to sound nonchalant. "There's a big hole in my double-ender, and I won't be able to use her again this season. So I guess I'll have to get the old dory overboard. I thought you might help me get her off the wharf."

"Somebody makes you trouble, eh?" Grampa pursed his mouth shrewdly. "Who put the hole in your boat?"

"I don't know," said Linn. "Maybe it was an accident. But that isn't what matters now. I can get her fixed some-time, I guess—maybe Wade'll patch her up again when he has some time, he's pretty good at boat-carpentering—but I still have to pay him what I owe on her. So that means I have to take the old dory."

Grampa put his hands on his hips and gazed fixedly at his grandson. "I did not want you to buy that boat. You made the deal without my permission. Now your boat has a hole in her, so you want my dory again. She was not good enough for you then, but she is good enough now. Is that it?"

"I guess you can figure it that way if you want to," said Linn wearily. "I'm not arguing about it. I just have to have her again, that's all."

"Yes." The old man wagged his head. "You don't argue. For there is no argument. You think all you have to do is tell me. You don't ask me what you can do, you *tell* me."

For Linn, the sight of his grandfather's face was like the cold breath of the sea. He could feel himself tightening against it, the way he would tighten his body against the violent attack of a gale. He sat up straight in his chair and put his hands in his pockets so the old man would not see his tense and twisting fingers.

It was a familiar scene, Grampa standing there with his hands pressed flat against his hips, tucked inside his belt and his thumbs sticking out; his small figure tense, his dark eyes beady-bright under the wrinkled lids. Linn sat still as a stone, waiting.

His grandfather cleared his throat and spoke in a deceptively mild voice. "You are like many people, my boy. You do not want to take advice, you think the old folk know nothing. Then something happens, and you just walk up and say, I must do so and so. You do not say, I made a mistake. Nobody ever says they made a mistake." His voice rose and his eyes glittered as he bent forward and stared into Linn's face.

"You say you must use the old dory again. You do not ask me if you can have her to use." He pointed a stubby forefinger at Linn. "You have long legs, and long pants to go on them, but that does not make you a man—not yet. You don't come and *tell* me what you do."

Linn answered quietly; he could not have raised his voice, he had no breath for it, only a dreadful weight on his chest. "I thought you'd understand the mess I was in, my double-ender being stove in and no good to me. I didn't think—"

"Young sprouts like you never think!" shouted the old man.

Linn was so tired that he closed his eyes for a moment. There was no use in arguing, no use in trying to explain, no use in anything. He could only sit and listen until Grampa had shouted himself out. But he wanted sympathy and understanding, not a lecture. In his mind's eye he saw the double-ender lying by the wharf, filled with sea water, the great jagged hole in the bottom, and a pain greater than any he had ever known cut across his throat in a great strangling ache, and he tried to swallow to ease it away. The pain spread to his eyes and they burned like fire. He opened them and saw his grandfather in a bright swimming mist.

Linn stood up, and his tall figure towered over the old man's. *"Well?"* The question came sharply.

"Nothing, Grampa." Linn was polite. "There's nothing for me to say. You don't want to listen to my side of things, you just want to hear yourself. But I'm so tired, I don't care what you say or what you think. If you don't want me to use the dory, say so. You don't have to beat around the bush."

He walked to the door. It was no lie he was telling when he said he was too tired to care what happened. It was not the fatigue that comes with hard work, but the exhaustion of the spirit which knows without question that it is alone.

The old man's voice followed him, strangely broken and muted. *He can't believe it, because I never walked out on a lecture before,* Linn thought. *But I just can't take it now.*

"If you go out that door now," said his grandfather, "you don't come back. You understand. *You don't come back.*"

And Linn, hearing and understanding with one side of his brain, also heard his own incredible answer. "I understand." He swung the door wide and went out, and down the path, his feet taking him where they would, for he had no mind for thinking. He was like someone numbed. There was just one idea in his mind, to find a silent, lonely place where he could lie down and put his face against the cold salt-rimed grass and wait for this weariness to pass away.

His feet took him across a field, through a thicket of alders and birches and young spruces, and out onto the western shore of the island. The land rose high from the sea in a great jumble of cliff-like rocks, cracked and split with the years. Back from the rocks the ground was covered with a coarse thick grass, dry and brown now, with an occasional granite ledge showing through. The sun was high, and the sea blue and rippling under a gentle wind, but he took no notice of the day. He went to one of the big granite out-croppings and dropped down into a grassy hollow beside it. He paid no heed to the clamor of the gulls and crows that had been feeding on the shore. He sat with his knees hugged close to him, and his forehead on his knees, his eyes shut, and gave in to his desolation.

He could not strike out, he could not raise his voice in fury. His instinct had been to beat Randy within an inch of his life; and he had wanted to rise up and shout back at Grampa, telling him everything that had been bottled up inside him for years. But because he was nobody, because he had nothing—not even a bed of his own, let alone a roof to set it under—he could not fight back.

He stretched out on his back and looked up at the gulls wheeling overhead in the blue. Only a gull could live in comfort, with plenty to eat, a place to sleep, and nothing to worry about, unless it was somebody who might take a shot at it for getting into his doryload of herring.

He got up and began walking again. The path he followed was familiar, between the tumbled and broken rocks on one side and the spruces on the other, stunted and twisted by the wind. Within the shadow of the trees the land rose and shut away the sky until he came to the outermost point of land, where the ocean spread before him in boundless acres of blue.

No trees grew here, only the coarse brown grass and clumps of dead goldenrod. In little damp hollows the cranberry vines flourished, and he crushed the hard bright berries under his feet as he strode along. The sea was a brilliant, restless surface, with white breakers marking the hidden ledges. Here and there a lobster boat rocked in the swells. Surf boiled against the shore below Linn, and outside the surf numberless sea birds rode at ease on the water. He realized suddenly that it must be noon, and he had had only two cold biscuits since daylight. A roasted black duck wouldn't taste bad at all. But he had no shotgun, and he'd settle for a cup of coffee and more biscuits. Maybe he could get them from Polly. And after he'd eaten something, maybe he could think what to do next.

What could he do? As if there were anything he could do. He stared across the water and saw Tom Lowell's white dory making her steady way over the bright swells toward some shoal spot where he would probably anchor to a pot buoy, and spend a tranquil few hours hand-lining for cod. He remembered another day when he had sat alone and friendless, trying to think, and Tom had spoken to him. Tom knew what loneliness was, but how serene and happy he seemed in his strange, solitary existence! Was there ever a time when Tom stood on these barren slopes and felt as desperate as Linn felt now? Linn couldn't imagine it.

At the Armstrong house he found Polly alone. "How about some coffee and a handful of biscuits?" he asked bluntly.

"You can have better than that. There's fish chowder, still warm." She set out a big bowl for him while he hung up his jacket and washed his hands. While he ate, she watched him silently. When he was ready for more, she brought it to him, and then said shyly, "You've had trouble with your grandfather again, haven't you?"

Linn flashed a wary glance at her, and she went on. "I saw him down at the fishhouse, prowling around. He was throwing some of your traps out of the way, and I could tell he was mad, just by the way he chucked them over toward the beach. He didn't break any, though," she added.

"He'd better not," said Linn darkly. "I've got troubles enough without having to patch pots."

She didn't ask him any more questions, but offered him a third bowl of chowder, and he shook his head. "I don't intend to eat you out of house and home. Can I get you some wood or some water? Do an errand to the store for you?"

"You don't have to do anything," she assured him. "I guess we can afford to be neighborly without having some kind of pay."

He slept that night in the fishhouse. A pile of ancient cod and mackerel nets lay in a corner of the loft, and he moved them into a semblance of a bed, flattening them here and there, lying on them to see if he could be comfortable. They would do, but he needed a blanket, and he went back to the Armstrong house. Once more Polly didn't question him, but went off without a word to find spare blankets. She must have primed the children, he realized, for none of them piped up with embarrassing remarks, and Bert went on smoking his pipe as if there were nothing out of the ordinary in Linn's request.

Polly, returning with the blankets, said, "You needn't sleep out, Linn. One of the boys could sleep with Pa, and you could bunk with the other one. Nobody would mind, if you didn't."

He shook his head. "I don't want to be that much bother. You're doing enough, letting me have blankets."

"Well, you know you're welcome," Polly said, and her father nodded.

Linn slept surprisingly well. He was stiff and lame when he first awoke in the morning, and depressed; he still didn't know what he was going to do. He was sure only that he was going to cling fiercely to the island. When he came out into the chilly sunshine and wind, Bert Armstrong hailed him from where he was chopping wood in his dooryard.

"Got flapjacks and molasses coming up! Want to sit in with us?"

Nobody had anything to say at the breakfast table—the business of eating was too important. The thick golden flapjacks and molasses, the mugs of steaming tea, all tasted too good going down for anyone to want to interrupt the pleasant interlude with words. But when Linn and Bert had finished and pushed away from the table, Bert lit up his pipe and frowned at Linn through the puffs of smoke.

"Well, son, I guess you're kind of betwixt and between these days. Anything I can do?"

Linn shook his head. "Thanks just the same, Bert."

"What are you going to do now? It's too rough to haul."

"I couldn't go to haul anyway, with a smashed peapod."

"That's right. I forgot about it." Bert fussed with his pipe. "It's a dirty shame, that."

Linn got up hastily. He couldn't stand sympathy. Once he gave in to self-pity he would be lost. "Need any water before I go, Polly?"

Polly, still filling the children's plates, answered gravely, "No, thanks, Linn." She gave him a quiet thoughtful look. He was glad of her friendship, but humiliated that anyone should pity him, and he left the house quickly.

Down at the fishhouse he went to work, stripping broken laths off traps and mending with new ones. He was conscious of every step and his head jerked up whenever anyone came along the path and spoke to him. Any moment now his grandfather might arrive and tell him to stop working, that he couldn't use the fishhouse if he was done with living in the house.

But the morning passed, and Mr. Swenson didn't come. By the time the mailboat whistled outside the point and then came rolling around it, Linn realized that his grandfather did not intend for the present to put him out of the fishhouse. A little of the strain was relieved, and he found himself even being grateful. As long as he had the fishhouse for shelter, he wasn't beaten.

CHAPTER FOURTEEN

Wiley Helps and Needs Help

The next morning someone pounded at the door of the fishhouse before Linn was up. Braced to meet Grampa, he went cautiously down the stairs. But it was Wiley, who looked as unconcerned as if Linn had been in the habit of sleeping in the fishhouse all along.

"Seeing as you've had an accident to your double-ender," he said casually, "I thought you might want the loan of my dory to go haul your traps. Help yourself." He put his pipe back in his mouth, nodded, and strolled off.

"Gorry, thanks, Wiley!" Linn called after him. "I sure appreciate it!" His mouth quirked ironically. He did appreciate Wiley's kindness; besides that, Wiley's dory was small, and easy to row compared to the yellow Banks dory. But what was there to go haul for? Probably Randy meant to go on either hauling or sinking Linn's traps, whenever he found himself near any of Linn's buoys, and out of sight of any of the other men.

But Linn kept up appearances and rowed out of the harbor in the cold, quiet morning. *I'll start bringing my pots in, a few at a time. What's left of them,* he decided. *As if I was going to dry them out and patch them up. That'll take up some time. After that—* Here his planning stopped. After that, he didn't know what; he couldn't think.

Randy had sunk only the traps on Long Ledge. He might continue to meddle with the remaining traps whenever he could, but even Randy wouldn't take a chance on sinking too many to go beyond the bounds of coincidence. Somebody might say, "Darn' funny the kid lost *every* trap! Poor judgment could account for losing some of 'em, but not that many!"

So, though Randy had already gone down the West Side at sunup this morning, Linn's buoys still floated on the still, shadowy water. Linn shrugged at that; but when he went through the gestures of hauling he expected to find the doors open again and the bait bags gone. Instead he found that the traps had not been bothered at all, and he would have some lobsters to sell to Wade after all. He was too wary to be overjoyed. Randy had wrecked the peapod, a terrible blow; and Randy knew, as everyone else knew, that Linn had had trouble with his grandfather, and had left his house with winter coming on. So Randy, Linn reasoned, could afford to sit back and watch until he decided his next big move. *The one that's meant to finish me,* Linn thought in a curious calm. *He's playing with me like a cat with a mouse. Well, whatever happens next, maybe I'll have some more paid out on the peapod first.*

Pushing his luck, he boldly set out ten more traps.

The weather had fallen into the little lull of hushed waiting that comes between fall and winter, in early November; and Linn was waiting too. He didn't know for what, he only knew he must keep his eyes and ears open because he didn't know from which direction the next storm would sweep into his life.

In this strange mood, with so much on his mind, he didn't want to talk to anyone. When he wasn't working on traps at the fishhouse, nervously expecting Grampa to appear at any moment, he escaped from the village. Hour after hour he tramped around the shores, piling up driftwood above the tideway for anyone who might care to collect it, dragging wrecked traps out of the rockweed, salvaging buoys, doing anything that would use up his nervous energy. When he was tired enough he sat down and stared bleakly at the ocean. Sometimes he thought of the Armstrongs' shabby kitchen and its cheerful confusion, but he knew that if he went there Polly could not help showing her sympathy any more than her father could help shaking his head dolefully.

And when Charles showed up at the fishhouse, with his grin and his bottle of strawberry pop, Linn couldn't make easy conversation while his grim secrets lay so heavy on him. To give Charles credit, he hadn't asked Linn what had happened between him and Grampa, but had only asked if Linn needed any money.

"No, thanks," Linn said, both pleased and embarrassed. "I've got enough for what I need." In the week since he had left home, naturally his earnings weren't going into Grampa's tin box. After he paid something on the peapod from each haul, and bought some food, he put what was left into a coffee can hidden in the corner of the fishhouse loft. There was something else hidden up there too—a gaily wrapped box of candy for Polly. He would take it to her when he felt able to face her eager sympathy.

One afternoon he went all the way around the rocky eastern end of the island. It was unusually mild and still, a real Indian Summer day. No surf exploded on the tide ledges Coot and Duck, where the islanders went gunning for sea birds. Linn hadn't planned to call on Tom, but by the time he reached the sheltered little cove where Tom's wharf and fishhouse were, and where the dory lay on her haul-off, he was sweating and thirsty. He climbed the steep bank and crossed the sloping field toward the house.

The low shingled cottage had been built many years ago, and was surrounded by twisted old apple trees that filled the air with sweetness in blossom time. A little beyond the house there was a small barn, but neither cats nor chickens appeared in the barnyard; no dog barked or rooster crowed, no cow lowed from the other side of the stone wall. There was only silence and emptiness, emphasized by the calm of the day and the pale sunshine. The spruce woods rose dark beyond the orchard, but a long meadow stretched from the stone wall to the open sea, which swept in summery unbroken blue to the misty horizon.

He went up on the doorstep and banged on the door with his fist. There was no answer. He opened the door and put his head inside, shouting, "Tom! You home?"

This time there was a faint answer that seemed to come from under his feet. "I'll be there in just a moment. Take a chair."

He walked into the tiny, sparsely furnished kitchen. The bare floor was unpainted, the windows were uncurtained. But everything was so scrubbed and immaculate that Linn glanced down uneasily at his boots to see if he had tracked in any mud.

"Who is it?" Tom's distant voice came again.

"Linn Robertson!"

"Come down cellar, Linn, and see my shelves. It's the door beside the sink."

Linn, with a thirsty glance at the water pails, had no interest in Tom's cellar or shelves, but it would have been unmannerly to refuse. He went down the steep steps into the dim low cellar; the posts that supported the house seemed to be big tree trunks. Tom's pale face appeared among them like an apparition in the woods. He beckoned with a long white hand, and led Linn to a wall of cupboards. They were filled with an impressive number of jars, all carefully arranged.

Tom named off the variety of foods. "This is my provender for winter, Linn. Berries I have picked in season, vegetables from my little garden, mackerel and herring I've bought from the men. I have even one shelf of pickles." Smiling, he smoothed his black mustache. "I won't starve for a while."

"I should say not!" Linn said fervently. "You've got enough grub here to fit out an army!"

"Not quite that." Tom's smile deepened. "But I would be quite well off indeed if I had as much money as I have food on my shelves. Yes, I should be quite content."

He led the way upstairs and Linn got his drink. When he had hung the dipper back, he found Tom's black eyes studying him with a kindly interest.

"You've had bad luck lately," he remarked.

"Bad luck!" Linn snorted. "Well, that's a mild way of putting it. Peapod stove in."

"You have the loan of Wiley's dory."

"Yes, and she's a lot lighter than Grampa's old dory." He flushed under Tom's steady gaze. "I'm thankful for that, all right."

Tom touched his mustache. His eyes moved to the horizon far beyond the windows of his little house. "Things will

come right for you, Linn. They must, eventually, if you just
have the strength and patience to keep on."

That was Tom's philosophy. Strength and patience. If
Tom lost those, by which he lived his days, he would have lost
everything. But in comparison with Linn, Tom was well off,
with his little house and land and dory. And if he wanted to,
he could set out some pots.

"Tom, why don't you have traps out?" Linn asked. "Don't
you like lobstering?"

Tom's eyes measured him thoughtfully. "Don't you know
why I don't go lobstering? Do you mean nobody has told
you?"

"I guess nobody ever thinks of it," Linn said candidly.
"You're just taken for granted, seems to me. Tom Lowell—
he comes and goes and nobody seems to think much about
it."

Tom nodded. "I suppose that if I just disappeared some
day, nobody would even mention the fact."

"Well, I don't know as you could blame them. You don't
live like anyone else, you know. You're kind of like the
birds, Tom. You have a different way with you."

"I know," said Tom somberly. "Folks used to make un-
kind remarks about poor Tom Lowell. Well, perhaps I deserved them. They say a coward deserves all he gets."

"Coward!" The word burst explosively from Linn.
"You're no coward!"

Tom gave him a brief smile. "When I was a little shaver
my father took me with him in his sloop. I liked it all, the
motion of the boat, the sail curving out and above my head
toward the sky. I had no fear of anything, and I was proud as
a little peacock when my father let me take the wheel. Then
one day—" He paused, and bit the edge of his mustache reflectively. "One day—" He shivered slightly. "My father was
hauling, and the warp was falling to the bottom of the boat,

as it always did, and I was hovering around, anxious to see what he would get in the trap. There was nothing in it, so he pushed the trap overboard with a sort of curse, and you couldn't blame him. We needed all the money we could get. My mother was expecting another child, and you know how that would be."

Linn nodded silently.

"Well, what happened next was so quick it was hard to know just how it came about. The rope slipped overboard after the trap, of course. But I was standing among the coils." He hesitated, biting his mustache again, and Linn felt his own body stiffen. "My father swung the boat over, the sail moved the other way with a jerk, and the coil came taut about my legs. I went down on my shoulders somehow, and then up over the side and overboard." He put his hands up to his face. "I can remember that water yet. The sensation of being dragged down by some terrible force—of choking—"

He was silent for so long that Linn wondered if he would go on. Then he began again. "My father saw me go, and he grabbed the gaff and hooked at the line and me. He pulled me back in. . . . And that's all I remember of that part. I remember next being carried in his arms to the house. He had come back to the harbor at once. I was soaking wet, of course, and he undressed me outdoors and took me in all naked over his shoulder. My mother thought I had been drowned, and she shrieked. It was a terrible sound. I remembered the water and shriek together, as if the wet and the cold and the sound are one thing."

He looked at Linn with eyes that seemed to be seeing other things. "It was a long time before I could even go in a boat again. They thought I would be better ashore on the mainland, so I was sent off to live with an aunt and go to school. But I was homesick and very lonely. I studied hard and learned many things, but as soon as I could, I came home to the island. I didn't go lobstering, but I farmed and had the orchard—it's much smaller now than it used to be. My father died, and then my mother—"

"What about the child?" asked Linn. He had been very moved by the story.

"The child? A girl, and she died very young. So you see, Linn, how it is. I can't endure the sight of a pot-warp on the bottom of a boat. That makes me a coward." He stood up. "Let's go outside, Linn. I've been saving a load of driftwood for Polly." His mouth quirked. "You know how she's always wanting dry stuff for a biscuit fire. Help me load the dory and I'll row you back to the harbor."

Down on the shore Tom pulled the dory in and Linn began gathering an armful of wood from the sizable pile on the bank. He hated the thought of returning to the harbor. There was a peace and self-sufficiency about Tom's place that he envied, even though he knew now about Tom's unhappy youth.

Neither the man nor the boy spoke as they went back and forth over the beach carrying the light dry wood; but both heads went up sharply as a sudden burst from a shotgun sounded from around the high rocky point that rose to one side of Tom's place. It was the extreme eastern end of the island.

"Somebody gunning for ducks," Linn grunted. Tom nodded. They put more wood into the dory, each lost in his own thoughts. But they expected the gunner to appear around the point, shotgun cradled in his arm. Linn dreaded meeting anyone who might want to hold conversation about his trouble with Grampa and his shattered double-ender. With luck, the hunter might exchange only a few words and then go his way, following the shore back to the harbor.

There was another shot, so close that only a jumble of big boulders seemed to hide the gun from them. But no birds rose up from the rockweedy shallows and flew wildly over their heads. Another shot came, and still not a bird. There were none on the water, either. Linn became uneasy. Meeting Tom at the dory he said tentatively, "Somebody might be hurt. Wouldn't do any harm to scout around a bit."

They went up to the turf, where the walking was easier than on the beach, and walked rapidly toward the rocky rise that stood between them and the gunner. As they topped the rise and started down the other side, they saw him. He was lying on his back among the rocks below the tide-mark; his dark clothes blending with the rockweed made him almost invisible.

Linn ran down over the slippery rocks as nimbly as a goat, and Tom, for all his moderation, was close behind him. "It's Wiley!" Linn cried, in something very like panic. "And I dunno if he's dead or not!"

"I'm not dead," said Wiley strongly, and Linn had never heard anything so wonderful. Wiley's long thin face was drawn as he stared up at the others, but he managed a wry grin. "I slipped on the cussed rockweed, and I guess I've broken my ankle. Thought I broke my back at first, the way it knocked the wind out of me."

A couple of wild ducks lay a little distance away, limp bundles of dark feathers, where he had dropped them when he fell. He motioned for Linn to take his shotgun. "Glad that thing didn't go off and puncture me. Now how are you two figgering to get me out of here?"

"Can you sit up?" Tom asked. He reached out his hands, and Wiley grasped them and pulled himself up to a sitting position. He winced, then nodded grimly. "Now what?"

"Darned if I know," said Linn helplessly. He turned to Tom, who stood stroking his chin. "What do you say?"

"I'll go back to my dory," Tom said at last, "and see if I can bring her in among the rocks just below here. If there's a deep hole down there, I can do it. Then between us, Linn, we can get Wiley down to the dory and aboard. The rocks are slippery, but we each have two good legs and Wiley has one."

"Sure, five legs are better than four, any time," Wiley drawled, and felt in his pocket for his pipe. "And there *is* a deep hole right off here. I thought sure I was going to drown in it when my feet went out from under me."

Tom went back over the rise, a black and agile figure. Wiley smoked, and Linn squatted beside him, too relieved to want to talk. The first sight of that long body sprawled among the rocks had been a terrifying one. And Wiley, too, must have been enduring frightening thoughts as he lay there, hoping someone would hear the shotgun and calculating how long it would take the tide to reach him.

Tom and the dory appeared soon. Tom maneuvered her skilfully among the half-submerged rocks, through narrow openings where the surge flooded and retreated, until he found the deep hole where the dory could take the weight of three men without touching bottom. He made the painter fast around a jagged peak of rock; then he came up to where the others were.

With Wiley's arms around their shoulders, and their arms about his waist, they made their way down the rocky, weed-covered slope to the dory. Wiley hopped on his good foot; they were infinitely careful about the placing of their own feet. At that, there was a good deal of slipping and sliding, and once Linn had a horrible moment when he thought he was going to lose his footing altogether and pull the others down with him. But it was a day of miracles—he knew that once and for all when they had Wiley safely in the dory. Wiley was sweating, but his lean face broke into a grin.

"Don't know how I'm ever going to pay you fellers back for this," he said.

"We just happened to be there," answered Linn.

"But if you hadn't just happened to be there, where'd I be by dusk tonight?" Wiley demanded. There was no answer to that.

Linn wanted to row back, but Tom refused pleasantly. "It's kind of you, Linn, but nobody knows my little dory as I do. And she's carried a heavier load than this one many a time."

It was true that the dory seemed to obey Tom like a willing little horse. A breeze had sprung up, but she rode gaily through the rough cross-chop at the harbor mouth and then glided across the sheltered waters in a way that made Linn homesick for his double-ender.

He roused himself from the mood and said, "What'll we do, Wiley? You'll be wanting to take that bad ankle to the mainland—no sense your trying to get up to the house, is there?"

"No, best to go in to Wade's car and see if we can't find me a good Samaritan with nothing wrong with his engine." Wiley tried to shift his position, and groaned a little in spite of himself.

"Wade's down on the car now, crating lobsters," said Linn, and at the same moment Wade's deep voice boomed across the harbor toward them.

"Well, you fellers been out on Cashes? Looks like a mighty big codfish you've got in the stern there!"

"Biggest one you ever saw!" Linn called back, and then recognized Randy on the car with Wade.

He had been dipping lobsters from one of the compartments with the long-handled dip net, and turning them into empty crates, but as the dory nuzzled the side of the car, he leaned the dip net against the scales and looked at the passengers with one eyebrow lifted.

"Well, Wiley," he observed, "you're in strange company."

"I'd be in stranger company still," Wiley said crisply, "if they hadn't heard my gun go off. Linn, you want to go up to my house and give Grace the news? Well, Randy, you're always wanting to go racing off to the mainland and spend your money, how about taking me in right now to get this ankle set?"

For once Randy looked surprised. "For the love of—what'd you do, shoot yourself? Sure, I'll take you." Norris Wade looked into the dory and shook his big head in awe.

"You could have killed yourself. Bad thing, going gunning alone."

Linn passed close by Randy without a sidewise look, went up the ladder, and headed for Wiley's house at a lope. Grace took the news calmly, with only a tightening of the lips.

"There, I always knew he'd do something like that, some day. I'm just thankful it's only an ankle. It could've been his neck. Maybe he'll take a lesson from this, but I doubt it." She shook her head, then moved toward the cupboard with an air of purpose. "Well, they'll just have to take him across tonight and I'll follow next boat day. I can't get ready in five minutes." She had what Wiley called her quarter-deck manner, speaking with brisk, breezy authority; she was short and stout, but all her movements were calmly efficient. "Linn, you go back and tell them not to start off till I come down with some blankets and a thermos of hot coffee."

Back at the wharf, a crowd had gathered. Randy had brought his boat in alongside the car. There was an atmosphere of excitement and emergency which everyone seemed to be enjoying, since Wiley's condition wasn't dangerous. Children scampered up and down the wharf, women stood in little groups with their hands pushed up into their sleeves against the frosty chill which came at sundown. In the to-do of getting Wiley into the big boat from the dory, Linn and Tom were quite forgotten. Tom looked on with his usual meditative expression, but Linn's loneliness increased to painful proportions. He and Tom had found Wiley and brought him home, but now they were pushed to the outside and ignored while everyone else made a holiday out of the unexpected event.

Grace arrived with blankets, hot coffee, sandwiches, and orders; Wiley was settled comfortably on a locker in the cabin. Randy, in a new leather jacket, went aboard, pushed his cap back, and grinned up at the crowd on the wharf.

"Well, who's going with me?" he asked. "Who wants a trip to the big city? Come on, Charlie! Give the city girls a treat!"

"Why, shore, Pardner! Don't mind if I do!" Charles, laughing, swung his stocky self down the ladder. "We'll be back early tomorrow, if it's fine, Pa!" he called to his father.

Linn felt a sudden, intense pang; he wished that he and Charles were the ones taking Wiley ashore, crossing the bay under the great arch of the night sky, seeing the lighthouses begin to show on the horizon all around; he saw himself and Charles standing by the wheel, talking or not talking, it didn't matter. It would have been good, either way.

Linn turned and left the wharf before the boat had backed away from the car. But as he passed the salt shed, someone called to him. It was Polly, who had been standing alone. She smiled at him, pushing up her stubborn little chin.

"Gorry, this has been quite a day, hasn't it?"

"It sure has," he said morosely.

"And I'll bet you ate cold canned beans for dinner."

He had to grin at that. She was a sharp one, all right. "How'd you guess?"

"Oh, I can read your mind, after all these years," she told him breezily. "Come on home with me. We had boiled salt herring and spuds for dinner, and there's plenty left over. I could warm 'em up—"

"No need," he broke in. "There's times when a cold boiled potato and a salt herring taste better than anything else in the world—and this'll be one of them."

Then he remembered something. "I'll go around to the fishhouse first. Don't wait for me. I'll be right over."

He could take the candy to her now.

CHAPTER FIFTEEN

Grace Makes an Offer

Polly was so surprised by the candy that for once she couldn't say a word. She had never had such a gift before, and she kept looking at the beribboned box as if she couldn't believe her eyes, then proceeded to pile Linn's plate so high with food that he was hard put to eat it all.

When he had finished with the meal, he took Polly's water pails to the well and filled them. As he left the well, Grace Abbott sang out his name from her front door and then came swinging down the path from her house, a stout and energetic figure who waved an empty pail at him.

"I'll get your water as soon as I deliver this," he called back.

She was waiting at the wellcurb when he returned, but the pails were full. "I thought I was supposed to tend to them," he reproved her, but she flung her head up scornfully.

"Land of love, it isn't the first time I've hauled pails out of that well, nor the last. But you can lug them home for me, though. I want to talk to you."

"What about?"

"Never you mind right now. I never was one to talk over my business in the face and eyes of the village."

Linn picked up the pails and started up the slope toward the Abbott place. Grace walked beside him, an absent-minded expression on her usually jolly face. She held the kitchen door open for him, and he passed through and set the pails on the dresser by the sink. When he turned away from the dresser, Grace pointed at Wiley's chair.

"I've got something special to talk about, Linn, so you might as well sit down."

"Ayeh," said Linn good-naturedly, and settled into the familiar captain's chair. Now what did she have on her mind? Seemed as if everybody had a bone to pick with some-one.

Grace set her back against the dresser and braced her feet as if she were aboard Wiley's boat in a southeasterly. "It's no secret to the folks on the island that you've had trouble with your grandfather," she said bluntly. "You've had to borrow Wiley's dory to haul your traps, and you're living in the fish-house. Things seem to be against you right now, and I don't know why they should. You work hard, and you've had to carry an old head on young shoulders while you've lived with old Swenson."

She paused, cocking her head at him, and then plunged on. "I've been thinking. Here Wiley's gone and broken his ankle, and he'll be on the retired list for a few weeks. There are his traps out in the water, needing to be tended. How about you taking his boat and tending his gear and your own at the same time? It'd help us both out, Linn."

He swallowed to ease a constricted throat. "Do you think Wiley would trust me with his boat?" he asked honestly. "I wouldn't want for you to let me take it, unless it was some-thing he gave consent to."

She thrust her hands decisively into her jacket pockets. "You take the boat, Linn, and tend the gear. I've got something to say around here, you know. I don't want those traps lying out there untended if something can be done about them. That'd be pure pig-headed foolishness."

"Grace, you're sure a one." It was weak, but it was the best he could do. "You sure are. All right. I'll take the boat and I'll be careful, just as if Wiley was leaning over my shoulder the whole time."

"And in the meantime, just so you'll rest easy," she promised him, "I'll get word to Wiley about this deal of ours."

The wave of gratitude that swept over him was almost too much to bear. He wanted to leap up and shout, to clap his heels together, to run, to turn cartwheels; anything wild and strenuous to let loose the fervent happiness that surged through him. He drew a long breath, and then his gaze fell on the woodbox behind the stove.

"Can't I chop some wood for you?"

"It'd be a big help," she admitted. "There's some stacked in the shed, but if you want to add to it, I won't stop you."

This was what he needed to loosen the tension that had bound him in the house. One by one he took the mighty chunks of spruce from the pile by the woodshed and split them; and with each swing of the axe, with each moment of contact when the blade sliced through the wood, his spirits rose, and his hopes came bobbing to the surface like so many unsinkable and irrepressible seals.

Having the use of Wiley's boat meant many things. It meant he could haul on days when it was far too rough for a dory; it meant he could set out traps of his own, as far out as Wiley set his, and haul them at the same time. It meant that if Randy decided to start molesting his traps again, thinking that Linn was getting a bit above himself with the use of Wiley's boat, Linn had a fighting chance to keep an eye on him. It meant that, given a slight share of luck, Linn could finish paying for the peapod in the next few weeks and put a good portion away in the coffee can in the loft.

It was only when he had finished chopping wood and had gone back to the fishhouse, where he could see the double-ender drawn up on the beach, her broken timbers and planking fully exposed to the sight of anyone going by, including Randy—it was only then that his hopes sank again. He still had plenty of troubles, in spite of the few weeks' respite while Wiley was off his feet. There was this business between him and Grampa, always gnawing away in the back of his mind; and there was Randy, waiting for his chance.

He turned disconsolately toward the fishhouse, stooping to pick up some broken laths and a handful of old rope for his fire. Now the harbor was all ripples and a sharp breeze blew past his ears. *Likely to be blowing a gale by morning,* he thought ruefully. *This time of year there's more wind than calm.*

He was bent over the stove, building his fire, when Norris Wade spoke imperatively from the doorway. "Guess you'd better give me a hand with that peapod, son."

Linn jumped and swung about, his hand clutching the stove lifter. "Peapod?" he stammered. "You taking her back?"

The big man standing in the doorway nodded. "Yes. Taking her back to patch her up for you. She's not doing any good laying on the beach with her bottom out. A few minutes here and there when I'm not doing anything else, and I'll have her tight as a cup in no time."

"But she's not your responsibility—"

Wade shook his head impatiently. "I know all about that part of it. Don't argue with me, boy. Let's get that peapod off this beach? You want your grandfather to get the laugh on both of us?"

Linn could see no sign of a smile on the man's ruddy face, but he knew that it lurked somewhere out of sight. Yes, it would be a chance for the old man to heap sarcasm on Wade, if the spirit prompted him. But still, it was adding favor on favor for Wade to repair the injured boat, when Linn had not paid for it yet.

Wade had already walked out to the peapod which lay like a beached sea creature. The boat was light as a chip from being dried out in the wind and sun, and they picked her up between them as if she were a birchbark canoe, as fragile and as vulnerable as those ancient craft. They carried her along the path to Wade's wharf and set her down in the low shed where Wade had a saw table and a long bench. When Linn stood back and looked at her, he knew what the word *humility* meant. Twice in the last few hours he had been hailed and assisted. It was not easy to understand. He was just a penniless young fisherman, with troubles on every hand. His grandfather, his only living kin, had set his face against him. Now two people had come to draw him toward them, not turn him away.

"There!" Wade seemed pleased with himself. "I'll send for some oak and some pine right off. Barring accidents, we'll have her ready for the water again in jig time." He winked at Linn. "Probably make old Swenson hopping mad, eh?"

But Linn could not smile back. There was something else he had to say. "Guess I'd better tell you that Grace wants me to take Wiley's boat and tend his gear while he's laid up. Then I can tend mine too, and get out even if it's too rough to row."

"Say, that's good!" Wade exclaimed. "Too bad Wiley had to go fall down, but I guess it's one of those things to prove the old saying—one man's loss is another man's gain." He put his hand on the boy's shoulder. "Keep that chin up, son. I'm banking on you, you know. Besides, we've got this peapod to get settled between us."

He chuckled deep in his throat. "We made a deal, son. And we've got to see that it's a good one. Just to spite old Swenson, if nothing else. I admit your grandfather's got his good points, son," he added seriously. "But he's not the only one. No, sir. There are others on here who know a little something, and don't you forget it."

"I guess I couldn't very well forget it now, not the way things have been happening today," Linn said. "I'm more grateful than I can say, Mr. Wade, for you fixing the peapod."

"That's plenty to say, Linn, plenty. Lots of folks don't know enough to say that much. So you just go along, son. Just go along."

Linn went back to the fishhouse, where he warmed up a can of beans and ate them with crackers and a big mug of strong tea. The dusk was settling fast, and the far corners of the fishhouse were hidden in gloom. The flames glowed cheerily through the cracks of the old stove, and the heat from the rusted round sides made him drowsy. Suddenly he was nodding, and he roused himself and went up to the loft, where he tumbled onto the nets and rolled himself up in his blankets. He heard the wind keening in the eaves of the building, and whispering at the small panes of the big window in the gable.

He smiled to himself in the dark. *I can go to haul in the morning, no matter if it does blow.* The thrill of the knowledge tightened his muscles, then he snuggled deeper into his blanket. Best to get a good sleep now, so he would be up and ready when the gulls started screeching at dawn.

CHAPTER SIXTEEN

Eviction from the Fishhouse

The wind went east and was blowing in fresh gusts when Linn turned out at dawn. No one else was stirring when he put on his oil clothes, a jug of fresh drinking water, and his box of bait into the skiff, and rowed out to Wiley's boat.

Like one in a trance he went about starting the engine and casting off the mooring. He saw where Wiley had brought aboard bait for his day's hauling and had it neatly stored in boxes under the washboard. As he moved about, doing the necessary things before leaving the harbor, he felt as though he were aboard an ocean liner. Wiley's boat was a solid forty-footer, built for years of work and rough weather, while Linn's double-ender was a fragile fifteen-foot shell. When he stood on the bow deck and let the mooring chain go, he had a sense of strength and accomplishment. *A man would have to be a success in a boat like this,* he thought. *Just being in it, working it, must make Wiley feel like a king.* He quickly ran down the deck to the cockpit. His hands knew what to do without being told, and he was thankful for the times he had been with Charles, running his boat, handling his engine, helping to haul his traps. Those times had not been very many—Grampa had seen to that—but enough so he had learned his way around a powerboat. He had thought it great fun to be with Charles, but it was tame indeed to what he was feeling now, as Wiley's boat began to move smoothly away from the other boats, toward the harbor mouth and the open slate-gray sea.

As soon as he was clear of the harbor ledges he moved the throttle and the boat leaped forward. He let her go free as a gull, cutting her way through the water as she sped past the western side of the island, toward the outer shoals where Wiley had his gear.

The height of the island sheltered him until he passed the southern point, and then the wind-driven sea rose up to smite the boat broadside and throw buckets of water over her. But Linn was in his oil clothes and they kept him dry and warm. The boat made her way straight to the line of orange and white buoys that seemed to gleam with a kind of radiance as they rose up on the tops of the crested waves and then swam down into the hollows. As Linn gaffed the first one and pulled it on board, he thought of his own traps, close to the island shores. If the wind was blowing much harder when he was done with Wiley's traps, he would skip his own, those on the east side, anyway. He wouldn't take a chance with a boat not his, on the rocky windward shore.

As he worked, he realized overwhelmingly all that he had been missing by not being able to range far into deep water. The lobsters that came out of Wiley's traps were big, dark, wide-backed creatures, satisfying to grasp and hold as he plugged the huge crusher claws before putting them in the barrel. And there was the ease and security, the wonderful strength that lay under his feet as the boat lifted and moved on over the rough water, dipping and rolling, but always with a self-containment that filled the boy's heart with delight. When he had finished with Wiley's gear, and had hauled all his own traps on the west side, he was in love as he had never been before in his life. He was still loyal to his double-ender, but this was something different. And Linn knew now that he could not rest until he had a boat like this for himself. Every waking moment would be spent toward that fulfillment. He didn't need to promise himself this, he knew it as a certainty, the way a person knows he lives.

Most of the other fishermen had preferred to stay ashore that day and work on gear. But Bert Armstrong was out, puttering around along the lee shore, and Linn waved proudly to him as he swept by. When he sold his lobsters and Wiley's to the beaming Wade, he paid something on his debt and had the gas tanks filled for the next day's work. When he was rowing ashore, Polly ran down to the beach to meet him.

"Come to the house and have some cabbage soup!" she called, before his skiff touched the small riffle of surf on the sand. The wind was blowing her hair around her face and whipping her skirt about her sturdy bare legs. The wind had stung her brown cheeks with red.

"Aren't you cold?" he asked, tying the painter around a log.

"Not very. You coming up and have some soup?"

"It'd taste mighty good," he admitted. "And thanks, Polly. I saw your father hauling outside the Point," he added. "He'll be ready for some hot soup before long."

She ran ahead of him to the house. He stopped by the fish-house long enough to leave his oilskins inside the door and then went on. The boys were already at the table. Linn glanced at the battered alarm clock on the kitchen shelf as he washed at the sink. "Is it that late?" he asked in astonishment. "No wonder I felt so lank on the way home."

"And you were gone right after daylight," she said. "You must have hauled them all."

"All I could find," he acknowledged and sat down to the table. He tasted the steaming soup, and grinned at her. "You're a good cook, Polly. You'll make some man a good wife."

She put her chin up. "Time I get through cooking for Pa and the kids, I'll want a vacation from such chores."

For several days this was his schedule, and he was duly thankful to Polly for the hot meals she had ready for him. He tried to pay her, but she refused, saying that he had done favors enough for her and her family. Now he could hardly wait to finish paying for the double-ender, and one day he took all that he had saved in the coffee can and gave it to Wade. It meant he had only twenty dollars more to pay. He made a daily visit to Grace and gave her the money from Wiley's traps, and an account of what he had done.

"Wiley's boat is a real craft, Grace," he said earnestly. "All a man could ask and hope for. You feel safe and secure and she handles so easy." He shook his head in envy and wonder. "Wiley sure got himself something the day he brought her home."

"I guess she's a good boat all right," Grace agreed.

Linn felt sorry for her, thinking how sad it was a woman couldn't know the joy in a man's heart for such things. She gave him a supply of bread and cookies, and a bag of freshly made doughnuts. "To help out with your cooking," she said. "Though I guess I don't need to worry about you. Polly seems to be doing that."

With the box of food under his arm he started back to the fishhouse, meaning to do some work on traps before dark. When he walked into the building, his grandfather stood by the workbench, looking at a hatchet that had been lying there. He turned it over slowly, staring at the blade, and Linn put down the box of food without a word, feeling a strange prickling at the back of his neck. He waited for his grandfather to speak, and the minutes dragged, while the old man studied the hatchet. Then he laid it on the bench carefully and turned around to look at Linn. "You seem to have quite a place here," he remarked. "I guess I'll have to charge you rent."

There was no humor in his tone, and Linn thought, *You'll probably do just that, to show your authority.* But he said nothing, only waited for disaster to strike.

The old man's gaze traveled slowly around the room, taking in the stack of canned beans and pea soup and corned beef on a little shelf near the door, the saucepan on the bench. "You do better here than at the house with me," he said slowly. "Here you can do as you please, with no one to see if it's the right thing to do. And you can be free to run with trash. You must like trash."

Linn's face blazed with anger. *Trash* meant the Armstrongs, simply because Bert was a ne'er-do-well. It didn't matter that he was kind, that Polly was Linn's loyal friend. All at once he realized how it must have gnawed at his grandfather to see him going into the Armstrong house so often, so openly. Grampa had sent Polly the eggs, but that didn't mean anything after all, as long as Bert was the way he was.

"Birds of a feather flock together," Grampa went on. "How much of your money have they begged off you?"

"None."

"They will." His grandfather nodded in sardonic satisfaction. "And then at last you'll be in the same box with Armstrong." He put his hands behind him and walked toward the doorway, and stood looking out at the harbor, peaceful in the afternoon light. Linn took a long breath.

"Polly and Bert have been good friends to me. I'll never turn my back on them for anyone."

Grampa didn't answer that but Linn was glad that he'd said it. It had been long overdue.

"Where is the double-ender?" his grandfather asked.

"Wade has her in his shed, repairing her," said Linn.

"So he had to take her back from you, eh?" The old man

turned a wicked black glance at the boy. "I could have told you something like this would happen. But you wouldn't have believed me. So you have to learn for yourself."

"He's not taking her away from me," cried Linn in a shaken voice. "And don't sound so happy about it! I'm not licked yet!"

"Don't raise your voice to me!" thundered the old man. He wheeled around and thrust his face close to Linn's. "You're still on charity. And folks who have to take charity have no right to lift their voice to those they owe. Not until you are a man, free and clear. Then you can raise your voice, to me—or anyone."

"I don't know what you mean about this charity business," said Linn hoarsely.

"This fishhouse that you are living in, using it to fix your traps, sleep in, make a roof over your head—are you paying for it? No. You pay nothing."

"But I will."

"Hah!" it was a sound of pure contempt. "*You* pay? So close to being a town charge, and you talk about pay!" He hooked his thumbs under his suspender straps and teetered on his heels and toes, his small bright eyes boring into the boy's steady gray ones.

"Say what you want for rent," said Linn doggedly. "I'll pay it, somehow." If only he hadn't just paid Wade all his savings! Then he could slap down a ten-dollar bill right now.

"Yes, somehow. And when?" The eyes bored deeper. "No." The old head shook slowly, almost sadly, but the eyes were still fierce. "You will have to take charity for a long time, unless you move in with the Armstrongs . . . then it can be the blind leading the blind."

"I don't have to take any more of your charity," cried Linn. "I can find another roof for my head, and not the Armstrongs, either."

"Go, then!" shouted the old man, raising his fist toward Linn's angry face. "Go, now! Take what is yours and go! I expect you to be cleared out by nightfall." He turned and walked out with outraged dignity.

Linn stood without moving, staring through the doorway at the harbor. Gulls swooped down to the water's edge, to wander about awkwardly in search of bits of food. Sometimes he watched them with an affectionate gaze, but today he hardly saw them. In the short space of a few minutes he had become a derelict, without a place to lay his head, to cook his meals, to fix his traps.

Suddenly he straightened his hunched shoulders and shook himself, as if to rid them of the weight of despair, and turned to survey the room. Take what was his, his grandfather had said. His small amount of clothing, packed in a cheap imitation-leather suitcase . . . oilclothes, boots . . . He studied the tools that lay on the bench and hung on the walls. *Charity*. Yes, it must look that way to the old man. Linn had nothing of his own except his traps, buoys, bait and clothing. He could take the clothing with him, but the bait and traps would have to remain where they were for the time being. Certainly Grampa couldn't expect him to move them right now.

He walked out of the building and back up across the wintery field of dead grass to the Abbott house. Grace was in the back yard, tying up some vines of rambler rose that the wind had torn loose from their fastenings. He gave her a hand wordlessly, and between them they soon had the vines snug and firm in place against the white clapboards. She said with a gusty sigh, "Well! I'm glad you came, Linn! I was doing some cussing under my breath when you showed up. Now let's go in and have some coffee and fresh doughnuts."

"I didn't come to eat," he said.

Instantly solemn, she stopped on the doorstep, "What's wrong, Linn?"

"Would it be all right if I slept aboard Wiley's boat for a while?"

"So that's it. Old Swenson's been at you again. Kicked you out for fair, eh?"

"Oh, I talked myself into it," said Linn with a wry smile. "I said I could find somewhere else to lay my head . . . talking kind of brave, that's all. He took me up on it so quick it made my head reel, said he wanted me cleared out by dark. So." He shrugged.

Grace didn't answer at once; her gaze moved beyond him to the black line of spruces against cloudy skies. Then she said abruptly, "You're welcome to stay here, Linn. I don't want to see you out in the cold."

He shook his head. "I'd rather stay aboard the boat—if I can. See if I can't work something out for myself by the time Wiley gets home."

"Or it gets really cold weather. You couldn't live there all winter."

"I suppose not," he admitted. "But I'd like to try it by myself for a little while, anyway. I have to do some thinking."

"Yes, I see what you mean," she said. "Well, you go ahead. Sleep aboard. But what about eating?"

"Oh, I can warm up something on the cabin stove," he said cheerfully. "I'll get along all right."

"You sure you don't want to be a hermit here, in comfort, while I'm off to the mainland?"

He kept shaking his head. "I appreciate it, don't think I don't. But it would put me too much in your favor—and I'm so deep in now."

She smiled. "You want to be independent, as much as you can. Well, after you've been so much under Swenson's thumb, I suppose it's only natural. Well, you go ahead and do your own figuring. But remember, there's a place at this table for you, anytime." She raised her hand. "Don't say 'Thank you' again. After all, you're tending Wiley's gear."

"I won't say a word," he promised. "But I can think it. Now I have to go pick up my stuff and take it aboard . . . just a few clothes and my boots. Don't sound too well off, do I?"

"Never you mind, now." She put an affectionate hand on his shoulder. "You keep your chin up. Things will work out. They *have* to."

He repeated her words as he went back to the shore. *Things will work out. They have to.* If they didn't, well— he was in a tough spot. But he shouldn't think of that now. He still had a place to sleep and a fire to warm his beans and tea. And friends. What was it Tom had said on that day after they had watched Randy sink the traps? *You may have more friends than you realize.* Well, it looked as if Tom was right.

CHAPTER SEVENTEEN

Linn Stands Accused

At the end of three days, the small cabin had fitted itself around him, and he felt very much at home. The lantern swung from a hook overhead and shed its warm glow on the lockers and the table where he sat to read and to eat his frugal meals. Later when he lay in his bunk in the dark, hearing the water slapping against the hull, he felt snug and secure. He knew that he would never forget this experience, or the feeling of being like a snail in its shell, taking its home wherever it might go. Now the boat was a part of him, home and shelter, where he spent his sleeping as well as his waking hours.

As the days were fair, though growing colder, he could work on his gear on the beach outside the fishhouse, but the bait remained inside. He let it stand, expecting any time that the old man would tell him to remove it. But when he did not, Linn realized that he had a sort of permission to let it remain under cover.

He was becoming quite adept at handling Wiley's gear with his own, and for the present his traps were being left alone. And, slowly, Norris Wade was getting the peapod repaired. Linn looked at her each day when he stopped to sell his lobsters and buy his food; he marveled at the careful way in which Wade bent and nailed the new timbers, the precision with which he measured and planed the new clean boards of pine for her bilge. No one had ever said anything about what must have happened to her. They had just glanced, and gone along. Linn knew that they wanted to keep clear of any trouble. He didn't blame them. When it came to them they just stood up to it, the way he was doing.

One afternoon when he had come in from hauling, and was setting his bait boxes on the wharf before he put Wiley's boat on the mooring, Polly's brother Raymond came running down the scarred planks, calling, "Hey, Linn. Wait!"

Linn caught hold of a spiling with his gaff and waited while Raymond hurried down the ladder. "Polly wants you to come to supper, Linn," the skinny youngster announced. "And can I go to the mooring with you?"

Linn grinned. "Sure. Glad to have you aboard. You can catch the mooring-buoy for me."

"We're going to have clam chowder for supper!"

"Who dug them? Not you, I bet. Your father?"

"Nope." Raymond shook his head. "Polly dug 'em. Took her quite a while, but she got enough for a chowder. And she wants you to have some."

Linn let the boat back slowly away from the wharf. He marveled at Polly's persistence. He knew what the clam digging was over in Seal Cove. You spent more time and strength turning over big rocks than in the actual digging. *Leave it to Polly,* he thought in admiration. *She got tired of asking her father and the boys to get some, so she did it herself.*

Raymond stood on the bow with the long gaff, proud and alert as the boat nosed gently up to the mooring. He caught the buoy and hauled it onto the deck. Linn shut off the motor and went up to the bow, pulled up the heavy chain and made it fast to the short, strong post that came up through the deck. Then they went aft and got into the skiff and rowed ashore.

The great bowl of chowder, steaming and fragrant, sat in the middle of the Armstrong kitchen-table. The children's faces were happy and anticipatory, and Bert gestured grandly. "Food for the gods, my boy! We had to have you share it with us!"

Polly winked at Linn, who answered her father gravely, "Thank you, I'd be glad to sit in."

Everyone fell to, and no one spoke except for the few necessary words in asking for bread or water. Polly kept an eye on the table as she ate, and got things quickly. When the bowl was emptied there was a sound of long sighing, and then Bert spoke reverently, "That was good. Mighty good! Makes a man send up thanks to his Creator."

Linn thought, *Polly needs some special thanks, too.* He caught her eye and said, "Thanks, Polly, for asking me in. It was a master of a chowder."

Little Jane went to play with her dolls, and the boys went

out. Their father called after them. "Now, you boys be in on time. No staying out all hours." He filled his pipe, and Polly began clearing off the table. Linn got up to help her, but she waved him back. "You set," she said. "You've done your work today. Now I'll do mine."

He sat down and Bert nodded through the pipe smoke wreathing about his head. "That's right, son. Never argue with a woman. Just set back and take it easy." He puffed a few times at his pipe and then gave Linn a strange shrewd glance from under his eyebrows.

"I just remembered," he said with odd reluctance. "Got something to tell you, son. Don't know as I should carry tales, but I don't know anybody else would tell you, and you've been a friend to me, letting me have bait when I knew darn well old Swenson would a skinned you alive if he'd heard about it. So I guess it won't do any harm for me to let you know what's being said about you around the shore."

Linn had taken off his boot to straighten his sock that had got twisted, and now he became motionless, his hands clasping his foot over his knee, his eyes wide and apprehensive on Bert's face.

"There's talk around the shore about me?" he asked slowly. So this was it; Randy was beginning his next move.

Bert nodded. "It's nothing I'd ever give a second thought to, but there's them that might, and I guess you know the kind they are. And who they are," he added.

"Bad talk, huh?" said Linn. He smoothed the sock, and folded his pant leg around his ankle, slid his foot into the boot, and stamped it on the floor. Bert watched him and then said, "Sounds plenty bad, son."

Suddenly Polly cried out, "Stop being so slow with it, Pa! Come out with it! And why didn't you tell me about it?"

"Didn't hear it till a couple hours ago. I meant to tell you, but it slipped my mind till supper, and then I thought I'd wait till the kids had gone out. Not saying they don't know it. There's mighty little they miss around the harbor."

"Might as well say it in short words," said Linn. "If there's bad talk about me, don't dress up what you heard, Bert. Let me have it straight." He tried to guess what it might be. Was Randy saying he hauled traps not his own?

Bert took a final puff and laid his pipe on the table. "Kingmans' have lost some of their best potwarp, son. Taken right out of their fishhouse. Brand new stuff, about sixty dollars worth."

"What's that to do with me?" asked Linn, aware of a disagreeable sensation in his stomach.

"Well, Randy got wind of it, and he's egging George Kingman into believing you took it." He leaned his elbows on the table and never took his eyes from the boy's face.

"What a lie!" Polly exploded, red-cheeked. "That's just like Randy, making such talk! I hope you told him a thing or two!"

Her father gave her a reproachful look. "How can you tell anything to anybody who doesn't want to listen? Nobody would hear me. They were all looking at Randy."

"I know." Linn was surprised that he could speak so quietly, after the first sick surprise. "I'm poor, without anything to my name. Rope costs plenty, and it wears out fast. It would tempt me, that rope, more than it would anyone else. That's what they think. You don't have to tell me what was in their minds . . . especially after Randy got spouting." He stood up and hitched at his belt. "But I'll bet Charles doesn't believe it."

"You're not going!" Polly objected. "I haven't even started my dishes. I thought you might sit and talk with Pa while I did them up."

Linn turned away from her disappointed face. He was too shaken to want to talk to anyone. He couldn't let this matter go through the night. How would he be able to sleep with this on his mind? He fumbled for words. "Don't think I'm ungrateful for the nice supper, Polly. But now that your pa has told me this, I have to do something about it."

"But what?" she asked.

"Yes, what?" echoed her father. "Rope is rope. Who can prove anything one way or the other?"

"I think I can prove something," said Linn. "In the first place, if I had new rope, where could I put it for safe keeping? In Grampa's fishhouse. Well, if there's none there—" He shrugged.

Bert sighed. "I think it's more than proving things. I think there's somebody after you for sure."

"So do I," admitted Linn. "I've known it for some time, but I couldn't prove that, either. But maybe I can prove this. At least I can make a try."

Bert picked up his faded old hat off the couch in the corner, and followed Linn outside. "Going over and talk to the Kingmans?" he asked.

"Yes. I'm going to—" Linn stopped in his tracks. "Look, Bert, I guess somebody is ahead of me again." He set his teeth together hard over his dismay and fury as he strode rapidly down the path to his grandfather's fishhouse. In the early dusk he could see several men standing near the doorway, peering in curiously.

As he approached, one of the men glanced around. "Make way, boys," he said amiably enough. "Here comes Linn. Let's see what he says about this."

The others stood back, their weathered faces noncommittal. Randy Mears' smooth dark cheekbones and black eyes stood out for a second in Linn's vision. Randy looked as blank as the rest. Then Linn went into the dim fishhouse, and Bert Armstrong crowded in behind him. Everyone was very quiet.

Linn crossed the long room, past the workbench, toward the corner where his grandfather and Mr. Kingman and Charles were standing, looking down wordlessly at a tumble of old canvas at their feet that showed up in the ray of a flashlight.

"What is this?" he demanded hoarsely.

Charles' face was red and worried. His father, usually so good-tempered and quick to laugh, turned a stern glance on Linn and didn't speak. He was holding a small coil of rope, a warp all measured and cut, ready to be tied on a trap.

"This," he said in a hard voice.

"Listen, Pa," Charles began, but his father ignored him.

Mr. Swenson asked suavely, "You think that is yours, George?"

"Of course it's mine. Nobody on here has been buying any of that red manila. Everyone else has been getting the green or the uncolored kind."

There was a general rumble of assent among the other men. "Looks like you're hemmed in, son," Armstrong muttered in Linn's ear. Linn was grateful for the man's presence. But if most of the others believed him guilty, Bert Armstrong's convictions of his innocence would certainly carry no weight at all.

Grampa turned to Linn now. "You got anything to say about this?" he asked Linn.

"Just that I don't know anything about it." Linn looked steadily back at the old man, trying to fathom his expression. But it was unreadable. "I've never stolen anything yet from anyone, and I don't intend to ever steal anything."

"Then how did the Kingmans' rope get in here?"

"I don't know." Gray eyes locked with black ones. "Do *you* think I stole it?"

Mr. Swenson didn't answer and Linn felt a new dismay, the deepest yet, rising painfully within him. Even his grandfather wouldn't come out before the whole island and say that he believed him innocent.

"Well, I don't believe the boy had anything to do with it," Bert Armstrong said unexpectedly, and Charles said, "Neither do I. Linn's stubborn as a hog on ice, but he's too darn proud to touch anything that doesn't belong to him."

"I know how you feel, son," Mr. Kingman said. "Linn's been your chum, and all. But you got to make allowances for human nature. Linn's had a tough time of it, we all know that, and when you're down and out it's awful easy to be tempted."

"I'm not down and out!" said Linn proudly. "I'm supporting myself! I don't have to steal what I need!" His fists clenched hard in his pockets. George Kingman looked at him almost kindly.

"I just heard today how many traps you've lost because your rope was so old and rotten—I can see where perhaps you couldn't resist taking that new rope. But it's made you a thief, you see, Linn, and you ought to know there's no room for a thief on Lee's Island."

"I'm *not* a thief!" Linn cried out.

"Pa, he's no more a thief than I am!" Charles blurted. "Somebody else hid that rope in here. They must have. Linn never did!"

"Son, by the time you're my age," his father said, "you'll know nobody's either all black or all white. There's a lot of shades of gray in between." He shook his big head heavily. "Carl, you'd ought not to have turned the boy out from under your roof, but I s'pose something like this would've happened sooner or later."

Grampa teetered a little on his toes. "Well, if that is your rope, take it and go. I don't want to stand here all night."

As Mr. Kingman stooped to gather up the coils, Linn felt

as if he were going to explode with outrage. "Those traps I lost—who said it was because the rope was rotten? Who dreamed that up? Is he scared to speak up?"

"No," Randy said softly from the crowd around the door. "I'm not scared to speak up." He came into the fishhouse and Linn walked toward him, his fists swinging lightly at his sides. "How do you happen to know so much about my traps?"

Randy smiled. "Because I've seen you lose traps while you were hauling. I can tell when a warp breaks before a man can get a trap onto the gunnel."

"You never saw me lose a trap that way!" Linn lunged toward that slim cocky figure and easy taunting smile, but the Kingmans caught him and held him back.

"Assault and battery won't make things any better for ye," George said warningly.

Charles muttered in Linn's other ear, "Easy, Linn, for Pete's sake."

Grampa cleared his throat and waved his arms at the gathering. "Get out, all of you. I am closing this fishhouse." He seemed absolutely undisturbed by all that was going on.

When everyone had gone outside, and most of them were strolling away uneasily in the dusk, Grampa pulled the sliding door shut, picked up the hardwood pin that hung on a string stapled to the doorcase, and put it through the huge old iron hasp. He went away without speaking. Although he had shown no emotion, Linn realized what a blow it had been to the old man to have his own flesh and blood accused of stealing. Linn was conscious of feeling a grim pride in his grandfather. But his grandfather had no such pride in *him*. The evidence had been too strong. Until Linn could prove he was innocent, he would be labeled a thief. He would be watched constantly, discussed endlessly, and if anything else happened it would be laid at his door.

Standing outside the fishhouse in the dark, hearing the sad little keening of the wind through a pile of traps like the voice of his own misery, Linn had forgotten Bert until the man cleared his throat. "Come on up to the house, son," Bert said to him.

"No, thanks, Bert." All at once Linn felt so tired that it was an effort to speak. "Maybe later. I—I'm much obliged to you for standing up for me."

"I'll always do that, son. Well, you come up when you get ready."

Linn stood with his hands in his pockets, listening wearily to Bert's footsteps die away on the path. Then another pair of footsteps approached and he spun around, his heart beating fast. Had Grampa come back? But it was Charles, grumbling. "I had to help the old man lug that cussed rope home. I argued with him all the way, but he kept telling me the flesh was weak, and all that stuff."

"I guess he really believes it," Linn's mouth twitched wryly. "Sounded real sympathetic to me until he came right out and called me a thief."

Charles sighed and sat down on the chopping block. "You're in a bad spot, Linn. Everybody believes the same thing as he does. And they won't stop believing it until they know just who put that rope there and why."

"I know who put it there," said Linn between his teeth.

Charles dropped his voice. "I guess I do now," he murmured. "Come to me all of a sudden, when you and Randy were having the towse about the traps. Funny how something strikes you like lightning. I didn't have anything to go on except my feelings, but I knew you were telling the truth when you said you never lost any traps from rotten rope."

"Thanks, Charles," Linn said huskily. "That's an awful little word, but it's the only one I can think of. Thanks."

"Ayeh." Charles got up. "Well, I don't know what he's got against you, but I knew he can be mean. You'll have to be pretty foxy to catch him. But you've *got* to catch him, Linn. A lot of people don't like the guy, on account of his lip, but nobody's ever seen him do anything crooked, and his family's known to be honest." He wheezed loudly. "Just listen to me. I'm dryer than a cork leg. I need a drink of hot coffee. Let's go and get a mug-up from Polly."

CHAPTER EIGHTEEN

Tom Lowell Comes to Call

It was good to sit again with Charles in the Armstrong kitchen, and laugh, and tell jokes with Polly, and as the evening passed there were moments when Linn almost forgot what had just happened.

Once Charles asked, "How much you paying Wade for fixing the peapod?"

"Nothing," Linn answered.

"*Honest?*" Charles sat back in amazement.

"What's so surprising about that?" Polly snapped. "Can't a person do something for Linn once in a while?"

Charles laughed at her indignation, his blue eyes bright. "Of course he can. But Wade? I always thought he had a price for everything."

"All I know is, I asked him once how much I owed him, and he said, 'Nothing.' Maybe he likes working on boats as

a change from keeping store. Of course I'm going to pay for
the materials he used. I didn't expect him to use his stuff."

"Yes, that would be charity," mused Polly.

Linn flushed. "I don't like that word."

"I didn't mean anything by it," she apologized. "Excuse
me, Linn. You've had enough things said today. I don't
wonder you feel sensitive about everything."

Armstrong came into the kitchen in his heavy socks, walking as quietly as a cat. He took up the old alarm clock and
wound it and put it back on the little shelf behind the stove.
"Time to hit the kelp, boys," he said affably. "Polly has to
be up and doing early, and I guess you have to, too."

Charles grabbed up his jacket in a great flurry of pretended wrath. "I can take a hint. It's a wonder you don't
shove us out with a pitchfork!"

Everyone laughed, and there was a confusion of good
nights. Charles walked with Linn along the path until he
had to turn to his own dooryard. "Don't forget what I said,"
he reminded Linn in a low voice. The island night was fog-
bound and utterly still.

"It's not likely it'll leave my mind," Linn answered dryly.
"Not when the rest of my life depends on it."

"Good. Well, g'night."

" 'Night."

Going down to the wharf, Linn thought with affection of
Charles. But he could not help a sigh as he considered the
difference in their circumstances. Charles was going home
to a good bed in a real house, where there was abundant love
and understanding for whatever he might try to undertake.
But for Linn there were the tight confines of the cabin, and
the narrow bunk, and the silence that was absolute. No
sound of others moving beyond the partition, no murmur
of voices, no greetings called out. Linn was alone, and as he
rowed across the harbor, he reviewed the scene in his grand-

father's fishhouse, and realized how empty and lost everything seemed.

How could he prove who did this thing to him? His mind was so bewildered that he could think of no plan. He would have to sleep on it, mull it over, watch and listen.

The skiff bumped softly against the side of Wiley's boat, and he drew in his oars and climbed into the cockpit. He tied the painter astern, and blinked at the small dory that floated ghostlike there. He hurried to the cabin and flung open the slide to the companionway. It was dark within, but he smelled the sweet scent of pipe tobacco. Into the blackness he said softly, "That you, Tom?"

Out of the blackness the reply came. "Nobody else. I was beginning to think you were going to sleep at Armstrongs' tonight. If you'd waited longer, you'd have found me in your bunk."

Linn went down the little ladder and fumbled for matches in the wooden box nailed to the wall. He lit the lantern, blinking against the glow, and saw Tom sitting on a locker, his back against the wall, his feet propped on the locker opposite. His arms were folded, and one hand cradled his straight-stemmed pipe. His black slouch hat was pulled low on his forehead, and from under its brim he stared broodingly at Linn through the mist of tobacco smoke.

"You're wondering why I'm here? Well, sit down and I'll tell you."

"Gorry, Tom, you gave me a start!" Linn dropped onto a locker. "It's been quite a night for starts, all in all."

Tom puffed at his pipe. "Did you see me standing at the back of the crowd by Mr. Swenson's fishhouse, when that rope hunt was going on?"

Linn shook his head. "I didn't look around much. I couldn't say for sure who stood there. I'm glad you saw how it was, Tom." He pounded his fist softly on his knee.

"What am I going to do about it? I've been named a thief, and I've got to wash the name off. It's easier said than done."

Tom nodded slowly, his eyes glinting like jet buttons in the lantern light. Linn watched the thin face, waiting patiently for Tom to speak his mind, and in the silence he could hear the lapping of small waves against the side of the boat.

Tom leaned forward after a time and put his pipe on the galley stove. "I saw it done, Linn," he said placidly. "But I don't know how you'll prove it. Wait," he put up his hand as Linn was about to interrupt. "Yes, I saw the whole thing, but you and I both know how people feel about Tom Lowell. He's touched, daffy, barmy. They did call me Barmy Lowell once."

"How could they?" cried Linn. "You never did anything to harm anyone!"

"No. But I have strange notions. That's what they say. Not to my face—oh, no. But I hear what is said. I just don't let them know that I've heard." His long white hand came up and caressed his chin. "They think I'm not right in the head, Linn. I know it, and I accept it. I realize that without proof I can't change their ideas. And without proof you're going to be called a thief."

He paused and sighed. "The world is strange, Linn, but the men who inhabit it are stranger."

He sat silent and finally Linn said, as casually as he could, "Do you mind giving me some details on what you saw, Tom. I'd be much obliged."

"Oh, yes, yes." Tom started up quickly, as if he had been miles away. He stroked his mustache, to the right and to the left, and the black lustrous growth gleamed in the light.

"It was like this." He spoke meticulously. "I was waiting in the loft of Swenson's fishhouse a few nights ago, waiting for you to come. I thought we might talk a little. I didn't know you were staying aboard here, then. I was sitting on a box near the stairs, when I heard someone sliding the door over, and it roused me. I leaned forward and was just about to call down the stairs, thinking it was you, when I saw these coils of rope tossed inside on the floor. 'That's strange,' I thought. 'Linn doing chores this time of night.' And then someone moving like a cat came inside and closed the door. I kept perfectly still. A flashlight was laid on the bench, pointing toward the far corner, and within the light I could watch a man carry the rope across and toss it in a pile and then pull the old canvas over it. I could see clearly who the person was, especially when he leaned down to tuck the canvas more neatly around the rope."

He stopped talking.

"It was Randy," said Linn in a colorless voice. His mouth felt stiff. It was one thing to suspect Randy, to feel sure that he had done it; it was another thing to anticipate his name on another's lips.

Tom nodded. "It was Randy. I never knew he was capable of moving so quietly. He went in and out of the building without a scrape of sound, except when he opened and closed the door. He couldn't keep the rollers from squeaking a little."

"He's really after me, Tom. In any way he can think of, he's going to try and ruin me. Drive me off this island."

"Then you've got to catch him the next time he does it."

"Next time?"

"Oh, there'll be a next time, don't worry." A faint smile flickered around Tom's thin mouth. "George Kingman got his rope back. He's a kind man, he might be inclined to give you another chance. It has to happen again, so there'll be no doubt that you're a menace to the community, and the community will tell you to go. Randy can't drive you openly, but he can do it this way. He'll keep trying until the rest of them get angry enough to put an end to it. They'll do his dirty work for him."

"And there are three ways he can drop the ax on me," Linn said slowly. "More stealing—more stuff stowed away in the fishhouse for them to find. Or he can go back to work on my traps. He starts out earlier than anybody else in the morning and stays out longer, so he can do a lot without being seen, if he sets his mind to it; and I can't afford the gas to chase him all day." He looked around at the snug lantern-lit cabin. "The third thing is to harm this boat somehow, when I'm responsible for her. Make it look as if I couldn't be trusted to take care of her." The thought of harm coming to Wiley's boat and himself being blamed made him feel sick in his stomach. He leaned back against the curved wall and laughed weakly. "The question is, do I wait for the ax to fall, or get out before I'm kicked out?"

"Or do you put an end to this mess," Tom asked in a soft voice, "before the rest do? Randy's watching for a chance to trap you. But who's watching Randy?" He took his pipe off the stove and tucked it into his pocket. "He's not likely to hurt the boat, since you're aboard most of the time. To harm your traps—well, that wouldn't discredit you before the others. No, it'll be thievery again, he's already laid the groundwork for that." Tom stood up to go.

"I thought once that all I had to do was hold out longer than he could," Linn said. "I was sure he'd make a slip sooner or later. But when he left my traps alone, he sank my peapod. I never expected that. And this—tonight—well, it knocked me galley west." He stared at Tom, his heart beating fast. "Do you think there's *really* a chance—"

"Strength and patience," murmured Tom. "And a little craftiness on your part." He smiled and went up the companionway to the cockpit.

Linn climbed up behind him, and stood leaning against

the slide as Tom went aft and pulled his dory alongside the boat. As he stepped in and took up his oars he said, "Don't let the weather discourage you, boy. A stormy night might be just the time you could trap your fox."

Without waiting for an answer, he rowed off into the dark. For a long time Linn stood listening to the rhythmic sound of rowlocks, until it had faded into the night.

Down in the cabin, he took off his clothes and got into the bunk. *Sleep tight, son,* he told himself. *From tonight on, you won't see this bunk till morning. No matter how much sleep the rest of the island is getting, you've got to be on your toes, with your ears and eyes wide open. You've got to clear yourself of a bad name, or else pack your bag and leave this place.*

I won't give up as quick as Randy thinks, he said to himself, as he moved into a comfortable position. *He doesn't know how stubborn I can be. Nobody knows. But we're all going to find out.*

The boat swung at her mooring, following the pull of the tide. The air was chill with fog from the open sea. When daylight came the wind sprang up and pushed the fog back to the distant reaches of the ocean. Linn slept heavily and was not awakened until a flock of crows clamored in the spruces of the harbor point.

He got up quickly and built his fire, made his coffee, and ate the cold biscuits and molasses that Polly had given him. Usually he whistled while he moved about, but this morning his thoughts were too sober for that. He knew it might be a long time before he whistled again in the morning.

CHAPTER NINETEEN

A Veiled Threat

Beginning on that day, Linn set himself a course of action that he hoped would be successful. *Patience and perseverance,* that was his motto. And as he waited through the long hours of the first night, he realized that it might take a great deal more patience and perseverance, than he had guessed. Supposing Randy waited two months before he struck again? Linn tried not to visualize the punishment he would have to take in the meantime.

His routine was a simple one. That night, as soon as all the lights were out on the island, Linn rowed ashore. He avoided the harbor beach, thinking that Randy would be sure to check all the dories, skiffs and peapods drawn up there. He went instead to a little cove just outside the harbor, and hauled Wiley's light skiff up to the grass where she would be safe. His long legs carried him rapidly through the small wood behind the village. Skirting back yards with their clotheslines and henhouses, keeping clear of the houses that had dogs who might hear even the stealthiest footfall on the hardening ground, he reached his grandfather's fishhouse. He could have gone inside, for the door was fastened only by the wooden pin through the hasp, but he wanted to trap Randy alone inside, not himself and Randy together.

Outside, near the door where the traps were piled, he fixed a sort of blind among them. The slats held off some of the wind, but not the November cold, and soon he was stiff and cramped from sitting motionless so long on an old lobster crate. He wished that Randy would become impatient and get started planning another theft. He wore all the extra pants and jackets that he could, and wrapped a woolen scarf over his ears, for after the first half hour the wind that came swooping across the harbor waters, whistling along the eaves and fluttering loose shingles on the fishhouse, bit to the bone.

The second night it snowed, and he crept to his blind among the traps by a roundabout way, so that Randy would not see his tracks; as he waited, the flakes came down and lay in little drifts on his still figure, filling the wrinkles in the sleeves, falling off only when he stretched his cramped limbs. He did not mind the snow as much as he minded the cold.

As soon as the darkness began to thin, he crept around the village and through the wood to the beach where his skiff waited. He was so cold as he rowed back to the harbor that he thought he would never be warm again. He crawled aboard Wiley's boat, and fell into his bunk. It kept on snowing all day, so he did not have to think about going to haul. And the day after that there was a high wind, making it too rough to find the buoys. So he had plenty of time to sleep. And if they wondered why he was keeping to himself so much, let them wonder. Let them think him morose and downcast. Let them think he had a guilty conscience. They could think anything they wished about him until he caught Randy.

He went ashore in the daytime only to get food at the store, and on the fourth day he met Charles there. Charles treated him to a bottle of pop and asked in a low voice, "Uh —you doing anything?"

"All I can," Linn said curtly, and Charles asked nothing more. There'd be time to talk about it when it was all over, time to laugh and tussle with Charles again.

Polly was frankly worried and she rowed out to the boat later that same afternoon and banged her oar against the washboard, calling, "Linn! You there?"

He awoke, groaning, and put his tousled head out the companion way. "Of course I'm here. Don't you see the skiff astern?"

"Can I come aboard?" She clung to the rail with one hand, her eyes pleading. "I want to talk to you. Why don't you come in any more, Linn? You don't think it helps to stay away, do you?"

He eyed her gloomily, and pushed his hand through his hair.

"Linn," she said anxiously, "you don't look good. I think you're coming down with something."

"Maybe I am," he glowered. "Maybe I've got the rising bum-flummox."

"I'm not joking," she said. "Please, Linn. Will you come over to supper? Nice hot biscuits and baked beans and cold lobsters. That sound appetizing?"

"Beans and hot biscuits," he mused. "Did I ever have any before in my life?" He grinned suddenly. "I guess it's true —the way to a man's heart is by way of his stomach. Polly, I accept your invitation, with many thanks." He put his hand on his chest and bowed to her.

She laughed delightedly. "I'm glad you can still smile, Linn. I was worried that all this stealing business was making you crack up. I don't want you getting like Tom Lowell . . . you know how folks call him off his head."

"Don't worry. It would take more than this stealing business to make me crack up. Now you go on home and tend to your beans."

"Okay, Linn." She pushed away from the boat and rowed ashore. He watched her; it was nice to know somebody worried about him. It helped a lot.

As he rowed to Wade's wharf in the wintry dusk, his clothes changed, his hair brushed back neatly under the old visored cap, he saw Randy standing by the store. Immediately he felt the tide of impotent anger that he experienced every time he saw Randy now; his hands tightened harder on the oars. There would have to be a real showdown, how could it be otherwise? All this talk about getting along with your neighbor peacefully! How was it possible when your neighbor hated you and wanted to do you harm? Never mind if the island was small, and the people had to use tact, diplomacy, or whatever they wanted to call it. There came a time when nothing counted but good straight talk, and—if necessary—a couple of good straight pokes to the jaw. Old Swenson didn't go around using tact. Maybe folks didn't like him too well, but they let him alone and didn't try to drive him off. Maybe they *had* tried to, once, but he was still here.

Linn tied up the skiff at the car and went up the wharf to the store. He went in without a glance at Randy, who in turn seemed so intent on the view of the harbor in the late light that he didn't see Linn. Wade was alone in the store, and greeted Linn jovially.

"Well, the peapod's all mended and prettied up good as new! You can put her back on the haul-off anytime now."

For Randy to sink again or cut loose? Linn thought. *But nobody'd dare tamper with her on Wade's property.* Aloud he said, "Do you think I could leave her in your shop for a little while longer?"

"Leave her as long as you like, boy. You want some candy, do you?" He moved around behind the penny-candy case, and Linn made a choice of a quarter's worth, for the Armstrong children. As the big man filled the bag, he said in a much softer tone than usual, which Randy couldn't possibly have heard, "What about this rumpus in Swenson's fishhouse the other night?"

It was the first time he had mentioned it to Linn since it had happened five days ago; whenever Linn had come to the

store or the wharf, someone else had been around. He smiled
faintly. "Oh, somebody mislaid something, that's all."

"Guess they went way out of their tracks to mislay it, didn't
they?" Wade chuckled deep in his chest. "Everybody fussing
and carrying on . . . I listen to 'em out here, when I'm in the
post office sorting the mail, and I think, 'You boys better
save your breath to cool your porridge. You may be feeling
pretty foolish one of these days.' "

Linn looked at him steadily. *He's telling me he doesn't
believe I stole,* he thought. Then he handed over his quarter
and took the bag of candy, saying, "Thanks, Mr. Wade.
Thanks very much." He knew the man would understand
what his thanks were really for.

As he turned to go, Wade exclaimed, "Oh, I meant to tell
ye. Had a card from Grace today, telling me to hold their
mail. They think they'll be home next week."

"Wiley will be some happy to get off the mainland," Linn
answered. "Well, good night." He went out, again passing
Randy without a sidewise look; but this time Randy's voice
followed him, deceptively gentle. "Where's the party? You
look so neat for a change, must be you got a girl. Is that it?"

Linn walked back to him. Randy stood with his hands in
his pockets, smiling, as if Linn were too insignificant to
worry about. "I know. You're going to have supper with
Polly. I saw her rowing out to the boat. I should be glad
that somebody takes pity on you and gives you a decent meal
now and then. But frankly, I'm not. I think you know where
you stand with most of the Lee's Islanders, though."

"I know where I stand with *you!*" Linn tried to keep his
voice unruffled. But the ache to grab Randy and shake him
till his teeth rattled put a slight tremor in it.

"Look," said Randy, and the silkiness was gone. "Why
don't you give up now and get off the island while you're all

in one piece? You know what's ahead of you, now, don't you?" His dark eyes seemed to glitter in their intensity.

"Ayeh, I know what's ahead of me," Linn answered stoically. "It never was clearer in my mind. But I'm not leaving the island—yet."

They glared at each other like two cockerels, and Linn remembered how they had faced each other on that day so long ago, each determined to possess the dinghy for his own; one sure of his right to it by discovery, the other sure of his right to it by force.

Randy's gaze dropped first and he turned away. "Go fill yourself with good food," he scoffed. "Do it while you can. Your stay on this island may be much shorter than you think."

"Thank you for the information," said Linn urbanely. "I will consider what you have to say." As he walked away, he was surprised and amused. He had sounded just like Grampa when the old man was up to something.

He arrived at Polly's house in a much better frame of mind than he had expected. The few words with Randy had amounted to an open gesture to which he could reply; it wasn't like the rope affair, a blow struck at him in the dark.

At Armstrong's and Polly's urging, which he did not need, he ate beans and fresh boiled lobster and hot biscuits till he was completely stuffed. But he was hungry for more than food; for the light and warmth of the kitchen, with its wood fire crackling and teakettle singing; for the children's chatter dispelling silence and loneliness.

When he finally sat back, sighing gustily, Armstrong laughed. "Polly had a good idea when she rowed off to see what was up with you! You shouldn't hang off there like that, son. We're your friends, you know that. Come in like you used to. We haven't much, but you're welcome to share it, any time."

"I know it," said Linn humbly. "I should have dropped in more, but somehow I just didn't."

"I guess I know how it was." Bert wagged his head. "You got kind of a shock. You don't need to explain about it. Anybody would be set back on his heels hard, if he'd come face to face with such a thing." He chewed at his ragged mustache. "It'd be too bad if it happened again like that, son. Been a long time since anybody stole anything on here. And that fellow was caught and sent off bag and baggage. Not room for a thief on here, son. You could see why."

"Of course. It would seem kind of peculiar having men lock their doors. I never saw a locked door here. Nothing but the hardwood pins in the hasps, to keep them from blowing open in a gale of wind."

"I wish you could find out who did it!" Polly flamed at him.

"I've got to prove what I find out," said Linn. "And that's the tough part."

"I suppose so!" She began clearing the table, and the boys went out to bring in some wood for the fire. "When are Grace and Wiley coming home? I know he must be pretty comfortable at his sister's, but I should think he'd be itching to come home."

"He is," said Linn. "Wade got a card from Grace in the mail today. She said they're planning to be home next week sometime." It was the first time he had thought of it since the encounter with Randy.

Polly opened her mouth, but closed it again. Linn knew what must have been on the tip of her tongue. Where would he sleep and eat when Wiley came back? Would he be able to stay aboard the boat as he was doing now?

But he couldn't think about that now; he would cross that bridge when he came to it.

CHAPTER TWENTY

The Trap Is Sprung

When Linn left the Armstrongs' at nine o'clock, the night wind was cold, the stars frosty bright. The boats pointed to the north as they rode on their moorings. At the wharf he got into the skiff, then he rowed around the corner of the wharf and tied the skiff to an out-of-the-way section, where the pipe from the gas tanks ran along the edge, and where there were many empty lobster crates stacked in long ranks.

Nimbly he climbed the spilings and moved across the wharf. The starlight gave him good visibility, the slosh of water around the spilings and on the rocks hid the sound of his boots on the planks. There was not a light to be seen. All the men were counting on tomorrow being a fine day to haul and had gone to bed in good season. He wondered if Randy would choose tonight for anything. Probably not. But Linn had begun this thing, and he must go on with it until something happened, one way or another. He shivered inside his jacket, not from the cold, but from the possibility of having to go through many more nights in this same fashion.

He went along the shore to the fishhouse and settled himself into his hiding place among the traps. Somehow it was harder tonight. Had the few hours with Polly and her family softened him, so that the thought of crouching here for hours made his muscles ache? However, he must go through with it. This *might* be the night.

As he sat with his back against the rounded sides of weathered lobster traps, he could peer through the slats of other traps and see a light flashing on the horizon, far to the north. But above him the stars were brighter than the distant lighthouse. He fell to marking their positions, and became so engrossed that he was startled almost into jumping to his feet when he heard the sound of someone moving cautiously over the pebbles outside the door. He held his breath and strained to see, but the traps broke his vision. Then he heard the door creak as it was pushed open. He stood up with infinite care, and against the grayish shape of the fishhouse wall in the starlight, he could see a black square—the open doorway. He slid out of his blind and crossed the littered yard in a long savage leap, grabbed the door and pulled it across and caught up the heavy hardwood pin to thrust through the hasp.

All in that moment, he realized that whoever was inside might smash a window and get out. Then, as though a weight lifted from his body, he remembered seeing his grandfather, only a few days before, nail heavy boards over the windows to prevent the violent storms of winter from loosening panes that might blow out, and to keep snow from beating into the building. The old man had methodically nailed each board hard and fast, and Linn had thought how Grampa always made preparations for any eventuality. He blessed the old man now. For whoever was inside would stay inside, until someone let him out.

The marauder made no sound. There was something uncanny about his trapped silence. Linn stood still, his heart pounding. Whom should he awaken? And then he knew that Wade was the man. He was the constable for the island; the men always laughed when they voted him in, saying that it was only for the book. But now it would be more than for the book. It would be for Linn's defense.

He ran along the shore, his boots thumping loudly against the frozen ground. Wade's house was only a little distance behind the store. Linn pounded on the back door and shouted, and his heartbeat was as loud in his ears as his fists on the door. Then he heard Wade's muffled roar.

"What in Tophet is all the touse about? Can't you let a man sleep?" The roar came nearer, and the door swung open. Wade stood with a lamp in his hand, staring sleepily out into the night. He had pulled his work pants on over his nightshirt. "Anybody sick?" he asked, his face sharpening.

Linn thought, *Yes, that's about all the trouble any body expects on here.* "Will you come with me?" he gasped. "I've caught that rope thief!"

Wade set the lamp down on a table near him. Linn kept talking as if he couldn't stop. "I've got him penned in Grampa's fishhouse. He might get out somehow. I don't see how he could, but he might. I want you to come and help me with him."

"Who is it?" asked Wade.

"I don't know. I didn't see his face. But somebody went in. And he had no business to, not in the middle of the night like this."

"What are *you* doing out in the middle of the night?"

"I was watching—oh, I'll tell you that later!" Was ever a man so miserably slow! "You've got to come with me! You're the constable. You're the law on here."

"Well—" Wade reached for his big mackinaw on the wall. "I don't know what this is all about but it better have some sense to it. I don't like being hauled out of bed in the middle of the night."

He called to his wife that he would be back soon, and lighted a lantern. They walked back rapidly, but to Linn it was as if they crept slowly. He kept saying to himself, *I hope Grampa nailed those boards with tenpenny spikes. I hope he's not gone when we get there.*

But there was no sign of a broken window in the wide circle of lantern light. Wade pulled the wooden pin out and opened the door just enough for him to put the lantern through and then his head.

"All right," a sulky voice said out of the dark. "You can stop shining that light around. I know when I'm caught."

"*Randy!*" Wade grunted in astonishment. He peered inside.

"That's right. Randolph Mears, Esquire. Who's with you? Linn?"

"Yes, Linn," said Wade. "He says he caught the rope thief." His whole tone changed and deepened. "What's all this about, anyway? What're you doing in Swenson's fishhouse like this? Answer me, son!"

"He's hiding rope, the way he did the other time!" Linn exploded. "So I'll get blamed for that, and get ordered off the island." He tried to get past Wade into the fishhouse, but the big man's arm held him back. "Let me go in first, son."

He stepped over the threshhold and Linn followed, his heart beating fast.

"It was just a joke, Norris," said Randy placatingly.

"Funny way to joke," growled Wade. "Trying to turn the men against Linn. Doesn't sound like a joke to me."

"Oh, I was going to come out and tell them the truth, later. I just wanted to get him worked up a little. That's all."

"So you brought more rope here tonight?" Wade was grim. "Let me see."

"Well, not exactly rope. I thought I'd vary it a little." He laughed, but the laugh was nervous.

"Let's see how you varied it," Wade said.

Randy pointed to the canvas in the corner beyond the workbench. "You can see for yourself," he said lightly.

"Oh, no!" Linn tucked his thumbs in his belt. "You drag it right out here yourself."

"Randy, I don't like the look of this," Norris Wade broke in. "It has a bad odor about it. In fact, it stinks to high heaven. Pull that canvas off so I can see what you've got here."

Randy pulled back the canvas, and Linn gasped. Glimmering in the lantern light, nested carefully on some rope, lay a couple of hammers, a new block plane, some bright chisels, and a small handsaw.

"*Well, now!*" Wade stroked his jaw. "This is valuable stuff, Randy. How did you think you could smooth it out for Linn, after you got everybody thinking he was a thief?" He cocked his graying head toward the older boy.

The lantern on the workbench cast a yellow glow over the room, on the three occupants, on the tools and the old rusty stove, and in its light Linn contemplated Randy, wondering what he would do next. He even felt a reluctant admiration for Randy; caught in the act, he seemed perfectly at ease, his yachting cap at a rakish tilt, his hands in his blue reefer pockets, his black eyes brilliant. He was about to be shamed before the whole village, before his own father, but he didn't seem to care.

"Maybe I wasn't ever going to smooth it out for Linn!" Randy answered Wade. "If you hadn't caught me, I'd have fixed it so he could never put a foot on here again." His smile was thin and taut.

"I didn't catch ye," said Wade stolidly. "I was home in bed, snoring. It was Linn who had the patience to catch you red-handed."

Randy leaned against the workbench and stared fixedly at Linn. "You're quite a smart guy to have around, I guess. Always right on deck to do the right thing at the right time. Isn't that so?"

"I want to do what's right, if I can," Linn said.

Randy mocked him. "So you want to do what's right! That's the biggest laugh I ever heard. And you're the biggest piece of conceit that I ever saw walking around. Why don't you take yourself away from where you're not wanted? Why do you insist on staying where you don't belong?"

"Because I *have* got a right here," said Linn doggedly. "I've got a right. My grandfather—"

"*Huh!*" The laugh was high-pitched. "Your grandfather doesn't want you either. He's shoved you around plenty— kept your nose to the grindstone, trying to drive you out without actually telling you in so many words to go. I've heard him giving you what-for in this fishhouse plenty of times. I thought you'd have brains enough to get out before I had to go to all this trouble—"

"You certainly did go to a lot of trouble," interrupted Wade. "Who does this stuff—" he jerked a thumb at the tools on the canvas—"belong to? You?"

"No. It's not mine, but I don't have to explain it now. I'm just telling this mainland dolt—"

"Oh, cut it out, Randy," Wade advised him. "It won't do you any good."

"Well, this might, then," cried Randy in a wild, broken voice. "Take *this,* you—you scavenger!" He picked up an old broken-clawed hammer from the work bench and rushed at Linn.

"Look out!" Wade yelled. "You crazy?"

Linn saw the hand with the hammer raised above his head, and his own hand flew up, clamping itself around Randy's wrist, holding the hammer away. The two boys wrestled briefly, and then Randy said breathlessly, "All right, I'll put it down. Let me go."

"Drop it," ordered Linn. "Just drop it."

Randy opened his hand, the hammer dropped to the floor,

and automatically Linn looked down at it. In that instant Randy came up with his other fist and struck Linn on the jaw.

It was a glancing blow, but it stung both Linn's face and his pride. The anger that had been held down for so long boiled up with such passion that he forgot everything except his great hunger to smash Randy's face. He had been wanting to smash it for a long time; to drive the hateful smile, the hateful words, back into that smirking mouth. Now he would do it, and nobody could stop him.

He leaped at Randy with savage pleasure. He felt Randy's fist on his cheek, but it didn't jar him. It gave his own arm extra impetus; he struck out hard and knew the blow landed, but Randy came right back at him. They both stood firm, trading blows, grunting, panting, and Linn barely heard Wade as he ordered them to quit.

"Cut it out, you two!" he shouted, and moved toward them, reaching out his two big hands to separate them.

Stop now? thought Linn, as he swung his right fist toward Randy's jaw, ducking the blow that Randy was throwing at him. *After all I've been through, after all this time? Stop now? I can't stop. This has to go through to the finish.*

Before Wade could grab their collars and hold them apart, Randy caught Linn in a wrestling hold and they went down with a crash on the chip-littered floor. They rolled and twisted wildly, each trying to gain the upper hand.

Wade shrugged his huge shoulders and moved back out of their way. "S'pose I might as well let you two have it out," he rumbled. "Nothing I can do about it, anyway."

They rolled across the floor, first Randy on top, clawing for Linn's throat, and then Linn holding Randy down; they came up against the legs of the bench with a bone-jarring impact. The lantern trembled, the flame flickered and smoked. In another moment they had jolted back across the floor, with a tremendous banging of heads and heels, and this time they collided with the old stove. A brick that held up one corner, where a leg had been broken, was thrust out of place by someone's elbow, and the stove lurched heavily down on one side. The blow didn't wholly dislodge the stovepipe, but soot rattled down inside it and showered from a crack in the rusty joints.

"Good thing there's no fire in there," Wade growled, but they didn't hear him. They rolled over and over, breathing hard through clenched teeth. As one of Randy's violent surges carried them toward the door, Wade pulled it shut so that they wouldn't fall out over the sill.

Both boys were gasping for breath and their clothes were covered with chips and sawdust. Linn felt himself tiring, his arms and legs ached with strain, but he knew he had to keep on. Randy must not win this battle. He had won out on all the other things, but this time he must not. He would still find ways to persecute Linn, unless he knew absolute defeat now. The thought gave Linn the last desperate burst of strength that he needed, and in a sudden convulsive motion he broke Randy's hold and pinned him heavily to the floor. It was the end of Randy's strength too; Linn felt the savage springiness go out of him. There was a sudden quiet, in which their labored breathing seemed very loud. Then Randy said slowly, "Okay. I'm beat. Let me up."

Linn got up and Randy struggled to his feet, wiping his bruised face. Linn's nose was bleeding and he held his handkerchief against it. Wade surveyed them unemotionally.

"Well, I hope this clears the air. You fellers must have been needing it for a long time, from the way you went at it."

Randy, his black hair rumpled, his face smeared with blood and soot, stared around him glassily, his lips moving without sound.

"I guess this settles everything," Linn said. "Wade is a witness. He'll speak for both of us, Randy."

"You're darn' right I will! I never thought I'd run up against any such actions on *this* hunk of rock and grass. It's plumb disgraceful when a couple of boys can't live and work and be neighborly, without there being this kind of trouble." He turned a stern glance on Randy. "You've set yourself in an awful awkward place, boy."

"I'm going home," Randy said. He pushed the door open and went out.

Wade shook his head after him, and picked up the lantern. "Well, this has been quite a night." He yawned mightily. "Guess I'll go home too. We can talk more about this to-morrow, or today, whatever the time is."

"It's near midnight, I think." Linn was surprised at how calm he felt. He brushed the chips off his clothes and picked up his cap.

They walked together as far as the wharf, and said good night. Linn went down to his skiff. The stars were still as bright and clear as they had been earlier. Nothing on the island was changed. The shadows of the houses looked as they always had; the wharves jutting out into the water were the same, and so was the sound of the water gurgling around the spilings. It was hard to believe that the long stretch of waiting had paid off and it was over, and that Wade knew the truth and could speak out for him. He was in the clear. *In the clear.* He wouldn't have to leave the island on that account now. He could stay and go on fishing his traps.

Back in the cabin at last, he looked into the small mirror tacked against the wall and saw his eyes puffed and red, the streaks of soot, and the bruises darkening on his cheeks and jaw. Randy had a good right fist, no mistake about that. He touched his face gingerly. But it was worth it, to have done some punching on his own account; and he had wrestled

Randy into hollering *uncle.* Now maybe Randy would believe that Linn could stand up for himself when the need
arose; maybe he would have a little respect for the mainland
dolt.

He got ready for bed slowly, his mind going over everything. Now he could relax. Now he could tell Charles. He
climbed into the bunk and let himself go loose against the
bedclothes, and immediately he felt the slow rocking of the
boat with the tide. It was like a cradle, lulling him into
slumber so deep that even the alarm clock did not awaken
him.

CHAPTER TWENTY-ONE

Reconciliation

He was taking off the mooring, preparing to come ashore
to get bait to go to haul, when he saw a group of men tramping around the shore from Wade's store toward Swenson's
fishhouse. Wade was with them. By the time Linn had
reached his grandfather's wharf and made fast, the men were
inside the fishhouse. He went up the wharf, carrying his
bait box, and stood in the doorway. Wade was making a
good story of the night's events, and Linn felt suddenly shy
and would have gone away at once, except that he knew it
was his right to be here. He saw that Mr. Mears wasn't
present; then he must know already the truth about Randy.

Nobody spoke until Wade was through with his account,
and then George Kingman bent down and took up the tools

from the canvas. He held up each implement, asking, "Who does this belong to?"

As each tool was recognized, its owner claimed it. When the last chisel went, Wade rubbed his huge hands together in a gesture of finality. "Well, I guess this takes care of the matter, doesn't it, boys? Linn's in the clear."

"Yes, *Linn* is," one man spoke up, "but how about Randy? It's one thing to have a kiddish grudge, it's another thing to let it hang on till it comes up with something like this. We could have given Linn a hard time and driven him off the island, if Randy hadn't been caught."

"There's a boy needs a good stiff talking-to," somebody said. There was a general wagging of heads and some grave mutterings, and then they turned to leave. When they saw Linn standing there, the expressions changed from dour disapproval and concern to friendliness, in some cases to outright smiles. "Glad we know the right of it, son," someone said.

"Glad you had the spunk to stay on the job till you caught him," Mr. Kingman told him.

Almost everyone had something to say, and Linn thanked them soberly, with his head up. Wade came out last, and slapped Linn on the shoulder. "Now you can go to haul with a real light heart. I hope you get a good catch, just to add to the general good humor." He laughed, and Linn laughed with him.

But when they had all gone, the men back to their own fishhouses and Wade to the store, he realized that his grandfather had not appeared. Mr. Swenson was not one to see people tramping over his property without showing up to find out what was going on. So he couldn't know yet that his grandson had been proved innocent. *And he should know*, Linn thought stubbornly, *whether he wants to listen to me or not.*

He threw down the bait box and started for the house. As he reached the yard he heard the cow lowing in the little barn. The sound of that dismal bawling made his stomach twist in foreboding. She should have been milked long before this! He wrenched the back door open and walked into a cold kitchen. No fire snapped in the stove or stirred the teakettle into song.

He took the stairs three at a time, and halted on the threshold of his grandfather's room. It was empty, the bed unmade. He ran through the rest of the house, calling, "Grampa! Where are you?"

But no answer came, and the echoing stillness disconcerted him. As he came back into the kitchen he saw that his grandfather's oatmeal stood untouched on the back of the stove. The old man hadn't even eaten his breakfast. The lowing of the cow came again to him. Without stopping to close a door behind him, he ran out of the house, across the yard and into the barn.

The cow in her tie-up bawled even louder at sight of him. But Linn saw only his grandfather, lying huddled and still on the floor near the ladder leading to the hayloft. Linn's mouth went dry. Suddenly very much afraid, he ran and knelt beside the old man who opened his eyes. Linn's heart slowed its frantic beating. At least Grampa was not dead.

"It's good you have come," the old man murmured. "I went up to pitch down some hay a little while ago, and I fell off the ladder and hurt my back. I can't seem to turn over."

"Can I turn you?" Linn asked anxiously, crouching over him. "You've got to get to the house. You can't stay here. You think you've got any broken bones?"

"No, not that. But I have got a bad sprain, somehow. If you could lift me—"

Holding his breath, Linn slid his long arms under the slight wizened body and lifted slowly, watching the old man's face, waiting for him to cry out to be laid back again. But the weathered dark face was set stoically, and at last Linn got to his feet with his grandfather in his arms. He was surprised to find him easy to carry, and realized how strong his arms and shoulders and back had become from years of rowing. Moving cautiously, he carried his grandfather out of the barn, across the yard, and into the house. He laid him down on the couch in the dining room and covered him with a blanket.

"Think I should send someone to the main for the doctor?" he asked.

"No," said his grandfather feebly. "Not yet. Let's see what we can do first. It did not hurt me too much when you lifted me. There are some pills in the cupboard for pain— get me two." He closed his eyes, and Linn hurried to do his bidding.

After Grampa took the pills, Linn rebuilt the dead fire in the kitchen stove, and set the teakettle over the leaping flames. Then he went back to the old man.

He opened his eyes when he heard Linn approach, and looked up at him with a long, speculative gaze. "What has happened to your face?"

"Oh!" Linn smiled faintly, and touched his bruises. "I came up to tell you about that, Grampa. I found out who planted that rope in the fishhouse. It was Randy. I beat him up last night." He had meant to be easy about it, but his voice hurried eagerly in spite of himself. "He tried to hide some more stuff. But I've got Wade for a witness this time, and everybody knows I'm in the clear."

"That's good." Grampa was surprisingly calm. "I knew you didn't do it."

"Why didn't you say so, that night?" Linn demanded, too amazed to be indignant.

"I wouldn't give you any sympathy or encouragement."

Grampa's voice grew stronger. His eyes sharpened. "I had gone my limit with you. You had to sink or swim by yourself. I had washed my hands of you."

"Completely?" Linn was aghast at the cold statement. He sat down because it made him feel so strange and empty. "I didn't know you hated me that much. Just because I walked out of the house that day. I *had* to, Grampa," he explained earnestly. "I'd reached my limit, too. I couldn't take any more of your tongue-lashing. I should think you'd understand that. You must have had times—"

"I understand more than you think," said Grampa. "I know what I did to you. I drove you, yes. I wanted to see how much you could take, how strong you were. You did pretty good. Sometimes I didn't think you would." He paused. Then he said quietly, "If you hadn't, I would have been disappointed."

Uneasily Linn ran his hand through his hair. "I don't understand. Why did you have to lay it on so hard? Drive me out of the fishhouse the way you did? Where could I have gone if Grace hadn't let me use Wiley's boat? I'd have had to leave the island."

"I know," said Grampa.

Linn's jaw tightened. "Did you *want* me to leave?"

"No. But it was up to you. It was always up to you. More than you realized." Grampa's eyes closed for a moment and then he opened them again, gazing at Linn with a curious birdlike brightness. "I may as well tell you, if you don't know it for yourself. I was hard on you, because you have to learn that life is always hard. It is never soft or gentle. *Never.* And only a fool will believe it can be so. So I have to prepare my grandson. You came to me a boy who was ignorant of everything. You didn't know the first thing—except that you wanted to live on the island."

Linn nodded. He was beginning to see a great deal. He

saw, suddenly, an image of Grampa when he had been six-teen-year-old Carl Swenson, aboard a square-rigger; a boy who had known for most of his short life that the world of-fered him no easy path. And now, many years later, he was trying to pass on some part of that knowledge to another sixteen-year-old. Trying to teach him while he was still young, so that when he was a man he would be strong and purposeful in himself, able to take whatever the world of-fered him, good or bad.

"So you've been hard as nails," he said thoughtfully. "Trying to see if you could break my spirit. Is that it? And if you had—?"

The old man's face was strangely sad. "It would have been a great disappointment. I wanted you to be strong."

"But if I didn't obey, you got mad!"

"Because some things you wanted were wrong for you; and because I am an old man who must have his own way, and when a boy defies me I must not give in to him."

"Is that why you wouldn't ask me to come back to the house?"

His grandfather looked at him steadily. "Yes."

"Would you ask me to come back now?"

The old man was silent.

"Still stubborn?" Linn asked. "But I *have* to come back. I can't leave you here alone. There are the chores to be done, fires to be kept going, while you keep still and let your back get well. And you don't have to ask me. I'm doing it on my own hook, see?" He stood, feeling taller in the small house than he had ever felt before. "The way I'm going to do other things on my own hook. Read in bed once in a while, and go out sometimes at night to sing or dance; and keep a little change to jingle in my pockets and maybe treat somebody to a bottle of pop. And—" his voice strengthened, "see my friends out in the open, the ones who've stuck by me, and show 'em I'm not ashamed of 'em." He smiled a little. "Can't you see, Grampa, nobody can teach me any bad ways. You ought to know that. You got your oar in first!"

Grampa's eyes were brighter than before. "We are more alike than I knew," he said.

"I've been thinking that for some time. . . Can you stand a cup of coffee? I know I can."

Grampa didn't smile, but his words were easy. "A cup of coffee—ja, it would be just the thing. Put plenty of cream in it. You know how I like it."

"Sure thing!" Linn's mouth puckered into a whistle as he went to the kitchen, but no sound came. A man with a sprained back didn't want to hear whistling. Better to save that noise for the barn when he did the chores. A man with a sprained back needed it nice and quiet and restful, so he could sleep and get well again. You could always save whistling for outdoors, where whistling ought to be. It sounded better in the open air, anyway.

After he had milked the cow, had things shipshape in the house and barn, and Grampa was asleep, he went down to the shore. As he passed the fishhouse door, Tom Lowell stepped out of the building, and Linn stopped short.

"Gorry, Tom," he burst out happily. "Am I glad to see you! Listen, everything's all right—they all know now I never stole anything, and—"

Tom lifted his hand. His lean pale face was smiling. "I've already seen Norris Wade. You did well, Linn."

"But you helped me, Tom," Linn hurried on. "I want everyone to know that. I'll never forget what a friend you've been to me. And what do you think? I'm back with Grampa again. He fell out of the haymow and sprained his back, so he needs me." His excitement died down before the surprise of it. "He never needed me before. But I needed him. It was sort of one-sided."

"Not as one-sided as you think, Linn. You're all he's got—you're his flesh and blood. He's crusty and tough, but he has your well-being at heart."

"I know it now," Linn admitted. "We've been talking. Seems as if we never really *talked* before. Anyway, he's been grinding me to see just how much I could stand. I'm kind of glad he isn't ashamed of me." He stared at Wiley's boat for a moment, and then turned back to Tom, who had counseled strength and patience from the very first. "Tom, if there's ever anything you want me to do, or help you with, like trying to get those copper fastenings from that ship on Bull Cove Reef, I'll be glad to do everything I can."

"You don't have to help me, Linn," Tom answered with an affectionate smile. "I've been looking for treasure all these years and I'll keep on looking. But you have your own interests, your own treasure to seek."

Linn frowned, trying to fathom the strange words. But Tom didn't explain. "I'll be on my way, then. I'll see you one of these days, maybe off on the Haddock Ground!" He lifted a black eyebrow quizzically, touched his mustache, and walked away. Linn looked after him. What Tom had said about treasure was the sort of remark that made people call him barmy. They didn't realize that Tom just thought a little *deeper* than they did, and you had to keep trying to understand. All the way to the mooring and back, he couldn't forget what Tom had said. *You have your own treasure to seek.*

Thinking hard, he went up the wharf, and bumped head on into Polly. Laughing, he caught her shoulders and steadied her. "You're liable to get hurt, pushing people around like that!"

She had been running, her cheeks were scarlet, her hair

flying, and she was out of breath. "Oh, Linn, I just heard the good news about Randy—I mean about you—and I saw you and wanted to tell you how glad I am!" She seized his hand and shook it hard between both of hers. "You did a wonderful job, catching Randy like that!"

"You mean we *all* did a wonderful job. You and your pa for feeding me and keeping up my courage, and Charles for sticking by me, and Tom for putting ideas in my head—" He laughed, got his breath, and went on. "Grace for lending me Wiley's boat to haul in and sleep in—and Wade for everything he's done—Lordy, Polly when I figure up all my friends, there's quite a list, and I'd have been a dead duck without 'em."

"Friends," said Polly sagely, "are better than money in the bank." Her hazel eyes were sparkling. "I'm so happy for you, Linn." Then, abruptly, she sobered. "If only your grandfather—"

"But he believed in me all the time, Polly. He just wanted to see how tough I was."

"Funny way of doing things." Polly pushed out her chin, and then grinned. "Well, I can't even be mad at *him* today. Now I've got to get back to the house, I've got bread in the oven." She ran up the path, turning to wave to him. "Be seeing you!"

As he walked home, he thought of what Tom had said about treasure, and what Polly said about friends being better than money in the bank. In a way, the two things belonged together. And accordingly he was quite well off already. Only a week ago he had thought he was nobody, but today he was enriched by a sense of belonging to Lee's Island at last.

A snowflake drifted out of the east and fell on his sleeve. His head went back alertly; the sky had gone leaden in the last hour. The wind had not yet sprung up, but there was this snowflake. He saw another one float down onto the wrist of his mitten. He walked faster. Let it snow. Let it blow. There wasn't anything to fret about now. He opened the door and went into the kitchen, and the warmth from the fire was a friendly, living presence. He gazed around the familiar rooms with satisfaction. He had his place now, his heritage, and nobody could deny him.

When he had put more wood on the fire, he went to the dining room and stood in the doorway, waiting for the old man to speak.

"How is it outside?" Grampa asked after a moment.

"Going to snow. Flakes drifting down now."

"Well, we don't need to worry about that," the old man said serenely. "We have plenty to eat and to burn. We can be comfortable, I guess."

"Sure, Grampa," Linn said. "We're going to be all right. Better than ever."

THE END